Doom of Namdaron Part Five

Michael Porter

Copyright © 2020 Michael Porter

All rights reserved.

ISBN: 9798633430974

DEDICATION

For my wife Jacqueline, her encouragement, and proof reading.
John Kenny for dragging me to that first writers meeting.
Lloyd R. R. Martin, fellow author and madman for some bird.
Katherine Angel, author your encouragement has been essential.
Thanks to Neil Mark Dave and Kim, amongst those that bought the first
four volumes, take the final steps along the glory road with me.
It's been a long road, more than twenty-five years.

"No matter how evil may assail you.
Remember, there is still love in this world."

CHAPTER FORTY-NINE

Alverana was walking across the central courtyard when he heard the scream, the soul wrenching sound that fell into a strangled gurgle, he sprinted into the main entrance drawing his sword as he ran, ahead of him he saw a figure standing in the doorway to the chapel, in a flash Alverana squeezed between the man and the door frame, a moment later he saw Kevana on the ground in front of the altar. Alverana dropped to his knees beside his fallen friend, his left hand reached to Kevana's neck, quickly found a pulse and slow respiration. Turning towards the man still standing in the doorway.

"What did you see?" The man simply stared.

"What did you see?" Yelled Alverana, as others began to arrive at the door.

"You won't believe me." Stuttered the monk.

"Tell me." Snapped Alverana.

"There were spinning lights, yellow, red and blue, turning around and around, then they spun back into the emblem and he collapsed screaming."

Kevana groaned. Alverana gently picked up his shoulders and cradled him in his arms.

"Where does it hurt?" Asked Alverana, softly. Kevana's eyes flashed open.

"Get Worandana." He whispered. Alverana looked up at the monk still in the doorway.

"Get Worandana." He shouted. "Run." The monk turned and fled, his black robe billowing like a dark sail behind him.

"What happened?" Muttered Alverana.

"You don't want to know, and you're not going to like it when you do, let's wait for Worandana, I'm not sure I have the strength to tell this more than once."

Miclorana came into the chapel, walked slowly to the two on the floor, together with Alverana they lifted Kevana onto a bench so that he was at least a little warmer, but maybe no more comfortable. The sound of rapid and heavy footsteps preceded the arrival of Worandana and Bruciana.

"What happened?" Demanded the younger of the new arrivals.

"I heard him scream and ran in, he was unconscious on the floor."

"Well, Kevana?" Asked Worandana.

"Clear the room, firsts and seconds only." Said Kevana. Worandana's eyebrows raised in surprise, then he nodded to Bruciana. The camp leader turned to the others in the room.

"Everyone out. You." He pointed at one of the monks, "Close and guard the door, no one comes in until we are finished here." In only moments the room was clear, other than the five.

"Now." Worandana spoke very quietly. "What happened here?"

Kevana looked into Worandana's eyes for a long moment before speaking.

"Zandaar spoke to me." He whispered.

"That never happens." Said Bruciana.

"Almost never." Said Worandana. "What did he say?"

"He said that we would bring the sword to him, and that the path would be hard, I asked about our survival, he said that was unimportant, the only thing that mattered was that we would bring him the sword."

"Did he say what he would do with it?"

"The old gods would leave or die, and the younger gods would be absorbed, Gyara would stay."

"I can see from your eyes there is something else?"

"Yes, not actually said but a feeling, a deep dread that something really bad is going to happen."

"What do you mean?"

"I'm not sure, I just get the impression that Zandaar is afraid of something other than the sword."

"How do you mean?"

"I don't know. Have you any idea just how powerful the thoughts of a god are? He almost wiped out my own mind with all that power, but somewhere behind there was something else, a worry, a fear, a deep concern, something was distracting him, something he didn't want to think about and certainly didn't want to share with me."

"So, we have something else to think about, something to protect Zandaar from, now that makes me feel a little better." Worandana almost smiled.

"Strangely," laughed Kevana, "I agree, we now have two enemies to defeat, the thieves and whatever it is that makes our god nervous, finally we have a foe worthy of our attention."

"You people are crazy." Muttered Bruciana, "you believe that something god is frightened of can be stopped by you?"

"Who can tell what we can achieve once we have the sword?" Asked Kevana.

"Or even without it." Laughed Worandana.

"I'm with Bruciana," said Alverana. "definitely crazy, but I'm along for the ride, I can't desert you now." He looked hard into Kevana's eyes as he spoke, then helped him to his feet.

"Can you walk?" He asked.

"I'm fine," replied Kevana, "getting stronger by the moment, Zandaar certainly knocks the stuffing out of a guy, but recovering just fine now."

"What are you going to do?" Asked Bruciana.

"Plans are unchanged," chuckled Kevana, "we go to Angorak, and wait for Namdarin to pass one side or the other, then we kill him and take the sword, travel to Zandaarkoon and kill whatever it is that is making god nervous. Heroes one and all."

"The survivors you mean."

"Even the dead will be remembered as heroes."

"Much good it will do them."

"Do you want to live forever?" Laughed Kevana.

"No." Whispered Alverana and Worandana together.

"Crazy." Said Bruciana, softly. "You people are just plain crazy."

"And we'll be gone with the sunrise, you could do one more thing for us when we have left." said Worandana.

"What more can you want from me?"

"You could get word back to the council that we are still chasing the sword, and that we plan to bring it to Zandaarkoon as soon as we can. If you can get our own people off our backs that would be a great help, it could even save some lives, and not just our own."

"I'll do what I can, but I can make no promises, it could be that once the leaders find out that I just let you pass through, they may decide that we should all have died in the attempt to stop you."

"Unlikely," laughed Kevana, "had we been carrying the sword, then they would expect you to give up your lives to stop us, but without it, we aren't that much of a threat."

"So, what are you going to do?" Asked Bruciana.

"I," said Kevana, "am going to get some rest, talking to Zandaar is very tiring, somehow I feel like I've run for miles, it's like he was draining my energy to maintain the link between us. I never want to do that again, especially over this distance."

"I have never had the privilege of talking to Zandaar over any distance." Said Worandana, "not even face to face, I am so happy to say. Kevana you get some sleep, I'll keep training these miners, for the rest of the day, and tomorrow we'll set off for Angorak." Kevana nodded and slowly climbed to his feet, he reached out to Alverana for assistance, by the time Kevana's arm was across his friend's shoulder, Alverana was carrying most of his weight.

"Damn, I'm weak as a kitten." Muttered Kevana.

"Miclorana." Said Bruciana, "Take him to his bed, then bring him some soup, he's too weak for anything else." Bruciana immediately showed Alverana the way, Bruciana opened the door to the chapel to lead them out, the monk set on guard duty, turned rapidly his hand on his sword hilt.

"Relax," snapped Miclorana, "we are finished in the chapel, this man needs to get to his bed, help him." In the narrow confines of the corridor there was little the monk could do other than hold doors open and keep others out of the way. Within a few short minutes Kevana was lowered into a bed and a blanket thrown over him. Miclorana delegated food service to the monk who was more than happy to get away from the visitors if only for a short time, the fear in his eyes was unmistakable.

"I am sorry," said Miclorana, "but I have things to do, Stevana will see to your needs, rest here until you feel strong enough to move, if supper needs to come to you then that can be arranged."

"Thank you Miclorana, you are a most gracious host." Muttered Kevana, with a nod. Miclorana bowed and left.

"He's a good man." Said Alverana. "Perhaps we should take him with us?"

"No. He's far too happy here, this place suits him far too well."

"How are you feeling?"

"I don't think I've ever felt worse, even that damned cold didn't make me feel this weak."

"That cold was bad."

"I'd advise you not to talk to Zandaar if you can avoid it."

"Did you get a choice?"

"No, I got sucked into the swirling pattern above the altar."

"So how did he know it was you sitting there?"

"Now that is a question I really didn't want to ask."

"Was he looking for you specifically or just someone from our group, Worandana would have been a better choice, he's a much more competent magician."

"Perhaps he didn't want someone competent?"

"You mean he wanted someone weak?"

"Perhaps, someone with low resistance, someone who could be easily subjugated." Kevana hitched up on the bed, looking up into Alverana's eyes.

"Be careful who you make that suggestion to, Kirukana would have very clear views." Alverana smiled, that smile was reflected in Kevana's face.

"Can you imagine how he is going to feel when he hears that Zandaar talked to me and not him?"

"Now there's a guy with so little resistance that he may as well just roll over and play dead."

"From the feel of things, I'm not so very different." At this point the monk returned, carrying a tray with a large bowl on it, and a group of small buns.

"Will you need anything else?" He asked.

"Wine would be good, or beer, for their restorative properties of course." Laughed Kevana.

"I shall bring you some wine." Said the monk departing quickly.

"Are you sure you should be drinking wine?"

"I am certain that I need something more than water to drink." Laughed Kevana.

"You be careful. In your current state that could be risky."

"I'll drink slowly, but then, I'm already on my back."

"It's good to see that you still have a sense of humour."

"If I can't laugh at this, it's going to drive me mad in a very short time."

"Agreed, but is it a good thing?"

"I'm just going to have to live with it, good or not, I'm going to have to be careful if Zandaar decides to talk to me, it could be fatal if he believes I'm actually laughing at him."

"That's a fact. Do you think it is likely?"

"Not really, but who can tell, he can now locate me in a heartbeat, so it could happen next time he wants to know what is going on."

"I hope that never happens again." Muttered Alverana.

"Me too."

"Have you any idea how it felt to see you slumped on the ground, as if dead?"

"No worse than seeing you after Crathen's dream was torn apart."

"I suppose, but I thought I'd lost you."

The monk returned with a large earthenware flagon, and a couple of mugs. He handed the items to Alverana bowed and left. Alverana poured a good measure into each mug, then took Kevana's arm to lift him up in the bed, Alverana reached behind and re-organised the pillows, as he lowered Kevana back against the pillows he hugged him fiercely. While their cheeks were touching Alverana whispered, "I couldn't bear to lose you."

"I feel exactly the same." Mumbled Kevana before the hug broke. Alverana looked away and filled two mugs with wine before turning back. He looked into Kevana's eyes again, for what felt like a long time, neither wanted to break the eye contact, but Kevana finally had to, he needed to take his mug and drink some of it. His eyes hidden from view for a while behind the rim of the cup. When the cup lowered Alverana's eyes were waiting, after a moment he reached down and picked up the bowl of soup, with every intention of feeding his friend, one spoonful at a time.

"I can manage." Mumbled Kevana, immediately afraid that he had somehow offended Alverana. The younger man simply smiled and held the tray so that his commander could feed himself. The bowl was just under half full when Kevana leaned back against the pillows, dropping the spoon in the bowl. Alverana snatched up the spoon and started shovelling the soup into his mouth as fast as he could.

"This soup is good." He mumbled between mouthfuls. More wine was poured and drunk slowly as the bowl emptied. A face appeared in the open doorway, followed by a loud knock, then a moment later Kirukana burst in.

"Did you actually talk to Zandaar?" Excitement prevented him from stopping there. "People are saying you did, how was it speaking to God? I can't imagine how it must feel meeting with God."

"You're babbling." Said Kevana.

"Sorry. How was our God?"

"Hungry." Laughed Kevana.

"What do you mean?"

"Talking to him took so much of my energy it almost killed me."

"But it is such a privilege to talk to god."

"Kirukana, next time he calls you can answer him, that sort of privilege I can do without."

"I would be more than honoured to do that."

"You might even survive the experience."

"What did he have to say?"

"That we would bring him the sword, and that the way would be hard, he made no promise that we would all survive, nor did he particularly care."

"Why should he care? We are his servants, we do as he wills."

"In the current order of things, you are my servant, and much as I hate to admit it, I do care whether you live or die. Our god should give us the same consideration."

"He is Zandaar, we live and die for him."

"Agreed, but it would be nice if he cared one way or the other."

"He has much larger things on his mind, especially now with the sword in enemy hands."

"I thought his mind encompassed the whole world?"

"Now that really is a good question." said Worandana from behind Kirukana, no one had heard his approach. Kirukana's head snapped around, spearing the old man with a look of hatred, if only for an instant.

"Yes, so it is taught, and I believe it to be true. There have to be priorities though, and a few soldiers must be a long way down the list."

"Good catch." Laughed Worandana, he looked round the younger man, "How are you feeling now?"

"I'm feeling better, still very tired, and weak, but I'm sure I will be fine by morning, we will ride at dawn, and we will ride hard. You better be ready old man."

"I'll be ready, not at all sure about this place though, their skills are woeful, there talent almost non-existent."

"Not our problem, we didn't send them here so badly prepared."

"Agreed, if we make to Zandaarkoon, I shall be having some serious words with Axorana, he needs to understand just how vulnerable these brothers are."

"I think he cares even less than Zandaar."

"You can't say things like that." Interrupted Kirukana.

"Of course, I can." Laughed Kevana, "I have felt the indifference of Zandaar, and it seems that Axorana has even less feelings for his men, for they are his men in every way. Perhaps this lack of care is something engendered by the closeness to Zandaar."

"It could be that the callousness of god rubs off on those closest, and there can't be any closer than the council."

"You are both talking of things you don't know." Snapped Kirukana.

"Do I finally sense some growth in Kirukana?" Asked Kevana.

"I believe so," replied Worandana, "only a few days ago he'd have been screaming 'heresy' by now. He may be learning." Alverana smiled hugely at Kirukana's discomfort.

"But is he learning to think, or just avoiding the use of the single word?" Asked Kevana.

"I really don't care all that much," smiled Worandana, "just so long as he stops screaming heresy every few minutes."

"Many of your ideas are deemed heresy," muttered Kirukana, "as you will find out when we get to Zandaarkoon." He turned to leave.

"Remember something," said Kevana, "even god doesn't care if you make it to Zandaarkoon, only the sword matters to him." Kirukana stamped off, the remaining three laughed softly.

"I'm just off to get something to eat," said Worandana, "do you want anything?"

"No thanks, I've had my fill of soup for now, I'll try and get some sleep, before we set off in the morning." said Kevana. Worandana nodded and turn away.

"I'll leave you to rest." Said Alverana, standing slowly to follow Worandana.

"Make sure everything is ready for tomorrow morning."

"Of course, rest, I'll be back later." Alverana closed the door and set off towards the refectory, not that he was actually hungry, but he felt like the silent company of others, his mind still a turmoil of complex feelings and doubts, the refectory was much as these places are everywhere, he picked a small table against one wall, and sat alone, nursing a large cup of steaming tea. He stared downwards into the rising plumes, trying to shut out the world, the chair across from him was slowly drawn back and someone sat down in it. Slowly Alverana looked up into the clear blue eyes of Petrovana.

"Are you struggling with something?" Asked Petrovana.

"Yes." Mumbled Alverana.

"Care to share? I may be able to help."

"I'm not sure about that, or anything really."

"Is it something about Kevana?"

"How do you know?"

"It's not exactly difficult to see, for those with eyes."

"What do you mean?"

"There are obvious feelings between you two, even if you can't see it, I can."

"I don't understand."

"After a while one learns to be sensitive to the small signs of attraction, though not actually prohibited, let's just say these things are frowned on. In a closed society without females this sort of thing should be expected."

"I am not sure I like what you are suggesting."

"That's not much of a surprise. I have a very simple question for you, you don't have to tell me the answer, just be honest with yourself. Will you think on it?"

"Ask your question."

"Close your eyes, now imagine your life without Kevana in it. What can you see?" Petrovana paused for a moment, then continued. "You don't need to tell me, just think about it."

"I see an emptiness, it's a place I don't want to be." Muttered Alverana.

"You didn't need to tell me that, but it does tell you something about the way you feel about him, perhaps he feels the same."

"But how can I be sure?"

"I have seen enough of the signs to know by now, he cares for you, ask him, talk to him."

"I am frightened how he will answer."

"He'll either admit his feelings or deny them."

"I couldn't bear for him to respond badly, it would change things, I'd know for sure that he doesn't have feelings for me, by all the hells, I'm not even sure how I feel about this."

"How long have you two been together?"

"Must be ten years."

"He's always been your commander?"

"Pretty much, every time he got a promotion and moved on, very soon he arranged my transfer to be in the same unit, once he made captain, my transfer was always part of his conditions for accepting a new position, we've been fighting side by side for a long time now."

"So how have things changed?"

"I don't know, this mission was supposed to be a walk in the park, and it looks like we are all going to die, even Zandaar is involved very personally in this one, that's not good news."

"I agree with that, much as I love serving him, having him looking over our shoulders is very frightening."

"I've never really considered the fact that I may die, it's sort of expected for soldiers like us, but this mission makes it so much more likely, I feel that even success is going to be fatal."

"I know what you mean. I have a really bad feeling about this one."

"Perhaps the feeling of impending death is bringing the other feelings to the fore? Anyway, how come you know so much about these feelings?"

"I've always known about these things, it's just the way I am, though it's not regarded as heresy, it can still get a guy in deep trouble really quickly, we have to be careful, very careful sometimes. One of the things I've always liked about Kevana, is that he doesn't care how his men feel, so long as they fight well. He may think that I'm a bit of a whiner, but he knows how well I fight, he's seen me in battle and had me standing behind him when it counted. He doesn't care that I prefer the company of men."

"I never knew."

"Neither did I, I thought you were firmly in the mainstream, not like me at all, I never even considered you, until very recently, only in the last few days have I seen your attentiveness for Kevana, and his for you."

"I'm very confused." Said Alverana, shaking his head.

"I think your feelings are only for him, not men in general, you're not like me."

"I didn't know you felt that way."

"Some things are better kept a little quiet. Not that anyone really minds, but I'd rather not create any more problems than necessary."

"I've always been more than happy with the occasional dalliance with women, visits to a whore house when one is available has always been enough for me." Whispered Alverana.

"You are actually feeling sexual attraction for Kevana?"

"I don't know, I'm not sure, I care about him, and about how he feels for me, but sexual attraction, I'm not sure about that at all."

"Could be that you only have an emotional attachment, not a physical one."

"All this is making my head hurt, do you know what I really need right now?"

"I think I'm frightened to ask."

"I need an enemy to fight, someone to kill, someone to hurt."

"I don't think we have anyone like that around here." Muttered Petrovana. "These people are friends."

"Not as much friends as Kevana."

"Please calm down, I feel that you are heading for berserker rage."

"I am getting angry about this whole situation." Alverana took a large draft of his now much cooler tea, then looked up at Petrovana. "Perhaps I'll find someone to spar with?"

"I'd suggest several someone's but try not to break any of them."

"Not until I'm considerably calmer."

"That may take a while." Smiled Petrovana.

"Maybe, perhaps they've got some practise dummies here."

"I didn't see any in the courtyard and that's where they should be, if they're going to be anywhere."

"I could always go and kick their heavy gates, that'd give them something to do, they'd definitely need some serious fixing, the walls aren't much better, an angry mule could kick them down. This whole place is a joke, what in all the hells is Axorana up to?"

"He's after the gold that's all, he needs money for something."

"I'm sure he's up to no good, but what it is, we can't find out until we get back to Zandaarkoon. I think I'll ask him directly."

"That could be interesting, what will you do if he won't tell you?"

"He'll tell me, it might take a while to convince him, but he'll tell me." Alverana smiled, thinking about the pain he would cause.

"Kevana won't let you," laughed Petrovana, "he has very clear rules about torturing council members."

"That could be changed by the time we get there."

"You could be right at that, if we get enough opposition along the road, caused by their warnings, he's going to be angry."

"I think you could be right." Alverana smiled broadly, an image of himself and Kevana standing shoulder to shoulder, battling the minions of the council. Swords flashing in the confines of the council chambers, blood splatters decorating the walls all around. The steady rhythm of sword play filling his mind as they advanced on the cowering old men of the council, the sound of steel sliding on steel, the screams of the dying, the stink of blood. Alverana drew a huge breath, and smiled even more, he blew out a long sigh.

"That's better," said Petrovana, "much more relaxed now, I dread to wonder what you were thinking."

"I'm a simple soldier, simple soldiering thoughts." Laughed Alverana.

"The dance of death, yes I know the steps, but I don't think I quite revel in it like you do."

"Probably not. It has a serious calming influence, given the warnings that the council have sent out about us, I think we are going to be dancing long before we get to Zandaarkoon, no matter if we have the sword or not."

"You could be right."

"You better be ready, Kevana won't hesitate, and I'll be alongside him, if any are foolish enough to attack us, then they will surely die."

"Even if they are our own brothers?"

"If they attack, then I will defend myself, as will Kevana, and so will you if you want to stay alive. Kevana says Zandaar is going to make our journey harder than it needs to be, god may even be trying to kill us all, if that is the case, then he's going to have to pay a real price."

"You would side with the thieves? Their intention, if we are to believe Crathen, is to kill Zandaar."

"Not really, but it does depend on how angry Kevana gets, mad enough he could go that way."

"Would you follow him?"

"We are all going to be fighting for our lives at that point, somehow I don't think there will be a choice."

"So, stepping back a little way, does considering fighting and dying make you feel any better?"

"Yes. It makes me more relaxed."

"You really are strange, but Kevana reacts much the same, you two certainly make a fine pair." Petrovana laughed aloud, climbed to his feet, clapped Alverana on the shoulder and walked slowly away, leaving the man to his thoughts.

Alverana sat for a while, thinking over old battles, old times, fighting side by side, with Kevana, and others. Large battles and small, always the song of steel ringing in his head. Gradually his mood changed, less worried, less stressed, more relaxed. Finally, he left the refectory to find something else to do. A quick check on the horses showed him they were properly looked after, and would be ready by the morning, he found Briana and Fabrana in the courtyard, lazing, staring at the clouds rushing across the blue sky.

"Busy?" He asked.

"Not especially, just worrying about the weather we are going to face tomorrow, if those clouds keep moving at that rate, we could have anything before sunrise." Said Briana.

"Plenty of time for that tomorrow, I need some exercise, you up for a little two on one?"

"Better that sitting around getting fat." Grinned Fabrana, not sure that two to one were good enough odds. The two stood and shed their outer robes, Alverana did the same, then drew his sword, with his left hand he drew a long knife from the back of his belt, he stood ready for the others to attack. Fabrana drew and stepped right, Briana moved left, in a flash they both struck, Alverana took their first strikes on his blades, and turned them away, he spun in between them sweeping the sword at one and the knife at the other, both attacks were parried, and counter attacks came in a flash, but Alverana was still moving, spinning and dancing, his blades striking with the speed of a snake, flashing in the sunlight, weaving a pattern round his body. Briana almost penetrated the defensive pattern with a sudden thrust, this was met by both blades, and a savage twist that spun Briana's sword from his hand, Fabrana knew that he now stood little chance against the more experienced soldier, mere seconds was all it took for Alverana's knife to appear at his throat. Both men stepped away, each panting hard, though the confrontation had taken only four minutes, it was more than enough exercise to get the blood racing, and the lungs pumping.

"Again?" Asked Alverana looking at Briana. who raised his recovered sword in salute and moved straight to the attack, this kept Fabrana behind Alverana, Fabrana's first attack started Alverana spinning, he swept Fabrana's sword aside then stepped past him, putting his opponents one behind the other, while Fabrana was turning to face Alverana, Briana stepped right and attacked, striking at Alverana's head, Fabrana struck at Alverana's legs, both blades were blocked and the counter attacks came inside their guards, giving the pair no option other than retreat. This retreat rapidly became a rout, as Alverana pressed forwards. Briana moved to his right, hoping to get to Alverana's weaker left side, Fabrana defending rapidly, trying to give Briana time to move around the bigger man. Once Briana was far enough away, Fabrana found himself under attack from both blades, only a heartbeat later the long knife tapped him on the belly to indicate a death stroke, Briana found himself alone again, and completely outmatched. He fought on, losing ground with every motion, until the wall was behind him, Alverana's knife forced his sword aside and then the sword appeared under Briana's chin.

"Well played." Panted Alverana. "Again?"

"No thank you," laughed Briana, "I, no we, have been humiliated enough. What's got you so riled today?"

"Nothing." Muttered Alverana turning away, sheathing his weapons and collecting his robe from where he had dropped it.

"He's definitely pissed about something." Said Fabrana.

"We'll find out, or not, as he chooses." Smiled Briana, shaking his head and watching their friend walk slowly into the main entrance.

Alverana went straight to the room where Kevana was now asleep. He sat on the second cot that had been brought into the small cell, he looked at his old friend, sleeping peacefully, like a child, a small smile on his lips, Kevana fidgeted briefly, as if he could sense someone watching him, before he sighed and settled down again, breathing slowly and evenly, not a single care in the world. 'How can this man mean so much to me?' thought Alverana, looking back on all the times they had shared, some good, some not so, battles won, and lost. Friends made and lost. He wondered briefly about Kevana's love life, his own not at all impressive, a few ladies of the night, whenever the opportunity presented itself, nothing of any real import, all his lasting relationships had been with fellow soldiers, and none of those as long as his friendship with Kevana. He thought back to a time before he knew Kevana, a small garrison many days north and west of Zandaarkoon, the town was growing fast, many farmers moving in to service it, more than a few bandits and other outlaws trying to take advantage of the growing economy. The garrison saw plenty of action, and had a high turnover for a while, Alverana rose quickly through the ranks, as a survivor. Any military establishment has a tendency to collect "camp followers", this one was no exception, one particular young girl caught Alverana's eye, Lindene, short, slim, huge brown eyes, and the best part about her, for Alverana at least, was the fact that she always smelled nice, he first met her when he was off duty, just wandering through a market place, thinking about a beer or two. He heard a scream from an alleyway, not unusual in a small town, there she was, draped over an empty crate, one man trying to hold her still, while the other was trying to remove her clothing, neither men were doing terribly well at their self-appointed tasks. Alverana tapped one behind the ear with his heavy knife hilt, and showed the sharp end to the other, as the first slid slowly to the ground.

"She's only a whore." Said the standing ruffian, releasing the girl's arms.

"Even whores are somebodies' daughter." Smiled Alverana, as the girl moved behind him.

"This one doesn't even have a pimp to protect her, he died in a knife fight last night."

"If you don't want to join him, I suggest you pick up your friend and leave, while you still can." He kept the girl behind him as he gave the ruffian room to gather up his friend and together they staggered from the alley. He knew that their short belt knives were no competition for his own, nor the sword as yet undrawn. Once they had left, Alverana turned to her. "How did you end up in this place?"

"That man was right, Jeorge was killed last night, he was supposed to look after me."

"I was more interested in your family, you look far too young for this, er, shall we say, profession."

"I'm almost seventeen years, or I will be next summer."

"And now you find yourself without a protector, how did you end up with this Jeorge?"

"I came to town about six months ago, Jeorge was very nice to me, he bought me fine clothes, and good wine, all I had to do in return is lay with a friend of his, a fine lord he was, big house, big black carriage, with four horses. He was kind to me as well." Alverana shook his head, wishing he hadn't heard the story before.

"Did this fine lord have a name?"

"I forget."

"A coat of arms on his coach?"

"I remember that, blue and red background, black stripe diagonal down to the left, black dragon above and three gold balls below."

"An old man?"

"Oh yes, white hair and wrinkled face, almost like grandfather, but not as scrawny."

"You should consider yourself lucky, the old lord is much nicer to little girls than his son, it's said he treats them much as he did his daughters, the younger lord treats them as his sisters before they died."

"So, what should I do now?"

"You are ill fitted for life on the street my dear."

"Yes, I had noticed that. There are girls that do it."

"Yes, but they usually have a knife at least and the willingness to use it to good effect, you, do not."

"So, what can I do to make a living?"

"I know a place, it's a whore house, the woman who runs it owes me a favour or two, I'm sure she'll take you in, you can clean and cook, and look after the other girls, give it a couple of years before you decide to take up whoring as a profession."

"Jeorge said that my youth was good for me, it put the prices up, I earned so much money with him."

"You mean for him. You saw next to none of it. Come with me let's go meet Alice." He held his hand out to her, as she walked alongside him, she looked so much like a child out and about with her father that Alverana almost cried when he looked down into her trusting eyes. It was a fair walk across town to the brothel run by Alice, as soon as they walked in off the street, one of the girls in the front parlour spoke up.

"Hey Alverana, you do know you're not supposed to bring your own girls!"

"Thanks." He laughed. "Where's Alice at?"

"I think she's in the back somewhere." Alverana set off towards the corridor that led to the back of the building, for a moment a large and heavily armed man stood in his way. A glare was all it took to make the security guard step aside, somethings just aren't worth dying for.

The corridor into the back was only short, but narrow enough to slowdown any invading group, Alverana and Lindene could hardly be considered an invading force. Together they stepped into a large kitchen area, a middle-aged woman in a long grey dress was issuing orders to a pair of girls who were washing pots in a huge sink. She turned as Alverana crossed into her vision.

"What are you doing back here?" She demanded.

"I have a friend who needs your help."

"She's more than a little young."

"Sadly, she has already been introduced to your profession, but I'd like that to stop."

"So, you bring her to a brothel?"

"No, I bring her to you."

"And you think this is something different?"

"Oh yes, I'm certain you will look after her, she's too small, and too young to be left on the streets, and all the others that I know would simply sell her to the highest bidder, until she's worn out and old."

"You think I won't do exactly that?"

"No," laughed Alverana, "you are making more than enough money, with what you already have here, you're even driving down the prices around here, the competition is going out of business. You don't need one more young girl."

"So, what should I do with her, if I can't rent out her body?"

"She could work the back room here, until she is of a decent enough age to make up her own mind how she earns her way in the world, currently she has been informed that she only has one talent that anyone will pay for."

"Who told her this?"

"Jeorge, he found her as soon as she came into town, looking for a new life, well she got one."

"Where is Jeorge now?"

"He's dead, seems someone killed him."

"You?"

"Not I, perhaps someone who was upset by the quality of the merchandise he paid for."

"How do you mean?"

"Maybe Jeorge didn't understand that you can only sell a virgin once."

"A lot more than once." Muttered Lindene. Alice laughed out loud.

"Name girl?" she asked.

"I am Lindene, for now at least." smiled the girl.

"That will do, have you any family likely to come looking for you, after all it could be a brother or a cousin that ended Jeorge."

"No family, a fever took them all during the spring."

"You've been fending for yourself ever since?"

"Yes, a hungry smile can get all sorts of treats, and I can run when I need to."

"At least you have enough sense to run, why not run from Jeorge?"

"I thought he was going to help me."

"He did I suppose, but he was mostly filling his own pockets. Do you know who killed him?"

"No, I woke up, and he wasn't there, and then I heard he was dead."

"So, she went out on the street on her own." Said Alverana.

"Were you successful, my dear?" Asked Alice.

"Not really, Alverana here, rescued me."

"Did you kill anyone?" Asked Alice.

"No, hurt, but not damaged."

"Good, I don't need that sort of trouble from the watch."

"Won't Jeorge's death cause any trouble from the watch?" Asked Lindene.

"No," smiled Alice, "no one will mourn his passing, especially not the guardsmen of the watch, their only thought will be surprise that he has survived this long."

"They knew what he was doing, but did nothing?"

"Unsavoury, but so long as the girls he was pimping were sort of volunteers, he wasn't actually breaking the law, as such. Offering a service, the girl couldn't provide, now that would be breaking a law or two, but so difficult to prove."

"Looks like someone chose an old-fashioned form of justice for Jeorge." Said Alverana.

"Trial by combat you mean?" Laughed Alice.

"He was found guilty." Laughed Alverana.

"So, what happens to me?" Asked Lindene.

"You can have a place here, if you so desire. We'll look after you, until you make up your mind to change your profession, but you are really too young to make this decision. Is that acceptable to you?" Asked Alice.

"What would my responsibilities be?"

"Cleaning, cooking, general maid stuff, nothing too strenuous."

"I accept." Lindene held out her small hand to shake Alice's. The older woman smiled and shook hands solemnly.

Over the next two years Alverana's relationship with Lindene changed slowly, they became lovers, first on an occasional basis, then much more regularly, after a year she took to trading under Alice's tuition, she became both skilled and affluent, by the time Alverana was posted elsewhere, they talked about her going with him, perhaps even marriage. Lindene was enjoying her life far too much to follow him, their parting was tearful, Alverana vowed as he rode away, that he would never become so involved with any woman ever again, it hurt far too much.

Alverana opened his eyes to see Kevana staring at him.

"Are you all right?" Asked Kevana, seeing a tear rolling slowly down Alverana's face.

"Memories, pain from the past, things could have been so different, if only."

"If only's, are the worst sort of pain."

"Agreed. Physical pain is cured and gone, or something we deal with daily, but the emotional pain just sneaks up, and hurts all over again."

"Nothing we can do about it, just ride it out." Sighed Alverana.

"It helps to have friends around."

"Yes, but some things are so difficult to share."

"Tell me." Whispered Kevana.

"I was thinking about my love life, and it's almost complete absence these days, there was a time when I actually considered quitting the order and marrying an actual woman, don't tell Kirukana, he'll have a fire built in a minute." Alverana smiled, slightly.

"An actual woman?" Smiled Kevana, "What stopped you?"

"I really couldn't see myself as a prostitute's husband, or more likely a madams."

"Was it the thought of her still, er, working?"

"No, that didn't bother me, most of my, er, lovers have been working girls, but Lindene was something completely different. She was a great person, sometimes I really wish I'd had the balls to quit soldiering to be with her, or that she'd quit whoring to be a soldier's wife."

"Given the current feelings about women, she'd have been in a very bad place by now, and you'd have had to quit."

"I know, but back then views weren't as harsh as they are today."

"Not a good move as far as I am concerned." smiled Kevana.

"Agreed, perhaps it's time we took our priesthood back from the woman haters."

"Not an easy thing to accomplish from out here." Laughed Kevana.

"I know, but sometimes I really miss Lindene."

"I can imagine."

"You probably can't."

"What do you mean?"

"It's not the sex that I miss, it's her smile, a simple touch, and a laugh."

"Somehow I can believe that of you."

"What of your love life?" Asked Alverana.

"Much as yours, nothing long term though, an occasional dalliance with a dockside doxy, never anything close to marriage though."

"Never thought about settling down with a real family then?"

"Not with any seriousness, in a drunken dream perhaps, but never serious when sober."

"Are you planning to die for Zandaar then?"

"Not today, but maybe sometime soon, though I do have my eye on an old soldiers home a day's ride from Zandaarkoon, it's run by a couple of madams, they have a retirement home for old whores next door as well, if I can amass enough of a pension I'll move there when I retire."

"Sounds like a decent plan, how much have you got saved?"

"Exactly?"

"Approximately?"

"Nowhere near enough," laughed Kevana, "but I've still got the dream."

"Maybe I'll join you, that could be interesting."

"Do you think they'll be able to cope with both of us?"

"If we live long enough to retire, we'll be no problem, some days I feel pretty much dead already."

"That's definitely how I feel today." Kevana smiled and settled back against his pillows.

Worandana came in through the door, looked at the two relaxing.

"You two got nothing to do?"

"For a change," said Alverana, "everything seems to be going well without us."

"And I'm far too tired to even stand up." Laughed Kevana, cocking his head to one side.

"You are not wrong, Crathen seems to have taken charge in your absence, he's keeping everyone working, the horses are all fed, watered and groomed, packs are ready for loading, everyone is planning an early start immediately after morning prayers."

"How did the training go?" Asked Kevana.

"These people had barely covered the basics before they were shipped out here, it's crazy just how badly trained they are. Really they shouldn't even be wearing the black." Worandana shook his head, as if in despair.

"As Bruciana has said, they are here for the gold they can mine, nothing else."

"Well, they are a little better prepared than they were, Bruciana can at least throw a decent lightning bolt now, how he'll perform under pressure I have no idea, I just hope he never finds out, such discovery could prove fatal."

"Once we are gone that is not our problem."

"Will you be well enough to travel in the morning?"

"Right now, even the thought of standing up makes my knees shake, but if I have to be tied to my horse, we are leaving here first thing, and at a gallop. Is that clear?"

"Why the hurry?"

"We have to be at Angorak before Namdarin gets there, if we are not there first, then we have lost the race."

"I understand, but do you really need to kill yourself to get there?"

"That would be a yes. If necessary I'll be tied to my saddle, but we will get to Angorak first."

"Fine. It's almost time for the evening meal, are you going to come to the refectory, or should I get some food sent here for you?"

"I'll go get it." Interrupted Alverana. "Solid food or soup again?"

"The soup was very nice, I'll have some more of that, if you don't mind?"

"I won't be long." Alverana left.

"Are you sure you're going to be able to ride in the morning?" Asked Worandana.

"As I said, if I have to be tied to the saddle, then, so be it. Here's a question, seeing as there's just the two of us here, how is it that communicating with Zandaar took so much out of me?"

"This may surprise you, I've never heard of Zandaar communicating with anyone outside the city before, only ever short range and to members of the council, not to some small-time troop commander out in the field." He shook his head, to emphasise the point.

"Never?"

"No, he communicates with the council, and then only a 'Come' command, instructions then given in person, in the actual presence, these instructions passed along to the rest of us, in written or distance communication. This is something huge if Zandaar is talking directly to you."

"Could it be that he has a valid fear of the sword?"

"I think so, the evidence suggests he wants it, and more important doesn't want the council to get it, he wants you to bring it to him, if you plan to do that we may be forced to fight our way into the city, and into the temple."

"Against the opposition of the council, and all their forces?"

"That could be the only way to get the sword to Zandaar, if either faction in the council takes control of the sword, things could go very badly, for us, or the opposing faction."

"The city guard number thousands, and the council members private guards, hundreds, we are very few, we stand little chance."

"I'm sure that Zandaar has a plan, perhaps he will tell us of it as we approach."

"He can talk to you next time."

"I hope so, I'll have better defences than you, he'll not drain me as easily."

"That's almost certainly true, I have another tactical thought."

"Go ahead."

"Having reclaimed the sword, we gallop towards the city with the sword held aloft, triumphant in the service of our god."

"Go on."

"I foresee a hail of crossbow fire from the top of the wall. One faction or the other takes the sword, and we all lose."

"That thought had already crossed my mind, I was going to wait until we actually had the sword to voice it though."

"I have another thought, it's not exactly as our instructions though."

"Please tell on."

"This thief, Namdarin, is planning to kill Zandaar with this sword, so we know where he is going, all we do is tag along, let him take the thing into the city, then hit him from the rear when he is least expecting it."

"That may be a workable plan, but we'll have to be awful close to his group."

"I'm actually thinking of us joining with him."

"Our group must be as large as his now, he'll not let us just join up, that doesn't make any sense."

"Agreed, we'll just have to hope we can tag along behind, without being seen, do you think that is possible?"

"No. Well not with any certainty." Said Worandana. "Far more likely, there will be battle as soon as we meet them."

"That's going to cost us some lives, and hopefully we'll take all of theirs."

"Here's a thought for you, we fight, they die, we lose a few, we take the sword, we head for Zandaarkoon, Namdarin comes back to life, and comes after us, he has no friends left, he's back where he was when he started, nothing to lose. We may have the sword, but do you really want to face him again?"

"I suppose not, but we can always kill him again."

"Every time we face him, we lose some lives, and he just keeps coming back."

"Yes, and your point is?" Snarled Kevana.

"We need to kill him, and capture the others, they can be used to control him, we take all their survivors to Zandaar, and let him decide their fate."

"That sounds reasonable, the accomplishment may be difficult though."

"Agreed, but at least it is a plan."

"So, we have a way forward, tomorrow we ride, and ride hard, we must get to Angorak first."

"Agreed, you get some food inside you, and some rest, and we'll be on the road as soon as morning prayers are finished." Worandana left just as Alverana was returning with a tray full of food and wine, more than enough for both of them, the two merely nodded to each other as they passed.

"Can you sit up?" Asked Alverana.

"I can at least do that." Smiled Kevana. Alverana placed a bowl of soup and a large hunk of fresh, and still warm bread on his lap.

"Decisions made?"

"Yes." Kevana nodded. "We ride hard after morning prayers, for Angorak. Then see where we go from there."

"Hard riding is going to hurt you." Alverana looked down to avoid eye contact, so that Kevana couldn't see the worry in his eyes. The crack in his voice was unmistakeable though.

"I've been hurt before, and probably will be again. Don't fret, we'll be fine."

"Unknown territory doesn't help matters."

"You worry too much, I'll be fine, in a day or so, all this will be behind us, and we'll have an entirely new set of dangers to worry about." Kevana smiled, looking hard into his friend's eyes. The two sat in silence for a while eating soup, Alverana re-filled the bowls, and then filled two cups from the second larger jug, this was wine, a deep rich red. Kevana took a quick taste from his cup.

"Where do they get such good wine, out here in the wilds?" He muttered softly.

"Perhaps it comes in on their supply caravans, I don't believe there is a source nearby that can make something this good, the terrain is just not right for vines."

"I'll have to go slow on this one, I'm too weak to be drinking too much of this."

"It might be good to help you get some more rest."

"Passed out drunk is not resting," laughed Kevana, "even I know that, no matter what the rest of you think about my drinking habits."

"Finish your soup, and we'll drink some of this fine wine, you need to get some sleep, we have an early start in the morning."

"Right. I want our horses on the road as soon as prayers are finish, is that clear?"

"Once you are settled, I shall go and spread the word, I don't think many will be too upset to be out of this place as soon as possible. Though I do have an observation to make."

"We've been friends a long while now, spit it out."

"When I was hurt, you slowed the ride down until I had recovered, why not slow down tomorrow for a while, until you are stronger?"

Kevana stared for a while before speaking slowly.

"We were simply in pursuit of the thieves, with no real hope of catching them any time soon, now, we have an urgency, we need to be sure to get to Angorak before they do. Hopefully days before, we need to be able to track their movements, we need to be sure they are heading to Angorak, if they're not then we need to have time to change our plans."

"I understand all of this, but do you need to kill yourself to do it?"

"I'll not die, it may take me a few days longer to heal, but if we can get to Angorak, with enough time to spare I can heal there, if not then we ride some more." Alverana nodded but said nothing more for a while. Once the soup was all finished and the bowls wiped clean with the last of the bread, he topped up the wine cups and placed the jug on the small cupboard, gathered the dirty pots and put them on the tray.

"I'll get rid of these and make sure the rest understand when we are leaving." He left Kevana to himself for a short time. Kevana sipped his wine slowly, thinking of the road ahead. He knew there were going to be some hard times ahead, Zandaar had told him so, but he had no clear idea what they would be, with these thoughts cycling through his mind, he settled down to sleep.

CHAPTER FIFTY

Jangor woke as the dull grey of pre-dawn lit the tent from above. He felt Mariacostte's slim form pressed against his side. Her head on his left breast and her thin arm across his belly. He looked down at her and smiled. It had been many years since he had woken in this situation. It was a feeling he enjoyed, but he knew it was soon to be replaced by separation, not so much fun. Still the task must go on, or these people of the forest will be wiped out by the Zandaars. This was a thought he really did not relish. He leaned forwards and kissed the top of her head. The straggled hair, a little matted and salty from yesterday's exertions. She stirred slightly, so he kissed her again, this time her purple eyes popped open, and she looked up at him.

"I suppose you must go today?" She whispered.

"I am afraid so, it's time to move on, we need to do what we can to help Namdarin."

"Will you be coming back this way?"

"Perhaps, if we survive, nothing in this world is certain."

"I, for one, hope that you do come back. I have thoroughly enjoyed our time together, you are a good man."

"But now I have to leave."

Her hand slid slowly down his belly, through the coarse hair, and wrapped itself firmly around his rapidly hardening manhood. Her smile told him everything he needed to know, he rolled slowly on top of her.

Namdarin was surprised when he woke in the full light of day, he had expected someone to have woken him before now. He kissed Jayanne and rolled to his feet, pulling on his trousers, he left the tent. A quick trip to the latrine and then to find some water to drink. Still the camp was in silence, well nearly so. The gentle sounds of lovemaking from Jangor's tent, brought a smile to his lips. He considered returning to the tent, and the sleeping woman that was there, but there was much to do, if they were to be on the road before midday.

He walked over to the place the horses were picketed, Arndrol tossed his head and snorted a rough greeting. The elves had already fed the horses and placed large vats of water where they could reach them.

"From the look of your coat," said Namdarin. "they've already groomed you this morning." He pulled Arndrol's ear affectionately. Arndrol snorted and stamped a foot, by way of a warning. Namdarin felt an approaching presence behind him. As he turned thoughts raced through his mind. He was weapon less, he braced his mind, to reach for the sword and call it to him. The turn completed he saw Gervane standing very close. Namdarin blew a long and relaxing breath.

"Is there a problem?" Asked Gervane.

"I just felt someone coming up behind me and realised just how defenceless I was, Jangor would be very upset with me right now."

"Why? You are amongst friends here, you have nothing to fear here."

"I understand that, but we have enemies that may be able to reach us from a distance."

"I think you should be safe here."

"Perhaps, how is King Fennion today?"

"He's awake, which is not something I would have bet on last night. He hit the wine quite hard once the party got moving last night. I think he was a little disturbed by the feelings engendered by the actions of certain people." Gervane laughed quite openly.

"He did seem a little distressed to be involved in Laura's first broadcast."

"Just a little."

"We need to get moving, we have a long way to go and much to do. I'm going to get my people together; can you arrange for the king to meet us after breakfast?"

"I'm fairly sure I can do that. He will be sad to see you go, as will some of the others."

"Go we must."

"I understand, I'll see you in a little while." Gervane turned and walked off in the direction of the central tree. Wolf came bounding up to greet Namdarin, he sat, his great red tongue lolling to one side. Namdarin knelt and ruffled the wolf's mane, as he stood, he saw Kern coming towards him. An elvish woman was holding Kern's hand, as they walked slowly, side by side.

"Hi Kern."

"Namdarin, are the horses looked after?"

"I can't fault the elves on their care of horses, even my own."

"That's good, we should be getting ready to ride."

"Agreed, I need to talk to Fennion first, Gervane is setting up a meeting for after breakfast."

"I'll go get the food started then." Kern set off towards the camp without introducing his friend, she smiled at Namdarin but said nothing. Wolf tagged along with Kern.

Namdarin stood for a while with the horses, talking to Arndrol, simply keeping the horse company. He became aware of an approaching figure. A strange looking elf, without the smoothness of gait that comes naturally to the elven peoples, at least until advanced age has affected them. This one looked both young and unsteady on his feet, his walking staff gave away his identity.

"Hail Namdarin." Called the figure.

"New clothes Gregor?"

"Yes." Replied the younger man, turning slowly so that Namdarin could see the complete effect. "A gift from one of the ladies from the party last night."

"Green and grey elven robes suit you well," said Namdarin, "far better than your previous attire."

"I agree, all that black was getting very depressing." Gregor laughed loudly, a couple of the horses spooked a little by the sound, ears flattened to the heads, and they braced to run. Gregor choked the laugh down to a quieter level and the horses relaxed. "What are the plans for today?"

"Breakfast, meeting with the king, and then south at speed. Simple really."

"Sounds reasonable to me, though I don't think it's going to be any fun. I'd suggest a fast run to the east, then a short sea voyage, then set up for a new life on a new continent."

"That does indeed sound like a lot more fun, but I have a task to complete first. If you choose to make that run to the east, I will not hold it against you."

"Looks like I'm along for the ride as well, you're going to need all the help you can get. Look who's coming." He pointed at two figures walking very slowly towards them. The two approached and stopped at arm's length. Both bowed.

"Good morning Tomas and Torral." Said Namdarin.

"Good morning Lord Namdarin." Replied Tomas.

"I am sorry for the loss you suffered yesterday. I don't ever expect you to forgive us, but I do hope that your pain will lessen over time."

"I thank you for your kind words," replied Tomas, "but respectfully ask of your plans for today?"

"We plan to be gone before the sun reaches its zenith."

"That is for the best, your simple presence here causes pain."

"Father." Interrupted Torral.

"Relax Torral." Said Namdarin, "I know that our presence is hard on some of your people, I intend to remove that pain as soon as I possibly can."

"That would be for the best." Said Tomas. "Many of our people will be sad that you are leaving, I will never be numbered amongst them. I'm sure you understand."

"I do." Namdarin tipped a small bow his way.

"That said, I wish you all the luck there is in your endeavour. It is in all our interests that Zandaar is removed from this world."

"I thank you for your honesty."

"I am interested to know how you plan to take the mindstone from the king's sword?"

"I actually have no idea as yet, I'm hoping for some sort of inspiration to present itself. Have you any thoughts on the matter?"

"Sorry I can't help you with that."

"Can't or won't?" Namdarin smiled.

"Interesting thought. Luckily, I don't have to make that choice, I have no idea how the removal of the mindstone could be achieved. I hope to find out later today." Tomas smiled and turned away, taking Torral with him.

"He's a strange old man." Said Gregor.

"He is that, but a good man none the less."

"Let's go and eat? I think Kern should have food ready by now."

Together they turned towards the camp, where the smell of cooking was drifting on the morning breeze. As they neared the camp, others were walking in the same direction. Granger was coming from the river, Brank and Laura from the central tree. Andel and Stergin from one of the outer trees. Jangor and Mariacostte were sitting outside his tent, Kern cooking with Wolf watching. Jayanne was a little way off, working with her axe. Swinging complex patterns against imaginary enemies, her hair flying loose all around her head as she exercised. Namdarin ducked into his tent briefly, returned with his sword. Shortly, the blue blade was sweeping rapid arcs in the sunlight as he and Jayanne fenced, sword against axe. The song of steel filled the air all through the glade. Long before Kern declared that breakfast was ready, both Jayanne and Namdarin, were dripping with sweat.

"You'd think they had enough exercise yesterday." Said Stergin.

"You'd think your sword was sharp enough." Laughed Andel, waving a hand at Stergin's whetstone, stroking along the edge. Stergin's only response was a lift of the eyebrows.

"Breakfast won't be long." Called Kern. He was toasting bread and frying bacon and mushrooms over the fire. Granger and Gregor were stood near the fire, close together, talking in quiet voices, almost whispers.

"What are you two plotting?" Asked Jangor, looking pointedly at the magicians.

"Ah," replied Granger, "we are discussing the events of last night. It seems my young colleague got quite mixed up in all the excitement, I just want to know what it was like, I have never seen or even heard of such a thing."

"It was certainly something different." Said Jangor, reaching out and taking the hand of Mariacostte.

"I agree," she said, "definitely different." She smiled, then looked away, as if embarrassed.

"It was fun." Said Laura.

"And today we leave." Muttered Brank.

"You'll be back."

"I'll try, don't wait longer than a year. If I'm not back by then, I'm dead." He scooped her up in his arms and kissed her quite firmly, tears flowed slowly down both their faces.

"Breakfast is ready." Said Kern, tipping stacks of bacon and buttered toast out onto a pair of huge platters. He snatched the first portions for himself and his lady friend. A general melee occurred until all the food was gone and in a short time Kern started on a second batch.

Jayanne wiped her greasy hands on her shirt, and then her trousers. She sighed, content with a full belly, and the tang of salt bacon on her tongue.

"We have to meet with the king soon." Said Namdarin, staring at the stains on her clothes. Her green eyes locked onto his clear blue ones, her clenched fists rested on her hips, her increased breathing put her shirt under some serious tension. Silence filled the glade, blazing blue and green stared hard. Wolf dropped belly to the ground and whimpered softly. She tossed her head and howled with laughter. With both hands she grabbed Namdarin's face and kissed him. In the next moments her clothes hit the ground, she set off towards the river, snatching the axe as she went, she paused as she passed between the last of the tents, looked back over her shoulder, every eye was on her.

"Namdarin." She called. "You stink." Then she continued her stately strut down to the river. Namdarin sniffed delicately.

"She's not wrong." He stripped off and took his sword, setting off to the river, presumably for a wash.

Mariacostte's eyes fixed on his flexing buttocks as he marched away from them.

"Jangor." She whispered.

"Yes, Mariacostte."

"Your people are all crazy."

"No, they're not, they just do a very good impression."

While they were all eating the second servings, the bathing session changed into a very wet fencing match.

"At least they'll not get sweaty." Observed Kern.

"They'll not get any rest either," replied Jangor. "and we have a long way to go today."

"What are those two doing?" Demanded Gervane, walking into the camp.

"Just blowing off some steam, they're not serious."

"How can you tell?"

"If they were serious, they'd be standing back to back, and the world would be shaking in fear."

"Perhaps. The king will meet you all in the central chamber shortly."

"That may not be a good idea." Said Granger.

"Why?"

"We have no idea what is going to happen, there could be a large energy release, when he tries to swap the stones over. Personally, I'd rather have that happen out here in the glade. Confined spaces are not ideal for large magics."

"And how, exactly, do I explain that to him? He wants his spectacle."

"I will come back with you and explain it to him, I'll use simple words." Granger looked at Gregor for a moment. "You're with me." He said, Gregor nodded. As the three left the camp Gervane turned back for a moment.

"Get those two," he nodded in the direction of the river, "dry and calmed down before we get back."

Jangor smiled.

"Namdarin, Jayanne." He yelled. "Time to stop playing games. Fennion is going to be bringing his entire court down to see us very soon now, so out of the water, and put some clothes on." The last statement caused some giggles through the camp.

"Did you really have to say that?" Whispered Mariacostte, watching a very wet, and naked, Namdarin walking towards them.

"Didn't you get enough entertainment last night?" Muttered Jangor.

"Of course, but you have to admit, he is an excellent specimen."

"He's not really my cup of tea." Laughed Jangor.

"I fairly sure he's exactly someone's cup of tea." She was watching Jayanne's eyes as she followed Namdarin from the river. The two vanished into their tent, the sounds emanating from the tent made it clear to all that they were indeed getting dressed to meet the king. It's very difficult for two people to get dressed at the same time in a small tent. In short order, Namdarin was pushed into the open air, to finish dressing in more public, but less cramped conditions.

A barked warning from Wolf caught all their attention. They turned towards the central tree, to see a procession of stately elves moving sedately towards the camp. The king flanked by the two magicians, staves flashing blue with every impact as they marched. Followed by the council of elders, and quite a crowd. Fennion carried his sword at his hip, one hand resting on the hilt, more to control the way it moved than to be ready to draw. Jangor almost laughed at the look of confidence on Fennion's face, he knew it to be false. Jayanne came into view fully clothed, Namdarin settled his sword on his back. They both formed up either side of Jangor and set off to meet the approaching party. Kern, Brank and Wolf one step behind.

With an unspoken agreement the groups stopped with four paces between them. The two magicians planted their staves and a column of blue fire jumped from the tip of each, up into the air. Jangor glanced at each, and received a wry smile in return, everyone knew they were simply showing off.

"Hail, king Fennion." Bowed Jangor.

"Hail Jangor." Replied the king, with a much shorter bow, more of a nod really. Again, Jangor smiled.

"Today we will leave, and continue our quest, hopefully one day we will return, though this is by no means certain. We only have one task before we go, the transfer of the mindstone to Namdarin's sword."

"It's not really mine, it belongs to Xeron." Said Namdarin.

"Have you any idea how this can be accomplished?" Asked Fennion.

"Actually none." Replied Namdarin.

"Then what do you suggest?"

"The stones themselves are such intrinsic parts of the swords, I don't believe they can be removed. I think the properties of the stones themselves can be swapped, the black becomes green and the green becomes black."

"That seems preferable to breaking them, but how?"

"I can't believe that Gyara would suggest this if we couldn't make it happen. I suggest we bring the stones together, and simply ask them to change places." Namdarin shrugged.

"Seems worth a try." Fennion drew his sword, making a much better job of it this time, Jangor nodded. He planted it point down in the grass. Namdarin drew his sword with a smooth overhand action, turned it over and planted it similarly. Now the two were close together, their similarity was un-deniable. The king of the elves and the lord of Namdaron each leaned their swords closer together, until the pommel stones touched. Fennion wished the mindstone to leave his sword, Namdarin wished it to come to his. Fennion wished the darkness of Xeron take up residence in his sword, Namdarin wished the darkness to leave the sword of Xeron. Elf and man each saw the gem in their sword appear to spin without moving, a spiral motion without action. The black slowly showed a core of green, and the green a core of black. These spiralling cores grew gradually until the black was green and the green black. Fennion looked into Namdarin's eyes.

"That was easier than I expected." The pair lifted their modified swords, each stared hard at the new pommel stones. Wolf yapped, and raced back to the camp, he stood beside Laura, mane bristling, his resonant growl deep in his throat. Though Wolf couldn't quite find his target, he could feel it approaching. Namdarin and Fennion raised their swords, stood back to back. Jayanne snatched the axe of Algoron to hand and stood with them, Jangor drew his sword and joined the three. The magicians stood ready, staves searching for targets. The familiar sound of distant wings was heard.

"Gyara comes." Shouted Kern. A rushing of wind and wings as the huge black bird came into view. Gyara was not alone this time, she stood to one side of the central group, to the other side, a vague figure appeared. The dis-embodied head of a grey bearded man with long hair, Namdarin had seen Xeron before, though not in this world.

"Craawk." Screamed Gyara, as the buffeting from her wings caused so many to stagger.

"Namdarin." Called the voice from the grave, the four warriors turned as a group so that Namdarin was facing the head of Xeron. Jayanne and Fennion changed places, so she now stood back to back with Namdarin. Fennion and Jangor protecting the sides.

"You have done well." Said Xeron.

"Very well." Croaked Gyara. "I could not have wished for better."

"You have created the weapons that can end Zandaar," said Xeron. "you can defeat him, you can destroy him, you can free yourselves from his power."

"You will free us all from servitude to this world." Said Gyara.

"He will never do that." Snapped Xeron.

"Perhaps, but she will, directly or indirectly, she is the one with the power."

"I will never do what you want." Screamed Jayanne, "I'll kill you first."

"Believe me when I say that I wish that you could." Sniggered Gyara. "Even death would be better than what comes this way."

"What does Gyara mean?" Asked Namdarin, his gaze on the spectral face of Xeron.

"Grinderosch spoke the truth, when the moment is right, you will know what to do, I can tell you no more. Gyara on the other hand."

"I will tell them nothing," interrupted Gyara, "they know what they need to do, that should be enough."

"Can anyone tell me, what in all the hells is going on here?" Yelled Fennion.

"I can tell you nothing." Said Xeron.

"I can tell you everything." Giggled Gyara.

"So. Both of your plans are in progress and can come to fruition." Snarled Fennion. "Be gone, both of you, neither of you are needed at the moment, if ever."

"We shall go." Said Xeron. "We will be nearby should you need us."

"I plan to plunge this sword into Zandaar's heart and end his time on this plane." Said Namdarin.

"Once he is gone, then I can be freed from this servitude." Said Gyara.

"Gyara believes that the hunger that cannot be filled will free her."

"He will, I will be free."

"That is in no way certain as yet." Xeron's already translucent face fades slowly from view. Gyara squawks one more time as her huge wings sweep her slowly into invisibility.

"Those two are really beginning to get on my nerves." Laughed Jangor.

"But what do they mean?" Demanded Fennion.

"Nothing they do or say is ever clear." Said Namdarin.

"So, what are you going to do now?" Asked Fennion.

"Simple," replied Namdarin, "we ride south, Xeron says we have what we need to kill Zandaar, Gyara thinks the same, after a fashion. From what they have both said there may be some other foe to face but face it we will. Fennion, I'd like to thank you and your people for all the help they have given us. I make a promise to you that should any of our party survive the confrontations to come, this sword and its mindstone will be returned to you."

"Lord Namdarin." Answered Fennion formally. "We thank you for this and hope that you bring the mindstone back to us."

Fennion bowed, then turned away, walked slowly through the throng of his people, most of whom followed.

Once the crowd had dispersed enough Jangor spoke in his usual military manner.

"Let's get this camp stripped and be on the road before noon. Now move." He turned and walked towards his tent, to begin tearing it down. Mariacostte stepped into his way. Her eyes held his for a long moment.

"You are really leaving?" She whispered.

"You know that I have to. You knew that before you insisted on my services." He turned his eyes downwards lest she see the sadness in them.

"I know, I understand, but I don't have to like it."

"I feel the same."

"Will you come back to me?"

He looked into her eyes again, no longer caring what she saw there.

"I promise if I survive, I shall return or get word to you of my death." He hugged her hard to his chest, kissed her. Sobs choked in her throat, her arms flew around his neck, and pulled him even harder against her. With a loud sigh, she broke the kiss and pushed him away, her tears leaving long tracks down her face.

"I'll help you." She muttered, "Let's get this over with."

Jangor swept the camp with his eyes, Namdarin's tent was already falling, packs were ready for the horses. Mariacostte went into the tent to start packing things away. In very short order, a bedroll and saddle bags came out of the tent to be caught and stacked for loading.

"Has anyone seen Mander?" Shouted Jangor. No one answered, a couple shook their heads.

"Damn him." Snapped Jangor, his eyes turned to Wolf lounging by the fire. He noticed that the fire was blazing higher than it had been, most likely caused by the presence in its midst of two staffs.

"Wolf." He said. Wolf stood and came to him. "Find Mander, bring him here." Wolf turned his nose upwards briefly, then set off to one of the outer trees, a grey and black arrow, seeking out its target.

"Kern." He called. "That wolf could indeed be useful." They both laughed and continued with the packing of tents.

"Namdarin, can you get the horses, we need to start loading them."

"I have already taken care of that."

Jangor frowned a questioning look.

"I told Arndrol to free them and bring them here."

"Interesting." said Jangor. "I hope there are no elves trying to keep them to their pickets."

"I hadn't thought of that, they tend to be pretty much left to themselves."

"Here they come." Across the glade the horses were indeed coming to the camp. Leading them was Arndrol, he was having some trouble, not with the horses, but with the picket line itself. He'd decided to bring that as well, carrying the rope in his mouth he kept stepping on it and dropping it. The continual stopping and picking it up again was really starting to get him angry. Namdarin rushed over to help the horse with the rope and to thank him for bringing the others. He threw his arms around the horse's neck and allowed himself to be lifted from his feet briefly.

"Time to be travelling again, my friend." He said, stroking the long white neck. Stergin and Andel started loading the pack horses, while Kern saddled the riding horses, other than Arndrol of course. That fell to Namdarin, the big grey wouldn't let anyone else do it. It had been far too long since Namdarin had saddled the horse himself.

There was some form of commotion in one of the outer trees, shouting and laughing, from the ramp came a naked human figure, chased by a large canine. Not so much chased, as herded. Guided by a gentle nip at an ankle, or a touch against a knee.

"Kern." Said Jangor. "Wolf or sheepdog?"

"I'd say a little of each." Laughed Kern. Behind the man came three young elven girls. Loosely dressed and carrying between them a man's clothing, they were laughing as they ran after the wolf. Mander fell on his belly at Jangor's feet, Wolf placed one foot on his back.

"Thank you Wolf." Said Jangor. "And you ladies for bringing his clothes, he needs them now. Mander get dressed, we are leaving very shortly." The girls threw his clothing on the ground and helped him to his feet. Each hugged him in turn, each kissed him, their robes fell open as they pressed their naked bodies against his, the last of the three laughed aloud as she pulled away, feeling some of Mander's tumescence returning.

"Can we expect angry fathers pursuing us to the ends of the world?" Asked Jangor.

"No. Definitely not." Mander started dressing. "Those girls are crazy, they're not broadcasters but they did insist on holding hands with someone every time, I'm completely knackered."

"Get the horses packed we will be leaving very soon." Called Jangor. "Namdarin, do you think we'll get some sort of escort, or should we just mount up and ride off."

"I think there are some that will want to say goodbye."

"And some that will want to be sure we've actually left." Jangor smiled.

A large group of tall elven horses came thundering into the glade, Gervane at their head. His troop made up the bulk of the riders, a few prominent exceptions, and two empty horses.

"Hail Gervane." Shouted Jangor.

"Hail friend." Called Gervane.

"King Fennion," said Namdarin, "come to see us off?"

"Perhaps escorting you off the premises." Laughed the king.

"Torral?" Asked Namdarin.

"Father wanted to come, but he's too frail for any serious riding, so I made him stay at home, and I took his place."

"That's a sensible thing to do, honour guard, or escort off the grounds?"

"Some of both, my lord, some of both." Torral smiled.

"It's good that you come along." Namdarin looked questioningly at the two horses without riders, then at Gervane. Gervane looked at the king. Namdarin's gaze moved on.

"They're nothing to do with me, not my idea at all." Said Fennion, looking at Laura.

"They're mine." Said Laura. "I'm coming with you."

"That's fine." Growled Namdarin. "When the rest turn back, so do you. If you have to be tied across your saddle, you will be going home, is that understood?"

"I accept your terms, Lord Namdarin."

"Good. Why two horses?"

"The other is a gift."

"A gift worthy of a king, for whom?"

"Brank." Everyone looked at the large man, his jaw fell open.

"Laura, you have to be jesting? That damned horse is huge." Groaned Brank.

"He is Luthien, the latest of our greatest bloodline, he will never fail you, nor let you fall. He will run a whole day after all these others have died. He will bring you back to me."

"But he's so big." Mumbled Brank.

"You'll do fine." said Jangor, "These elvish horses are famous."

"Famous for what?"

"Famous for being seen only in the distance, no one ever gets that close to them, or at least never reports the fact."

"That is not entirely true." Laughed Gervane. "Not entirely."

Brank stared up at the horse that Laura was now holding for him. The fear in his eyes was obvious for all, even Luthien could sense it. The horse stepped forwards and placed his chin on the big man's shoulder. Brank reached up, and held on to the horse's neck, until the pair of them settled down together, Brank looked even more frightened standing so close to the horse.

"Luthien," said Laura. "this is Brank, you are to look after him, and bring him home to me. Is that understood?"

Luthien nodded his head as if in agreement. Laura accepted the horse's word and indicated that Brank should mount up. Laura held on to the reins until Brank had hauled his not inconsiderable bulk up into the saddle. Luthien glared at the woman but made no other indication of his feelings. Laura released Luthien's head, then adjusted both stirrups, just to be sure they were set right for Brank.

"The saddle comes with the horse," she said, "you'll have to look after it, and you'll have to get used to it, our saddles are a slightly different shape to yours." Brank groaned, and everyone else laughed.

"What's wrong with him?" She asked of Jangor.

"Well he's barely got used to a human shaped saddle, he's going to hurt all over again, learning one of yours." He laughed.

"Oh, you poor little lamb." She laughed and blew Brank a kiss, which only caused him to groan again.

"Let's get this party on the road." Yelled Jangor, he turned towards his horse, only to find Mariacostte standing squarely in his way. She reached up with both arms and pulled his head down for a long kiss.

"I shall miss you." She whispered as the kiss broke.

"And I you, perhaps we shall be back this way, if you want, that is?"

"I'd like that. Now run, before I decide to hold you prisoner." He glanced around, only himself and Kern were still on the ground. Kern was turning to his horse as his lady friend moved slowly away. Jangor swarmed up into his saddle, with a final look around, and a meaningful glance for Mariacostte.

"Let's ride." He yelled, laying heels to his horse's flanks and setting off south for the river, knowing full well that the others would catch up.

CHAPTER FIFTY-ONE

Alverana woke with a start, the light from the window had barely a touch of the grey of pre-dawn. He felt an arm across his chest, and the slow steady breathing of the person next to him. He remembered how during the night, though Kevana had been sleeping, he was shivering and shaking in his sleep. Alverana added his blankets to his friend's and crawled carefully under them, simply to warm them both. Now here he was, laying on his back, with Kevana's arm across his chest, Kevana's left thigh across his own, far too much naked skin touching. With every slow and careful breath, he took, he could feel the coarse hairs on Kevana's arm moving through those on his own chest. He could feel every beat of Kevana's heart against his shoulder. These feelings were strange but not too discomforting. The same could not be said for the feeling of Kevana's morning erection against his hip, or Kevana's thigh pressing against his own, these were quite disconcerting.

He gently took Kevana's left wrist in his right hand and shook it slowly.

"Wake up Kevana." He whispered. There was no response, so he tried again, a little louder. There was a sudden intake of breath and a tensing of Kevana's entire body. Alverana held him tightly and whispered. "Relax."

"Relax." Gradually Kevana did just that, blowing warm breath into Alverana's shoulder.

"What has happened here?" He whispered.

"You were cold and shaking in the night, I shared my blankets and you warmed up. We find ourselves like this. How are you feeling?"

"I feel quite good, nothing like as tired as I was, I'd say not exactly top form, but capable of riding hard today, as we had decided."

"You decided. You were quite firm about it."

"I'm feeling even firmer right now."

"I had noticed that."

"So are you."

"I had noticed that too."

"You're not moving away." Whispered Kevana. Alverana released his wrist.

"Neither are you." He mumbled.

"What are we going to do about this situation?" Kevana's hand slid slowly down Alverana's chest, making a gentle rustling sound as it passed over the coarse hairs.

"Well," muttered Alverana, "we're going to have to get out of bed very soon. Your plan was to be on the road after dawn prayers after all."

"I know that, but somehow I am loath to move from here."

"Me too. I'm just far too comfortable." Kevana moved his thigh slowly further across the body of his friend. Rubbing across Alverana's erection and pressing his own harder into his hip.

"That feels strange but good. I am sorry, but we need to be moving. Miles to go before we sleep."

"Sadly, I agree. We will share our blankets again?" Kevana's voice shook as the question passed his lips. Alverana nodded a little. Kevana smiled, then slid his leg further over his friend, until he was above, and astride Alverana. "No underwear next time?" Again, Alverana nodded. Kevana slid across him and snatched his outer robe, which he threw around his shoulders as he rushed off to the latrine. Alverana rolled slowly to his feet and started dressing, he felt the same need for the latrine, but somehow, he didn't want to meet Kevana there.

Kevana met Petrovana in the hallway.

"Get the others moving." He said.

"Already done that, the horses are being loaded even now. How are you feeling?"

"Better, much better."

"That's good, I was worried."

"Why?"

"You don't want to know."

"Pray tell."

"You insisted." Petrovana paused, looking hard into Kevana's eyes. "I don't want to be part of a group run by Worandana. If that happens, nothing is going to end well."

"Thank you for your honesty. I'll do what I can to make sure I don't die."

"Thank you Kevana." Petrovana nodded and turned away.

Having completed his ablutions, Kevana went straight to the refectory. Where he found Worandana and Bruciana talking quietly at a table.

"I'm hungry." He declared, "What food is ready?"

"Custom dictates we eat after morning prayers." Said Bruciana, trying his best to sound confident.

"Bugger custom." Snapped Kevana, "I'm hungry now."

"Are you planning on getting dressed at some point today?" asked Worandana, indicating Kevana's open robe and underwear.

"Maybe, after I've had something to eat." He waved Bruciana away as he took a seat at the table.

"You're feeling better I see," said Worandana, "if more than a little peevish."

"I'm mainly hungry. I've never felt this hungry in my life."

"The drain of talking to Zandaar must have been dreadful."

"It certainly is, I dread it ever happening again."

"The thing is you may be his contact point for the group now, he knows your mental signature well now. You'll be very easy for him to find."

"That is the real scary thing." Said Kevana as Bruciana returned with a few slices of bacon, between some bread and a small cup of wine.

"Thank you Bruciana, that is greatly appreciated." Kevana snatched the sandwich and took it in three bites, barely chewing, swallowing huge chunks, washing it down with the wine. With a huge belch he was finished. "How long until sunrise?" He asked.

"Not long," replied Worandana. "we better get ready for prayers, and you should get dressed."

"Fine." Said Kevana as he left the refectory, not quite at a run. He returned to his room, to find that Alverana had almost finished the packing, by the time Kevana was dressed it was complete. They picked up their saddle bags and went out into the courtyard. The horses were lined up against one wall, together they loaded their saddle bags, then turned towards the central chapel.

"Have you any idea, just how much I don't want to go in there?" Whispered Kevana, one hand on Alverana's arm, slowing them both.

"I understand." Replied Alverana. "I feel the same sometimes, especially around the temples of Gyara. Do you know how many of those we have seen together?"

"Yes, one."

"Oh my, do I wish that was true. We have walked through at least seven in the last five years."

"Seven?"

"Yes, and each one calls to me, every time. And each one frightens me, every time."

"So why did you summon Gyara in the mountains?"

"Because Worandana was going to do it and do it wrong. That could have killed us all." They watched the last of the black robed figures go into the chapel. "We really need to go inside."

"I don't want to, but I suppose we must. I'm going nowhere near that altar, I'm not even going to look at it. Do you understand?"

"Close your eyes and I will guide you." Alverana took Kevana's arm in his own and led his friend into the chapel, together they took seats at the back. Even though, as guests, there were pews set aside for them at the front. All through the ceremony Kevana missed the strange glances he was getting from the residents. Once it was over, Alverana guided him outside, Kevana opened his eyes and breathed deeply of the fresh air. Which for some reason had never tasted so good.

"Are you feeling alright?" Asked Alverana.

"Better, and better by the minute, let's go eat." Kevana's turn to lead, straight into the refectory, he went to the serving table, and collected plenty of food, perhaps even enough for two. They sat down at a table to eat, and gradually their group gathered around them. Kirukana scowled at every one, especially Crathen.

"What's your problem Kirukana?" Demanded Worandana.

"Him." Kirukana pointed at Crathen, this caused many raised eyebrows around the table.

"Crathen has caused no offense to the rest of us, so what is your issue?"

"He was present in the chapel and participated in the ceremony, this should not be allowed."

"And why is that?"

"Our ceremonies are secret, and devoted to god, not for the uninitiated."

"Our services are not secret, and outsiders are always welcome, where do you get this idea?"

Kirukana thought for a moment before answering.

"I'm not sure, I can't remember any specific instruction, or edict from the council, it just seems to have happened."

"Kevana." Said Worandana, "Did you notice that?"

"What?"

"Kirukana actually paused for thought before he spoke."

"And I missed it? Perhaps your training is finally taking root, I don't expect it to happen again. At least not anytime soon." He laughed.

"I had to think about it." Said Kirukana, "I couldn't remember anything, it just happened."

"So." Said Worandana, "The instructions and edicts are engraved in large letters in your head, so you can't forget them. You need to be careful, big letters take up a lot of space, you will soon be running out."

"It's not that so much," replied Kirukana, "it's the meditation ritual, I recite the one hundred and twenty-three edicts, the two hundred and sixty-nine instructions and the suggestions as a way of relaxing. It helps to keep things fresh in my mind."

"That in itself is interesting. Edicts, instructions, these have precise numbers, the suggestions on the other hand, seem a little vague. Why?"

"They just are, not just vague, but sometimes contradictory."

"So, you choose which ones to remember and which ones to forget?"

"I suppose." Kirukana frowned, unsure as to where Worandana was taking this conversation.

"Your council, whose entire purpose is to reveal the word of god, makes suggestions, that you decide are not worth remembering?"

"So it would seem, I'd never actually thought about it that way."

"I suggest that you have never actually thought about anything, you are only just beginning to think. I have an idea for you. Pick one or two of those suggestions that you have rejected, think about them and the reasons for your rejection. Then work out just how stupid you would have to be to turn this suggestion into an instruction."

"I shall do this, but it makes me feel very uncomfortable."

"Why?"

"You will want me to explain why the council is wrong and why I am better than them."

"Well done, you begin to think. Will you do it? Will you be honest, not to me, but to yourself?"

"I shall try." Said Kirukana, after a moments delay.

"Oh my." Said Kevana, "He did it again." A big smile on his face.

"There's no need to be rude." Snapped Kirukana.

"Not rude, a congratulation, your education is beginning to take hold."

"You plan to turn me into someone just like you?"

"No." Said Worandana, "Our plan is to turn you into your own person, not someone indoctrinated by the council."

"I'm not sure that is a good thing."

"That is also true. Being a free thinker and trying to live in their rigid world, this can be very dangerous. Never boring. Occasionally fatal. Learn fast, once you leave their controlled boundaries, anything can happen." Smiled Worandana.

"Enough delays." Called Kevana. "It's time to ride. Bruciana." The local leader looked up at the sound of his name. "Thank you for all your help, the supplies and the people. Please try and get word to the central monasteries. Tell them that we are not a threat and are committed to the mission Zandaar has assigned us."

"I'll do what I can."

"Thank you, and goodbye." He got to his feet and looked around the room, picking up each of his people with momentary eye contact. "Assemble for departure immediately." He left the refectory without a backward glance, knowing his men would be following him. The sound of scuffing chairs and heavy boots told him this was true. He didn't actually look back until he was standing by his horse, in the courtyard. Immediately on his heels was Alverana, with the rest in close pursuit. In very short order they were all mounted.

"Alverana, do you know the quickest route to Angorak?"

"East past this small mountain range, and across the river and then south, that'll get us there, if there is a quicker or better route, I have no idea."

"That'll do for me, lead out, and keep the pace up, we cannot afford to get to Angorak second." Sweeping the compound with a glance he caught Bruciana's eye. "Bruciana, thanks again, see to the gate for us, will you?" Bruciana waved at a man standing near to the gate.

"Kevana, I wish you all the luck in the world with your mission, sadly, I feel you are going to need it." Bruciana bowed deeply as the gate swung inwards. Alverana kicked his horse up to a trot before he was through the gate, Kevana behind him leaving the rest to sort out their own order. Alverana turned east and pushed the pace to a smooth canter, Kevana pulled alongside, his black horse enjoying the run, if not the terrain. The plateau looked smooth and flat from a distance, but up close it was criss-crossed with shallow gullies and sudden potholes. Perhaps the burrows of animals, none of which were visible. Alverana kept the pace as high as he dared to keep some modicum of safety. Seeing as they had a destination in mind, and he knew that their quarry would be heading that way. Alverana wasn't wasting time checking for trails, or tracks, he was simply looking for the best path that they could ride along at a decent clip. Much of the time he was actually letting the horse choose its own path, the rest of the group just followed in his tracks. After an hour they reached the edge of the plateau, here their pace had to be reduced. The tracks down into the valley were quite well defined, though they didn't look like they got much in the way of horse traffic. Smaller animals were responsible, most likely sheep, goat and deer. As the trees closed in along the path it became quite narrow. Occasional branches whipped at his horse and his own face; this caused another reduction in pace. Each time he came to a fork in the path he picked the one that looked the best for the horses. By mid-morning, they were deep into the forest, the paths were now even steeper. In places Alverana considered dismounting but he knew that his own riding skills were good enough and the others can see to their own rides. The trail levelled out, and then opened out into a small open glade. The sun cast hard edged shadows, the brilliant green of the grass was too tempting to pass. Alverana dismounted and released his horse to eat for a while, grabbed some food from his saddle bag. Kevana followed suit.

"Rest break." He called. Releasing his own horse to graze alongside Alverana's. He turned to the newest members of the group.

"How are you three doing?"

"We're just not used to so much hard riding." said Astorana. Alverana laughed out loud. "What's so funny?"

"This isn't hard." Said Alverana. "The horses aren't breathing, I see no foam on their chests, and the riders shouldn't be tired at all. You'll learn soon enough what hard riding is, and perhaps hard fighting as well."

"If this is easy, perhaps we should go back to mining?" Astorana mumbled to his two friends.

"No, I'm not going back there, it's far too boring, with these guys we stand a chance of seeing some of the world." Replied Davadana.

"But we could die tomorrow."

"I'd rather die out here, than in that dreary mining camp. The sun is shining, the grass is green, and my arse feels like it's been beaten with a stick." He laughed loudly, and wandered off into the trees, most likely to relieve himself.

"Canteens are getting low." Observed Alverana, shaking Strenoana's water bottle.

"We'll stop at the next stream for refills." Said Kevana.

"I thought that Worandana was in charge?" mumbled Strenoana to Kirukana.

"Worandana is the leader of the clerics, Kevana of the military, this is a military situation."

"So why did god choose a military commander to speak to?"

"It could be something as simple as the fact that Kevana was in the chapel, in front of the altar, staring at the symbol, at the moment god reached out."

"You people are really complicated."

"You don't realise the half of it yet."

"What do you mean?"

"You know the mission we are on?"

"Yes. We heard."

"And you were told to attack us on sight?"

"If Worandana was wielding the sword."

"He wasn't and still you considered attacking."

"I suppose."

"Do you suppose that yours was the only place advised thus?"

"Probably not."

"So, your aborted attempt to kill us is likely to happen again?"

"I suppose."

"And you joined this group knowing that?"

"We didn't really look at it like that." Strenoana looked to both his friends, eyebrows raised all around. Kirukana simply smiled at them and turned away.

"Did we do the right thing joining with these men?" Asked Strenoana.

"I think so." Replied Davadana. "We are now travelling with the intention of meeting Zandaar. What could be better?"

"We could be killed by our own people."

"Look around you, carefully, these are now our people. For better or worse, we have chosen their path, now we have to learn to live with it."

"For such a young man you have a real feel for drama." Said Worandana.

"Am I wrong?"

"In some ways no, but in others yes. There are many who would want to kill us, at least half the council of elders would be quite happy if we were to die along this road. Equally unhappy if the opposing faction got their hands on the sword, the sword we don't have as yet. Let's hope we get it fairly soon, it will certainly simplify things more than a little."

"I'll definitely agree with that, but first we've got to get to Angorak."

"Right. Kevana, how much longer for this rest, we need to be moving?"

"Give the horses a few more minutes, then we can get moving again."

"Seeing as we are looking down on the tops of nearby trees, I'd say the path gets quite steep and very soon."

"I'm hoping that Alverana can find us a path down from here that was not created by the local goats."

"I'm sure I can see a rabbit trail just over there." Laughed Alverana, pointing at a small gap in the long grass at the edge of the glade.

Worandana walked into the middle of the glade, and slowly turned a complete circle, scrutinising everything that he could see. Finally, he turned to Alverana.

"Can you think of any reason there would be an open glade here?" Alverana's turn to look more carefully than he had before.

"No fallen tree, no young trees competing for the light, no underbrush struggling to spread across the open ground." He stamped his heel into the ground, it left a shallow impression in the grass that sprang back almost immediately. "The ground is good and dry; the grass is green and well fed. I can see no reason that trees shouldn't be growing here, at least no natural reason."

"What sort of un-natural reason then?"

"Someone or something is preventing the trees from claiming this open ground. Not even the tiniest of saplings are sprouting here."

"Do you think god or man?" muttered Worandana.

"No idea, if this is a temple of sorts, it's not dedicated to Gyara, no summoning tree. I see no altar for any of the other gods that I know of. As far as I know this place is too remote to be maintained by men from the nearest village."

"How can you be sure of that?"

"The paths are all game trails, nothing bigger than deer come here on any sort of regular basis, though some deer do like to eat saplings, they don't generally dig them out. There is something else about this place though."

"What?"

"It smells funny."

"What do you mean?" Demanded Worandana.

"I don't know, it's smells like something I almost remember." Alverana walked over to one of the trees on the edge of the grassy area. Looking closely, he noticed high above his head a series of parallel vertical grooves cut into the bark. He looked nervously around.

"Everyone mount up. Fast and quiet. Move it." His voice barely above a whisper. Kevana bounded to his feet and jumped into his saddle, he snatched the reins of Alverana's horse and walked slowly over to where his friend was standing.

"What is it?" He whispered as Alverana levered himself upwards in to the saddle.

"I remember now." Was the return, his words almost drowned by a deep resonant sound, "hugg, hugg, hugg." All around men were now climbing onto the backs of horses, these were getting more and more restive, as the sounds came closer.

Astorana was struggling to get his horse under control, it kept moving away as he tried to mount. Alverana rode over and snatched its reins, holding its head still against his leg, while the younger man mounted.

"Kevana." Said Alverana quietly. When the leader looked at him, he went on. "I'll lead, you and Worandana cover our retreat, keep your horses under control, use fire only, it will be more effective, but under no circumstances run, if you run you are lost. Am I clear?"

"Your instructions are clear, but what in all the hells, are we facing?" Alverana pointed to the far end on the glade, stalking into the dappled sunlight came a huge cat like creature. His enormous mane filled out as he saw them, the deep tawny coat with dark vertical stripes, made him almost invisible in the shadows of the trees. His hugg, hugg, hugg, sound was replaced by a roar.

"Follow me." Called Alverana, "And keep those damned horses under control, tight reins at all times." He turned and walked his horse from the glade and into the darkness of the trees.

Before the roar was ended, three more cats stepped into view, they had been walking behind the leader, these were only slightly smaller, without manes, two kept to the edges of the glade, half in the shadows, the other walked alongside the leader, she was most obviously a female, with babies to feed, her low-slung teats clear evidence.

"He said fire." Muttered Worandana, reaching into his jacket, trying to hold his horse still with one hand. "Kill or scare?"

"Scare first." Said Kevana, taking several silver flames from inside his coat. His horse needed no control, though its breathing was strained it showed no signs of bolting, it trusted the man. Kevana threw the first flame, it formed in the air and exploded on the ground in front of the male. He pounced on it, trying to bite the roaring fire, only to have his head engulfed in flame. He jumped back with a howl, face blacked and whiskers gone.

"Ware." Shouted Worandana, the two cats in the shadows had started their own runs towards the men. Two flames flashed out this time, one to each side, and then a third into the middle, more for emphasis than anything. The two females aborted their runs, a little singed but not really damaged. They returned to the centre of the glade, to where the huge male was roaring in fine style. Kevana threw another flame, which burst on the grass in front of the cats, with a snarl they all took a step backwards.

"I think we can leave now." Muttered Kevana. "You first." Worandana nodded and walked his horse slowly under the trees along the path that the others had taken. Kevana walked his horse sideways until it was blocking the exit path, then he turned to face the cats. He sent one more flame towards the cats, willing all the power he could drive into it, the flash and flare were huge. The cats turned and ran, Kevana turned and walked his horse into the darkness. He didn't even glance over his shoulder.

Once out of sight of the glade, Kevana pushed his horse to a greater speed. Risking low slung branches, he caught up with the rest in only a little time, squeezing past the others he pushed up until he was behind Alverana.

"How did you know about the cats?" He asked.

"I saw scratch marks high up on the trees, and I've been told of their calls in the past. I was told to run as soon as I hear the call, if they see you, running is too late. You've got to admit, they are very beautiful?"

"That big male isn't so pretty today, he took a snout full of fire. He's not seriously damaged, but he better not put his head in any holes until his whiskers grow back."

Alverana chuckled softly to himself, guiding his horse gently down the steep gradient. The path began to open out and the slope reduced, very soon they were out of the densest part of the forest, into more open woodland. As soon as the ground was open enough Kevana pulled his horse alongside Alverana's. Kirukana's voice came from behind them.

"Is that the river ahead?"

"No." Said Alverana. "It's too small, we can follow it to the great river, then all we have to do is cross that one and follow it to Angorak."

"Sounds simple." Laughed Apostana, from a little further back in the line.

"Nothing about this is simple." Said Worandana.

"That river can't be more than an hour or two's ride from here." Said Apostana.

"And downhill all the way." Said Crathen.

Kevana glanced meaningfully at Alverana, together they kicked their horses into a smooth canter, still being careful, for the terrain was rocky and uneven. Slowly the scrubland opened out into the grassy flood plain of the river they were approaching. Kevana didn't allow the pace to get any quicker though, it's always better to keep something in reserve. His stallion was not happy about the slow pace when the ground was so smooth and open, and with all those horses behind. He just wanted to leave them even further behind. Kevana had to keep pulling him up.

Once they reached the river, Kevana turned downstream. The banks were high and dangerously crumbling, until they came upon a large bend, the inside bank was quite low and lead onto a gravel section. From the footprints in the muddy puddles it was clear that many animals watered here. Alverana stopped his horse by a long patch of soft brown mud.

"Something amiss?" Asked Kevana, as the other horses were being led to the water to drink and canteens were being filled.

"Yes." Alverana looked around, then back down at the mud. "I see sheep, deer, cattle and rabbits." He looked around again. "Where are they?"

"They're frightened of people, so they ran off to hide, until we are gone."

"Why didn't we see them running away?"

"They run too quick?"

"No. Something ran them off before we got here."

"What? Not more of those cats?"

"No. The cats are forest hunters, mainly. No, something else."

"What now?"

Alverana shrugged his shoulders and led his horse to the water's edge. He remained seated while the horse drank, scanning the much-shortened horizon, the banks were as high as his horse's saddle. He waited until Kevana had filled his water bottle, then passed his own down. Kevana filled it without a word, as he passed it back Alverana gave him his large waterskin to fill.

"You're that worried?" Alverana nodded.

"Of what?" Alverana shrugged, but maintained his watch on the land around them, he was paying close attention to a large copse. One that reached to the banks of the river, it was only about half a mile downstream of their current position. Kevana handed the filled waterskin up to Alverana, who checked the stopper and dropped the skin on the small pack behind him. His horse flinched a little as the cold weight was added but gave no other notice of the event.

Crathen was gathering driftwood for a fire. Kevana considered this for a moment before stopping him.

"We have more than a few hours of daylight before we need to camp."

"There's so much easy to find firewood, and ready water, we'll not find a better camp site than this."

"Alverana, what do you think?" Asked Kevana.

"I think it's a great site, a sloping bank in front of us, the river behind us, great place for a late-night ambush."

"You think we are in danger of an ambush?" Asked Crathen.

"Our own people have put out kill on sight instructions, what do you think?"

"They can't be serious, surely?"

"Oh, they are serious." Interrupted Astorana. "Any group carrying a sword with a black pommel stone is going to be attacked on sight. Given the warnings sent out, any commander that knows you people will attack on sight, as soon as Kevana or Worandana are recognised we will be attacked."

"And you joined us?" Asked Worandana.

"Have you any idea how boring mining is?"

"Not as such, tell me."

"Imagine shovelling sand and gravel from a freezing cold river, sun rise to sun set, every day, nothing ever changes, only the depth of the water, the temperature is unchanged, from the depths of winter to the sweaty heat of summer, that water is mind numbingly cold. Your arrival was a chance to get out, even if short lived." Astorana held out his hands and looked at them. "Do you see? They are pink and warm, not blue and cold, like they normally are. My heart has never raced so much as it did at the sight of those cats, I wasn't sure it ever would. I believed it would just slow down and stumble to a halt, in the cold of the mountains. Our time with you may be short, but at least we'll live it." The other two new additions nodded.

"This is all sort of irrelevant," said Kevana, "mount up, we are moving on." Slowly all the ones on the ground climbed into their saddles and prepared for departure.

"If we are going to follow this river." Said Alverana. "We are going to have to pass through those trees."

"You see that as a problem?" Responded Kevana.

"Perhaps, an even better place for an ambush than here?"

"We'll just have to stay alert then." He glanced round, and seeing that everyone appeared to be ready, or very nearly so, he led out. Alverana was alongside in only a moment, they walked the horses up the incline to the grass plain, then lifted the pace slowly, so that none were left behind.

"I'm still seeing no animals." Said Alverana.

"You worry too much." Laughed Kevana. His right hand almost on his sword hilt, and his left loosely holding the reins. Slowly the darkness under the trees became more ominous, Kevana's hand moved from his sword to the inside of his jacket. He slowed the pace to a walk, to pack the group together a little more. The complete silence of the trees was beginning to get to him. They were about fifty yards from the trees when the silence suddenly changed. There was a rumble of horses and the shattering of many branches, as twelve horsemen came charging into the daylight, swords drawn, and battle cries on their lips. Kevana's hand snapped from his jacket and a bolt of flame flashed out to flare up in front of the horses, one shied so violently that its rider fell from the saddle but failed to clear his foot from the stirrup, the frightened horse dragged him along the ground, back towards the safety of the trees. Kevana and Alverana galloped to engage the strange horsemen, swords drawn and more than ready for battle, before they came into contact, Strenoana's bow thrummed and one man fell, an arrow through his chest. Kevana and Alverana charged straight through the attacking line and each slashed an opponent from his saddle, one without a head, the other without an arm. As they made their turn to return to the fight, Kevana saw that Worandana was stationary, with two others, Apostana and Kirukana. They were making no attempt to close with the attackers. Worandana gestured casually with his right hand and a man fell from his horse, a few seconds later another, this one was thrown clear out of his saddle by the force of the impact. Alverana and Kevana cut down another two while they were looking for the source of the strange force that was attacking them. Fabrana took two in quick succession before dropping his bow for the close quarter use of his long knife. The resulting melee was short lived and brutal. As the last of the attackers fell dead from his saddle, Kevana yelled.

"Injuries?"

"Scratched." Shouted Fabrana, wrapping his left hand around a small cut on his right arm.

"Likewise." Called Briana, holding a shallow belly wound.

"Good." Responded Kevana, angrily. "Any of these assholes breathing?"

"Over here." Shouted Alverana, pointing at a man who was attempting to crawl away, with one hand holding a large belly wound. Alverana dropped from his horse alongside the man, turned him onto his back, and roughly examined the injury. Alverana looked up at Kevana. "He'll live if he has the sense to lie still, till I get him bandaged, and to take things easy for a few days." A pointed glance at the man on the ground was all it took to make him stop moving.

"You killed them all bar one." Called Kirukana, "These aren't assholes they're our brothers."

"They were our brothers." Said Kevana slowly and clearly, "Then they attacked us, they made no attempt to talk, there was no meeting of brotherhood. They attacked and died for it. You had your own action in this meeting, you killed them just as we did, now let's find out why."

"I need to know." Muttered Kirukana. Kevana walked over to where Alverana had the fallen monk almost completely undressed. Kevana looked a question.

"He needs more than a bandage, we go no further today." Alverana looked back to the man on the ground. Kevana looked briefly and nodded.

"Camp." He called.

"What about the danger?" Asked Crathen.

"I don't think there is another group nearby, they'd have joined forces before attacking us. Am I correct?" He looked at the injured monk.

"The nearest group is most likely a day away at least. There are a few around here."

"Well if that is true," said Kevana, "we can afford a little time for you."

"He won't be fit to travel for a couple of days at least." Said Alverana.

"Then we patch him up and leave him behind. I'm not letting this survivor slow us down, he's already costing us too much time." Snarled Kevana. "Might be better he didn't survive at all." Petrovana slapped a hand over Kirukana's mouth and whispered in his ear.

"If you speak now, you will die."

Alverana looked up at his friend.

"You cannot mean that."

"Damn it, you know I don't." Snapped Kevana, he drew his sword in a flash of steel, and screamed in frustration, before stamping off towards the trees, his sword whistling as it moved from side to side.

"I am Willowana, in the third year of my novitiate, I am currently stationed at Angorak north monastery. As were all my friends." Said the fallen monk, establishing name, rank and location.

"Well Willowana." Alverana smiled, the name had some strange overtones, what had it been before? "If you can follow instructions you may just stay alive, but we will be leaving you in the morning." The young man nodded slowly before speaking.

"Just how crazy is Kevana?"

"Right now, very, we had been advised that the word was out that we may have allied ourselves with an enemy, but he didn't actually believe that our brothers would attack without warning. Now he knows, this could go any way at all."

"What do you mean?"

"He may decide that Zandaar is no longer worthy of his loyalty."

"What would he do?"

"He's very angry, he might go so far as to take the sword from the thieves, take it back to Zandaarkoon and shove it so far up Zandaars ass that it'll knock his hat off."

"Surely not?"

"You expect sureties in this world?" Alverana laughed, then continued. "Your wound is too bad to be just bandaged, it's going to need sowing, and I don't have the time, or the drugs to be gentle about this. Do you understand?"

Willowana gave a small nod, then laid back on the grass. Alverana signalled for Apostana and Astorana to lend a hand. Apostana took Willowana's hands in his own and pressed them into the grass above the injured man's head, Astorana placed Willowana's heels together then sat on his shins. Alverana took a glove from his belt and stuffed it into Willowana's mouth. He took his sewing kit from his belt, selected a short-curved needle, placed that needle on his thick leather riding glove. Briefly he focused the power of his mind and projected that energy into the needle, which flashed red before he poured cold water on it. This was a tiring process, but far quicker than waiting for a fire. Methodically he set about stitching the long, if shallow, wound in the writhing belly before him. He paid no attention to the moaning and twitching of the injured man, he looked over at Worandana.

"Worandana." He said, calmly, "Your magic is just great for killing people, plotting to kill people over great distances, and burning down houses with people in them, have you thought of doing something like healing people?"

"If a man dies, it is gods will, who are you to question gods will." Interrupted Kirukana. Alverana looked pointedly at the thread he was using, then spoke quietly.

"I should have enough left to sew up your stupid mouth." The sneer on his lips showed that he meant it, if only for a moment or two.

"Ignoring what Kirukana has to say," said Worandana, "which is something we all should do most of the time, it has always been easier to destroy than mend. Healing is a difficult and delicate process, there are those that specialise in it, not many, nor well-travelled. Wounds such as you are currently dealing with are the easiest, hold him still and I will do what I can. I wish I had my staff; this sort of thing is always easier with a tool to focus the power. Kirukana, Apostana start me a slow cycle, steady no major surges, just a smooth feed of power. Worandana knelt beside the injured man, and gently placed his hands on each side of the wound and carefully pulled the jagged edges together, with the first surge from his companions Worandana started the healing process, the cut gradually shortened, as the edges sealed together, very slowly Worandana closed more and more of the wound, until he reached the section that Alverana had already stitched.

"Enough," said Alverana, "leave that section, if it starts to fester, he'll need something left to be opened to let the pus out."

Worandana broke the link to his friends, and slumped to the grass, breathing heavily.

"Damn, that's hard work." Muttered Apostana, his breathing no less harsh. Kirukana slumped to the grass, without a word.

"This is why we don't do this too often." Mumbled Worandana, "One man is healed and three are out of the battle."

"He's not really healed, there's still a lot of damage that needs to heal on the inside. Are you paying attention Willowana?" Said Alverana. The injured man only nodded, the wound may be closed but the pain wasn't all that much less. "You had better stay as still as possible for a couple of days, then take the stitches out, between five and ten days, don't leave it any longer or they'll never come out. I don't expect you to have any problems, but if your belly gets hot and swells open the stitches and drain the pus out. It shouldn't be a problem, most of us keep are blades relatively clean, whose blade was it that cut you?"

"It was yours." Muttered Willowana.

"Then you have been very lucky already, I hope that sort of luck holds. I must have been pressed for time or I'd have cut you in two." Smiled Alverana.

"You were being attacked by two others at the same time, I fell from my horse as you struck."

"Fortunes of war."

"All the fortune seems to be on your side."

"You're still breathing it could have been worse." Alverana turned to Worandana, as the old man was getting his breath back a bit. "If you could get a tighter focus on your power you would need less of it."

"That is correct, it would be a lot easier with a tighter focus, I'm not bad at this sort of work, but a focusing instrument would certainly help."

"When we get back you can design something, and learn the tight focus needed to heal people without the massive drain."

"That could certainly be interesting, what sort of focus device though?"

"I really don't care," said Kirukana, "anything that reduces the load on the rest of us would be an improvement."

"I thought you were against healing people?" Asked Alverana.

"Yes, but now I've seen the good it can do. I mean this man would most likely have died, if we hadn't helped him."

"Agreed."

"His chances are doubled at least now, though I can barely walk, we have done a good thing here."

"Even though the general thinking of the council says it is wrong?"

Kirukana paused, looked around at all the expectant faces, then he turned to Worandana and bowed deeply. "You are right, this is a good thing, and we must learn to do it, together?" the last word, both a question and a plea.

"Kirukana, we will learn this new lore together, while we still can, it may take us some time, but in the end it should be worthwhile. I already have an idea for a focus device."

"Fine." said Kevana, stamping into the middle of the group. "You two go off and work on your medical magic, the rest of us have work to do. Alverana, how long before we can leave this man." He waved at the fallen monk.

"I don't want to leave him for an hour or two at least, he should be mobile by then."

"How long before he can ride?"

"Couple of days and he'll be able to mount a horse, if he goes careful."

"Fine. You three." He pointed randomly. "Get these corpses into the woods, they'll not stink the place up so much. Crathen, small fire, lots of firewood, so our friend doesn't have to move far to keep his fire lit. Quick meal then we ride."

"Excuse me." Said Willowana, diffidently. Continuing as Kevana turned back to him, "Aren't you going to bury the dead?"

"I have neither the time nor, to be brutally frank, the inclination. We'll move them into the woods out of sight, I would advise against you trying to dig them graves, I suggest that as soon as you can ride, you head for somewhere that can care for you. I am sorry, but this is how it must be. Now here's a thought, did your leaders have a check in schedule?"

Willowana, looked around the group, searching faces for clues as to how to answer this question. Alverana tipped his head to one side, then spoke quietly.

"Don't think about it, if you lie, he'll know."

"Fine." Muttered Willowana, "Check in is one hour after dawn, sometimes it got as late as two hours, we just had to sit and wait until contact was made, and instructions given."

"So, the commanders of this search have a lot of groups to contact, every day." Said Kevana. "So come tomorrow morning, they'll know exactly where we are."

"Actually no." Said Willowana. "Long range communication not really my thing," he laughed, "I'm really bad at it. I don't see how it can ever work, and I can't do it. Swordplay, now that is my thing, you may not believe it, given my current state. So, come tomorrow morning they'll think that Gaffana has fallen asleep, or is too busy to hear them, he's none too good at this either, sorry was. That may just get you another day, beyond that they are going to send someone to investigate this area, they know were each group is."

Kevana looked at Worandana for a moment before speaking.

"Have you noticed that communications are becoming a problem, more and more are finding it difficult?"

"What I have noticed," replied Worandana carefully, "is that the skill levels of the military members are dropping."

"Have you also noticed that their mortality rates are also climbing?" Snarled Kevana.

"If they keep attacking us, then that's going to climb some more." Grumbled Alverana.

"What I'm saying," said Worandana, "is that the entry qualifications for soldiers have been reduced, so long as the officer corps has enough skill to communicate, the common soldiery have no need, as they only follow orders."

"Nice to know I'm just a commoner." Said Alverana.

"I think I'm in the same class." Growled Kevana.

"Worandana." Interrupted Kirukana. "Exulted leader, there comes a time when it is sensible to stop digging." He laughed loudly at the looks on every bodies faces. "You never thought you'd hear me say that." He laughed even louder, in a few moments the others joined in. Looking at the dark faces around him, his smile just kept on getting bigger. "Come on fellows, let's not take council policy too much to heart." At this point Kirukana fell to the ground, paroxysms of laughter preventing him from breathing properly.

"You know," said Kevana to Worandana, "he's enjoying this far too much, I think I'll kick him."

"You can't. In far too many ways the fool is right. Why should we worry about our relative standings? As far as the council is concerned, we are all traitors and should be killed anyway."

"I intend on making that as difficult for them as possible, perhaps they'll give up?"

"Unlikely, but we can hope." Worandana prodded Kirukana with a toe. "Get up fool. Time to make camp."

"I'm not sure that fool is the right title." Chuckled Kirukana, wiping the tears from his face.

"Fool is the right title, you may be their favourite, but you'll die alongside the rest of us."

"Tis a sobering thought, but not new to me." Kirukana climbed slowly to his feet and went off to unload the pack horses, still smiling.

Kevana turned to Alverana. "How long do we need to stay to look after this man?"

"I'd prefer to give him a couple of days, despite Worandana's help, but the morning should tell us everything we need to know."

"What are his chances?"

"Very good now, without our help, not so."

"I hate losing the time, but I suppose he was our brother once."

"I'm still your brother." Said Willowana.

"As were all your friends. I'm sorry, but in my world, brothers don't attack without warning."

"Gaffana thought we had a good chance until you moved away from the river."

"You were watching us even then?"

"Gaffana talked about catching you in your cups."

"In the dark, from behind, whilst drunk, my estimation of your leader has fallen quite considerably. Sadly, he learned that he wasn't up to a frontal attack."

"We were surprised that you weren't more surprised by the suddenness of the attack."

"Zandaar told us he was going to make things more difficult for us, so we were, and are on alert. Even more so now."

"That is obvious, you talked to Zandaar?"

"No, he talked to me, he knows we don't have the sword, but he's not going to stop the hunt. Damn him."

"Be careful, he can hear you, you know."

"Somehow that no longer fills me with the fear it used to, tactically speaking, his only option other than sending my brothers against me, as he did with you, and no doubt many others, his only option, is to call down black fire on us, and that won't bring him the sword, all it will give him is more corpses, just like he achieved here today. Willowana, a thought for you, our wonderful all-seeing god, he set you and yours against me and mine." Kevana swept his friends with an arm. "He knew how you would react, he knew how we would respond, he knew the outcome of this battle before it was even joined, your survival may be the only surprise. He would have been fairly certain that I would leave no witnesses." A wry smile twisted Alverana's face.

"That's true." Said Alverana, "Surviving enemies are a rarity for us. Are you our enemy?"

"No." Mumbled Willowana. "I am not your enemy."

"Then who is?" Asked Worandana.

Willowana looked round at all the expectant faces, unsure as to how he should answer this, but certain his survival depended on the response. The dreadful truth was solidifying in his mind, finally his eyes fell on Kirukana's, that man's hand firmly on the haft of his belt knife. Worandana observed the exchanged looks, and with a speed that belied his advanced years, he drew his own knife and pricked Kirukana just above his kidneys. Kirukana's head snapped round, his eyes caught by Worandana's. The look said it all, Kirukana released his knife, and held his hands out to the sides, empty palms upwards. Without breaking eye contact Worandana spoke softly. "Willowana, speak, only the truth."

"Brothers, I am sorry to say this, but logically there is no other answer. Our god is your enemy. He sends forces against you, and even tells you that he will not make things any easier for you, this is not the action of a friend." Kirukana twitched but made no other response. Worandana slowly returned his knife to its sheath at his belt. Worandana broke eye contact with Kirukana, and turned to the recumbent man, Willowana's brow was beaded with sweat, from more than the pain in his belly.

"Kirukana, what do you think?" Asked Worandana. Kirukana looked down on the fallen monk.

"This man speaks heresy, he speaks against god, he needs to die immediately."

"He speaks against god, that is true, but is he wrong?"

"He is a heretic, that is enough."

"He's a heretic, but is he wrong?" Kirukana paused for a moment before spitting a reply.

"Damn him, he's not wrong. You people have turned our god against us, now we will all burn."

"What have we done to bring the curse of the one we serve?" Asked Kevana.

"You use forbidden magics and break the traditions of the church at every turn, how can our god respond in any other way to such disobedience?"

"You poor fool." Smiled Kevana. "You are still just a stooge for the council. You'll never see the tactics as I can. Zandaar wants this sword so desperately, but he can't trust his own council with it, he needs it to come straight to his own hand, not through them. The only way that can happen is if the sword turns up at the gates of Zandaarkoon in an angry fist, mine!"

"They'll simply set the whole army against you, can you stand against them?"

"I believe that Zandaar will have removed that option from them by the time we get there, I've no idea how, but the local army, and the city guard, perhaps even the councils personal guards will not be an issue. How much confidence do you have in our god?"

"I trust Zandaar completely, but we are acting like heretics as far as the council are concerned, and theirs is the power."

"So," Worandana interrupted. "we are heretics in the council's eyes, but not in god's?"

"If Kevana is right, then that is correct."

"If Kevana is correct, and we are working in the interests of Zandaar, who are the heretics?"

"You know there's only one logical answer to that. If Kevana is right, then the council are the heretics, but how do you prove that Kevana is right?"

"Given all that has happened to us already, the evidence is certainly stacking up in Kevana's favour."

"I still don't believe it."

"You don't need to, you're only along for the ride, perhaps you can learn a few things along the way. Now, let's get this camp set up, because we need to be moving targets before dawn."

"What do you mean old man?" Snapped Kevana.

"Dawn, the morning rituals, can you think of a better time to search for us?"

"You're right. Early to bed, early to rise, you heard him, get this camp set up." Kevana's parade ground voice took over gradually until the last was almost shouted. Pack horses were unloaded, tents were being assembled, Petrovana and Briana were carrying the dead to the forest.

"Petrovana." Shouted Kevana. "Stop wasting effort, use the horses, just drag them into the forest, and don't forget to empty their pockets of silver." There were some harsh looks, but none said anything about Kevana's treatment of the dead. Even the horses were unhappy, the smell of death disturbed them.

"I'm not stupid." Muttered Petrovana, who wasn't just collecting the flames and the lightning bolts, he was emptying their purses as well, despite the disgusted looks from Briana.

Once the grizzly task was completed, they returned to the camp, Petrovana dropped a sizable collection at Kevana's feet, many flames and lightning bolts, a good purse of gold, a few choice daggers, a couple of these quite ornate, a fancifully painted bow, and quiver full of arrows. After he'd had a look through the spoils of war, he said to Petrovana.

"Divide up the silver, bow and quiver goes to Fabrana, he's the only one that can use them." A quick glance round, then he continued. "Apologies gentlemen." Looking at Davadana and Strenoana. "You're new, I am sorry that I overlooked you, on seniority Fabrana gets first choice. Well?" He turned to Fabrana.

"I'm happy with my bow, I'm used to it, and it is used to me. A pretty new bow is not something I need."

Strenoana took the new bow, hefted it, pulled the string to the limit, slowly he released the pressure, and nodded. He offered his own bow to Davadana, who shook his head. Strenoana dropped his old bow and now empty quiver onto the pile, the arrows were almost the same length, and would be good enough, at least over short range.

"There is something I don't understand." Said Kevana turning to Willowana. "Look at all that silver, and you came charging out of the trees waving swords?"

"Gaffana, was a soldier, we all were, throwing lightning bolts wasn't really our style."

"Your style got you all killed, in fairly short order, you could have at least killed a few of us in the initial surprise."

"We have been trained, but we have been warned that your mystics are extremely skilled."

"That is true, but surprise would have killed a few of us."

"Gaffana didn't like the uncertainty, he knew that our skill level is basic at best, he thought we stood a much better chance with swords."

"He was wrong, even your archer managed to miss all those targets."

"Archer. Don't make me laugh, it hurts too much. His daddy was rich enough to buy him all the best gear, but he'd struggle to hit the side of a barn, he was more likely to hit one of us than one of you."

"I see." Kevana paused for a while, his thoughts running in circles. "Used to be that being a soldier of god was something to aspire to, now it seems that anyone can qualify."

"You have been away from the capital for a long time, haven't you?"

"It's been a few years, yes."

"This may not be something you want to hear, soldiering is now considered a fairly safe occupation, there are no wars going on, and not even any serious suppression actions, an average soldier can expect to put in ten years, come out with a good pension, and minimal risk. I've got five years' experience and the most dangerous mission I've ever been on was collecting a few lost brothers, only they killed my entire troop, in less time than it takes to name them all."

"Your troop had no field experience at all?"

"Depends how you define 'field experience', we've camped out a few times, generally within sight of the city walls, not always Zandaarkoon either, sometimes wilder locations."

"These things will change when I get back." Snapped Kevana, turning on his heel and stamping off, he needed some distance between himself and the others, he was trying to make some form of sense from what he had just been told. By the time he had calmed down and returned to the camp tents had been erected, food was being prepared by Apostana and Strenoana, Briana was just returning to camp, his horse festooned with five heavy water skins.

"Where's Willowana?" He demanded. Apostana pointed at a tent, Kevana opened the flap and looked inside, Alverana was tending the wounded man, who was grimacing in pain as Alverana probed the wound. "How's he doing?"

"Surprisingly well, I'm seeing no signs of festering, and very little pain."

"Little pain?" Choked Willowana.

"Little pain." Said Alverana.

"Good," said Kevana, "I haven't been away from Zandaarkoon that long, maybe four years, when did it become safe to be a soldier?"

"It started in earnest about six years ago, many of the councilmen's relatives are in the army, or city guard, and they decided that soldiers from other cities should do most of the dying, Zandaarkoon soldiers have become more involved in parades and ceremonies, less in the actual fighting."

"So how did you end up all the way out here?"

"There are many groups searching for you, but we aren't allowed contact with the local forces, either the council or Zandaar want you stopped, but quietly."

"That does explain something that had been puzzling me."

"Go on."

"We passed through a large town, no one was looking for us, but a monastery only half a day's ride away had already had warnings about us."

"Only the priesthood is searching for you."

"That should make things easier, we just have to keep away from monasteries, and their roving patrols."

"That should keep you safer, but it is no guarantee."

"There are only two things in this world guaranteed, death and taxes."

"That's for sure." Willowana smiled.

"Get some rest we will be leaving early in the morning, before sunrise, we'll leave you enough provisions to keep you alive for a few days, and horses to take you home once you are fit to ride, I wouldn't do anything too strenuous for a couple of days."

"I understand. Thank you for all your help, I'd be dead without it."

"I know, please don't make me regret this."

"I'll put off making contact with our people as long as I can."

"That would be good, they'll be focusing on this area in a couple of days, but we'll be long gone by then."

"I don't believe there is anyone who knows me well enough to make direct contact, so they'll be blundering around in the dark until someone can catch up with me."

"If Zandaar comes looking for you, he will find you."

"Yes, but he'd have to know to be looking for me specifically, and I'm a long way down the list."

"I hope, for your sake, that you are right. I've talked to god and it hurts, in your condition it would most likely kill you. I'd hate for Worandana's efforts to be wasted." Kevana smiled.

"Thank you, commander. You need to get some rest, you have an early start and I believe, you have much worse to come."

"You may be right." Kevana stood and walked the two steps to the fire where Alverana was resting.

"Will he be all right on his own tomorrow?" Asked Kevana, in a voice that he hoped was low enough not to be heard by Willowana.

"Does he have an option?" Alverana shrugged.

"Not really, we leave early. What are his chances?"

"If he doesn't move around too much, for a couple of days, he should be fine. There are no major predators that would think of him as food, except a passing wolf pack, and that's very unlikely."

"So, you think he'll survive?"

"He stands a good chance, a much better chance if we stay with him another day or two."

"We can't afford that, once the controllers find out this party is dead, they are going to be flooding this area with troops, we need to be far enough from here so as not to get caught. I really have no wish to kill any more of our brothers, I'm going to talk to Worandana." He turned away to where the older man was resting in front of his tent.

"Walk with me." Said Kevana, helping his friend to his feet, and together they turned towards the river. They walked in silence until they were far enough from the camp not to be overheard.

"We need to consider a course of action that is going to meet some resistance." Said Kevana.

"We need to look like something other than what we are." Replied Worandana.

"I expected at least token resistance from you."

"I'm not stupid, our own brethren attack without a word of warning, we need to be someone else."

"I suggest we become horse traders, we have enough horses, good saddle horses at that, even if we leave three behind for Willowana, what do you think?"

"That would give us a sort of cover, we need to lose all this black, and the saddles from the horses, they are valuable, but they do mark the horses as belonging to Zandaars."

"Agreed, we cover our own saddles with cloth, so the emblems are hidden, but what can we do about our clothes, we have nothing but black."

"There may be something we can do about that. It's not going to be pretty, but it may be enough to convince people at first sight, and that is all we need, we need questions to be asked before battle is joined."

"Agreed, and at the first town we buy some new clothes."

"Certainly, it'll make a change not to wear this dreary black all the time."

"Great, what do you need for this colour changing magic?"

"It's not magic, it's simple chemistry. I don't expect we have enough time to achieve anything magical, but greys should be possible by morning."

"Explain please."

"Those trees over there are ash, and when the wood is burned, and the ashes washed with water, the resulting solution is caustic, this should bleach our clothes from black to grey before morning."

"I suppose thinner, lighter cloth would be easier?"

"Cape and outer clothing are impossible, underclothes and shirts, they may work. We don't need much, just so long as most of us are wearing something that would be considered 'heretical' in Zandaarkoon." Worandana laughed loudly.

"He's never going to allow that."

"If he's the only one dressed in black, he'll be the prime target, which is definitely good enough for me."

"Agreed, let's get things moving." Together they returned to the camp, men were dispatched to collect the requisite wood, and a large fire laid on the downwind side of the camp, the wood still being wet was bound to generate an amount of smoke. Worandana oversaw the process, until a large pan of rather pungent liquid was sitting over the fire bubbling gently. Worandana dropped one of his older undershirts into the water, this one was already a little faded, and as he stirred is around in the pot, it could be seen to be fading even as they watched.

"Get me a large pot of clean water." Said Worandana, to no one in particular. Once this had appeared, he pulled the garment from the liquid, and let it drip back into the pot, when it had cooled a little he wrung it out quickly then immersed it and his hands in the cold water, rinsing the shirt thoroughly. As he withdrew it from the rinsing pot it was clear that the black had faded quite considerably, it was a long way from white, but it was certainly not black anymore.

"It may not be the prettiest of colours," said Kevana, "but it's definitely not black, I'd say grubby looking grey." He laughed as Worandana shook the garment out and laid it to dry beside the fire. "Everyone present undershirts for lightening." Kevana went to his pack to retrieve a shirt.

"How does this help?" demanded Kirukana.

"Just when you think he's starting to think he goes slipping back into old habits." Laughed Petrovana. Before continuing. "Cloaks will be worn mostly on horses' rumps, grey shirts become outerwear, it's not like it's really cold just now, and we are heading south."

"I am not going to commit this sort of sacrilege."

"I have no problem with that," smiled Kevana, "while our enemies are targeting the only Zandaar they can be sure of, the rest of us will have a few moments to kill them all."

"Kirukana." Worandana's quiet voice was filled with threats. "You can take over the bleaching process, it's not hard, don't put your hand in the hot bleach, once the colour has faded enough let the clothes drain for a while, then wring all the liquid back into the pot and plunge the cloth and your hands into the cold clean water as quickly as you can, the bleach will damage your skin if you aren't fast enough." Kirukana looked around into hard eyes at every turn, he knew further resistance would have been to his detriment. So, he nodded and took Kevana's shirt from him. Worandana stayed to supervise, the first few shirts, until he was certain that Kirukana wasn't going to injure himself.

"You understand that Kevana will sacrifice your life so that the rest of us can survive?" He asked gently.

"Yes, I understand, but I've been wearing black for so long, in the service of our god, that I cannot turn away simply to survive, if god wishes me to die then so be it."

"I'm fairly sure that god would prefer that you died in his service for something other than the colour of your clothing. I will not force you on this matter, neither will Kevana, his tactical thinking is most likely correct. You may just buy the rest of us the few seconds it takes to survive."

"I don't like it."

"Think on this for a while, the council has sent brothers with specific commands to kill us all and take the sword from our cold dead hands. Kevana is not taking this well. He hasn't said anything yet, but I am fairly sure he now plans to take the sword straight to the council, when he walks into the council chamber with Alverana on one side and me on the other, there are going to be some seats up for re-election, perhaps even all of them. Stand in his way, and he'll gut you like a fish without breaking stride. Think on it, your council have created this situation, each faction hoping to profit, they may even be lucky enough to stay alive."

"You said 'your', why?"

"They sent people to kill me too, I'm hoping to get the chance to explain to them how this is a bad thing to do."

"You plan to kill them?"

"I'm considering something even better than that, if I find out who turned our brothers against us, I'm going to bury a flame in his belly and keep it burning until there is only ash left. In some ways Kevana and I are the same."

"Can that even be done?"

"You want to stay alive long enough to find out?"

"You people are crazy."

"If you want to stay alive, get one of your shirts in that bleach." Worandana walked away leaving Kirukana to his task and his thoughts.

CHAPTER FIFTY-TWO

Jangor pounded across the river, water scattering from his horses hooves, over the sound of his own horse he soon heard the familiar sound of thunder, Arndrol pulled alongside to his right, and moments later a strange counterpointed rhythm came up on the other side, a glance left shocked Jangor, there was Brank on his new horse, a huge grin on his face, he seemed to be enjoying the ride for a change. The others pulled in behind, matching pace with the three.

"Does anyone know which way we are going?" Yelled Jangor over the sound of their passage.

"Not me." Laughed Namdarin, he waved a hand in the air and soon Gervane pulled up alongside them.

"Did you summon me?" He asked.

"I suppose, do you have any idea where we are going, because we don't?"

"You're on the south road, so you can't get lost."

Jangor laughed at this comment.

"We can't get lost," said Namdarin, "but how long is this sort of speed safe on this road?"

"A few miles yet before the road narrows down to a single cart wide, but it is a fairly heavily travelled road, so galloping always has its risks." Gervane shrugged and smiled.

"Good." Said Namdarin, showing no signs of slowing.

"What's the rush?" Asked Gervane.

"I'm not sure," frowned Namdarin, "but your home has a lure about it, that almost feels like a trap."

"I don't think I like the way you think about my city."

"Not in a bad way, but I could quite easily see me just turning round and going back there to hide out for the rest of my life, and that would be wrong."

"I'm sure my people would welcome you with open arms, very open arms."

"That is the greater part of the snare. If we went back, then the thing that I am hunting is going to be looking for me, and it would find you in the process, that would not be good. No. I have to leave, and the quicker the better."

"I understand, but I'm not so sure that Wolf does." Gervane looked down and in front of the four horses was Wolf, in full flow, his tail streaming out like a flag in the wind, his head bobbing with the pulse of his galloping pace.

"He's a healthy animal he can keep this up all day, it's not like he's pushing hard." Wolf responded with a short yap, which Arndrol took as a challenge, his first kick pulled him half a length ahead of the other horses and right up onto Wolf's tail. Wolfs next bound was a full whip of his spine, and he was reaching out. Namdarin snapped his reins tight pulling the horse back to a more reasonable pace, even slowing down, to a canter, he looked over at Gervane.

"Less likely to have an accident at this speed."

"Agreed, and the pack horses are more likely to be able to keep up, they're not racehorses you know."

Namdarin settled the pace down a little more, Arndrol shook his mane in disgust. As the pace came down the group gathered closer together, Gervane dropped back, and Fennion pulled up alongside Namdarin.

"It's been a long time since I rode like this, it's fun." He said.

"This isn't too tiring for you, is it?"

"No, I can cope, but I'd rather not have to do it all day, and I'm sure the horses feel the same."

"Once the road narrows we'll slow down, and rest the horses for a while, I just have this urgency at the moment, I have no idea why."

"You do have a great distance still to travel, and who knows what along the way."

"That maybe it, while the going is easy, let's keep the pace up." Having said that Namdarin slowed the pace down a little more, thinking about the slower horses in the group. Fennion turned in his saddle and shouted to Gervane.

"Send outriders, clear the road." Gervane only nodded then made a few hand signals to members of the escort group, six of the tall elven horses surged into the lead, as they went passed the leaders Arndrol had had enough, he snatched the bit, and set off after the elves, Namdarin dropped the reins, he knew that Arndrol was not going to stop for a while yet, a glance to his left showed that Brank had come with him, he appeared to have lost his fear of horses, the smooth stride of the elven steed surprised even Namdarin. Even Arndrol's prodigious best wasn't enough to catch the outriders, Namdarin looked down to see that Wolf had come along too, he was pushing hard, it didn't look like he had much left, but he was keeping just ahead of Arndrol. They kept up this punishing pace for a few minutes, until Arndrol was covered in white foam, his breath coming in huge gasps, Namdarin picked up the reins, and slowly pulled Arndrol down to a much slower pace, even the elven horse carrying Brank was showing signs of fatigue, its chest was white with foam, and it's breathing rough in its throat. Namdarin slowed down some more, until Arndrol settled into a gentle trot.

"Hey Brank." he called. Brank looked across.

"These elvish horses are fast, I mean really fast."

"Mines not."

"You are three times the weight of an elf, even a large one."

"You're not wrong." Brank laughed. They continued at a steady trot until they caught up with one of the outriders, he was standing beside a small cart, pulled by a single horse, the driver looked a little unhappy, to be held up so, but waved a hand as Namdarin and Brank passed by.

"The new king will be along shortly," said the outrider to the driver, "you wait until his party has passed before you move on."

"What do you mean the new king?"

"The undead king has been replaced by a living one."

"How did that happen?"

"Those men that just passed by killed him."

"Is the new king leaving with them."

"No, he's just escorting them out of the forest."

"Making sure they don't steal the silver on their way out of town." Laughed the cart driver.

"Perhaps." laughed the outrider, "It's a large party and moving quickly, so stay here until they have passed."

"Yes sir, will I recognise the new king?"

"Probably, but try not to laugh, it only makes him angry." The outrider turned and galloped off after Namdarin and Brank, he flashed past them at a full gallop, almost as if they were standing still. Namdarin laughed and flicked the reins at Arndrol's neck, the horse turned its head a little and glared at the man with one eye.

"I think he's tired." Said Brank.

"He could be." Smiled Namdarin, patting Arndrol's neck and releasing the reins. They continued at a steady trot, even wolf looked tired. The road narrowed until it was only wide enough for two horses' side by side, well, two horses and a wolf. They came around a sharp bend in the road and there in front of them was one of the outriders, his horse turned sideways, completely blocking the road.

"Be careful my lords." he said. "There is a cart just around the next bend, and we can't get it out of the road."

"Thanks for that." Said Namdarin, "Why don't you carry on, my friend and I will wait here until the rest of the party catch up." The elf nodded and turned away, he was gone in a heartbeat. Wolf looked up at the men, wondering why they weren't moving, after a moment or two he sniffed around and wandered over to a nearby puddle, and drank it until it was dry, then went looking for another one. Finding one at the edge of the road, he drank that one dry as well.

"Hey Wolf." Called Namdarin. The wolf looked up at the man.

"Can you find a bigger puddle; the horses are thirsty too?" Brank laughed as Wolf looked around, but he found only small and shallow puddles at the edge of the road. He came and sat at the horse's feet whilst they all waited for the rest to catch up. It was only a few minutes when they heard horses approaching. They weren't moving too quickly so were able to rein to a halt before there were collisions.

"Well?" Asked Gervane loudly. "did you catch the outriders?"

"No. Your horses are just too damned fast."

"And I'm way too heavy." Laughed Brank.

"What about you Wolf?" Asked Laura. Wolf just dropped to his belly on the ground, looking very embarrassed by his performance. Laura flung herself from her saddle and fell on the disgraced predator, she threw her arms around his neck and hugged him tight to her chest. Slowly he recovered and licked her face. Together they rolled on the ground.

"Daughter." Said Fennion. "Is this appropriate behaviour for a princess?"

She looked up at her grandfather, and came to her knees, with one arm around Wolfs neck.

"Anyone here with the balls to challenge my behaviour, with my four-legged friend so close?"

She allowed the silence to stretch out for a short time before she spoke again.

"I thought not." She turned to Namdarin. "Why are we waiting here?"

"Apparently there's a cart stuck around this corner, and it can't be moved. Proceed with caution I was told."

"Let's go then." She said returning to her saddle. Namdarin and Gervane led off with Laura and Brank behind, Wolf was undecided, he wanted to be with Laura and he wanted to be in the lead, in moments lead won, he dodged between the horse's legs and ran on a few yards. As they went around the corner they heard a man scream in fear. The man was on top of a broken cart, his sword drawn and shaking, a small girl hiding behind his legs, too frightened to even make a sound.

"Wolf. Down." Shouted Namdarin, Wolf followed the instructions but didn't move back, or take his eyes off the man waving a sword. "I am sorry friend, Wolf won't harm you, or your daughter. You can put up your sword."

"What has happened here?" Asked Jangor pushing to the fore.

"Pin failed. My son has gone to get help."

"You have a spare?"

"Yes, my lord, they do fail quite often, I was sleeping, and the wheel actually fell off before I woke up. If it doesn't fall off, we can usually fix it on our own."

"I sure we can sort this out in no time. Namdarin, Brank, Kern, this one is for you." The three dismounted, as did Jangor.

"Driver." he said. "Be ready with the wheel. You three loose the weapons." Jangor hung his own sword belt on his saddle. As the others did the same. "Brank, Namdarin, in front of the axle, Kern with me, right gentlemen backs up to the boards, bend the knees, take a good grip on the bottom edge. This is only a small cart, we are not going to let it embarrass us now, are we?" There were a couple of grunts in reply, but that was all. "This cart is carrying a valuable cargo of...." he looked at the driver, now holding the wheel in his hands.

"Potatoes, my lord." Was the diffident reply.

"Potatoes." Muttered Jangor, the driver nodded. Jangor shrugged.

"It's a small cart with a valuable cargo of potatoes, there can't be more than a couple of tons here, we are not going to let that beat us, are we." A chorus of quiet no's.

"I don't hear you gentlemen, this cart isn't going to beat us, is it?"

"No sir." Three shouts this time.

"Better, pump some air up, let's hear those lungs working. Are you ready!

"Yes." Three again.

"More. Are you ready?"

"Yes." Louder.

"That'll do. Here we go. Breathe out. Tense. Lift."

Eight boots pushed down into the road surface, eight thighs flexed, eight arms strained, slowly the cart started to rise, once it was clear of the sticky ground it came up quicker until all the men were standing upright, Branks knees still a little bent. Jangor nodded at the driver, he rushed in, and jiggled the wheel into place, then drove it into place with a few hard blows from a heavy hammer, with a shoulder against the wheel, his left hand reached behind himself, his daughter dropped the replacement pin into it, he slid the pin into its hole and tapped it gently into place. He stepped away.

"Down slow." Called Jangor, the four slowly lowered the cart until the wheel touched the ground, it sank slowly into the surface, the axle groaned as they gradually reduced their lift until the wheel was carrying the weight of the cart again.

"There you go friend." Said Jangor, "I suggest you need a bigger horse to pull this load, that one looks just too light for the task."

"There are normally two, my son took the other one to get help."

"We may not have got you back on the road, but we've saved you some time and effort."

"Even with the help my son is bringing, we'd have emptied the cart first, fixed it and reloaded, so we'd have been lucky to be moving again before nightfall. Many thanks to you all. Now you're not elves, and I was told the king was coming this way."

"I am king Fennion." The driver looked up and the man on horseback.

"You'll not be king for long, you're very old."

"I came late to the crown, that is true, but my daughter will be next in line, she's young enough to provide a certain stability, once I am gone." He waved one hand in the direction of Laura, who was on her knees beside Wolf, keeping one arm around his neck.

"Is she a witch that she communes with animals?"

"Careful fool, your words carry your own death." The driver tensed and glanced around. "Brank is now within arm's length of you, wolf is further away, if you offend my daughter Laura, I'm not sure which will kill you first, the wolf I think."

"Wolf." Said Namdarin, Brank looked at him rather pained. "You just lifted that cart, Wolf is fully recovered from this morning's run."

"Wolf." Said Jangor.

"Wolf." Said Kern.

"I'm not completely dead you know." Muttered Brank.

"My money is on Wolf." Called Stergin from the back of the crowd.

"No takers on that one." Said Mander.

"Three to one." Said Stergin.

"Not even at those odds." Replied Mander.

"My king," said the driver, "are these people actually betting on the manner of my death?"

"Not with any seriousness, you really ought to be more careful how you speak to people, I believe that my daughter will make a great queen. She has a certain hardness of heart and a softness of soul. She'll do very well, once people get used to the idea. I see a turbulent time for her, but she'll ride out the storms with some good friends to help her, it'll be rough for a while, but she'll be a good queen in the end. I feel that there may be a level of mortality amongst those that stand against her, don't be with them."

The driver looked around at the faces. He focused on Brank.

"Would you really have killed me?"

"I'd have pulled your head back and watched Wolf rip your throat out." Branks cold voice more than his words reached the drivers young daughter, she ran in and threw her arms around her father's legs and started crying. He reached down and gathered her up in his arms.

"Don't be frightened little one." He whispered, kissing her wet face.

"What is your name, little girl?" Asked Fennion. She glared at him but didn't answer.

"Tell the king your name." Said the driver, she frowned at him for a moment before turning to Fennion.

"I am called Angelina, you are not to hurt my daddy." She scowled.

"I will not hurt your daddy, but he was very rude to some people and a large and angry wolf, this could have been very bad for him."

"Mummy says he is rude to people, she's always telling him off for it."

"I see." Smiled Fennion. "You will make sure to explain to her what has happened here today, won't you?" Angelina looked at Fennion for a moment then nodded slowly, she turned to her father and scowled at him. He turned his head to the sky and sighed hugely. He turned to Laura.

"Please, my lady, release the wolf, a quick death is far better than what awaits me at home."

Laura smiled at him, then laughed, and slowly released Wolf. The driver flinched and turned away to protect his daughter with his own body, he heard a small sound, the yap of a puppy. There was no growl, no scrabbling of claws, and no heavy weight on his back. He opened his eyes, and looked up into Branks, Brank lifted his chin a fraction to tell the driver that he should look behind him. Slowly he turned, surprised to see, belly down on the ground the huge wolf, his tail sweeping the road surface from side to side, he gave a little yip and looked from Angelina to Laura and back again.

"Angelina," said Laura, "would you like to meet wolf?" Angelina looked at her father, he glanced at Brank.

"Wolf loves children." Said the big man.

"Yes." Said Kern, "I've never seen him eat a whole one."

"Kern." Snapped Laura. "You are not helping." Kern laughed.

"Is it safe?" Asked the driver.

"Safer for Angelina than for you." Said Kern. The driver frowned an unasked question.

"If wolf accepts her, then she's safe because he'll die to defend her, you're not so safe because he'll also kill to defend her. Do you understand?"

"I think so." Slowly he lowered Angelina to the ground and looked at Laura. "How do we do this?"

"Easy. Angelina, hold your hand out flat in front of you and Wolf will come to sniff it, if he likes you, he'll lick your hand, and you can stroke him."

"And if he doesn't like her?" Asked the driver.

"He'll walk away and show no more interest in her. Wolves place a lot of importance in scent."

"Hold your hand out Angelina." He said. She backed up against his legs but held her hand out as instructed. Slowly Wolf came to his feet, standing at his full height, Angelina was looking up into his huge yellow eyes. With a smoothness more feline than canine Wolf stepped towards the girl, his long red tongue fell from his mouth, then vanished back inside again. All too quickly his nose was pressed against the palm of her tiny hand.

"Cold." She giggled, then the huge tongue swept across the hand. "Hot and wet." Wolf stepped forwards again and placed his chin on her shoulder, letting her stroke his mane.

"This day is just full of surprises." Said the driver, he looked back to the king. "I thank you for your help and apologise for my rudeness and for delaying your obviously urgent mission." He bowed deeply and stole a touch of the wolfs fur. As he straightened up Jangor called loudly.

"Mount up. We have a long way to go." He looked disapprovingly at Namdarin as he re-seated the sword on his back and climbed into his saddle.

"Namdarin." His command rang out. "Your horse is crusted with sweat, when we stop for the night you can see to him." Jangor set off along the road, Kern to one side and Gervane to the other, at a quick trot, to burn up the miles. Namdarin, Jayanne and Fennion, in the next row, Brank and Laura next, Wolf quickly fell into his usual wide-ranging pattern, never far away, but not always in sight. They had only gone about a mile when they came upon an out-rider who was guarding two people on horseback, one a young boy, riding bareback, on a horse more suited for hauling carts, and an older man, on a horse more fitting for a saddle.

"Why are we being held here?" Demanded the older man.

"You know why." Said the outrider angrily.

"Why should we be held up for some king I've never seen? I have family in trouble on this road ahead." Fennion pulled hard on the reins, and his horse slid to a stop, almost reared.

"I am king Fennion, now you have seen me, what say you?"

"All I see is an old man in a silly hat."

"Let me guess," laughed Fennion, "your brother drives a cart, and he's lost a wheel this morning?"

"How do you know that?"

"Because rudeness seems to be a family trait. You understand that these are royal guards all around you?"

"What of it?" The man looked a little nervous, but no less belligerent.

"The humans here killed the undead king."

"I don't care for any of that, just get out of my way so I can help my brother. There are wolves here about you know." Kern laughed and watched as Wolf came forwards to where the man could see him, and he bristled his mane. Wolf stood silent watching the man.

"I have only one last question for you, would the lovely Angelina miss her uncle if he lost his head today? Namdarin." The last word an instruction. Namdarin's right hand rose and the sword leapt from the scabbard on his back to join it. The green stone started to glow, even in the full light of day, it was turning the surface of anything that was visible to it a brilliant green.

"Your majesty." Said the boy. "You have seen my sister today?"

"I have, my child."

"You have met my father?"

"Yes."

"Did he survive that meeting?"

"He did, but he came as close as your uncle is to failing."

"I apologise for my father and my uncle here. They do have a tendency to be rude, but they are good people."

"After we fixed his cart for him, he was rude to my daughter and Wolf."

"Sometimes they're not very bright, but they are good people."

"His cart is fixed, all he needs is the horse you are riding, and yourself, he doesn't really need his rude brother now does he."

"Probably not, but Angelina will certainly cry."

"Your words carry much weight. He can live for today, but you need to teach them both some manners, or the next time we meet it may not go so well for them."

"You have my word. I shall explain things to their wives when we get back."

"I am surprised that they are still married."

"As I said they are good people."

"I bid you fair well young sir and wish you luck with the training of your relatives."

"Thank you, your majesty." The boy bowed as far as is possible whilst still mounted on a horse. The king nodded and shouted. "Ride on." Namdarin sheathed his sword, and they all turned along the road, and set off at a fast trot, except for the royal guard who had been designated outrider, he pulled away at a full gallop. Namdarin settled alongside Fennion.

"Would you really have had me kill him?"

"No, but he didn't need to know that, he needed to learn, dead men can't learn anything, they already know everything."

"You know that I would not have killed him."

"Of course, that's why I picked you, soldiers can play a little rough, but I knew that you would tell me not to kill my own rude people, and then you'd have gone on to explain that there wouldn't be too many left by the time I had finished."

"You know me better than I thought."

"You are a leader, not a captain following orders, nor a general hiding at the rear of a battle, you lead the only way you know."

"How did you get to be such a judge of people?"

"You mean other than the many years of watching them? I have an advantage, given my age, many are unsurprised when I suddenly fall asleep, that's when many of them reveal their true intentions."

"You are a cunning old fox, aren't you?"

"I hope so, I've managed to stay alive a long time, I hope I have enough time to pass this on to Laura."

"She'll learn quick, she's quite sharp in her own way. When will we reach the end of the forest?"

"It'll be dark before we reach the end, even at this pace."

"Is there any where to camp, or stay at the end of this road?"

"There is a village just outside the forest, it's a farming community, but has a large open area in the middle, and a fair inn, or so I hear. Gervane." He called.

The younger man dropped back to talk to his king.

"Yes, my lord."

"Have the men brought tents and such?"

"Of course, we knew it would be late by the time we got to the edge of the forest."

"How about the inn in Breewood?"

"It's not big enough for our party, but it could sleep a few, it's not very good from what I hear."

"Then we'll camp on the green, and they can service us there."

"They may not like that."

"Then perhaps you'll enjoy explaining things to them. You could even threaten to set these crazy king killing humans on them, they certainly look like desperate people."

"What if they call your bluff?" demanded Namdarin.

"Well." said Fennion, "I see Kern, Brank and Wolf, storming into town and growling at anything that even gets in their way, and just when they can't get any more frightened in comes the demon lord on his white charger, wielding his blue bladed longsword, with the mind stone in the pommel, beside him a witch wearing the skin of a white bear and wielding a wicked axe. What farmer would have the balls to do anything other than crap in his pants?"

"Fennion." said Namdarin coldly. "My people will not be used to frighten farmers, just to make you look better."

"I know that, but an old elf can have a dream, can't he."

"Are you worried that these people won't accept you as king?"

"That could be it, I'm certain of my power in my home, out here is something else."

"Just behave as a king should, you have enough muscle to back you up, just don't expect too much of people whose king has been dead for a hundred or so years."

"That's easier said than done."

"You'll manage, your farming folk are going to be impressed enough when we come trooping into their village. Gervane, tacticals on the village?"

"It's just a collection of houses, around a green, and along a river, no wall, no stronghold, just a village of elven farmers, on the borders of our forest."

"That should be no problem," said Namdarin, "let's just hope we get there before they all go to sleep."

Gervane checked the position of the sun, before speaking. "The sun will be down, but it won't be full dark when we get there, if we can pick up the pace a little, we may even have some sun."

"Kern." Called Namdarin. "Pick it up, we need to get out of this forest before the sun goes down."

"Gervane." He continued. "Your outriders should already be at this village, so the villagers will know we are on the way, what preparations will they be making?"

"Most likely they are laying out a camp site for us even now, they know we won't want to be returning home in the dark, even for our horses these roads aren't safe in the dead of night. They'll have picket lines set up, and hopefully a fire for cooking, they may even have the sense to arrange for food for us."

"So basically, Fennion's fears are groundless. Any resistance from the farmers will have been quelled before we arrive?"

"Most likely, I just hope they haven't found reason to be too firm."

"I'm sure your officers can deal politely with a little resistance."

"I'm the captain, they are sergeants, sergeants can be a little terse." Gervane smiled.

"Terse?" Laughed Namdarin.

"What are you two giggling at?" Demanded Fennion.

"It seems," said Namdarin, "Gervane's force has no officers other than himself, the force currently riding into the village of, help me here."

"Breewood." Said Gervane.

"Breewood, the men, sorry, elves, in charge of this force, are the backbone of any army, sergeants, any sergeants major?"

"Only one." sighed Gervane, "He's the meanest drill sergeant you have ever met."

"That I doubt, but all soldiers say that, whenever two platoons meet, and drink together, they compare the brutality of the sergeant major that taught them, until it degenerates into the usual formula, 'our bastard was meaner than yours.' That's when the fight starts."

"I still don't understand, explain in words that a, erm, a, I hate to say this more than you can understand, a politician, can understand." Said a distinctly disturbed Fennion.

"Fine," said Gervane, "my king, who is the man that all soldiers are both frightened of, and most respectful to?"

"I don't know."

"Their drill instructor, the hand to hand combat instructor, the sergeant major, who's parade ground voice strikes terror into hardened veterans, and who's merest whisper sends men running to die."

"Please will someone explain this to me." Cried Fennion.

"Tell me he's armed." Namdarin looked hard at Gervane, who slowly shook his head from side to side.

"He carries only his stick."

"Crap." Snapped Nandarin, then his own parade ground voice came to the fore. "Kern, pick the pace up, minimum trot, but I want canter and gallop when the way is clear enough."

"I don't understand." Yelled Fennion.

"There are two sorts of sergeants major," answered Namdarin, "the ones who are armed to the teeth, and proficient in every weapon they carry, and the other sort. The man who carries only his cane, it's a small thing, not long enough to be a walking aid, nor thick enough to be a serious weapon, it's shiny silver top, often polished as he struts around, this is all the weapons and all the armour he needs. He ambles casually through a battlefield, passing warnings and commands as he goes, he'll slap a sword aside, and render the wielder unconscious with an empty hand, for someone else to finish off. He knows that his confidence is all that keeps his men fighting, he'll never break, never show an instant of fear. His only emotions are pride in the men he trained, and sorrow when they die. He is riding into Breewood to prepare it for your arrival, if it puts up any resistance, he will suppress that brutally."

"Damn." Fennion glared at Gervane.

"I am sorry my king, generally I am not separated from them, he looks to me for instruction."

"That doesn't help my people in Breewood." Fennion's own parade ground voice came out. "Kern, faster, fast trot minimum, I want full gallop any time it is even possible." Namdarin nodded, then called his own instructions.

"Mander, Andel, Stergin, look to the pack animals, they're not going to be able to hold this pace, I'll make sure there is beer and food when you catch up." As the three and the pack horses were left behind.

Kern was pushing hard, every straightening of the road lifted the pace to a gallop, hills and tight bends dropped to a canter, but a rolling gallop became the pace of choice. They passed a few groups of riders held at the side of the road, and one cart that caused some near collisions, but even that didn't slow them down too much. In less than an hour Arndrol was beginning to show signs of stress, the occasional stumble, the odd slip in a high-speed turn, nothing that actually slowed him down, but he was definitely getting tired, and more and more disturbed by the fact that the elven horses weren't, their stride flowed as smooth and effortlessly as ever, other than the one that was hauling Branks weight. The earlier hard run was taking its toll on the big grey, Namdarin could feel his friend starting to fail, something that had never happened before, but then he'd never been put under this much stress. The path started downwards, Namdarin hoped that there were no more up hills, 'Please let this be the end of this ride.' he prayed. Then in a heartbeat they rode into open space, green fields around them and a shallow river ahead, Namdarin pulled hard on the reins before they entered the water, the other horses went streaming passed. "I'll catch up." He yelled, as Arndrol stumbled to a halt, on the edge of the water, Namdarin allowed him to drink for a few moments, when he looked up he saw that Jayanne was stopped in the middle of the stream, the water swirling as it passed around her horse's legs.

"He's a big horse to be running so hard all day." She said, in a voice loud enough to be heard above the noise of the river.

"He's just about done in." He snapped the reins, too much cold water would not be good, at least not until Arndrol has cooled down some. "Come on my friend, last mile to go, I can see smoke from houses, or let's hope it's chimneys not houses." They walked slowly across the river, Jayanne fell in alongside, up the bank and onto the level ground, ahead a large collection of houses, none of them actually burning. Behind them the sun was sinking into the trees as the day was ending. Arndrol stumbled more than once as they walked into the centre of the village, there were no gates, and no fences, just open grassland. Namdarin was looking around for the fields, this was supposed to be a farming community, but one without fields of crops. Gervane appeared to guide them through the rapidly growing camp. He led them to the picket lines, where they dismounted.

"I'm going to look to Arndrol." said Namdarin, unloading the luggage from the big horse and just dropping it on the ground, he hitched Jayanne's horse to the line, then set about grooming Arndrol, all the time he talked to the horse in soft and reassuring tones. Brushing the mud and salt residue from his legs and chest. A bundle of hay and a bucket of water at the horse's head, meant it wasn't going anywhere. He checked all the hooves and shoes carefully, oiled the hooves until they shined. He checked the legs and knees for the slightest hint of lameness but found only fatigue. The man paid close attention to the part of the horses back where the saddle rests, brushing first with the stiff bristles, then the soft brush to burnish the short hair to a glossy sheen. By the time

Namdarin had combed mane and tail he was struggling to see, and Arndrol was on his third bucket of water, and second bundle of hay. Arndrol shone almost luminescent in the falling gloom of night. The major moon came up over the horizon, it glistened off Arndrol's shining flanks, Namdarin stood back, then reached forwards, and put his arms around the horse's wide neck.

"I am sorry my friend, for the pain I have put you through today." He whispered, as the large white ears twitched.

"I don't believe it would have made much difference." said a quiet voice behind him. Namdarin turned slowly.

"What do you mean? Gervane."

"He'd still have chased off after the elven horses, wouldn't you Arndrol?" The big horse snuffled and flicked an ear but made no other comment.

"Your horses are very fast." said Namdarin.

"They are, but only in our forests, once they get out into the open they seem to lose some of their power, they become just like normal horses, a bit taller, a little faster, but nothing like as quick as they are within the confines of our woodlands. Even there they don't have the raw power of this brute." He reached out to gently stroke Arndrol's neck, saying, "You did well today, very well, not many would even attempt to keep up with our steeds in the forest, let alone make such a good showing."

"How is that horse of Brank's doing?" asked Namdarin.

"Tired but still strong, Brank is so much heavier than any of our people."

"How will he fair once he is away from the forest?"

"He'll be fine, he'll most likely match Arndrol on the short, but don't expect too much in the way of speed over a long haul, you've turned him into a sprinter." Gervane laughed aloud.

"Hopefully we won't need any long-distance runs. I've been a little pre-occupied since we arrived here, what's been happening?"

"My sergeants acquitted themselves adequately. They were perhaps a little terse, but not harsh, when they met some resistance to the idea of a living king. Everything seems to have been smoothed over now, though it is good that Fennion is king, anyone else would have really struggled to maintain order here. Speaking of that, you need to make your presence felt among these people, they need to see the mindstone, and feel it's power, then they will truly believe."

"Now that I am sure Arndrol is going to be fine, I have some time before bed to meet the leaders of this community. Are there any specifically that I should know about?"

"Not specifically, though I'd expect some issues with the elected leader here, he's called Condulaine, he just feels a little more self-serving than he should."

"Should I offer to liberate his head?"

"That may be going a little far but might not be a bad idea. We'll keep that option in reserve, it would be good if he knew that it was only in reserve." Laughed Gervane.

"I'll see what I can do about that, shall I?"

"Please follow me." Gervane led the way across the green towards the inn where almost everyone was gathered. As they approached the crowd Jayanne fell in on Namdarin's left, she switched the axe to her left hand and leaned in close.

"I don't like these people." she whispered.

"Why not?"

"They are giving Fennion a hard time, never quite rude enough to be challenged for what they say, but certainly not showing the deference an elderly king is due."

"Let's see how they react to the mindstone."

"You two worry me sometimes." Said Gervane.

"Why?" asked Namdarin.

"Your sword hand keeps twitching like it's looking for a sword, she's switched her axe to her left hand, and it looks just as happy to be there as it is in her right. You are a war looking for somewhere to happen."

"Are you frightened of us?" Whispered Jayanne.

"When I hear that cold voice of yours, I get a shiver down my spine."

"Will it help to keep the locals in line?"

"I hope so, if not take a head or two and they'll all kneel for you."

"I don't want them to kneel for me, they should be kneeling for their king."

"I'm fairly sure they will be no problem."

The three of them approached the crowd gathered around the inn, Gervane was surprised that the crowd just seemed to melt away in front of him, then he glanced over his shoulder to see the scowls on the faces of the two people following him. He headed through the crowd, towards Gregor's staff that was just visible above the heads of the crowd. They could hear raised voices and became more worried, Namdarin and Jayanne stepped to the front, putting Gervane behind them, shoulders dropping and pushing people out of their way, they forced a way through the crowd, which became more tightly packed as they approached the centre. Finally, they broke through into the open space in the centre, where Fennion was arguing with an elf almost as old as he was.

"Ah, my friends." he said turning to them.

"So, these are the ones you say killed the undead king?"

"They are indeed."

"And you gave them the mindstone?"

"I did, and gladly."

"Small price to pay to be king."

"Fennion, my friend." Interrupted Namdarin. Condulaine snorted, in derision. A glance from Namdarin's cold blue eyes silenced him. "Do you need help with something?"

"Just a little local politics."

"I thought we had sorted the politics of this situation, there were some dissenters, they died, revolution over. Don't tell me we have to do it all over again?"

"I don't think so," said Fennion, "I'm sure if you show these people the mindstone, they'll all understand that this is for the best."

"Best for you maybe." Snapped Condulaine. A silence descended over the crowd as Namdarin stared hard at Condulaine. A quiet voice spoke "He really doesn't know when to shut up, does he?"

"Perhaps he'll learn." A soft answer. Silence again.

"Show him." Said Fennion.

Namdarin turned to face Condulaine, the old elf stepped back and placed his hand on his sword hilt. Namdarin simply looked at him and raised his eyebrows. The unmistakeable slap of wood into a delicate feminine palm made some of the people jump. The sword of Xeron appeared in his hand, it didn't move through the air, there was no sound, it just vanished from the scabbard and appeared in his hand, pointed straight at Condulaine's heart.

"If you draw that sword you will die." Said Fennion. "I don't believe you can draw it; can you move at all?" The glow from the mindstone was very bright, and it was lighting up all the faces around, a sickly green tinge showed in all the eyes. "Now you feel the real power of the mindstone, no one can move against the rightful wielder, and Namdarin won that right in battle, when he killed Grinderosch."

"What do you want?" Asked Condulaine, his voice harsh in his throat.

"I have told you, all we need is food, drink and a place to camp.

In the morning when my human friends leave to complete their quest, only then will we discuss your refusal to acknowledge your true king, and the implications that has on your life expectancy."

"I'm sure we can come to some form of agreement." Said Condulaine.

"I'm not looking for agreement, I'm looking for obedience." The last word so loud that many in the crowd fell to their knees, followed in a heartbeat or two by all the others, except Condulaine, who was still held within the thrall of the mindstone.

"His projection is improving." Said Jangor quietly, to no one in particular. "Well Namdarin, are you going to kill this fool, or let him live."

"Not my call." Said Namdarin, glancing in Fennion's direction.

"Not really mine either." Said Fennion, "Well Condulaine?"

"My king," said Condulaine, "please forgive me, my words were rash, and my intentions were good."

"I'm not sure about that," laughed Fennion. "I feel an example coming on."

"I am sorry if I caused any offence, please my king."

Fennion looked straight into Condulaine's eyes.

"My lord Namdarin, end this fool." He spat. The look of terror on Condulaine's face made Fennion's day.

"No." Said Namdarin. The sword returned to its scabbard and Condulaine fell to his knees.

"Would you really have killed me?" He asked.

"I know Namdarin far better than I know you, he would never kill a man begging for his life, well not unless the man really needed to die. I knew he would not kill you, but your face was a picture I will take to my grave." Fennion threw back his head and laughed. "I think it's time for a celebration of my coronation, don't you?"

"Wine, beer, food, let it all be made ready." Yelled Condulaine, stumbling to his feet, he bowed deeply to Fennion. "With your permission, my king?" Fennion twitched his head by way of dismissal.

"Fennion." Said Namdarin. "You are learning far too quickly about being a king."

"King's not too different from eldest."

"Not this far out of town, it's very different here. How would you have felt if I had taken his head?"

"You would never do that, you are far too honourable a man."

"Are you so sure of that that you would bet your life on it?"

"Oh yes. Not a worry in my heart. You carry your honour in

your face, in your eyes, and in your heart. I knew without any shadow of a doubt that you wouldn't kill him. He, on the other hand has no knowledge of you, other than that you are a thief and a killer, you stole the sword and killed a king. What do you mean, my life?"

"Look around, if they all turn against you, we all die."

"But they would not, they are after all elves."

"Fennion, my friend, I am going to miss you, but I will be glad to get back to people simply wanting to stick a knife in my guts."

"What do you mean?"

"You make things too complicated, I am a simple man."

"You my friend, are anything but that. Let's eat, then sleep, in the morning we part ways, hopefully, only for a while."

"You actually believe I can survive this thing?"

"It is my fervent hope that you do, this world is a better place with you in it. Oh, it will survive without you, but it won't be as good a place to live."

"I am not entirely sure of that, I intend on ending a god, and with him will go many of the others, perhaps the only one left will be Gyara, I'm hoping that the lack of the other gods will reduce her power, at least to some extent."

"I don't believe she'll have much power with all the elder gods gone, what worries me, is the last words that Grinderosch spoke as he died."

"Something in the darkness."

"Exactly, but what?"

"Just something else for me to kill probably."

"Are you not worried?"

"How can I be any more worried? The thought of facing down Zandaar makes my bowels run like water, I couldn't be any more frightened if I tried."

"You don't look frightened."

"The others don't need to know just how scared I am, I don't need to know either, because I'm going anyway. The bastard burned my family, one and all, and for that I'm going to kill him, or die trying. What more can a man do?"

"That's the truth. Sometimes the only way to control the beast is to grab it by the nose and twist it until it submits."

"We're talking about a god here, not some recalcitrant hog."

"Same number of letters, same piggy little eyes, perhaps even the same curly tail." Laughed Fennion.

"Have you actually seen this god?"

"I'm not sure anyone has, all representations, and there aren't many of those, show him as a ball of light, or a glowing nimbus, no real physical form."

"I saw him as a glow that hung below a ceiling."

"How is a sword going to damage a ball of light?"

"I don't know but I'm trusting Xeron to his word, and Zandaar for his fear of the sword, he's frightened for a reason, I've just got to work out what it is before I get there. Or I'll just stick the sword in him and hope the sword knows what it is supposed to do."

"Well, I wish you all the luck there is in this endeavour, please come back to us."

"I will certainly try my very best to do that, but it may take me a while, we still have some days to travel yet, and I've no real idea how many, have you?"

"I am sure that someone here knows how many days it is to Zandaarkoon. I think it's actually quite a few, Gervane find someone who knows will you?" Gervane left their impromptu camp and returned a short time later with a rather strange looking elf. Rather than the thin features of the other elves this one had a much fatter face, was shorter and considerably stockier than all the elves around them.

"This is Hardain, he's a Wagoneer." Said Gervane.

"Greetings Hardain." said Fennion.

"Greetings to you too yer kingship." Said Hardain, bowing low.

"Hardain, you are an uncommon looking elf."

"Ay, some say my mother was frightened by a troll when she was carrying me, some say she had a closer meeting with the troll, but they usually only says that the once." Hardain's right hand rested meaningfully on his quite functional short sword.

"That, though interesting, is of no real importance right now. We need to know about the roads to, and the time, to get to Zandaarkoon, what can you tell us?"

"This time of year, the roads are good, not too wet, nothing worse than miles of mud and cold rain. Zandaarkoon is too far to carry much in the way of perishables, taters is about all that can make it undamaged, oh and turnips, turnips be good, don't like turnips though, they smell funny."

"How many days?"

"Good weather twenty-five days, bad weather, more like forty."

"Those are wagon days, though aren't they?"

"What would I know about fancy horses, them be wagon days."

"How many days into the city?"

"Three days hauling, and two days empty."

"It took us best part of half a day, and we were pushing hard, so his twenty-five days becomes eight, or better still twelve. That's still a way, but we are in no rush, at least I don't think we are." Said Namdarin.

"So," said Fennion, "you could be back in less than a month."

"Possible I suppose, but I wouldn't bet any money on it."

"I plan to do exactly that, one month after we get back to the city I shall be hosting a party in your honour, you will do me the courtesy of attending, is that clearly understood?"

"Yes, my king." Laughed Namdarin.

"Good, it's always better to have something to look forwards to. Gives an elf a reason to stay alive."

"Do you think I need a reason to stay alive?"

"Actually, I do. You started this quest with every intention of dying before it's completion, now you have a real chance to finish this once and for all time, but you still cannot see yourself surviving. Now you have a party to attend, if the guest of honour doesn't turn up, I will be very cross."

"I am certain that your anger will keep me alive."

"You and at least some of the rest."

"I shall try."

"If Brank dies, then Laura's wrath will make mine pale into insignificance."

"If he dies, I think I'll miss passing on that news."

"Don't you dare, you bring that in person, you face her, you tell her, she deserves that at least."

"You are right, my friend, one of us will return to give her the bad news. I just hope that it is not needed."

"Now you are talking like a survivor." Whispered Fennion.

"Damn you."

"I know, I'm a bad person, but you really need to come back to us. You will always have a home amongst the elves of the great forest, or what's left of it."

"I thank you for the offer, I shall attempt to take you up on it."

"That's better, if you are successful you will certainly deserve at least the chance of some happiness."

"So long as Zandaar is dead, that will be enough for me."

"Fair enough, for now, we both need sleep, early start in the morning, and many miles to travel."

"Yes, good night, I'm going to check on the horses first." They both went their separate ways, Namdarin approached the picket lines as quietly as he could. Arndrol was standing very still, his head hanging low, one rear leg cocked up, so the point of the hoof was resting on the ground. He was sleeping, Namdarin smiled and turned back to the group of tents, out of the darkness came Wolf, he came and stopped alongside Namdarin's leg, and sat. He looked up into the man's eyes.

"You are ready for whatever is to come. Aren't you?" Wolf said nothing, just continued to stare.

"Sometimes I wish my life was as simple as yours." Wolf said nothing, a voice came from the darkness, it spooked the horses a little.

"Your life is quite simple right now." Kern stepped from behind a tree.

"What do you mean?"

"Right now, we are riding to a meeting, that meeting may be complicated, but the riding is simple."

"Nothing in this is simple, not like Wolf's life."

"His life is anything but simple, he's struggling right now, he looks up to you as alpha, but he's not certain that you are. He'd like you to be, he trusts your strength and your instincts, but our whole pack is confusing for him, things change too fast, alpha changes in a moment, with no fighting, and no blood. He is struggling to get to grips with it, and his confusion could cost us lives, his and others."

"So, what should I do to make this overgrown dog happy?" Namdarin reached one hand down and ruffled the fur on Wolf's head.

"His stance beside you says that he'll be beside you, if you take the alpha position, but you have to take it firmly."

"But we're not a wolf pack."

"He thinks we are, and he could be a great asset, but he needs a clear leader."

"We don't need that so much."

"Don't we?" Kern turned back into the darkness and wandered slowly off on his slow patrol of the camps perimeter. Namdarin shrugged and looked down at Wolf. Then walked slowly to his tent where he knew that Jayanne was waiting. He smiled as Wolf curled up outside the tent.

CHAPTER FIFTY-THREE

Worandana woke in the cold light of pre-dawn, as old men often do, the pressure in his bladder was enough for him to crawl rapidly out of his tent, his wrinkled nightshirt barely covered his rumpled backside as he staggered into an empty space between the tents and the picket lines to release the pressure. A quiet laugh made him turn towards the camp, his stream still flowing, where Petrovana was on early watch.

"Those are some ugly legs." Laughed Petrovana softly.

"You, young man, have no idea what ugly is."

"Sorry old man but those legs ain't pretty."

"Ugly is turning brotherhood into a knife in the back, legs, no matter the ravages of time, or injury are not ugly, they are simply legs. All this is by the by, get everyone moving, we need to be on the road very soon." Petrovana walked into the circle of tents and tapped on the top of Kevana's tent, making the guy ropes thrum like rigging in the wind.

"Wake up sleepy heads." He said gently, almost sniggering.

"We're awake," said Kevana, "most definitely awake in some ways." He continued in the quietest of whispers, so that only Alverana pressed up against his naked back could hear it. After a few moments luxuriating in the warmth they shared, Kevana hitched back against Alverana, pushing against his hardness and his belly.

"Come on, we need to get moving, you've got to check that injured man."

"His name is Willowana, and I have a slight issue with going out in public right now." Whispered Alverana.

"I'm the same," muttered Kevana, "put some pants on and stuff it down the leg."

"Such sage advice," laughed Alverana, "I'd never have thought of that. That's probably why you're a leader. Either that or your fat ass from sitting on too many horses." Kevana twitched the said item back against Alverana again.

"Move it fool." He said, with a smile in his voice.

Alverana rolled away and crawled from the shared sleeping roll, he pulled on a pair of shorts and a heavy pair of trousers before he left the tent, he went straight to Willowana's tent, knowing that he wouldn't be able to take care of the usual morning activities until the swelling had gone down some. He untied the thongs holding the tent flap shut and looked inside, straight into the eyes of Willowana.

"How are you feeling?" He asked.

"You'd probably say in a little pain, but damn this hurts."

"No hot spots, or redness?"

"No nothing like that, just a damned heavy, dull, throbbing pain that gets worse when I move."

"You know the answer."

"Yes, don't move."

"That's right, try to stay as still as you can for as long as you can."

"There are certain things that require motion, or things will get quite unpleasant in here."

"I understand, now listen very carefully, when you try to sit up, the natural way to achieve this is to tense the stomach muscles and use those to lift your body, that will do more harm than good for the next few days, so don't do it. Use your arms to lift your body, too much pressure on that wound and it could open up again, and once we are gone, you are on your own."

"That's not going to be easy."

"At least you're still breathing, not something I would have bet on yesterday."

"Agreed, now help me up."

"Actually no. You go back to being a baby."

"And what exactly do you mean by that?"

"No standing up, roll slowly and carefully onto your hands and knees, and you crawl. Minimum load on that belly wound. At least two full days and nights before you even attempt to stand up. And even then, you go very slowly, is that clear."

"There are certain functions that are impossible from a kneeling position."

"Not impossible, just different."

"Trousers are going to be a problem." said Willowana with a grin.

"No, they're not. Once you're out of this tent, I'm going to help you out of your trousers, and you can't put them on again until you can do it alone without injury. Is that clear?"

"I'll get cold."

"You'll be in your bed most of the time and wrapped in blankets the rest of it."

"Is all this really necessary?"

"Only if you want to stay alive, that wound opens after we are gone, and you die, it's that simple, so come on baby, let's go for a crawl." Alverana backed out of the tent and waited for Willowana to follow. Slowly the injured man rolled towards his belly and up onto hands and knees. There was still some pain, but nothing serious, once he was out of the restrictive space of the tent Alverana had him roll onto his back, boots trousers and underwear were removed, and put back into the tent. Alverana led the crawling man away from the tent, saying. "This way is currently downwind, but that will most likely change soon."

"This is so embarrassing." Mumbled Willowana.

"That is a great idea." Said Worandana, "What made you think of that?"

"It just seemed logical, to keep body tension down and take the strain off the wound."

"You do know that after a shock like that the water works come back real quick, but the bowels can take a while to restart."

"Yes, I know," said Alverana, "but I hadn't told him yet. Willowana, it may be a couple of days before your bowels start to function properly again, but under no circumstance push, is that clear?"

"Painfully and graphically clear." Willowana looked up at the men standing around him, he was expecting to see laughter in their eyes, given his current state of undress, but he saw only sympathy, most of these men had suffered some injury or other, to greater or lesser degree, they had all stared death in the face, and lived to tell about it, now, with their help Willowana was getting the same sort of chance.

"Fast breakfast, for us, and someone make a big pot of broth for the injured brother." Called Kevana.

"Breakfast already on its way and a couple of days' worth of soup for the poor guy that's staying here." Laughed Petrovana, looking around as the camp was rapidly packed away. Long before he had finished with his cooking horses were loaded and ready for travel, other than the cooking pots of course.

"Briana." said Kevana. "Go and fill a couple of water skins for Willowana." Briana rode off to the river, returning quickly, as the light was getting stronger.

"Willowana." Said Kevana quietly. "I am sorry that the council set you on a course that led to your current situation. I sincerely hope that you get well very soon. Remember one thing if nothing else, when you are recovered by the brotherhood, and I think you will be quite soon, tell them the truth, the whole truth, it may not be what they want to hear, it will certainly not be what they want to believe. The truth, all of it."

"Kevana, I will tell them everything you have told me, and everything that has transpired here. It may not show you in a good light."

"I'm not the one that sent brothers to kill me, they are."

"Be careful." Said Worandana, "Your very survival may be an embarrassment to the council. It could be that they won't like having a witness around, at least not a living one."

"You think they would kill me in cold blood."

"I don't think the council or any of its members have anything that would pass for blood in their bodies." Said Kevana. "I may even prove their lack at some point in the future."

"We need to ride," said Worandana, "the sun is almost up, and further east, say Angorak, it's already up. Searchers could be reaching this way already." The group started hauling themselves up onto their horses. Willowana crawled backwards into his tent, turning around in the tight confines would have been far more difficult. Once they were all mounted and ready to depart Kevana looked at Willowana's pale face, the pain clearly visible there.

"Good luck Willowana." He said, before calling out. "Alverana, fast pace head east and south, Angorak is the target. Move out." Alverana did exactly as he was told, heading south through the small wooded area, a narrow game track gave him an easy road to follow, soon they were out in the open, pounding across empty scrubland, the sun rose slowly, to their left, as they ran southwards. Only Kirukana was struggling with the omission of their normal morning rituals, his unease was passed on to his horse, the animal started to get jumpy, it veered to the side, or lost its pace suddenly. Until Worandana fell in alongside the younger man.

"Just relax, will you? You are disturbing your horse and everyone else."

"It just feels so wrong, the dawn rituals have been a part of my life, well, my whole life."

"Even before you joined the priesthood?"

"Yes, at least that's the way I remember it, morning prayers, evening prayers, prayers for special days, prayers for ordinary days, it's very hard to step away from all that."

"I understand, but you do understand the need right now. If the leaders can find us, with a search, then behind every hill, and in every copse, will be groups of our brothers like the one we met yesterday. Kevana would rather not have to kill any more of our brothers."

"Intellectually I understand, but emotionally it is still wrong." Kirukana shook his head, "For some reason the hairs on the back of my neck are standing up, like someone is watching me."

"Or looking for you." Worandana yelled forwards. "Alverana, full gallop, someone is looking for Kirukana, let's make it as difficult as we can." After a moments glance backwards, Alverana laid his heels to his horses flanks, and together they all accelerated to a rolling gallop. The pack horses were more reluctant, but Petrovana's not so subtle application of a long switch soon got them moving. Alverana kept their course changing to keep them as far from the scattered copses as he could, without diverting too far from their intended direction.

"Kirukana, has that feeling lessened?"

"It's gone completely, but that could be because I'm concentrating on riding this fast. It does tend to focus the mind."

"And as such makes your mind more difficult to find. We may have to find some way to block them from searching for you, your task masters have a good feel for your mind in particular."

"I am sure that Kevana already has a plan for that." Laughed Kirukana.

"We'll try to find another way, he does tend to be a little extreme."

"That would be good, I'd like to keep my head where it is." Kirukana laughed even harder, until a sudden lurch from beneath him, focused his mind back on the activity of riding. His horse returned to its smoother more measured gait, and he looked back at Worandana, and smiled.

"How long do we have to keep this pace up?" Asked Kevana, over the noise of the pounding hooves.

"How long could we hold a search given only a rough direction and distance?" Responded Worandana.

"Minutes only, certainly not a quarter of an hour."

"So, if we run for half an hour, then even a large group of highly skilled clerics would run out of energy."

"How large a group would be needed to last half an hour?"

"Perhaps fifty."

"Could they have that many?"

"Not likely." Interrupted Kirukana. "They can perhaps put twenty skilled clerics in a room without them fighting."

"Why so few?"

"There are two main factions amongst the council, but many smaller sub-groups, some of these disagree to such an extent that they can't even be in the same room, it's really sad to see how they behave, sometimes they are like unruly children."

"And you believe these people are right to be running our world?"

"They represent the will of god."

"Sounds like they can't agree on anything." Snapped Kevana falling back alongside the two.

"Oh, they can agree on some things, it's generally the small things they disagree about."

"Like what?" Demanded Worandana.

"One of my favourites is an older cleric, who's name I can't even remember came up with a theory that there is only one god, and all the other gods are simply aspects of the one."

"I can see that as a possible interpretation of the gods we have." Said Kevana.

"Please explain?" Asked Worandana, smiling.

"All these minor gods are simply aspects of Zandaar." Kevana's reply was pitched almost as a question.

"I see." Said Worandana laughing, joined by Kirukana.

"What is funny?" Demanded Kevana, looking from one to the other.

"That is one way to look at it." Chuckled Worandana, "The other way is to suggest that Zandaar is an aspect of the one god."

"Surely that is blasphemy." Said Kevana looking straight at Kirukana.

"Oh yes, most assuredly, however, this view does have some followers, as does the other view, and just as many say these theories are completely wrong." Kirukana's sad look said it all.

"Just so I can get this straight in my head." Said Kevana slowly. "The members of the great council of our faith will fight over the theory that either our god is a minor part of a collective, or the major part of the collective, or not part of a collective. Over this they will fight, but if a man wears a shirt such as we are today, then he goes straight in the fire?"

"That." Laughed Kirukana. "Just about sums the situation up."

"These people are completely crazy." Snorted Kevana, heeling his horse and catching up with Alverana again.

"You do understand," said Worandana, "he is right, and he will set about changing things as soon as we get to Zandarkoon."

"I know." Said Kirukana. "There are going to be some interesting conflicts when and if we get there."

"Yet you keep howling blasphemy at every turn, that doesn't make too much sense to me. Which faction do you support?"

"All and none, as always."

"You do know that someone is going to hack that fence out from under you at some point, and most likely quite soon?"

"It's possible, but prevarication has kept me alive for a fair while now, by being useful to all, I am tolerated, with minimum personal risk."

"So, this venture has been the most dangerous of your life."

"Definitely, in the capital, people tend to talk before they kill you, out here, it's not the same."

"And still you push, Kevana would take your life before you even knew it. So, would I for that matter."

"Yet, still I breathe."

"That may become difficult when we get to Zandaarkoon, especially if Kevana is carrying the sword."

"He's really angry just now, that may mellow by the time we get to Angorak."

"I wouldn't count on that, he may appear to be calm, but that fire will relight in a heartbeat, or less."

"I know. It's going to be a hard time for us all."

"But it doesn't need to be so hard on our horses." Then he shouted. "Kevana, I think we can slow down, let's not kill the horses, we'll let you know if we feel any more searches coming our way." Kevana looked at Alverana and nodded, together they slowed down to a slow trot, gradually the horses breathing settled to something a little less frantic.

"You keep your ears open for searchers." said Worandana.

"I'll try, but ears isn't exactly right."

"I know, but I'm sort of stuck for the words. You know what I mean."

"It is difficult to put these things into words, perhaps we need to work on a new vocabulary to deal with this phenomenon."

"Fine, keep your phenomenal ears open." Laughed Worandana.

"That doesn't sound to good either. These are very ordinary ears."

"I don't know, they stick out a fair way."

"I need something to rest my hat on." Laughed Kirukana.

"You are taking all this surprisingly well."

"It makes a change to see Kevana's life threatened, it sort of gives my heart a lift."

"You surely understand that your very survival is in his hands?"

"Of course, either he'll kill me, or they'll kill me, given the way things are going, I have a very small possibility of living through all this. Acceptance of this fact does give one a certain sense of freedom."

"Have you no wish to fight against this control of your destiny by others?"

"I am a small person in this world, and I accept that station, why should I rail against the oncoming storm? You are the hurricane, he," Kirukana nods in the direction of the leaders, "is the tornado, and Zandaar is a typhoon of ice and fire. This battlefield is far too large for me, as I see it my best chance of survival is to let the storms fight it out and hope they don't notice me."

"Where does Namdarin fit in to this conflict of weather formations?"

"I'm not entirely sure, but Crathen seems to think he is a force to be reckoned with, he could be anything from a gentle spring rain to a volcano. Though he did make a mess of the cave exit, so perhaps he's an earthquake."

"I think there were three striking that exit tunnel, him, the woman, and their magician Granger."

"And now they have Gorgana with them, and the two of them beat us, didn't they?"

"Them and that green woman in the fire, it felt really strange to be beaten with such calm, she didn't actually attack, she just took all our energy and fed on it. Working at such long range we had nothing else to give, only power, and she just mopped it up like a sponge."

"So, they have, Namdarin; Jayanne; Granger; and now Gorgana, not forgetting this un-named Green Goddess. And if we get close their soldiers will be able to act, that conflict could be quite something, suddenly I'm not so worried about the council and Zandaar, we have something else to face first, I don't see Kevana going to Zandaarkoon without the sword, do you?"

"Never, and yes that's going to be a hard fight, let's just hope we get to Angorak first, we'll be able to track the sword and get to them as they ride past."

"How far are we from Angorak?"

"I've no idea, we need to cross the river, and head south, that is all I know, I'm not familiar with the maps or the terrain hereabouts."

"Surely the two are the same?" Kirukana looked quizzically at Worandana. The elder man laughed heartily.

"The map is not the territory." He laughed some more before going on. "The most detailed of maps can only give an impression of the territory, there is so much more to a physical place than can be described in the best of the cartographer's art, think about our recent encounter with large cats. Had the map included the legend 'here there be cats.' would we have been prepared for what came across that clearing?"

"Until those cats came towards us, such a legend would have been considered a map makers joke."

"And if they hadn't actually shown up, it would still be a joke, until the damned cat is gnawing on your leg." Laughed Worandana.

"So, you have no idea at all?"

"The river is east of us, we have to cross it, then south takes us to Angorak, if the river is too wide where we cross, then we are already too far south, so north to Angorak. There are no major mountains in the way, nor cities, and only the one big river. But I have no idea as to the distances involved, it's certainly not going to be a day or two, more like a week, or two."

"A week or two to Angorak, then how long to Zandaarkoon?"

"By river, a day, horseback maybe two."

"And we may have to fight our way every step."

"That may be the case. Are you afraid?"

"Not so much, we will die on the road to Angorak, or at Angorak, or on the road to Zandaarkoon, or at Zandaarkoon, friend Worandana, we have entered the time when the hands of all men are turned against us."

"Be careful who you call friend."

"I see now that I have not been careful enough in the past, that has changed, if you would have me as a friend I would be most grateful."

"You are a spy for the council, a bigot, a zealot, and in many ways a fool, why should I accept you as friend?"

"Because all those things can change with your help and tutelage."

"I am not sure I have the life to waste teaching you."

"None of us can be sure how much of that we have left, this is truer for the people in this group, than for any people in the world."

"Agreed, but can you change?"

"Just look at me, I'm wearing the latest fashion, grey not black. I ride with a group of renegades, on the road to hell. I have changed. In our most recent conversation have I used the 'B' word? No. I have changed, I now see that the council and its factions are the fools, once our god has the sword all these petty squabbles will be sorted out by him, not them. I thought the whole world revolved around the opinions of the council, I was so wrong. Please master hear me, I have changed."

"You have changed? If Kevana is right, when he walks into, or storms, the council chamber with me on his left hand, the sword in his right will you stand beside him?"

"Yes. The council with all its infighting and back biting has done nothing to aid our god in his purpose, I will stand with him and you."

"And what exactly do you know of Zandaar's purpose?"

Kirukana looked around for a few moments, trying to find something to tell Worandana.

"I have no idea what our god wants, or needs, I have only the words of the council. I shall ask him when we meet."

"You are either mad or a fool."

"Why?"

"No one wants to meet god, and they definitely don't want to ask him what he wants."

"I don't understand, Zandaar is the central force in our lives, why should we not want to meet him?" Kirukana looked confused.

"He may be the core of our lives, but holds those lives in such low regard, he would spend all our lives to achieve one of his purposes."

"Surely his purposes are ours, that is why we follow him."

"We follow him for all sorts of different reasons, some for power, some for fame, some because it is the only life suitable to them. And there's you, why are you here?"

"I seek only to serve god."

"That's hard to believe, I'm here because I wanted to study the magics, Kevana is a soldier, and the army of god is one of the most powerful and active, so why don't you follow one of the other gods, they tend to be less demanding."

"We can worship no other gods; such a thing is B..." The last word choked in Kirukana's throat.

"Who decided that?"

"Zandaar, of course."

"Have you even looked into any of the other gods?"

"No, of course not."

"Why not?"

"Zandaar says that it is wrong."

"I nearly got the B word again. Who else says researching other gods is wrong?"

"I don't know who does?"

"All of them, all gods with any sort of following say that all the others are wrong, bad, evil, and only they are the true god. This is a standard formula for them all except one."

"There is a god that allows followers to think about other gods?"

"Just the one, that I know of, investigations are difficult when all their teachings are banned by Zandaar."

"Which god is that one?"

"Gyara."

"The trickster, we met her."

"Her, him, even that isn't clear, slippery sort of character is Gyara, and you ought to be more careful."

"What do you mean?"

"In that one statement, you admitted the existence of another god, and that you met her. In certain circles in Zandaarkoon that would get you your own personal barbecue."

"But it is true, she appeared out of thin air, as a huge black crow, and spoke to us, we all saw it."

"Zandaar has said that this cannot have happened, Gyara does not exist, and anyone who follows her is a heretic and should be killed. You know because this is what you are taught."

"But we met her, she is real."

"And you didn't even notice, you are starting to think but you really need to pay closer attention to what people say."

"What did I miss?"

"Zandaar has declared that Gyara doesn't exist, most religions say that there are no other gods than ours, be it a single, or a group, ours are the only real ones. I have researched a few of the old religions and they all say much the same, except for one, only one specifically names gods that are prohibited."

"Zandaar names two gods that are especially bad, Gyara and Xeron."

"Don't you think that it is interesting that we've met one and Namdarin carries the sword of the other?"

"Could it just be a coincidence?"

"I don't think so, Zandaar has something to fear from these two elder gods. One cannot leave, and the other wants to, but needs to take Zandaar with him, or so I believe from what we have been told."

"Can we believe what Gyara and Crathen tell us?"

"It has been said for more years than are recorded in our libraries that the black crow tells no lies, never the whole truth and always with intention to deceive. She said that she cannot leave this place until all life is ended, and that we, or Namdarin can bring this about. That is the part that scares me. Doesn't it you."

"I'm sorry, but we are only a roving band of mystics and warriors, I just can't see us ending all life on this plane, just so Gyara can leave."

"Perhaps we set something in motion, maybe killing Namdarin or taking the sword from him, or, I don't know, something that starts the end, so Gyara can leave."

"According to Crathen, killing Namdarin is impossible, taking the sword from him is going to be difficult. I'd say that given the magical weapons that they are carrying it's more likely to be them that ends the world not us."

"Maybe we are the catalyst that triggers the whole thing."

"You are giving us too big a part in all this, we are simple soldiers of god, we leave the ending of worlds to the bigger boys."

"I hope that you are right." said Worandana, at the front of the column Alverana's suddenly raised fist grabbed his attention, the fist snapped down and to the right, the hand opening flat.

"Turn right and ride hard." Said Worandana, unsure Kirukana would understand the military hand signals being used. The whole column turned as one and increased speed, to the limit the uncertainty of the ground would allow, Alverana seems to be heading for a large group of trees, only a short distance away. The whole group followed him, not entirely sure why, but trusting the man to have their best interests at heart. Alverana crashed into the wood with Kevana at his side, not an act to be undertaken lightly, a low branch can sweep a man from his horse, a lower branch can break a horse's legs, luckily neither of these happened, though Alverana's sudden stop only fifty yards into the wood did cause somewhat of a pile up of sliding horses. Alverana fell from his saddle and ran back through the pack of milling horses.

"Keep these animals still and quiet." He snapped, as he approached the place where they had entered the wood. The hole they had made in the trees forcing their way in at speed was clear for all to see, he stopped almost at the edge of the wood, he leant against a tree, and draped his arms along the branches, he began a slow, deep and wordless chant. The power of his magic soon became clear, the broken branches healed themselves, the grass reformed, the signs of the horses passing were erased in a matter of minutes, the woodland looked like it hadn't been disturbed in years. Once his task was complete he slumped away from the tree and stopped the chant, his song was replaced by the sounds of the birds, none had noticed that they had stopped singing until their sounds returned. Alverana crawled to the edge of the wood, Kevana pushed through the crowd of horses.

"Keep these animals quiet, and still, no noise." He said quietly, as he crawled up to where Alverana was lying.

"Why are we hiding?"

"I saw a group of riders, dressed in black."

"Did they see us?"

"We'll find out fairly soon. They'll either turn this way or they won't."

"Which way were they heading?"

"North, we were lucky, a fast turn put a small rise between us and them, and the wind was blowing our sounds away from them, we may have got away with it this time. Quiet." They both hunkered down as low as they could into the undergrowth, as a column of black clad riders came into view, riding in strict formation, two by two. One of the leaders carried a long staff, which rested in a cup on his right stirrup, the other had a longsword strapped to his back.

"Shit." Whispered Kevana. Alverana nudged him hard in the ribs, a glare told him to be quiet.

Sounds of voices drifted to them on the wind.

"What did you see?" Asked the swordsman.

"I'm not sure I saw anything, it was more a flash of movement, and then it was gone, it vanished, perhaps behind that hill there." He nodded in the direction of the rise.

"Well if a troop of fast-moving horses came this way there is no evidence, that wood hasn't seen any riders for a good long time, how many are we looking for?"

"We're not even sure of that, could be as many as twelve."

"Twelve horses have not forced their way into that wood in the last few minutes."

"I can see that, but I know what I felt, we are looking for Worandana and Kevana, they are both skilled and cunning, they may have a way of hiding their presence."

"If they do, then we will never find them, no one will."

"I could break their concealment spells given some time."

"We don't have time, our patrol area is north, they are much more likely to be north of here, we need to move."

"Agreed, it is unlikely that they are here, let's move on." The swordsman stood up in his stirrups and called out.

"Northwards move out." The column set off in military fashion, turned north and accelerated to a rolling trot. In a few minutes they were far enough away for the two lurkers to slip backwards into the wood. Once they stood up and started walking back to the rest Alverana spoke softly.

"You know who they are?"

"Yes, someone is really serious about not taking us alive. They don't let those two loose for simple tasks."

"But at least they are sending them the wrong way."

"I'd have thought they would stay closer to Zandaarkoon." Said Kevana, walking up to Worandana's horse. He looked up before speaking.

"The damned council have set the dogs on us."

"You mean Picarana and Broudana?"

"Yes, the damned hunters are looking for us, but they have been sent northwards. They'll turn around as soon as there is confirmation as to where we actually are."

"At least I know who I have to block now, Picarana is a very powerful searcher, he's been trying to catch me out for more years than I care to remember. Kirukana, how do you feel now? They're not looking to capture us, they are serious about our deaths, the dogs never take prisoners."

"This isn't exactly news, the last group we faced, tried to kill us, they failed, why should this new lot be any different?"

"You really have led a sheltered life, haven't you? You've never heard of the dogs, they do prefer a more ceremonial title 'The hounds of Zandaar.' You've heard of them?"

"The Hounds. Yes, I've heard of them, never met them, or knew their names. They hunt down renegades and heretics. No survivors."

"And their group is at full strength." Said Kevana. "Nine by nine, nine clerics and nine warriors. If they find us we are going to be in some trouble."

"Well," laughed Worandana, "they missed us today, their sense of smell must be off."

"Picarana was almost sure he'd seen someone riding into this wood, but when they arrived there was no physical evidence, so they turned away. Well done Alverana." Said Kevana.

"What was that magic you used?" Asked Kirukana.

"Alverana here," answered Kevana, putting an arm round his friends' shoulder, "used to be a follower of Gyara, and still knows some of their magic, it can be useful occasionally." All eyes turned to Kirukana, the uncomfortable monk looked around, plucked absently at his grey shirt, he thought for a moment or two, that seemed to him a very long time, he looked straight into Kevana's eyes before speaking.

"That's very interesting, I wasn't aware that Gyara had any magic, let alone shared it with her followers."

"See how much he has grown." Said Worandana, slapping Kirukana on the back.

"Surprising." Said Kevana.

"Not really." Said Alverana. "The people he trusted set the damned dogs on him, on us all. Things are going to get exciting now."

"When can we move on?" Asked Worandana, looking at Alverana.

"Give them a while to put some distance between us, then we'll go south for a while before turning east again."

"Good idea, Picarana does have a certain sensitivity to things going on around him, and he'll be looking just now." Kirukana was fidgeting with his shirt again, then he spoke up.

"We need to find a village and get shut of all this black, grey shirts don't really do much to hide who we are, and we need a cover story for any of the priesthood that we meet along the way. This is now more urgent than ever. I never thought I'd be running from the Hounds."

"Let's get one thing very clear here." Said Kevana, firmly. "We are not running from the hounds, we are attempting to avoid a confrontation that would result in the deaths of our brothers, the ones that go by the name of damned dogs."

"I'm sorry to say." Kirukana, almost whispered, "I don't have the same feeling of brotherly love for those men."

"Who said anything about love," said Kevana, "they are fellow soldiers, and they have been given a task that is likely to get some or all of them killed, a task that should never have been handed out, if the council want us dead they should come and do it themselves."

"They're tired old men, sitting in their comfortable chairs, I don't see them riding twenty days to see to us, most of them couldn't ride a single hour without dying." Laughed Kirukana.

"Now he's poking fun at the leaders of the council." Laughed Worandana, "What sort of monster have we created here."

"Not you, old man, them. The damned council and their machinations, my lord Kevana, when we face this council of fools, do I have your permission to stand at your side?"

"Kirukana." Replied Kevana. "You know these fools better than we do, when we face them, I will stand at your back, with the sword in my hand and death in my heart."

Kirukana looked hard at Kevana for a moment before quietly answering.

"Sounds like we have a plan."

Worandana looked around before saying.

"By all the old gods, what have I done?"

Kevana laughed out loud. "You my friend, have turned a cringing sycophant into, well, for want of better words, a god killer. He'll stand in front of his council of elders and demand that they fall on their swords, and when they refuse, he'll give them to me. You know, I could get to like this young man."

"Please tell me we can ride now?" Asked Worandana looking at Alverana.

"They should be far enough away by now, let's ride." Alverana led them slowly through the wood and out onto the plain, before pushing the pace up to a slow trot, Kevana moved up alongside Alverana, so that his friend was on his right, he heard rather than saw another horse, he glanced to his left just as Kirukana moved in on that side. Kirukana smiled at Kevana, Kevana turned to Alverana, caught his eyes, then looked left and back. Alverana had already felt Kirukana moving into position, Kevana and Alverana locked gazes for a moment or two, before they both shrugged and looked forwards to continue their journey southbound.

CHAPTER FIFTY-FOUR

Jangor had given himself the last watch before dawn, and done so deliberately, he watched the sky slowly begin to brighten in the east, there wasn't going to be much of a sunrise, far too much cloud, some of it low and dark. 'Perhaps there will be rain today.' he thought, adding some firewood to the campfire, the rush of sparks up into the air, and the crackling as the wood caught, caused Wolf to look up. For a change he'd spent the night outside Namdarin's tent, yesterday's run had been enough for him to want a little rest, but rested now he was, and raring to go, he sat up, and stretched, yawned hugely, and watched Jangor closely.

"It's going to get noisy round here." Said Jangor quietly to the wolf, who merely looked at the man. Jangor smiled at the wolf in an attempt to show him that there was nothing to worry about. Jangor took a deep breath, then another one, this time he shouted that particular soldiers rousing call, in true parade ground fashion.

"Hands off cocks. On with socks. Out of your pits you lazy blackguards." The cry rang around the camp, and even echoed back off the trees some considerable distance away. Wolf threw back his head and howled, that deep booming resonance filled the whole town and had people running into the camp.

"Jangor my friend." Called Fennion from inside his tent. "I could get to hate you. It's still dark."

"It won't be for much longer, the sooner we get on the road the sooner we'll get this thing done. Up and at em gentlemen."

"Excuse me." Shouted Jayanne.

"And lady, I am sorry that I momentarily considered you to be one of the men."

"Your apology is not helping." She shouted, laughing as she came out of the tent, only partially dressed, displaying beyond any doubt her gender. She placed her clenched fists on her hips, tipped her pelvis to one side, thrust her chest out, and laughed loudly at the lightening sky.

"Cover yourself woman," screamed a strange voice, "you display yourself like a common street whore." Jayanne's laugh stopped, she looked at the elf running towards her, her green eyes snatched his almond shaped ones and he stumbled to a halt, she stood straight, and strutted slowly towards him. The elf was unaware of the action going on around him, his eyes were held, but he couldn't avoid noticing the bouncing of her breasts with every stride she took. Soldiers moved into position all around the camp, facing outwards, but ears tuned inwards. No swords were drawn, but their readiness was clear. Another step closer, and Fennion fell into view from his tent, shirt only half on, and sword still in its scabbard in his left hand, Namdarin came through the flap of his tent, wearing only shorts, but the sword of Xeron in his right hand.

"Lady Jayanne, please forgive this fool."

"Who are you calling fool?" Shouted the elf, breaking eye contact for only a moment. Fennion ran to stand in front of Jayanne.

"Please lady, he has no idea."

"Lady?" laughed the elf. A deep vibration filled the air, a thrumming that shook everything, then the slap of wood on flesh made Fennion step backwards.

"Please lady, let Wolf have him." He waved to call the canine, Wolf looked to Namdarin and stayed where he was, close enough, but not too.

"You offer me to an animal? What sort of king are you?"

Fennion turned his back on Jayanne, and pushed the elf firmly in the chest, forcing him back a step and then another. "Wolf will only kill you, that axe will take your soul. You will apologise to the lady and do it soon."

"Why should I?" Fennion's jaw fell open for a moment, he

shook his head for a moment then yelled. "Gervane, perimeter, keep the rest of our people out of this." Gervane's people started moving towards the edges of the camp.

"To arms." Called Namdarin. Swords were drawn, and magicians' staffs were raised, the deep throated growl added to the tension in the camp.

"Gervane." Yelled Fennion. "Keep the rest of our people out of this, I will sacrifice this fool myself if I must." He turned to the elf and spoke quietly. "Are you beginning to get an idea, just how deep, is the pile of shit that you are standing in? Have you any clue at all?"

"I don't understand any of this." He mumbled.

"If you kneel and beg the lady for forgiveness you may just live long enough to find out, if not I'll take your head myself, rather than let that axe take your soul. The axe of Algoron." The elf's eyes snapped wide open at that name, Fennion nodded. He stepped back, dropped the scabbard from his longsword and raised the sword to strike.

The elf looked from sword to axe and back, then fell to the ground, he grovelled slowly towards Jayanne.

"I am sorry my lady, I had no idea who you were, or who you were working for, please forgive this fool." He moved his head enough so that he could look up into her eyes, somehow the breasts that had been such a problem weren't even noticed.

"I work for no-one, I follow Namdarin, we go to kill Zandaar, the axe was Algoron's, now it is mine, why should you live?" She spoke slowly and clearly.

"Lady, my words were spoken in haste and without thought, I am beneath your notice, you name gods as your enemies, I am insignificant by comparison, please forgive me."

Jayanne turned to Fennion. "He grovels quite well, what do you mean about souls?"

"Amongst our people it is believed that the axe of Algoron, so long thought to be lost, eats the souls of its victims, and sends them somewhere to perish in pain. For us this is un-bearable, our souls only wait to be reborn in a later generation, to be removed from this plane of existence is unthinkable."

"Why wolf first?" She asked, everyone around the camp could feel the tension dropping away, the soldiers were breathing easier, and the villagers were less anxious.

"With your anger so great, I thought a fast and bloody death would defuse the situation quickly, equally I knew that you probably wouldn't allow that. It was a cynical tactic to buy some time."

"You think you know me that well? What of the effect on this groveler?"

"You are a good person, if a little hot headed, as to the groveler, once we are gone, his self-righteous indignation will rapidly override any fear and embarrassment he feels right now. He'll survive, though somehow I'm not sure he is entirely safe just yet."

"My king." Whispered the crouched figure.

"Speak groveler."

"Would you two please decide my fate, the suspense is making me insane, I'm so frightened I'm peeing."

"Stand up groveler." Snapped Jayanne, slowly the figure rose, and faced her. The growing dark patch on his clothing showed that he was indeed in some distress. Her fists rested again on her hips, the axe fell to hang from its strap again. Fennion sighed.

"What do you see groveler?" She asked. His eyes flashed down her body then returned to be captured by the intense emerald.

"You are the sun and the moons and the stars, your presence lights the world, I cannot believe that in my blindness I failed to see this, forgive me for my harsh and stupid words. Or end my miserable life, I only ask that you don't allow the axe to take my soul." This time it was Jayanne who broke eye contact, she turned to Fennion.

"He does grovel quite prettily, but should he live?"

"He has given that choice to you, because he knows that is where the decision lies." She turned back to the elf.

"You live, but you serve until we leave, it will only be a short time, and there won't be much for you to do."

"Thank you, my lady, may I be allowed to get cleaned up first."

"No, there isn't enough time, we shall be leaving after a fast meal, go fetch the horses, and watch out for the grey, he bites." The groveler turned and fled to where the horses were picketed. The soldiers returned to their tasks, tents started to collapse, and packs were readied for loading. The people from the village knew that the crisis was passed but were still confused as to how they should react. The elder came over to Fennion, stepping slowly, and carefully.

"My king." He said bowing.

"Yes." Said Fennion a little sharply, but still nodding his thanks to Mander for the plate of food he was presented with.

"Would you really have killed him?"

"Yes."

"For a shameless human female?"

Fennion swallowed a mouthful of food, before looking back at the elder.

"Were you not sufficiently embarrassed last night? That woman carries the axe of Algoron, that man over there carries the sword of Xeron and the mindstone, they go to end Zandaar, or die trying, will you ride with them?"

"No, it is not my fight."

"Oh, but it is. Zandaar will swallow the whole world, maybe not in our generation, or perhaps the next, but he will have it all. Are you sure it's not your fight?"

"He's a god for the humans, it's up to them to remove him."

"They are trying just that; do you know what Zandaars first precept is?"

"No."

"Worship me or die. The choices are simple."

"If we turn away from our trees then we die anyway."

"True. So what choice do we have?"

"None. Shouldn't we go with them?"

"No. An approaching army of elves would only bring on a huge battle, and these people would never get through all that. So long as Zandaar thinks the sword is coming to him to be his, they have a chance of getting close enough. You asked if I would have killed that elf, know this, if I knew, beyond doubt, that feeding my race to that axe would mean that Zandaar would die, then I would line us all up to be killed. There are other tribes of elves to carry on."

"This is the act of a king?"

"Certainly, I look to the future, though I know I have precious little of it left to see."

"You are a madman."

"This also has been said before."

"Grandfather." Said Laura from behind Fennion, he turned. "Would you really do that?"

"Yes daughter. The survival of our race is all that matters in the long run, Zandaar will kill us all, eventually. His reasons are simple, his path clear."

"So why have we done nothing about it until now?"

"There has never been a visible possibility of victory, not until Namdarin turn up in our forest."

"No hints? No auguries?" Nothing?"

"No daughter. I have been aware of Zandaars growth for many

a year, but I could see no viable way to attack him, his city is huge, and well defended. I have considered so many ways, poisoning their water, or food, these were the best options I could come up with, but even so I couldn't guarantee that Zandaar himself would die, he's a god, I have no idea if he even eats food, or drinks water."

"I know what he eats, and I know what he drinks." Said Namdarin.

"What?" asked the elder.

"He eats people, their very lives, only a little from each at a time, but he feeds on his people."

"You mean that their prayers support him, and give him sustenance?"

"No. They walk through his temple and come out weaker and drained, I nearly got sucked into that myself on one occasion."

"He must be stopped."

"Finally, you see." Said Fennion.

"I am sorry, my king. I knew that the Zandaars could become a problem, but I was hoping for the normal outcome."

"Normal outcome?" asked Namdarin.

"Human religions," answered Fennion, "they generally tend to end the same way, they grow until they become so big that they lose control, they splinter, and schism brings them to civil war, they destroy themselves, and the survivors are too weak and scattered to be a problem for many a year. Usually another takes over and the cycle starts all over again. I am sorry but our long lives mean we see further into the past than you do."

"You've seen this?"

"Not personally, Zandaar has brought an unprecedented consistency, he's been around longer than I have."

"Grandfather, I don't believe that." Laughed Laura, as Brank came up behind her and placed a huge hand around her waist, she held his arm and leaned against him.

"Daughter it is true. Generally human religions grow and consume themselves within our lifespans. Zandaar first came to eminence when my father was young and shows no sign of division even now."

"Lord Namdarin." Said the elder. "How can we help you in your quest?"

"You have done enough, we have supplies and horses, all we need now is some luck."

"Luck I am afraid we cannot bring you, but know this, while we breathe the forest will never turn against you, nor betray you."

"You have rhanarill?" Interrupted Fennion.

"Yes, my king, he is young and not certain in his power yet."

"Present him immediately, this is most certainly a sign."

The elder turned to a member of his village standing on the edge of the camp, none wanted to come too close to these strangers.

"Bring Joe." He shouted.

"Joe?" asked Fennion.

"His mother's idea."

"He wasn't special enough, she had to give him a name like Joe?"

"She's a strange woman."

"Is Joe so special?" asked Namdarin.

"Joe is one of the great heroes of our history, it is said he killed the last of the fire drakes."

"Joe killed a dragon."

"So, the tale has come down the years."

"We have a similar hero in our past." Laughed Namdarin.

"Your tale was stolen from us, the last dragon was killed by an elf called Joe." The tension in Fennion's voice was climbing as he spoke. Walking into the camp came a woman and a young elf, not a child, but by no means fully grown. She moved with the smooth grace of all the elven peoples, but the youngster took that grace to an entirely new level, he didn't walk, he flowed from one step to the next. His skin was different from the paleness of the elves, his exposed arms were tanned brown, like a man who spent his life in the fields, but his hands had a pale tinge of green to them. They walked straight to Fennion and both bowed.

"King Fennion please meet my son Joe." She said calmly.

"Hello Joe."

"My king." Said the young man, his voice had a strange resonance.

"Are you truly rhanarill?"

"I think that I am. I have an affinity for the trees than many don't. I do carry the outward signs, but I'm not certain I will ever be any better than I am already."

"I have a favour to ask of you."

"I am yours to command."

"This cannot be commanded."

"Then ask."

"Can you extend the blessing of the forest to these humans and their quest?"

"Is their quest important to our people and the forest we serve?"

"Their quest is important to all life that doesn't support Zandaar."

"Then I shall try."

"Jayanne." Called Fennion, "please come here, this young man needs to talk to you."

"Talk is not necessary." Said Joe.

"But contact is." Said Fennion, Joe just nodded. Jayanne finished strapping a bundle to the saddle of her horse then came over. Joe reached for her hand and Namdarin's. She smiled and presented her left hand. Namdarin did the same. Once he had both hands Joe suddenly became rigid, his breathing harsh in his throat.

"Fennion." He rasped. "These people are carrying so much power, how can we help them?"

"I felt the power they hold, but even this may not be enough, they need all the advantages they can get, will the forest help them?"

"The trees are afraid, they carry fire in their hearts."

"That fire is not directed at the forest, it is reserved for Zandaar."

"Not only Zandaar."

"Zandaar and his followers."

"Their fire carries at it's source both hate and love, this contradiction causes the concern for the forest. Explain this." Joe looked straight at Namdarin.

"My love for my family triggered my hate for Zandaar, there is no contradiction there."

Joe turned his gaze upon Jayanne. All eyes turned to her, she flinched a little.

"This man died for me, I can never turn away from him when he is in such need." Her voice shook slightly.

"The trees can feel the truth, so please tell them." Whispered Joe. Jayanne twitched, tried to pull her hand free, and failed, Joe's hand didn't move at all.

"Truth." Said Joe, louder and firmer this time. Jayanne glanced at Namdarin, her eyes pleading. Namdarin nodded.

"Truth." She spat the words in Joe's face. "I hate men, all men, for the power they have over women, for the way they run the whole world, I hate them all, and have to power to kill them all." The axe snapped into her right palm.

"And Namdarin?" asked Joe. She looked at Namdarin before

speaking.

"I love him, more than life itself, and hate myself for doing so. Is that truth enough for you?" The axe fell to hang from its strap.

"There is the contradiction that frightens the trees, your anger is your energy, your hate is your power, your love is the source of your victory. You walk on the edge; can you give your life for him?"

"I won't know that until the moment of choice comes, I hope that I can, I pray that I can." She paused to draw a breath, her face reddened as the anger came to the fore again. "Damn you all, I will die for him, I will kill for him, I will burn the world for him, and all of you with it." Again, the axe leapt to her hand, her eyes flashed green and hot. The sword of Xeron jumped from its scabbard and slapped into the empty right hand. Joe closed his eyes for a long moment, then he smiled.

"There is the trigger, there is the power, the trees believe you will prevail, and they give you their support and power, for good or ill, they are with you." He released their hands, the two staggered backwards, not realising just how hard they had been pulling on those thin arms. Joe turned to Fennion and bowed.

"My king." He said, softly.

"Joe, you understand that once you're grown and come into your full power. You will have to come to the city."

"I know, I shall have to move to the city, so that I can support the trees, and the people that live there."

"I shan't be king by then, we'll have a queen for you to help, Laura will be the one you will be dealing with."

"I understand. We are unlikely to meet again, my king."

"You cannot tell, I may come out here to visit with you and learn the feelings of the trees. Most likely in the next month or so."

"I understand." Smiled Joe, he bowed again, turned and left with his mother.

"Did I miss something there?" Asked Namdarin. Fennion smiled but said nothing.

"You did." Said Laura. "Now that the trees have given their support, we will know as soon as you fail, they will feel your deaths, and pass that news on to Joe. He will of course pass that on to the rest of us."

"What about success?"

"That maybe something different, you measure success by the defeat of Zandaar, they feel things a little differently, they feel his end, but they may not consider that an actual success, he could be replaced quickly by something better or worse. This will give them a level of uncertainty."

"But failure they'll get immediately."

"Yes."

"Fine." Said Namdarin. "It looks like our camp is almost cleared, we have a long way to go, I suggest we get started. Fennion, my friend, thanks for all you help, and I hope to see you sometime soon." He held his hand out to shake that of the king, in the normal manner for humans. Fennion took the hand and shook it solemnly, then stepped back and bowed in the manner of the elves.

"Goodbye Namdarin." He said. "I wish you all the luck in the world in this adventure of yours, come back and see us when you have finished it, you will find peace and relaxation amongst the elves of the great forests. I shall be sending messengers out to all the tribes, there will be a meeting of the elders in the near future, it could be that war will be joined if you fail."

"I hope it doesn't come to that. The costs would be far too great."

"I'll agree with that. Goodbye my friend." Namdarin and Jayanne turned to their horses and climbed up into the saddles. Namdarin turned to Jangor.

"I didn't get any breakfast."

"You didn't do any packing either, you were too busy talking, you get to do without. Kern, move out." The last a shout. Namdarin looked back at Fennion, and shrugged, before tagging into the line of horses leaving the village green. Once they were clear of the houses and the spectators that had come out to watch them leave, Kern picked up the pace, soon they were heading south at a rapid trot, along the road, between cultivated fields, some worked by elves, others empty. In less than an hour they passed the last of the fields, this one had a lone elf, following a team of three horses and a multiple bladed plough. The elf waved a salute as they rode by, Jangor waved back, but they carried on, pushing the pace harder while the road was still in good condition. Kern knew that as they got further away from the village the road would begin to deteriorate. Southward they rode, through countryside that gradually became wilder, the occasional trees came closer and closer to the path, no longer a road, more a track, just wide enough for a cart, certainly not enough for two to pass. Soon the ruts faded to almost nothing and the path was almost impossible to see, merely a depression, that ran ahead of them into the distance, it was going generally in the direction they wanted to go, so Kern followed it.

So it went for day after day, riding hard through the day and camping through the dark, the only changes were the mountains passing slowly to the west, the terrain changed little. Brank became used to his new horse, he even became a decent rider, though that was more the horse's skill than his own. One miserable grey morning as they came through a break in a small forest, more a strip of trees following a small stream, as they crossed the ford, Kern, Namdarin and Jayanne side by side, the steady pace of the horses had lulled them into a state of somnolence, Namdarin glanced back to make sure everyone had cleared the ford before he sped up. As he looked forwards again there was a strange hissing sound, as Jayanne looked at him a red fletched arrow appeared in the middle of Namdarin's chest, slowly he toppled backwards off the horse, Jayanne howled, turned to the front, a group of men were coming toward them, one with a bow, he was drawing a sword as they ran towards Jayanne and Kern. Jayanne screamed and rode straight at them the axe weaving a complex pattern in the air, the six lasted mere seconds, each stroke was instant death, just off the road were a group of horsemen, they were turning away, she was hot on their trail.

"Kern, Brank." Yelled Jangor. "On her, keep those fools off her, bring some horses." Kern and Brank set off after Jayanne, Wolf already far ahead of them.

"Magicians ward." Jangor called as he dropped from his horse beside Namdarin, it took only a glance to be sure he was dead. Jangor grabbed the arrow and yanked it out, he hurled it away.

"Looks like you're going to have to prove what we've been told about you." He whispered. A heavy soft nose pushed against his shoulder, Jangor turned to Arndrol. "What are you doing here, go help Jayanne?" As if he understood Arndrol turned and set off ripping turf and chasing after Jayanne.

The horsemen were barely moving when Jayanne caught them, the first turned towards her, his sword raised, as it came flashing down the axe intercepted it and it vanished in a shower of sparks, the axe took the man in the belly and carved upwards until it stopped in his ribcage, blood pouring from the wound vanishing into the blade, passing energy onto Jayanne, she looked into the man's as he died, the horror there told her this was no ordinary death, as she pulled the axe from his collapsed chest, a bag of bones and skin fell from the horse, by the time she moved on to chase the rest Kern, Brank and Wolf were with her, as she closed on the next man he whipped his horse with the flat of his sword, but it didn't have anything left to give, Wolf came up on its right and the horse shied away so fiercely that the man toppled from the saddle, before he had stopped rolling along the ground, just as he was getting his feet under him, the axe took him in the back, Jayanne grinned as the axe paused for the moment that it took to drain the life, the blood and the soul from the man, his dying gurgle was filled with terror, but still she let the axe feed. With a wave of her hand she sent Wolf after the fleeing horses, only ten left, two were archers, each attempting to nock arrows, Jayanne heard the thunder as Arndrol started to close on them. As one the riding archers stood in their stirrups and turned, they pulled aimed and loosed, they weren't shooting at Jayanne, they hit the target they wanted, her horse, two arrows in the chest, it coughed, and stumbled. Jayanne screamed in pain for the horse that had served her so well. As its head started to drop she reached out and snatched the saddle horn of the big grey, she hauled herself across into the saddle, her horse fell to its knees and rolled end over end as it died.

"For that you all die." She screamed, Arndrol's pace was far faster than her own horse, in moments Brank was struggling to keep up, howling like a banshee she crashed into the fleeing horsemen, one archer fell from his horse right into the jaws of Wolf, he barely broke stride ripping the throat from the man and off after another. The other archer was cleaved completely in two by Jayanne, the axe flashed clean and again a dry corpse fell to the ground. Seven men turned to encircle the woman, one came up behind her only to be swept from his saddle by Brank's longsword, Kern slashed another, Arndrol slammed into one of the horses as the rider wobbled, Jayanne separated his head in a heartbeat, the fountain of blood was pulled into the shining axe as it flew around her, and slammed into the next, this time it got to feed properly, his dying scream was dreadful to hear. Wolf snapped at the belly of a horse and as it shied it crashed into one of the others, the two riders got tangled, before they got separated Jayanne had chopped one from crown to belt and Brank had the other, only one left, surrounded by three riders, and a Wolf somewhere in the grass. With a move so fast it couldn't have been seen she struck, straight down into the shoulder and diagonally across the man's body, he slumped, he died. There was little blood, as the corpse fell from the saddle. Wolf sniffed and then set off through the grass in the direction the other man had taken, up the hill towards the trees on the crest. Jayanne and the others fast on his tail, Jayanne was leaning well forward in the saddle, giving Arndrol the signal for more speed. The fleeing horse shied from the trees and turned away so fast that the man fell from his saddle, and staggered to his feet, running into the darkness of the trees. Arndrol was only a few moments behind him, but in the sudden darkness Jayanne was struggling to see anything at all.

"Wolf. Find him. I want him alive." She yelled, signalling the wolf. Wolf cast around then suddenly yapped and set off through the tightly packed trees. She turned Arndrol along the narrow path that Wolf was forcing through the brush. Eventually she was forced to dismount and lead Arndrol, they came into a small clearing some sparse scrubby grass grew in clumps on the bare ground, Wolf was sitting at the far side, staring at the last of the attacking group. Jayanne walked up to the wolf and patted him on the head, then she looked upon the frightened man.

"Who are you people?" he cried.

"I am Jayanne. Why?"

"I want to know who I've been hunting."

"Not that, fool, why did you attack us?"

"I heard that the Zandaars were looking for you, I thought we could make some gold selling you to the black robes."

"So, you're simply greedy robbers?"

"We have done some of that, we're blank shields currently looking for employment."

"So why did you stop running? Wolf would have caught you and kept you alive until I found you."

"I didn't have much of a choice, these damned trees won't let me go." he said, pulling hard on the branches he seemed to be holding on to.

"So, the trees are holding you not the other way around?"

"How the hells did you do that?"

"I didn't, but then we do have the support of a local tribe of elves, they did say that the trees would help us, seems they were right."

"So, what are you going to do now?" he asked.

"I'm going to kill you, after all that's what you did to my man."

"Please you don't have to kill me, just release me, you'll never see me again."

"I don't think so, your man put an arrow in his heart, without a moment's hesitation. It's the sword you're after, isn't it?"

"Yes, that's what they want, the sword. Though it's supposed to have a black pommel. If you must kill me, please, not that damned axe." He looked at Brank. "As a soldier, please a clean death, not that axe."

"The lady decides." said Brank. Jayanne patted Brank on the arm and smiled up at him.

"You know the worst part for you?" She asked of the mercenary.

"What?"

"Not that you are going to die, no not that, the worst part is that Namdarin is going to come back, unlike you he will live again." She smiled broadly, then she buried the axe in his belly, his groan came from the depths.

"Oh, my soul." He whispered as he died, the axe kept feeding until there was only a dried-up husk left hanging from the trees. As she turned away she thought 'He looks like he's been dead a hundred years.'

"Let's get back." She said. She slapped her left hand against her thigh, and Wolf fell in to that side, Arndrol followed to her right. Brank and Kern stared at the hanging corpse for a moment then followed. As they walked into the daylight, Kern turned to Brank.

"We need to collect as many of those horses as we can."

"Why?"

"You'll see, and Jayanne is going to need to pick a new ride for herself."

"Look at them, they're scattered all over, and frightened, how are we going to round them up?"

"We're not. Wolf." he shouted, Wolf came back to Kern, and looked up at him.

"Wolf my friend, we need all those horses rounded up, go get 'em." He gestured with his right hand, it took a few different hand signals for Wolf to get the idea, then off he went, a black and grey streak through the grass.

"Is he going to round them up for us?" asked Brank.

"I'm not sure, round them up or kill them all, we'll find out in a moment or two."

Much like a sheepdog Wolf ran off very wide until he was beyond the horses, their natural tendency to herd together was in his favour, he circled them until all the loose horses were gathered together, then he pushed them slowly towards Jayanne, Kern and Brank, again the horses training helped the wolf, though the horses were frightened of wolves, they were used to people protecting them, so naturally they gravitated to where the people where, very soon there were eight horses, Jayanne looked round at them as they arrayed themselves behind Kern and Brank.

"Looks like Wolf missed a couple." She said.

"He's no sheepdog, and these aren't sheep, eight out of ten is good enough, how many do we actually need?" Asked Kern.

"One will do the job, or it has before,"

"But how long will it take?"

"Hours, but not a day."

"Can you be sure that he will return?"

"He has so far, you saw him return, once didn't you?"

"Yes, he was dead when we approached but he came back to life with a scream, and more than a little disorientated."

"Not a surprise."

"And now he's going to have another memory of dying, how many of these can a man recover from?"

"He still has a quest to complete; he'll not give up until it is finished. Gather the horses, we don't want them running off now do we?" Kern nodded and started collecting the reins of the captured horses, they were getting close to where the others were waiting. The new horses were getting nervous, more people and an extreme excitement that they couldn't understand. She led the way around the site of her first encounter with the foot soldiers, the smell of the blood alone would have been too much for the horses, she came down onto the path and turned back towards where Namdarin had fallen. Granger came around the group and stood on the path his staff held horizontally, blocking the whole of the way.

"Stop there." He called. Then waved Jangor to the fore. Jayanne paused on the path, her displeasure clear for all, the axe held loosely across her knees.

"What's the problem, old man?" she called.

"You are." He turned to Jangor, "Can't you feel her power? She is rife with it. I can see it crawling around inside her skin. Like it's looking for a way out. Can you feel it Jayanne?"

"The only thing I feel is anger that you are standing in my way. We need to bring Namdarin back and quickly."

"I understand the process takes a while." said Granger, his staff became dark as ebony.

"Granger you are charging your staff, why? You plan to use it against me?"

"That is not my plan, I just suggest some caution before you are allowed too close to Namdarin."

"You think I would actually harm him?"

"Not deliberately, but that energy you are carrying is like nothing I have every felt before."

"I have felt it's like before." Said Gregor.

"What is it?" asked Granger.

"Jayanne," said Gregor, "did the axe take longer to kill than normal?"

"Yes, and it sucked the bodies dry, they looked like they had been dead for a hundred years."

"It sucked more than blood from these, it took all their energy and I believe, if the elves are right, it fed on their souls."

"How can you tell?" asked Granger.

"We used some old magic to conjure a dead soldier from a monastery, we wanted to know how he died, it turned out that Namdarin had killed him and all the others, but the energy we trapped inside a summoning spell felt just like that Jayanne has inside her."

"So," said Jangor, "the axe ate their souls, why?"

"Ate their souls and gave the power to Jayanne."

"Again, why?"

"I don't know, but the power she now carries should be used and soon. I sense no personalities in it, it's just raw energy, she needs to use it, I'd suggest she heals Namdarin with it."

"Can you do that?" Asked Jangor.

"I've never done anything magical in my life, so how would I know?"

"Could this be part of Gyara's plan? Fill Jayanne full of energy she doesn't know how to use, and get her to kill him permanently?" Said Jangor.

"I don't think Gyara would risk something like that, he needs Namdarin to do something with the mindstone. He needs them both alive." Said Granger.

"So, what do we do?" Demanded Jangor.

"Perhaps Jayanne can use the energy she has accumulated to revive Namdarin." Said Gregor.

"Do you know how to do that?" Asked Granger.

"I have no idea." Said Jayanne, Arndrol stepped from foot to foot, he wanted to be with his friend, and didn't understand why these people were in his way. With a tentative step forwards, he stamped his front hoof quite loudly, causing some of the other horses to shy briefly.

"Well you must try," said Granger, "let her by." He stepped aside and followed as the grey walked towards Namdarin's motionless form.

Jayanne turned to Kern, "Find me a new horse from amongst

these new ones, Namdarin is going to want his back." Kern dropped back and with Branks help he looked over the captured horses. Jayanne dropped to the ground, the axe held loosely in her hand, slowly she stepped up to Namdarin's body. Arndrol sniffed at his friend then shied away.

"Don't worry, he'll be back soon." Mumbled Jayanne as she stroked the horse's neck. She knelt beside Namdarin.

"Hang on." Called Jangor, stepping forwards, he bent down and slowly slid the sword from Namdarin's back. Jayanne frowned a question up at him, as he stepped backwards.

"I was present at his awakening, if he'd had his sword to hand, things could have gone very badly, and mighty quick."

"I see." She said softly, staring down at Namdarin's still form. She looked over her shoulder, at Granger. "How does this work?" Her voice stuttering over the question.

"It's a feel thing, most likely, feel the power, and pass it through the axe into Namdarin. The oath should make it go where it is needed, or Xeron has really made a monumental mistake."

"If Xeron has made a mistake?"

"Then Namdarin dies for good, and we have some hard choices to make."

Jayanne looked down into Namdarin's half closed eyes, her own filled with tears.

"Xeron." She called. "I don't know how to do this, so help me, I offer blood and souls to bring him back, hear me Xeron." She placed the shining face of the axe, over Namdarin's wound, covering his heart. Everyone felt the surge of power, it flowed from the axe and into Namdarin's chest. For a dozen heartbeats the light scattered around the gathered people and horses, Wolf dropped belly down on the ground, but didn't run. Surges of electricity pulsed through the air, slowly the light and the tension in the air faded. Jayanne noticed that his chest was rising as it filled with air, she slid the axe off his chest and waited for his eyes to open. The scream came first, that soul wrenching howl of rebirth. The scream finally ran out of air, as the chest refilled, his eyes opened, the cold blue latched onto the concerned green eyes looking down on him. The second scream died aborning.

"How do you feel?" She asked.

"Like some bastard killed me again, where is he?"

"Dead, everyone is dead."

"Well that's something."

"I killed them all. The axe took their lives and their souls, I fed the power back into you and brought you back, you've only been dead a very short time."

"Who were they?"

"Mercenaries, they heard that the Zandaars were looking for your sword, they thought they could take it and trade it for gold, lots of gold. They were wrong."

"The sword." Said Namdarin reaching for it, only to find it already in his hand.

"By all the hells." Yelled Jangor.

"What's wrong?" Asked Namdarin slowly rolling towards Jayanne and offering his hand so she could pull him to his feet.

"That damned sword."

"What about it?"

"I had it in my hand, I had a firm, and I do mean firm grip on the thing, then suddenly it wasn't there, you had it again. I didn't feel it move, it didn't slide out of my hand, it was just gone."

"Nothing to worry about then, and we've not even lost too much time." He rose slowly and a little unsteadily to his feet. "Let's keep moving there's still a lot of daylight left." Jayanne stepped in close and threw her arms around him, she pulled him tight against her body, placed her head on his shoulder, and whispered, "Please don't do that again, I couldn't stand it if I lost you." He stroked her hair and mumbled in her ear, "I'll try not to, but it's certainly not going to be my choice, if it does happen." She looked up with tears in her eyes, and he kissed her, soft and long.

"Kern." Said Jangor. "Have you chosen a horse for Jayanne?"

"Yes, calm bay filly, big enough and with good definition, she'll do fine."

"Fine. Get Jayanne's gear switched over, and we can be on the road."

"Jayanne, you want to try this saddle? It looks like a really nice one, they probably stole it from someone rich." The saddle he indicated was indeed quite good looking, nice tool work along the edges, a horn that was quite ornate and certainly big enough to hang her bow and axe from if needed. Jayanne stepped over to the horse and looked over the saddle, while Arndrol walked up to Namdarin and placed his head on the man's shoulder, expressing his gladness that his friend was alive.

"It looks nice." said Jayanne. "Not too wide or too deep."

"It looks like it was made for a woman, about the same build as you."

"I didn't kill any women today?"

"No, you didn't, perhaps they did to get this saddle."

"The bastards more likely wanted the contents than the saddle itself."

"Sad, but true." Kern held his hands out to help her mount, her scathing look was enough to make him step back, she took the reins and pulled herself up into the saddle. She bounced experimentally a few times.

"Shorten the stirrups." She commanded, Kern did as he was asked. Two notches short was enough for her quite long legs. She stood up in the stirrups, her backside cleared the saddle enough so that a jump over some obstacle or other wouldn't cause her any problems by way of sudden collision between ass and saddle. She rocked from side to side, causing the horse to step left then right, either way the girth didn't slip.

"That will do nicely." She said, smiling. She snapped the reins from one side to the other, causing the horse to turn first one way then the other. "She's quite light on her feet," said Jayanne, "she'll be good in a melee."

"We'd rather not test that out." said Jangor, "Can we get moving now?"

"What about the dead? Aren't we going to do something for them?" asked Gregor.

"No." Snapped Jayanne. "Let the other scavengers finish them off, I suppose we could empty their purses, they have no need of gold now."

"Surely that makes us no better than them?"

"Oh, we are far better than them, we don't attack people on the road for the gold they may be carrying. Their kill ratio was dreadful, they killed one of us, without warning I may add, and then I killed them all, every last one. The only real surprise is that this inept band were still alive at all. No, we're better than them in every way that matters."

"Stergin, Mander, go see what they were carrying." Commanded Jangor. The two set off to follow the instructions they had been given.

"I'm still not happy about leaving the dead out in the open."

"Look at it this way, the scavengers will find them easier, and clean them up faster. Look over there." Said Kern pointing at the nearby trees. There in the underbrush was a small red fox, she looked more than a little hungry, and her cubs even more so. "They'll eat for days on this lot, at least the ones that Jayanne's axe didn't drain completely. It's the cycle of life, even Gyara has to respect that, well, to some extent." Kern laughed and mounted along with the others.

"Kern, point, slow to start, those two can catch up. Move out." Shouted Jangor. Brank took two horses over to Stergin and Mander, then returned to catch up and fall in alongside Kern. Jayanne and Namdarin rode side by side, not talking, but occasionally glancing one at the other. Granger fell in alongside Gregor.

"They are good people."

"What do you mean?" Asked Gregor.

"In some ways they can be barbarians, but they are good people."

"But they just leave the dead unburied, somehow it just feels wrong."

"They're soldiers and mercenaries, currently without an employer, they did nothing to provoke the attack today. They were attacked by a force with superior numbers, and still they won. We really can't afford to waste half a day burying some roadside robbers, let someone else take care of that."

"There is no one here to take care of them."

"There will be, this road isn't well travelled but I'm sure someone will be along in a day or two, and there will be enough metal left to pay for the funeral and other costs, anyway, a different question, would your previous leader have wasted time on burials?"

"Probably not, after all these robbers weren't Zandaars."

"So that would make a difference? Unbelievers warrant different treatment?"

"There are rituals necessary, so the dead can come home to Zandaar."

"Would your leader waste half a day burying every dead Zandaar we leave behind?"

"Actually no. We had a whole monastery of dead Zandaars, he brought one back briefly and then left them all unburied. That was still wrong."

"But he did it, and you didn't complain?"

"Well no, Worandana is a respected leader, and renowned teacher."

"What does that mean?"

"Well, he's not the sort of man you question."

"And now you question everything?"

"I suppose so."

"You, young man, are learning. Question everything, and if no one can give you the answers, then find them for yourself. This may be a little difficult for you, 'The will of Zandaar.' is not an acceptable answer. Can you understand that?"

"I think I can, but where can I find the answers?"

"I have a great deal of knowledge, mainly from books, Namdarin was a landowner and lord, so he's not stupid, Jangor has a mountain of experience behind him, many cultures and many cities, he's so well-travelled you won't believe what he has seen. You have an entire library right here, use it."

"I'll try and remember that."

"Jangor." Called Stergin as he galloped up to the slow-moving column.

"What?" Shouted the commander as Stergin pulled up alongside.

"Look." Stergin held up a large bag.

"And?" Demanded an impatient Jangor.

"It's full of gold, those men may have been bad robbers, but they were successful."

"How can that be? Perhaps we should set up around here, we'd make a fortune."

"Yeah, like you'd do that." Laughed Stergin. "You'd hire us to the nearest city and get paid for doing what Jayanne already did for free."

"If they were so successful, and nobody knows they are dead, we could still do that."

"You could never keep a straight face making that sort of deal." Laughed Stergin.

"You're not wrong, it goes in the fighting fund. Fall in further back."

Stergin did as he was told and dropped back to where Andel was struggling with the increased number of empty horses, he settled into the line, and took a string of horses from his friend, with a big smile on his face. Jangor turned in his saddle to look back at the two, now silent, magicians.

"I wonder where they got all that gold, and more importantly how much the Zandaar are willing to pay for that sword?"

"You'd swap the sword for gold?" Asked Gregor, his voice showed his dis-belief, Granger laughed aloud.

"No, stupid." Said Granger, before Jangor could answer, or take offence. Gregor's look was enough to make Granger laugh some more. "The more money there is on offer, the more 'free-lancers' we are going to meet. Every one of those 'free-lancers' has the chance to end this quest, small chance, but chance still the same. We may actually spend our entire journey fighting every step."

"You're joking." Said Gregor.

"No, he's not." Said Jangor. "Don't forget, we ourselves, could be regarded as free-lancers."

"I hope we don't meet too many of them."

"I hope we don't meet any." Laughed Jangor.

"That doesn't explain, where this lot came up with all that gold?" Asked Granger.

"Let's just hope the damned Zandaar aren't paying mercenaries up front." Jangor frowned.

"That would make things even more difficult." Said Gregor. "I don't see it though; the abbots are too tight with the gold they have."

"If they are handing out gold, we'll find out about it pretty quickly." Said Jangor.

"Let's hope not." Said Granger.

"Kern." Called Jangor. "Pick it up, many miles to go, but can we be a little more alert?"

"Yes boss." Kern looked down at the ground in front of his horse. "Wolf find someone." He spoke quietly, Wolf looked up for a moment then raced off ahead. Kern turned and looked over his shoulder.

"Namdarin, are there any horses nearby?" Namdarin thought for a few seconds, before he replied.

"Only one, in those trees back there, nothing else that I can feel at any close distance. I do sense a group of horses, more than a little nervous, a good distance south, but that is all. I'll keep an eye on them all."

"That would be a good idea."

"I know." Mumbled Namdarin, "If I'd been more alert, they wouldn't have surprised us."

"I think you are the one most surprised."

"Only for a very brief moment. Then it all went dark, for a while, then the pain came back."

"Grinderosch mentioned something about the dark before he died." Said Jangor.

"He said that something was coming, but I felt nothing," replied Namdarin, "perhaps it was a different darkness."

"I'm sure we'll find out in due course." Said Jangor, he frowned briefly at the back of Kern's head, before calling, "Faster, we have an appointment with destiny." Kern snapped his reins and pushed his horse to a slow trot, they'd covered a lot of miles the day before, and he didn't want to strain them too much. The journey continued uneventfully until the sun was approaching the horizon, and Kern was looking for somewhere suitable to camp. Above the path to the east there was a large meadow, with a stream running alongside. Kern turned in his saddle, caught Jangor's eye.

"Camp?" he asked, then looked up the slight hill to the meadow. When he looked back Jangor nodded his approval. Kern turned off the road, such as it was, and climbed the short slope to the flat area, it definitely looked good enough for a camp. The nearby trees should furnish enough dead fall to give them a decent fire for the night, he dropped from his horse alongside the remnants of a fire.

"How long ago?" asked Jangor.

"Not days, but not months either."

"Namdarin, those horses?"

"South, they haven't moved, and they are more nervous than ever, something is really bothering them."

"How far?"

"Not far, perhaps a few minutes fast riding."

Jangor thought about it for moment or two.

"Kern." He said. "Take Brank and Wolf, go find out what's wrong with those horses. Be careful. The rest of us will get the camp finished."

Kern remounted, called Wolf and returned to the road, the three set off at a canter in the direction they had been going. The rest started setting up the camp, tents were unloaded and raised. Horses were strung on a picket line, near but not too close to the trees, Mander went into the trees to collect wood for a fire.

"Jangor." Said Andel loudly. "Look at all those horses, we now have two mounts each at least."

"Is this a problem?"

"Yes, you're never given the task of watching over them, we need to sell them as soon as we can."

"I know, we will do exactly that when we get to the next town, or even a small village will do, we have more than enough gold to last us a long time. We can trade the horses for supplies."

"Look over there." He said waving his arm in the direction they had come.

"They do leave quite a trail." Said Jangor.

"We'll be so easy to follow, we need to get rid of them."

"How many can you eat in one sitting?"

"Horse meat isn't good even when you are really hungry. It needs careful treatment before it can even be considered edible."

"You've never been hungry." Laughed Jangor. "We'll get rid as soon as we can, is that all right?"

"Yes, I was just saying."

Jangor slapped him on the shoulder and turned towards the now blazing fire. Jayanne and Namdarin were already cooking as he walked towards them.

"Namdarin. They've been gone a while, how close are the two groups of horses?"

"There is only one group, and it's coming this way now."

"How far out, and how fast?"

"Slow and only a few minutes away."

"At least we'll have food for them." Jangor laughed. Jayanne stirred the large pot of beef broth and moved it away from the fire, she served it into large bowls for each of the men, once she had served herself, out of the falling gloom two riders came towards them, pulling a string of horses behind them. Wolf came out of the dark, and yipped at Jayanne, she spooned him a small portion of broth into a bowl, she placed slowly on the ground. Kern dropped to the grass and pulled four bottles of wine from his saddle bags, he passed the bottle to various people, then fished a fat, round, yellow coin from his pocket, he passed this to Stergin.

"Is it the same?" He mumbled. Stergin glanced at the coin and nodded. Kern turned to Jangor.

"You don't look good." Said Jangor. "Are you well?"

"I don't believe I will ever be well again." Mumbled Kern, yanking the cork from the bottle he was holding and drinking half its contents in one draft. Jayanne brought him a bowl of broth, Kern failed to look her in the eyes.

"I am sorry, but I have no appetite at all just now."

"Where did all this wine come from and what does that coin mean?" Demanded Jangor.

"I think we know where those assholes got all their gold. A wine merchant with a lot of wine, and even more gold. More accurately a wine merchant and his family. They missed the coin when he opened his strongbox for them, they must have got all the rest, but missed just the one."

"Family?" Asked Jayanne, her voice catching in her throat. Kern still didn't look at her, but he nodded.

"Wife?" She whispered.

"And children." Stuttered Kern.

"Dead."

"All of them."

"Had they any defenders?" Asked Jangor.

"Some, but not enough, and one that will surprise some."

"Explain."

"A large man, dressed in long black robes, by the time he died he had so many arrows in him, he looked like a hedgehog."

"Were any of the bodies burned?" Asked Gregor.

"A few, some with small burns and others burned over much of their bodies."

"At least he got some of them before he died." Said Gregor.

"How many of these bastards did they kill?" Growled Jangor.

"It's difficult to say, but maybe ten, it's difficult to tell the attackers from the defenders. No uniforms on either."

"So that was a large group of bandits, before the last few days. How many days ago did they attack the merchants?" Said Jangor.

"I can't be sure," Replied Kern, "I'd say the fires had been burning for a couple of days, maybe as many as five."

"So, what were they up to for so long?"

"I'd rather not say." Muttered Kern, glancing in the direction of Jayanne, she noticed the look.

"Tell us, we'll find out tomorrow, when we go there." She whispered.

"I said family, the merchant had his wife, a daughter and a son with him. It looks like they provided some, er, entertainment, for the bastards."

Brank moved slowly to stand in front of Jayanne, tears streaming down his face, he fell to his knees and spoke softly.

"My lady Jayanne, I have been a soldier for a few years now, I have seen my own share of the brutalities that men can inflict on each other, I've inflicted enough of my own. Had there been the slightest chance that you hadn't killed them all, I would not be here, I would be hunting them down to make them pay, I still want to go and smash their corpses up some, but they wouldn't feel it. Never be ashamed for the ones who paid with their souls, they were already lost to the world of men. I have a small favour to ask, will you listen?" He dashed the tears from his eyes with his large hands and looked up into the raging green lights of the woman's. After a moment she nodded.

"If we meet their like again, please lay your heels to your horse, and try to keep up, watch my back, and take the souls of any that live."

"And mine." Said Kern, "I'll be at his side."

"Gentlemen." She replied. "Your words are a credit to you, but you will have to ride hard to be ahead of me." She reached down and pulled Brank to his feet, and threw her arms around him, she hugged him while he cried on her shoulder. Jangor turned to Namdarin, caught his eyes, and whispered.

"Crap."

"What's wrong?"

"I just got a picture of those three riding side by side into a group of robbers, say fifty, or a hundred of them, with every intention of killing them all."

"Between them they could do it." Chuckled Namdarin.

"That's the real scary part, they could. And we get to clean up after them."

"Is that a bad thing, the world will be a better place without the robbers in it."

"Those bastards created a monster here today, I'd rather not see it unleashed."

"Let's just pray we are following it, not running from it."

"I'll go along with that." Laughed Jangor, looking over at Brank, Kern, and Jayanne, huddled together, crying.

"Jangor." Said Granger. "Did you notice the axe when she attacked those foot soldiers?"

"What do you mean?"

"It blocked every arrow, just shattered them on its face, and she didn't have to lean down to take their heads, even if they were ducking. It grew to reach the targets."

"Not only that." Said Namdarin. "The head changes shape in combat as well. Stay well clear of that thing if it's in a battle."

"Let's eat, I have a feeling tomorrow's going to be a long and trying day." Commanded Jangor.

CHAPTER FIFTY-FIVE

Kevana kept the pace at a steady trot for the rest of the day, except where the terrain became to uneven, or steep for the horses, it was late afternoon before Alverana finally spoke up.

"These horses are going to need some time to feed and some rest, it's been a long and hard day for them."

"I suppose we ought to let them rest a bit, next good patch of grassland, we'll camp and leave them on long lines for the night, would that be enough?"

"It should be, we wouldn't want to kill them, except for that prancing black fool you are sitting on." Laughed Alverana.

"Don't be mean, me and him have been through a lot together. So what if he is a bit of a showoff?"

"A bit?"

"Fine, a lot. At least he's not boring."

"Agreed, not boring, equally not bright."

"He's supposed to be pretty, not intelligent."

"It is possible to be both, isn't it?" Together they looked at Kirukana, then looked back at each other and laughed loudly.

"Have I missed the joke here?" Asked Kirukana.

"It's unlikely that you could miss it." Chuckled Kevana.

"You two are making fun of me, aren't you?"

"Only a little bit." Smiled Kevana. "You'll probably get used to us, if you can relax a little."

"I am trying, but you people don't make it easy."

"There are few things in this world that need to be taken seriously, friendship and loyalty are top of the list."

"What about your devotion to our god?"

"He's a powerful guy, I don't think he cares too much about my devotion, so long as I get the soldiering done, I don't think he cares one way or the other."

"He is the central figure in our lives, we are his servants, his followers, his people."

"And you think one tired commander is going to make a massive difference in his world?"

"You, very specifically you, and the rest of us, are very high in his expectations right now, he's hoping that you will bring the sword to him."

"Actually, he told me that I will bring the sword to him. I just hope that his prediction is correct, he also said it wasn't going to be easy."

"You think it's going to get more difficult?"

"I can't believe that one small and almost painless skirmish, could qualify as making things hard. Though letting the hounds loose, will definitely make things different."

"I'm sure that if we put our trust in Zandaar, everything will come out right." The other two looked at Kirukana quite sternly.

"Do you actually believe that?" Asked Alverana.

"Of course. Our god will protect us."

"Who do you think set the dogs on us?"

"It was probably one of the council, or one of the factions."

"The hounds only answer directly to Zandaar, they are his and his alone." Said Worandana from behind them.

"That's as may be." Said Kirukana, "But I cannot believe that."

"Why not?" Asked Kevana.

"Think carefully and speak true." Whispered Worandana, he looked at Kevana and Alverana, motioning them to silence, giving Kirukana time to get his thoughts and feelings straight. Gradually the silence became oppressive, Kevana started fidgeting in his saddle, again Worandana waved him into stillness.

Kirukana took a deep breath, all faces turned to him, expectantly. He breathed out heavily, without speaking, then snatched another breath.

"My life was so much simpler before I got myself drafted in with you lot, I didn't have much of anything to think about, follow the rules, don't make a fool of myself, and then I get to come out here. I follow the rules and make a fool of myself at the same time, you people break so many of the rules I find it hard to believe that you are true followers of Zandaar. What was that magic that Alverana performed in the wood today? No one even questioned it, and for a change, neither did I."

"That was magic of Gyara, as you know he was once a follower, and that saved our lives, the hounds would have seen the damage we did to those trees and been on us in a heartbeat. I'd rather not face them in such confined conditions. I was also on foot, not a good way to face horsemen."

"I understand that, but I do struggle with the fact that a god, that has been decreed to be powerless still has some power and presumably some followers."

"I declare that the sun is now green." Laughed Kevana, then he looked up. "Do you like my nice green sun?"

"The sun is unchanged, it is still yellow, you are no god."

"I may not be a god, but then Zandaar is not all powerful, if he were, why would he be so bothered by this sword, that we have yet to see?"

"Zandaar tells us that he is the only true and living god, all the others are false."

"Yes, he does say that. That message is quite prominent in the book."

"You don't believe it, I can tell that from your voice."

"I am sorry to say that I don't, I never really did, but this mission, which started so well, has taught me many things, not least of which, or perhaps the most important, our god is as fallible as any man."

Kirukana spluttered for a moment or two over this comment, then he noticed the amused look in Kevana's eyes.

"Are you trying to bait me?"

"No, teach, yes."

"If you say such a thing in Zandaarkoon, you will be dead before you hit the floor."

"I think the only people that could do that are currently riding northwards."

"There are others in the capital, you know."

"None with sufficient skill or speed. That is why we got the job of hunting the sword down, Zandaar knew it was going to get loose, so he set the best to collect it."

"Aren't the hounds the best?"

"They are very good at what they do, but they are more than a little limited. Hunter killers, not at all subtle like us."

Kirukana threw his head back and howled with laughter. Alverana looked across at his friend.

"Well, I don't think it was that funny, quite funny, but not howling and falling off your horse funny."

"He's right, it's definitely funny." Said Worandana, "I have never heard anyone accuse either of us of subtlety. You're far too quick with your sword, and I'm way too fast to fry people that get in my way. Kevana, subtle is the one thing we aren't." He smiled hugely at Kevana.

"I see a likely camping place just ahead and right, looks like it even has a stream."

"It's a bit early in the day, but as has been pointed out the horses have been working quite hard. So, let's set up an early camp." Alverana turned right and uphill towards the clear area of good green grass. As soon as they slowed down to a walk even Kevana's horse was pulling down on the reins, trying to get at the lush grass. It actually became quite insistent, though it couldn't quite manage the complexity of holding its bit in its teeth, and cropping the grass at the same time. Kevana yanked hard on the reins. The horse shook its mane and glared at Kevana for a moment.

"Be patient, my friend." Said the man, patting the horse on the neck. "You'll get plenty of grass in a little while."

With the usual efficiency camp was set up, tents pitched, water collected, fires laid, food started. Horses were tied on long lines and very busy with eating. Kevana went and sat beside Worandana, in front of the elder's tent.

"Do you think they'll search for Kirukana again at sundown?"

"Perhaps, they might even search for us, there are many who know us both well enough. We'll just have to keep our heads down." Laughed Worandana.

"Can we do that?"

"Of course we can, it's not that difficult to ignore a communication, one simply has to turn away from it."

"And how, exactly, does that happen?"

"It's not something that is generally taught, our wonderful leaders don't want it to be known that it is even possible. They have a terrible fear of being ignored."

"I only want to ignore them until I meet them face to face." Growled Kevana.

"I feel exactly the same. There are a few things I want to say to them."

"Well you better make it quick, they won't have long to listen."

"That's as may be. Blocking a long-range communication is easy, the hard part is stopping them getting a location, we can simply refuse to talk to them, it will get harder as we get closer, I'm hoping we will get better with practise."

"So how do we do it?"

"We have to stop the connection being established, it goes in our favour that they don't have a real clue as to where we are, so the good and powerful searchers will be spread thin, they can't cover the entire realm in one go, they'll have to search small patches, most likely radiating paths leading out from Zandaarkoon, with luck they'll pass either side of us, with the other sort of luck we'll be right in their path. Even so at the range we are now, it's going to be difficult to find us. They'll most likely not be looking for me, they know I'll be hiding from them, but you and especially Kirukana will certainly be targets. The process is simple, and as always with something that is simple, it is also difficult. The best way to describe it, is that you have to pretend to be someone else. You have to get inside someone else's head, and be that person, pick someone you are close to, and attempt to think like them, this will mask your own mental signature. Can you think of someone?"

"I can," said Kevana, "Alverana, he has shown that he has a secure centre that cannot be breached mentally."

"Agreed, that's from his early training." Said Worandana, "Kirukana, have you anyone in mind?"

"No, my whole time in the priesthood, I've never been close to anyone, and I am adept at communication, and many people know my signature very well."

"What about someone from before your time in the priest hood, how about a parent." Worandana's voice tapered off and his face went blank.

"I can't remember my father, and mother is no use, she never had a serious thought in her head." Said Kirukana, but he got no reaction from Worandana, he stared hard at the old man and got no response.

"Something he said, triggered him. He's thinking," said Kevana, "I've seen this before."

"Are you sure he's not just died?"

"No, he's chasing some logic in his head, or digging some memory out, something he hasn't looked at for a few years, he'll be back in a bit. You still need someone to be, you have anyone you can think of that you got to know quite well?"

"Well, the only one that comes to mind is old Jermana, he was one of my teachers when I first became a novice. He was a great old man, very patient, and very kind. It really hurt me when he died."

"That's great, they're not going to be looking for him, it's surprising how quickly someone's mental pattern fades from memories after they die."

"His damned mother." shouted Worandana, making them both jump. "His damned mother."

"Please make some sort of sense." said Kevana.

"Gorgana, his green goddess is his mother, he's switched back to his old mental patterns, and wrapped himself up in her image, presumably assumed, or re-assumed his old name. He's far smarter than I thought, and much more knowledgeable than I imagined."

"And he did all this while standing next to the great Worandana." Laughed Kevana.

"You know what this means?"

"I'm sure you'll explain it to us poor ignorant peasants." Smiled Kevana.

"We'll never be able to break his protection, his name and his mother will protect him, when we attacked him we used the staff to find him, and simply assumed we had the right man, but without a name to start from, we really don't have a chance of breaking him down."

"Gregor." said Petrovana. "He was called Gregor."

"How do you know?" Worandana turned to Petrovana.

"We were talking about where we came from, his name was Gregor, and he came from a place I had never heard of, and now cannot remember."

"Well at least we have a name now," snapped Worandana, "but that's not going to be too much help, as we don't have anything of his mental pattern."

"And he did all this under your very nose?"

"Yes, he did. I had no idea how much he had learned, and how skilled he is, I wish I had more students like him."

"You really want to train more traitors like him." Demanded Kirukana.

"Isn't your protector supposed to be a kind and patient old man? An outburst like that fair shouts your pattern at the world. Look at me, I'm Kirukana, bitching about heretics and traitors as normal."

"This being someone else isn't easy." Muttered Kirukana.

"But it might just save your life and ours. And yes, I'd love to train more traitors, have you any idea how good it feels for a teacher to have his own pupil surpass him?"

"You think he has surpassed you?" Said Kevana.

"In some ways, he may not know as much of the old magics as I do, but his power is undeniable. I wish I had known how he was feeling before he left us, we could have explored so many of the old manuscripts together."

"Surely this is not within the present teachings, students need to be guided away from non-approved avenues of research." Said Kirukana. All faces turned towards him, several mouths fell open in disbelief.

"Sounds good." Said Worandana, "If you can focus those words into the centre of your thinking, then no-one that knows you will recognise you."

"I'm staring at him and I have no idea who he is." Mumbled Petrovana.

"That's great." Said Kevana. "I'm going to link with Alverana, who no-one can ever find, Kirukana is going to link to a long dead teacher, what about you old man?"

"I have a different plan," smiled Worandana, "I'm going to focus my mind on something that only one other person in the whole world knows about, and if he remembers that, no one will ever find him."

"Please explain to us stupid people." Snapped Kevana.

"At the first sign of any searching mind, I'm going to tune my mind down to the speed of that rock in the cavern. A few seconds of that will pass as hours in this world. Searchers will never find me, they'll be running around far too quickly."

"What about the rest of us?" Asked Petrovana.

"I don't want to sound patronising," smiled Worandana, "but I'm sorry, small fish, the searchers aren't going to waste energy looking for you. Now here's a thought. They might just look for Gorgana, he has a very sharp mind, the sort of thing that is easy to track, if they do, then, number one they'll be looking in the wrong direction, and, number two, his damned mother is going to eat them whole." He roared with laughter.

"What about the rest of us?" Demanded Petrovana, his right arm sweeping a gesture that included the whole camp.

"I wouldn't worry, you're not likely to be targets, but if you all relax and try not to think of anything, or at least nothing of any importance, then you'll just get lost in the background noise."

"That's easier for some." Laughed Briana, looking directly at Petrovana.

"What do you mean by that?" Shouted Petrovana, his hand going to his sword.

"Stop." Shouted Kevana. "Strong emotions they can pick up in a heartbeat. So relax, everyone, think small and happy thoughts, that way we might live to get to Zandaarkoon, and there I can explain to the council the error of their ways."

"I thought we were supposed to be thinking small and happy thoughts?" Asked Kirukana.

"That does include you Kevana." Said Worandana, smiling broadly. "Those thoughts are neither small, nor happy."

"How long before searches are likely?" Asked Kevana.

"Given our current position, sunsets in Zandaarkoon and Angorak are imminent, so anytime soon."

"You think searches could be launched from Angorak as well?"

"Why not? We have a large presence there, and some of the council originate there." Worandana glanced at Kirukana and got the nod of acknowledgement he was expecting.

"How far apart are their sunsets?"

"No real difference, Angorak is due north of Zandaarkoon, and only slightly higher, mountains to the west, may just make sunset a few minutes earlier, but not to any real degree."

"Right people." Said Kevana loudly. "We have a sort of plan, all we need is for everyone to keep their minds as quiet as possible, until we have full dark, though that is no real defence, it's only going to be a matter of time before they start searching at all sorts of random times of day."

"That's right." Said Worandana. "I hadn't thought of that, it's just that it is customary for communications to take place with the dawn and dusk prayers. It's a time when people know to be receptive to outside contact, or in our case as unreceptive as possible. We are going to need watchers, I know that I can feel a search before it becomes established, is there anyone else?"

"I can feel searchers." Said Kirukana.

"So can I," said Briana, "though I am more used to opening the communication channel, it's going to be very different ducking away from it."

"It's not going to be as simple as merely dodging, you're going to have to warn everyone else first."

"That makes it even harder." Muttered Briana.

"Me too." Said Apostana. "Blocking is not something any of us are used to, if anything the exact opposite is how we are trained."

"I understand that," said Worandana, "but the people that trained us all, they're the ones that set the hounds on us. I'd really like to meet them before I die."

"So, what are we to do?" Asked Briana.

"Watch cycles, short time on watch, longer off, with four of us, we should be able to manage." Said Worandana.

"What about sleep time?" Asked Kirukana.

"I'm not sure," said Worandana, "can contact be established with a sleeping mind?"

"That never happens," chuckled Kirukana, "something the great Worandana is unsure of."

"At least I don't make proclamations like some." Snapped the older man.

"Gentlemen, gentlemen," interrupted Kevana, "you both know how strong emotions broadcast, so calm down before you give us all away."

"I don't think so." Said Alverana.

"Please make some sense." Said Worandana.

"I don't think the sleeping mind can be contacted, it is generally turned inwards, dealing with its own problems."

"How do you know that?" Demanded Kirukana.

Alverana looked at him coldly for a few moments, then spoke slowly and quietly.

"You don't want to know."

"How can you say that?"

"Because it is true. The knowledge comes from a source you don't approve of."

"You mean your previous training?"

"Yes. It's not that contact can't be made with a sleeping mind, it is used as a weapon occasionally, but the information gathered there is utterly unreliable at best, at worst it's complete gibberish."

"Yes." Said Worandana. "The secret is to invade, take control, make it believable and then kill the target, his sleeping mind has to believe, or it doesn't work. The information in the dream scape is unreliable at the very best."

"You think they'll try something like that?" Asked Kirukana.

"They don't believe it can be done from extreme range, so no, but perhaps we can take out a few of them from afar, that might just get their attention." Said Worandana.

"No." Said Kevana. "If we are to kill any of them, it has to be face to face, they have to know why, and they need a chance to make their peace with god."

"You will give them more chances than they give you." Said Kirukana.

"I know, I can't help it, it's part of who I am. Once they have made peace with our god, then I'll kill them."

"That still seems more than a little dangerous."

"What I'd really like is for the entire council to come riding over that crest, swords drawn, howling their battle cries. That would make things so much simpler."

"That's not going to happen."

"A man's got to have a dream." Laughed Kevana. "Right everyone rest, those most likely to be targets for the searchers, assume your protective identities. Once the danger is passed, then we can return to a more normal pattern."

"What about evening prayers?" Asked Kirukana. Kevana thought for a short time before replying.

"How about moon rise? It's currently only an hour or so after sunset, would that be all right for you?"

"It just seems so wrong to completely abandon everything we have held true to for so many years."

"I agree, we have been forced into this position by our brothers, but we shouldn't turn away from everything. Worandana will lead the prayers at moonrise, attendance is mandatory." With this he turned away and followed Alverana into their tent, to relax and hide from the searchers in privacy.

Kevana lay down on his left side, with Alverana behind him, they were pressed tightly together, Alverana squeezed his friend close with both arms wrapped around him.

"Tell me of the teaching of Gyara." Whispered Kevana.

"Are you sure you want to know?" Came the almost silent reply.

"No, but I need something to focus on to hide from any searchers that come looking."

Alverana started to tell Kevana about the stories he had from his youth, how the world was made, and Gyara made part of it, how the different peoples were created, and how their lives were linked to Gyara's. Quickly many of the peoples turned away from

Gyara, because she was capricious, wilful, and oft-times malicious. So, the elder gods came into being, the dwarves had gods of stone and gems, the elves made gods of their trees, the men of the north made gods of ice and snow, the people of the desserts had gods of water and fire. These elder gods drew their power from the people who worshipped them, the same is not true for Gyara, she takes power from all the peoples of the world, and shares that power as she sees fit, which is rarely. The elder gods waxed and waned depending on the number and intensity of their believers. Gyara seems to have spent most of her time making them look stupid, or powerless. A small number she has driven insane.

"Have you any idea what it is like to follow a mad god?" asked Alverana.

"At the moment, I'm not entirely sure we don't." Kevana twitched, suddenly, and whispered hoarsely. "Searchers." Alverana gripped him fiercely and threw a leg across to hold him even tighter, then started the wordless chant that served so many purposes in the religion of Gyara, a plainsong that was both a summoning and a forbidding. Kevana immersed himself in the sound and tried to vanish from the world. The chant went on, Alverana never seem to draw a single breath, it just kept on rolling, the deep vibrations in his throat shaking through both their bodies, turning them almost into one flesh.

"It's gone." Whispered Kevana, Alverana slowed the chant, decreased the volume, but didn't actually stop. "Definitely gone, they were looking for me, but passed on by. Thank you, my friend, you may have saved all our lives today."

"I hope so." Muttered Alverana, "We should tell the others."

"Agreed." Together they crawled out of the tent and walked slowly to Worandana's tent.

"Worandana." Called Kevana softly. He got no reply, so he tried again, still no reply. Just as he was reaching forwards to open the flap of the tent Kirukana came up behind them.

"A powerful search just passed by, they were looking for me. My disguise worked."

"As did mine." Said Kevana. He opened the flap of the tent, just in time to see Worandana sit up, and take that first deep breath. "Searchers?" Worandana nodded.

"Yes, and looking for me, very specifically. I slowed right down, and they couldn't feel me, it only seemed like a second or two, before I came back, the slowing down is quite easy, but the speeding up again is hard work. Did you two feel them as well?"

"Yes, but they were looking for each of us. They were searching for my mental pattern, not just calling my name."

"Me too." Said Kirukana.

"Did you get any sense as to how focused they were?" Asked Worandana.

"I felt that it wasn't a tight focus like a location or a direction." Said Kirukana. "More like a spread, sort of somewhere over there."

"Same for me." said Kevana. "Specifically looking for me, but looking here, or this way, more over there. What did you get from them?"

"Nothing, I felt the search coming and shut down, I wouldn't like to have to do that while riding a horse."

"What are the chances of them trying again?" Asked Kirukana.

"From the sound of things, that wasn't one search looking for the three of us, it was three searches, and powerful ones at that, and with only a vague direction. No, it's going to be hours before they have enough power to relaunch that sort of thing, they might still be following their direction yet. Zandaar on the other hand, he could relaunch right now, if he could be bothered looking for us himself, but he knows we don't have the sword, and that's what he really wants."

"Moonrise is almost here." said Kirukana. "Have you any thoughts as to how this unusual celebration should go?"

"Actually I do, there is a little used ceremony for the first full moon of spring that used to be held at major moonrise. That should do nicely, it's all about renewal, and return of growth."

"I've never heard of it."

"It's very old, and almost never performed, at least not in the cities, it's a farming thing really, thinking about it, it was most likely assimilated from an older belief."

"An older belief?" Kirukana's voice rose.

"Remember, calm, patient, elderly teacher." Worandana smiled. "Yes, how do you think religions form? They absorb some of what went before and add some new stuff, it doesn't just happen by magic you know."

"Even one such as ours, so entrenched in the magic of our god?"

"Even ours, look at the morning and evening prayers, these go back into the ages to a time when the sun was worshipped as a god, now we have Zandaar and still we have morning and evening prayers. It is more for the coordination of the long-range communications, but it is still sunrise and sunset."

"I am really struggling with these concepts." Muttered Kirukana. "Zandaar is the only true god, all the others have always been false."

"That is how it is taught," smiled Worandana, "do you honestly believe it?"

"It is taught, it should not be questioned."

"That is the main difference between us. Between us members of the old guard," he waved his hand to encompass almost all the group, "and you of the new followers. We question things, we demand proof, you say 'will of god' and any discussion is over."

"Surely you cannot actually see things that way?"

"How else can they be seen? Only in the last day you have reduced the number of times you speak the 'H' word. Why is that? It's because you have chosen to hide behind the persona of a dead man, this most certainly puts you in the 'H' class, as far as your leaders are concerned. We all need to hide who we are simply to stay alive, they have set the hounds on us. On us!"

"I can see why they would do that, they seem to believe the worst of us."

"And they are so wrong, we are doing exactly as we were instructed to do, we chase after that damned sword, all the way to hell we will chase it, only they have moved hell closer, the damned hounds."

"That is not entirely true, you were tasked with something different."

"Yes, and it turns out the man currently carrying the sword, Namdarin as we now know him, is the one, and I repeat one man, who reduced that monastery to a mausoleum."

"Don't forget that you did the same to his house and his family." Said Crathen.

"That may have been an ill-judged action," said Worandana, "in hindsight. He must have really upset someone high up in the order."

"From what he described to us, his house, his wall, his courtyard, looked exactly like that mining camp we passed through. Readymade to be a monastery."

"You are suggesting that someone started all this just to save money on building a monastery?" Demanded Worandana. Kevana started laughing, so loudly that everyone joined in.

"It's not that funny." Muttered Worandana.

"Oh, but it is." Said Kirukana. "It's so tragic, that it's hilarious. Namdarin should be standing on his wall, watching carts full of stone and stonemasons trooping past, selling them food and wine, offering help and assistance, instead we burned it down, he should have been inside, but those sorts of things cannot be guaranteed. Even burned out with black fire, it's not going to take much to repair it all, except that now Namdarin has released the sword, and plans on using it on Zandaar. The irony is just delicious." Kirukana slowly pulled his knife from his belt. "If we survive this, I'm going to find the abbot that decided to save a little gold, I'm going to stick this knife in his guts, and twist it until the lights go out in his eyes."

"Kirukana." Said Kevana. "You are beginning to sound like a true soldier of god."

"And a heretic." Laughed Kirukana.

"It could quite easily be that when this is all over, the death of a certain abbot could be a holy mission decreed by god himself."

"If not, I may just have to make that decision for him."

"And there he is, back as a council member." Laughed Worandana.

"I don't think you are taking this at all seriously." Kirukana's smile, brought more laughter from those around him. "Don't you understand that our own people are trying to kill us." His smile lessened in no way at all.

"This is the curse of the soldier." Said Kevana. "We spend our lives improving our skills, until we get to be so good that we are a threat to our own leaders, then they set the hounds on us."

"Thinking of the hounds," said Kirukana very quietly, "they are supposed to be the best, how is it that they are still alive?"

"Thereby hangs a seriously secret tale." Said Worandana.

"Please go on." Said Kirukana.

"Are you sure?"

"No, but I think I need to know."

"It is not something that is spoken of, nor written down, and in most parts not even thought."

"Now you are just messing with us old man."

"You asked. It has long been thought that the ones designated as the hounds of Zandaar are special, not just the best, but actually enhanced in some way, now you all know my feelings about any sort of knowledge, it's alright to try and hide things from the ordinary folk of this world, but not from me. So, I went hunting for this rumoured magic, this ghost of a suggestion, in the deepest libraries of Zandaarkoon, the ones that no-one is allowed access, at least without special permission and escort from a member of the council. I found an older and unknown entrance, secret, and concealed, I spent months in that library, and what did I find, nothing, not a damned hint of the power that made the hounds who they are, I did find one important fact, and that was that something was missing."

"You just said you found nothing, make sense, old man." Said Kirukana, in an irritated tone.

"You misunderstand, I found nothing, but the nothing I found had a sort of pattern, there were blanks in the accounts, empty patches, by the shape and feel of this emptiness, I knew I was getting close to something, I had no real idea what it was, or even where, but I kept feeling out the edges of the removed parts, for it became obvious that someone, or several someone's had done a real job of concealing something. Eventually I got a feel for the minds of my enemies, that is how I saw them, I started looking in places they hadn't thought of, I went back in the records, I started taking real chances, I would smuggle a group of books, and scrolls out of the library to examine at my leisure, to be caught with a single one of these documents would have been instant death, but still I persevered. Eventually in an ancient scroll I found a reference, just the one, in an obscure dialect of a long dead language, it pointed to an ancient repository, in the birthing place of god."

"You had already found the most ancient library, in the depth of the catacombs, under Zandaarkoon." Said Kirukana.

"So, you know of the place?"

"Yes, I even went there a time or two, but found nothing of any real import, just confirmation of things I already knew."

"Were you escorted?"

"Yes, but not hindered in any way."

"Your escort helped you to find the documents you were looking for?"

"Without hesitation, he showed me where the records were, and I followed the information to its logical conclusions, I could sense no duplicity in his actions."

"The wardens of the place know it too well, they lead you to the beginning of a path, when they already know where it ends."

"Not so, old man, I found a reference to an old chamber, one hidden from the world, and I went back in after dark, found this chamber, and followed the information I found, it was most enlightening, it showed me where the real power of Zandaar comes from."

"The golden path."

"Yes, that's the one, did you find it as well?"

"Yes and no, I found the reference, as I was supposed to, and then I let them follow me around for months, I never went near the golden path, it was too obviously a trap."

"If it was a trap, then why am I still unharmed."

"Wrong sort of trap, they watched you follow the golden path, enter the hidden chamber and find all the answers to your questions, and all the answers they wanted you to find, your research was complete, there was nothing more for you to do."

"I never thought of it that way."

"They give the most inquisitive minds an opportunity to step outside the normal controls, or at least have the impression that they are doing that, the path is so hard to follow, and so rife with illegality, that anything discovered gains such intellectual weight that it can never be doubted."

"How did you know it was a trap? It certainly got me."

"As soon as I saw the reference to the golden path in the swari dialect, I knew it was a trap, and one aimed specifically at me, there are only a few people even aware of that long dead dialect, and I know them all, they are all dead now, but then they were still breathing, not walking right well, but breathing."

"I found the golden path from a different language entirely, it was buntu, the reference I saw."

"How many do you know of that understand that language?"

"Not many, perhaps as many as fifteen."

"And this is the most obscure dialect that you know?"

"Definitely."

"It seems their pattern doesn't change, for you it was a rare language, for me, if I'd found a reference in buntu, I'd have ignored it as too obvious, but swari, that almost had me, less than a handful that I was aware of knew that dialect, obviously the devious bastards in the council knew it, but perhaps they weren't aware how few outside their ranks understood it."

"Hey." Said Kevana, all faces turned to him. "Interesting though this conversation is, it's actually boring, back to the main plot please."

"Sorry." Said Worandana. "There is an old and hidden library at the birthplace of Zandaar."

"Everyone knows that Zandaar was born in Zandarkoon." Said Kirukana.

"Just because everyone is told something does not make it true. Zandaar came into his power when he arrived at Zandaarkoon, though it wasn't called that then, it was Zaronia. He started building his religion from his original disciples."

"Oh yes, the nine." Said Kirukana.

"Actually eleven, but two of them were later decreed not to count as they were women. He was actually born, if that is the true term, in the fires of a burning mountain, far to the south."

"You mean, the mountain where the blind seer makes her divinations?" Asked Kirukana.

"The very same."

"So, her power, could be linked to his?"

"It's a possibility, she has been raving in that mountain for more years than most people know."

"But they could be the same?"

"No," said Worandana, "her power is too small to be the same as Zandaar's, I've just had a very strange thought though."

"Go on." Said Kevana. "Share your new insight."

"This is only a theory, and not one that I believe can be tested, remember the rock that is alive, in the caves." There were many nods from all around. "Suppose, just suppose, such an entity was engulfed in liquid rock, the magma that drives volcanos. And the entity absorbed the heat, and energy into itself, it became powerful, taking the power from around itself, the liquid rock always moving, keeping the heat energy flowing into the entity, until it no longer needed the confinement of physical form to maintain its life force. He most likely stayed within the warmth of his birthplace, for a while, until his presence caused the disciples to come to him, and he joined them to come north to were there where more people, these converted to worshipping him, once they witnessed the golden aura that is Zandaar." At this point all faces turned to Kirukana, waiting the outburst that didn't come. After a few moments he spoke slowly and carefully, as if exercising extreme control.

"An interesting theory, as you say old man, the only test is to ask Zandaar himself. I can't imagine that his answers would be very helpful. Once you discovered his birthplace, what did you do?"

"I took a little time away from the church, you know, rest, recuperation, solitary meditation. As soon as the watchers had been drawn away by some juicier scandal I skipped out of town and headed to that very volcano."

"You talked to the blind seer?"

"I did, and at some length, Mauraid is crazy. No real surprise, too much time spent inside her visions, but it is possible to gather some semblance of reason from her ramblings."

"Hang on, you accused the council of distorting her words for their own ends?" Said Kirukana.

"And I have no doubt that is what they did, I simply listened, I asked simple questions, and I asked them over and over again, it took me six months to get any form of sense of what she was actually trying to say. The feeling I get is that there is a good mind in there struggling to make itself understood."

"You mentioned a repository?"

"Yes, there are a large number of books in a cave, soon after the council of Zandaar was formed a mission was sent to collect her insights, they recorded everything for a few years, but the thing with her madness is that when her words make sense they are meaningless, and her confused nonsense carries the most meaning,

"So, what did you discover from her mumblings?" Sneered Kirukana.

"First and foremost, she wants him dead." Shocked faces and total silence abounded. "Not dead, in the normal sense, the idea is ended. It appears her existence is tied to Zandaar, and she wants out, after all these years of madness, she wants to die."

"You mean she's as old as Zandaar?" Mumbled Kevana.

"Yes. And some, she was old when he was born, already lived an entire life, and now she just goes on."

"People have been following Zandaar for over a thousand years."

"I know, can you imagine living blind for that long, it was the light of his birth that destroyed her eyes, the two are linked by his birth, only she is tied to the place, and he is not. She has a desperate need to die, only she can't. Her ramblings did give me a clue to a special power that Zandaar occasionally shares with his most trusted. These are generally those chosen to be his hunting dogs, they have a direct link to him, he can feel their minds, and knows what they are doing and thinking. This gives him complete control, though I don't believe he can feed them much in the way of energy, they are more like his eyes and ears, as well as his killers."

"So, if he knows where we are, he can simply direct them?" Asked Kevana.

"Yes."

"So why hasn't he?"

"I can only think of one reason that makes any sense."

"Go on."

"He's keeping them close, waiting until we have the sword."

"And then they come in and take it from the survivors, leaving none."

"It makes some sort of sense."

"You are saying that our lord is planning to have us killed as soon as we get the sword?" Asked Kirukana, in a far quieter voice than any expected.

"That is the most likely interpretation of the facts as I see them."

"There is another interpretation." Said Alverana slowly.

"What could that be?" Asked Kirukana.

"The hounds are present as escort, once we have the sword, they will guide us into the city, and protect us from the council's lackeys, and take us to Zandaar."

"Is that likely?"

"It's a possibility I hadn't thought of." Said Worandana, he looked meaningfully at Kevana.

"I don't believe that anyone could look on the hounds as escort, unless it was to the gallows." Said Kevana.

"Possibility?" Muttered Kirukana, a hopeful look in his eyes.

"Perhaps," said Kevana, "if Zandaar knows more than we do of the future and how the sword will arrive, then maybe they are to be our escort, rather than the escort of the sword, and not us."

"If they are to be our executioners, I hope that you shove that sword up the arses of the entire council, now that's a kebab I would like to see." Said Kirukana, firmly.

"He's definitely beginning to think like a soldier of god." Said Worandana looking straight at Kevana.

"That's as may be. We still have a sword to find and some surviving to do." Laughed Kevana. "I think is time to get some sleep. We missed moon rise with all this talking, Watchers can take guard duty as well, no point in more people being awake than need to be." He stood and waved Alverana towards their tent with a smile.

"Hey." said Alverana.

"What?"

"Does this mean we don't get guard duty?"

"It does, no point in us being awake if we can't watch out for the searchers."

"I'm so not used to this, how am I going to be able to sleep, without spending hours alone and cold just watching for nothing to happen?" Alverana smiled at the rest as the pair crawled into their tent.

CHAPTER FIFTY-SIX

The predawn sounds of birds woke Namdarin, he opened his eyes to the dimness of the tent, there in front of him was Jayanne, her face lit by the soft light that passed through the walls of the tent, green eyes wide, breathing slow and even.

"Are you alright?" He whispered.

"I'm worried about what we will find today, it frightens me how I will feel, I don't want to feel so bad, I know I am going to be angry all over again, I don't want to feel that much pain again, but I know it is going to happen."

"We could go another way, not see it all?"

"No. I need to see it, I'm going to face it all and try not to hate the men around me, how can men be so bad to people?"

"I have no idea, until they burned my house I could never have been as I am now, oh, I'm not saying that I was perfect, when punishment was required, then I was prepared to administer it, I didn't enjoy it, but it was a necessity. The evil in the world needs to be controlled or destroyed. Now I, or we, plan to control one of the greatest evils that our world currently faces. I'm fairly sure that once Zandaar is gone, then he'll be replaced by something as evil, or worse. I can only hope that this replacement will take a while before it comes to power, and the people will have some small respite. It's a vain hope I know, the power vacuum that I intend to create is going to be filled quickly. All I hope for is a few years of peace." His voice stumbled into silence.

"I only wish that people could be good to one another, but they don't seem to want to be that way."

"I am sorry, my love, but you are wrong."

"What do you mean?"

"Remember Betty?"

"Yes, what of her?"

"If I had failed to kill Dorana, she'd have done it, she'd have tottered up to him, on shaky old legs, stumbled, fallen against him, and plunged her knife into his heart, she'd have died to free her people. Myself, I'd die to avenge my people, it's not quite so noble, but it's the best I can do."

"The two cases are different, completely different, she could free her people, yours, sad to say, cannot be freed from death."

"Very true, but, if I can end Zandaar and his power, then his people can never do that again. Never burn a house because the people there won't do as they are told, because they believe they are free of the whims of someone else's god."

"You think Zandaar will be replaced by another worse god?"

"Not immediately, his followers may be strong enough to recreate him, but it should take some time before he is as powerful, it could be years."

"How could he be re-created?"

"Many people believe that gods are created by our belief in them, the more who believe, the more powerful the god, Zandaar has many believers. I think that people would want a kind and benevolent god, someone to help them in times of need, in general terms Zandaar did a good job of those sorts of things, his people cure the sick, help end famines, but they are greedy, they want the whole world to be beholding to them. If they don't get what they want, then things get nasty, and here we are."

"Let's hope that Zandaar's replacement will be better than him."

"It's the only dream that we can hold at the moment." Namdarin sighed. Jayanne rolled on top of him, resting her arms on his chest and lifting her body so that she was looking down into his blue eyes. His eyes glanced downwards for a moment to see the heavy breasts hanging onto his chest, she felt the coarse hairs of that chest rubbing gently and bringing her nipples to full hardness, for a moment her breathing stopped as she focused on the feelings.

"If they hadn't become greedy," she whispered, "we'd never have met, my village would still be slaves to Dorana, and I'd most likely be dead, killed by a white bear, who's pelt lies over there." Her head twitched in the direction and the red hair swirled around his head.

"Much as I would like to, I cannot turn away from this path, my people are all dead, your's will no doubt be ensnared by some new force before long, I can't see Zandaar letting the silver for his weapons get away from him that easily. He must know by now that we are coming for him, his forces will be arrayed against us, their numbers are as the leaves on a tree. I hope beyond hope that this thing ends with the two of us alive and able to start a new and more peaceful life together, would you want that?"

"I think so." Her voice barely audible, almost swamped by the song of a nearby finch, warming up for the impending sunrise.

"Even though you hold a hidden hatred in your heart."

"Damn that elf." She snapped, pushing herself upwards, until she was kneeling beside Namdarin, her hands still firmly on his chest. "How could he see that inside me?"

"It is simply part of their magic. I have a novel idea for you to consider."

"Go on."

"It goes something like this. All women are good, and all men are rapists in their hearts, am I correct."

"That is pretty much as it is." Her eyes flashed, wondering where he was going with this.

"How about a third group? Not men, not women, but people, who have transcended their original designations by acts of valour, or kindness, by words of truth and love, this new group could be called true friends. What do you think?"

"Do you believe I could do that? Simply ignore the fact that people are male or female?"

"Now male, female, and friend?"

"You are asking a lot." She said, rolling down onto her back alongside him, staring up at the tent as his hand found and softly enfolded hers.

"I'll ask more, do you believe that I would ever rape you?"

"No, you could but you won't."

"Do you believe that Jangor would sneak up behind you and cut your throat?"

"No, if I did something to anger him enough, he'd come at me from the front and challenge me to single combat and die on my axe just to prove how wrong I was."

"Don't these two fit into your new group?"

"Perhaps, I'll have to think on this some."

"Good, while you're at it, think of the others who have proved themselves time and again. While you are doing all this, you could even kiss me." He rolled towards her and smiled down on her, slowly his lips approached hers, she did nothing to pull away, and smiled back. The kiss started slow and soft, but quickly became more urgent and excited, finally he broke away, panting slightly from lack of oxygen.

"Jangor is going to be yelling for everyone to get up any moment now, the sky is lightening with the gold of sunrise."

Her arms snaked around his neck and pulled him down into the kiss again, but only for a moment, a moment that felt like a lifetime in so many ways, then she pushed him away and rolled to her feet.

"Time to be moving friend." She whispered. He caught her hand and turned her back towards himself.

"I was actually hoping for something a little more than friend."

"You have to earn that." She laughed, released his hand and stepped out into the golden sunlight of the dawn. Jayanne stretched in the morning light, she turned as she heard a tent flap open, she looked into Jangor's eyes as he crawled into the open air. She smiled, he took in her naked form and shook his head slowly.

"You want to wake them all?" He asked quietly, she smiled, he watched her breasts rise as she filled her lungs to their prodigious limit, he saw the muscles of her abdomen bunch as she built the tension in her diaphragm. Her eyes flashed as she looked at him and watched his smile grow.

"Hands off cocks, on with socks, out of your pits you lazy blackguards." She called in a voice almost as loud as Jangor's more practised bellow. Jangor smiled and chuckled softly, slowly shaking his head. Groans filled the air all around them as people came swiftly to wakefulness. Wolf came out of the morning glare and sat beside Jayanne, his head level with her waist, he rested his shoulder against her right thigh, and licked her hip, just to be sure she knew he was there, her hand fell to his head and ruffled his ears gently. He stared up at her like a lost puppy, all big eyes and wagging tail, she smiled down at the predator and laughed so quietly that it could be heard by no one other that the wolf.

"By all the gods," said a soft voice, "now that is a sight to wake up to, on a cold and lonely morning, she is like a goddess all of her own." Jayanne turned to the tent where the voice came from, to see Mander's unruly hair and white smile flashing in the morning sun.

"It's neither cold nor lonely, you are amongst friends here."

"I agree it's not cold, but it is lonely, I am here with only male friends and you, the goddess. I am afraid I shall have to do something dreadfully adolescent before I can pee this morning. Woman, you are just too much for us mortals." He turned and walked towards the river, looking for a little solitude.

"I agree entirely with him." Said Jangor. "Though I am older and don't have all the problems of these younger men, I'll merely have to think of something like cold porridge for a little while." Then he too wandered off to the river, in a slightly different direction. Kern came into view, a sadder look on his face.

"It's going to be a hard day, let's get this camp stripped and loaded, Stergin, Andel, you start on breakfast, and the rest of us will start packing things away. Jayanne are you planning on getting dressed at all today, there are unlikely to be any complaints, but it would seem a little undignified chopping the heads off our enemies while they are ogling at your tits."

"Fine." Laughed Jayanne. "I'll get dressed." She crawled into her tent just as a fully clothed Namdarin came out. He turned back briefly to watch as she vanished from view. He looked at Kern and smiled.

"Namdarin my friend, you have to be the luckiest man alive, to wake up next to her every morning."

"Kern, that is as maybe, for me this is definitely the best of a bad situation, but the situation is still bad. Until Zandaar is gone there can be no peace."

"I understand," Kern stepped in close and whispered, "she's going to have a very bad day, you need to keep her close and keep her calm, she is going to find that controlling her feelings is going to be very difficult." He glanced at the opening to Namdarin's tent and turned away because Jayanne was emerging. The camp adopted its usual morning activities, everyone had a task and things got done in the right order, so that by the time breakfast was ready the tents were down and packed away, the pack horses were loaded, each one much lighter than yesterday, as there were so many more of them.

"We need to get rid of some of these horses." Said Gregor loudly.

"Yes." Agreed Jangor. "As soon as we find somewhere to sell them, we can trade them for supplies, gold we no longer need, if this quest gets any more profitable, we are going to need a wagon to carry our gold."

"I am sure there will be a price to pay sometime soon." Said Kern, dipping an oat cake into his breakfast, saving the last bite to wipe around the bowl.

"How far to the merchants camp?" Asked Jangor.

"No more than half an hour," mumbled Brank, "but I can find no reason at all to rush."

"Fine, let's get things moving, I've a feeling we aren't going to get too far today."

"You'll definitely not be interested in lunch." Said Brank.

It wasn't long before breakfast was finished, the mess cleared, the fire doused, and people started mounting horses, the baggage train was certainly longer than it used to be.

"Brank, Kern, lead on." Shouted Jangor.

"Can we not go another way? I have no wish to see that again." Said Brank, his eyes turned down.

"I want to see first-hand the barbarity of those men that I killed, I feel a little bad for the way the axe took their souls and their lives, to feed them to me and Namdarin." Said Jayanne.

"Please lady, remember you asked for this." Said Kern as he led the troop out of camp and along the river, pace set at a slow trot, Wolf ranging from side to side as he normally did, in rapid succession they crossed three feeder streams that joined the main flow, crossing on the shingle beds at the edge of the main river, the shallower water there offered easy crossing for the horses, not so much for Wolf, each exit was accompanied by the usual fountain of scattered water droplets glistening in the morning sunlight. After the third crossing Wolf stopped his ranging, he dropped back along the column and fell in alongside Namdarin and Jayanne. A sudden swirl in the wind brought the stench of death to them all, the horses twitched and shied away, only to be pulled back into line, to continue the journey, Kern reassured his horse with a gentle pat to the neck, which brought a ripple of the mane by way of response. Very soon the burned out remains of a wagon came into view, Brank slumped in his saddle. A hand signal from Jangor told the men to stop a little clear of the camp, and the remains of the fire that used to be its centre. Mander and Andel were having a hard time with all the pack horses, they really didn't want to be there. Kern and Brank walked their horses to the central fire, around the blackened embers were many bodies. Gregor almost fell from his horse and raced to the side of a black robed figure. The elderly man had been killed by the piercing of many arrows, finally his throat cut so deep that the cervical vertebrae were visible. He turned away and swept the surrounding space with his reddened eyes. The approach to the camp, from the nearby grove of trees was littered with corpses, some burned to a crisp, some just with heads and chests burned in small areas.

"I count eight, he killed five with fire and three with lightning, before they overran him." Gregor turned to Granger. "If only we'd been here to help him, they'd most likely have survived." Gregor reached inside the man's robe and found both pockets to be empty. "He ran out of silver, he wasn't sufficiently skilled with a sword to do any more."

"Without uniforms it's very difficult to say which is which, the burned are obviously the invaders, this one was one of the defenders he only got two with his bow before they reached him and swarmed him under. These bastards seem to have a sort of pattern though, hands, feet and let the victims bleed out."

"Not these." Whispered Jayanne, still mounted, her eyes held by the broken body of a child. Her knuckles white with the tension in her grip on the handle of the axe. Jayanne slid from her horse, Namdarin followed, as she walked towards the naked fallen child Wolfs huge head pressed against the empty left hand, which grabbed a handful of the coarse fur. Jayanne fell to her knees left arm around Wolfs neck. The girl can't have been more than thirteen years old, what was left of her breasts were barely more than small bloody mounds, the nipples cut away, the horror of her death was plain for all. Bruises on her wrists, thighs and neck show that she had been tied or held whilst the robbers raped her. Her younger brother fared no better, the same bruises, his small body twisted in the final moments of his death. Judging by the damage on the mothers body she gave the robbers a little more sport, overseeing all this carnage was the merchant and father, his hands gone and his feet broken, his arms bound tightly, presumably so he didn't bleed to death too soon, at least not before he'd witnessed the deaths of his family, each impaled on a sword through their lower orifices, the son's body so small that the sword tip was resting against his ear, the daughter slightly taller, the sword tip barely visible at the base of her throat, the mother taller still, the sword entirely encased in her body. Each sword hilt pressed firmly against the broken bodies. Looking at the father Jayanne assumed the robbers had waited until everyone else was dead before cutting open the merchants' trousers and removing his genitals, leaving him to bleed to death. Brank fell to his knees, tears streaming down his face, one hand reaching out to the naked foot of the boy, never quite making contact, to withdraw and try again. His sobs filled all their hearts with pain.

"We need to do something for these people." Whispered Kern. The spell of immobility was broken, Jayanne spun to her feet, the axe whistling as she rose, she faced Kern, axe ready, edge glinting in the sunlight.

"What more can you do to them?" She screamed. "Men like you did all this, and they enjoyed it." She spat.

"I could never do something like this." Said Kern slowly, his hand tense on his sword hilt, but he knew he'd never get time to draw it.

"Remember, friends not men." Said Namdarin, his sword had

materialised in his hand. Wolf cowered on the ground, totally confused.

"Lady." Said Brank, still on his knees, his hands held wide, his wet face looking up into her blazing green eyes. "If you must kill a man today, let it be me, I'm not sure I want to live in a world that lets shit like this happen." His eyes held hers, motionless he stared, the only sound was her laboured breathing, without looking away, she moved, the axe swung wide and fell, fell from her hand into the churned grass. She fell on the big man with both arms wide, he surged to his feet and caught her, her strong arms around his neck, his around her waist, they stood one against the other, well she sort of hung there, her feet well clear of the ground, together they sobbed their hearts out, heads on each other's shoulders, as the tears flowed the tension drained slowly out of the situation.

"Shit." Muttered Andel. "I don't need crap like that at my age, I thought for a moment she was going to take his head. Shit."

"I'm with you." Mumbled Mander. "I think we're going to need a bonfire."

"Good idea." Said Jangor. "We're not short of horses." He nodded in the direction of the trees. "Start hauling timber, perhaps once she's calmed down a little, she'll put that axe to some good use."

"I can hear." Sobbed Jayanne, not moving her face from the warmth of Branks large shoulder.

"I know." Said Jangor, "but there is no rush, you two cry it out for a while, we'll start with the pyre for these poor people. Before we disperse to our respective tasks I have an announcement to make. Once our current task is completed it is my intention to travel the world hunting down the animals that do things like this and teaching them the final lesson. I hope that some of you will come with me."

"What about landowners like Melandius?" Asked Mander.

"We may just pass by his way and make an example of him first."

"I'm in." said Mander, and all the others quickly followed suit.

"That's good." Said Jangor. "Now let's do what we can to lay these people to rest, before we leave this place."

Mander, Andel and Stergin unloaded some pack horses and set off into the nearby wood, they'd be collecting dead falls first, but they knew they'd be needing some felling before long. By the time they were hauling their first heavy logs into the open air, Jayanne had stopped crying quite so much and was cleaning up the little girl's body. Wiping the blood from her pale flesh and then she started to comb her hair.

"Why are you bothering with that?" Asked Andel, "They're only going on the fire." Jayanne stared at him for a moment, then glanced at the axe where it had fallen, then back into Andel's now frightened eyes.

"Sorry." He mumbled turning his eyes to the ground. "Their clothes must have all burned in the wagon." He muttered so quietly that only Jayanne and Brank could hear.

"We shall make them as beautiful as we can, before the fire consumes their bodies and sets their souls free." Said Brank, he took the girl from Jayanne and placed her gently on the ground, straightening out her limbs, uncertainly his hand reached out for the sword embedded in her, once, then again.

"Leave it." Snarled Jayanne, Brank looked hard at her.

"If they meet their tormentors in the afterlife, then they are going to need the weapons they have been given." Brank nodded in agreement and brought the boy to her, together they set about removing the mud and blood from his body, wiping the injuries, and the bruises, straightening his hair, and laying him down, but whatever they did, he just didn't look right lying on his back, the curved sword hilt sticking out of his behind made this just look so uncomfortable, that it felt wrong. Jayanne laid him on his side next to his sister, his left arm across her body, this looked far more natural.

"Is it just me?" Asked Gregor. "Or does that just look wrong? We should remove the swords that took their lives."

"No." Snapped Jayanne. "Think for a moment, you are one of the lucky ones, killed by Brank or Kern, not by the axe of Algoron. You meet this young man in the afterlife, he slowly draws his sword, from the place where you or your friends placed it to end his life. Imagine the fear as he approaches to shred your very soul with the weapon you gave him. Their swords stay." Gregor retreated, not wishing to anger Jayanne anymore.

Jayanne and Brank turned to the mother, her injuries more extensive required more cleansing, it looked like she had put up quite a fight before she had been subdued, the damage to her anus would have been fatal given enough time, if the sword in her vagina hadn't taken her life. The wife cleansed they turned together to the merchant, his injuries look somehow less, because of his clothing, a moments glance was exchanged between the two, no words, but Branks flashing knife made short work of his clothing, in a very short time he was as naked as his family, laid out next to his wife, one handless arm around her shoulders, the other around his daughter, the open wound of his pubic mound gave feeling to the manner of his death. Jayanne looked down at the family group laid out on the grass, they appeared quite peaceful in their repose.

"We need a pyre for these innocents," she called, "a big one." She looked down at them again, and slowly removed her clothing, perhaps in some expression of singularity with the murdered. Once she was naked she glared at Brank who had been helping her all along with the preparation of the bodies. He held her gaze for a moment before starting his own dis-robement. Once he was naked, Jayanne selected the first of the large logs that had been hauled into camp, a few flashing strokes of the axe and she had four good lengths, the wood was damp, but that wouldn't be a problem, with Branks help she laid them out in an open square. Two more trees arrived by the time the base of the pyre was arranged, smaller branches were removed with a simple slash, the major trunks cut to suitable lengths, a second and a third layer raised the pyre to three feet high, the brush cut from the trees filled up the base. Brank and Jayanne collected the bodies of the soldiers and laid them on the brush in the midst of the pyre, even the robbers were collected and placed in there with the others, Gregor came running over to help with the body of the Zandaar monk, his was the last of those not of the merchant's family. Jayanne looked around.

"We need more trees." She shouted.

"There are no more dead falls close enough, do you hear the axes?" Asked Jangor.

"I hear." She snatched up her axe and marched off into the wood land, following the sounds.

Brank followed her, a little like a lost puppy, a very large lost puppy, Wolf did not, he stayed by the pyre, a little confused by the smells and sounds. She suddenly came upon the tree felling party, Mander and Andel were swinging their small axes and Stergin had three horses pulling on the tree they were hacking at.

"First." She called. "Stergin, longer ropes and pass them round a tree, so the horses are pulling away from the tree when it falls. Second, you two stand aside." She waited not so patiently while Stergin and Mander changed the ropes and the position of the horses, the ropes now passed round a heavy tree, which was likely to get hit when the tree they were felling finally surrendered, but at least the horses would be out of the drop zone. Jayanne stood at arm's length from the tree and went over in her mind the instructions Namdarin had given her so long ago. The first stroke came in at a downwards angle, driven with the full power of her more practised arms, deep it struck, almost a third of the way through the trunk, she felt a surge of power, not the level of influx that the sleeping willow gave, but certainly a large jolt. She lifted the haft and pulled the blade from the wood. The second stroke came in low and fast, it struck almost as deep, a huge triangular wedge of wood leapt from the trunk, she felt a slightly smaller surge from the axe. The tree was swaying as if in a strong wind, though there was none to be felt. She slowly lined up the next stroke, aiming for the centre of the wedge. Jayanne pulled hard on the axe all the way into the strike, taking energy from it as the blade accelerated through the air, the whistle grew loud before the impact stopped it. The axe pulled even more energy from the tree, feeding it into Jayanne, the blade stopped when it was just more than half way through the tree, it stopped there, feeding on the life of the tree, passing on the power, as she watched the leaves on the tree started to wilt, with a crack and a groan the tree started to move away from the axe, the horses pulling on it started to move as the tree started to fall. Soon they were running just to get clear of the falling branches, as fragments of shattered wood fell all around, some pieces almost as big as a horse. The heavy trunk finally hit the ground and broke into several large pieces.

"Do we have enough, or do you want more?" Shouted Jayanne, over the susurration of falling leaves.

"One more I think," Yelled Stergin. "You'll want a good fire." He laughed and started moving the horses back into the centre of the clearing. "Any particular tree that you would like?" He asked, a huge smile on his face. Jayanne walked over to a slightly larger tree.

"This one I think." She looked round, "You can run the ropes around the same tree, we'll drop this one in the same place." She didn't wait for them to get the ropes set up, she attacked the tree immediately, two huge blows, and fully a third of the trunk leapt out in a wedge. Each blow fed her more of the tree's life force. She stepped round the bole and waited for them to set up the ropes and get the horses into position to pull. Stergin gave her the nod when they were in place, and they started the horses to the task of pulling the tree over. She raised the axe high, and pulled it in hard, using the energy she had already collected, the blade went in true and deep, the tree shuddered, it trembled and shook, its leaves started to fall, power poured through the axe into Jayanne, she pulled upwards on the haft, to give the tree that little extra push, with a groan and a shiver the tree started to move, moments later it was a shattered wreck in amongst all the rest.

"We better get to hauling this lot to the pyre," said Stergin, "You start chopping them down into manageable pieces and we'll be back in a little while." Each horse was tethered to one end of a large trunk and started dragging it from the woodland. Jayanne attacked some of the more difficult pieces, lopping off side branches that would make dragging complicated. There was enough life left in the recently fallen trees that she didn't get tired, generally a single stroke was all it took to separate the heaviest side branches. When the men returned with empty horses, they bundled up the largest to haul off.

"Make us some more like these," said Stergin laughing loudly, as the three hauled a second load away. Namdarin came to see how she was doing, for a while he stayed concealed in the trees, just watching. Jayanne walked slowly along a fallen trunk, swinging the axe smoothly, with what looked like the minimum of effort, branches falling and splinters flying almost continuously, he could see the muscles flexing in her arms and legs as the axe fell, its wide silver head flashing in the dappled sunlight falling into the newly created clearing.

"I can feel you watching," she called. "Care to join in the hard work?"

"This is definitely axe work, not swordplay." he said walking into the clearing.

"Your sword may enjoy the change of pace, this is just too easy for my axe."

"I would never have thought of using such a fine-looking weapon for so menial a task."

"Menial enough for the axe of Algoron, but not suitable for the sword of Xeron?"

"I suppose one god's weapon is no different from another." He smiled and drew the blue bladed longsword. "What would you like me to do?"

"That trunk," she pointed at a section, "just lop off the side branches, once you've done that I'll chop it into three parts, that should be more than enough for a decent bonfire." Namdarin nodded and stood up on the wide trunk, he walked slowly along it, the sword falling first one side then the other, each blow chopped a branch off, and each blow fed him a little energy.

"This gets easier with every strike," he laughed, capturing her green eyes for a moment before moving on. He was half way along when he felt the trees bark kick under his feet, he looked back.

"You could wait until I've finished cutting the side branches." he said. Again, the axe fell, and a large chunk of tree flew away.

"Why?" she smiled. Again, the axe fell, the lower section of the trunk was separated, what was left, rolled a short distance to the left, almost throwing Namdarin from his position on top of it.

"That is why, you nearly made me fall."

"You can handle it, you'll be better prepared next time." She laughed.

"Right." Namdarin said, going back to his task of clearing the side branches, as he progressed along the trunk these got thinner, and easier. By the time Jayanne was splitting the trunk into another haulable section he had finished the side branches, he stepped of the trunk and with a single strike cut the top ten feet off it.

"Ready for some more to be moved?" Mander asked, as the three returned.

"Yes." Jayanne said, "there should be enough now, I'll go back and help with the building, Namdarin, with me, I may need your sword, these three can haul all the wood now."

"You expect all this in one trip?" Asked Stergin.

"Of course not, just keep it moving." She laughed, walking away with Namdarin following.

"I wish she'd put some clothes on." Stergin said, quietly.

"I never thought I would say this," mumbled Mander, "I'll agree with that sentiment she's very distracting, and the splinters from every axe stroke are making a real mess of her pretty pale skin. She may not be feeling them right now, but tomorrow she will. She may have trouble riding tomorrow, a good-sized splinter caught her right on the ass, sitting a saddle may be difficult."

"If she asks for volunteers to kiss it better," Andel giggled, "Then you'll be on your knees faster than anyone."

"And you wouldn't?"

"No, she scares the crap out of me."

"Me too, she's just far too, I don't know, she's just too big for me."

"What?"

"I don't mean physically, I've loved many bigger than her, Jayanne has this really huge presence, she fills all the space around her, she's so beautiful and powerful, when those green eyes flash in my direction, I get the feeling of a great viper, you know what I mean?"

"Sort of and no," Stergin replied. "Snakes have no emotion in their cold black eyes, hers have far too much, sometimes I get the impression that her head is going to explode with all that pressure going on inside it."

"Namdarin is a brave man, and he is welcome to her." Said Andel.

"All this is entirely by the by, how angry is she going to be if this wood stops moving?"

"Right." The three busied themselves with the attaching of the trees to the horses, who had actually begun to enjoy their little rest.

"Another thing," said Mander, "why did she have to make Brank get naked? He's big enough with his clothes on, without, he makes me feel inadequate."

"Don't you worry," replied Stergin, "he's not so happy about it himself, watch his right hand."

"I don't understand."

"His right hand keeps crossing his body to his left hip and finding that the sword isn't there. Then he looks at Jayanne and the axe hanging from its strap." Laughed Stergin. "He's naked and defenceless, and she's still got the axe. Oh, how he hates it."

"Somehow I don't think I'd feel comfortable watching his right hand, it is generally too close to something else that makes me feel small." Said Mander.

"I wasn't aware you had those sorts of inclinations." Laughed Andel.

"I don't," snapped Mander, "just, checking out the competition, you know, and feeling small."

"I wouldn't worry about that," smiled Stergin, "his ass belongs to Laura, and all the other bits as well. We all made some promises this morning, but I am fairly sure that Brank is going to be racing to Laura, just to make sure it is alright with her that he goes off on another quest, a quest to end the brutality of men."

"She'll tie the bastard to a tree." Howled Mander. Together they mounted their now loaded horses and started the slow walk to the camp. They came out into the daylight and started down the gentle slope to where the pyre was taking shape, it was now so high that only Brank was tall enough to lift the branches on to the top, his sweating body covered in green and brown stains from his labour, Jayanne looked no better, the stains showed even more on her pale skin. Her face streaked with tears, she slowly climbed up one side of the pyre and started taking branches from Brank to add to the top. She was facing away from the approaching riders when she bent over to pull up another branch, the view was too much for Mander, he choked and shut his eyes. Stergin smiled, but no one else noticed.

"Jayanne," called Jangor, "get down it's high enough. Stack the long branches against the sides, then it's ready to go." She turned to the old warrior, nodded and slowly climbed down, one branch moved under her weight, and trapped her ankle. Her grunt of pain brought Brank the three strides to catch her before she fell, he slowly lifted her weight so that her ankle became loose, and then he lifted her down to the ground, her naked body pressed hard against his. She smiled at him, looking up into his eyes, her arms around his neck, then slowly the smile faded, her eyes hardened.

"I am sorry my lady, but when a beautiful naked woman presses her body against a naked man, one who is not actually dead, certain things happen to him, things that he has no control over, I have no control over that particular part of my anatomy. Please forgive me, I would ordinarily not be in this situation, and I would never force myself on a lady." Her arms stayed around his neck, he felt the weight of the cold blade of the axe of Algoron against his back, still hanging from its strap.

"Don't you want to make love with me?" She said quietly.

"Jayanne." Jangor said, tersely. "Stop teasing Brank, he's already offered his life to you once today, don't drive him to take his own." Jayanne glanced at Jangor, then looked back into Brank's eyes, slowly she smiled up at him.

"Thank you, friend." She whispered, then she tried to step away, his arms on her waist, failed to release her, she looked a wordless question at him.

"Lady, my current condition, please."

"What is your problem?"

"You can feel my problem, it's embarrassing."

"How can you be embarrassed by something you have no control over?" He looked down into her eyes for a long moment, then released her, and swallowed, his mouth suddenly dry. She didn't step away, her hands pulled his head down, and she kissed him softy on the lips, she felt the panic building in his heart, she released his head and dropped her hands to her sides, then the kiss broke.

"Thank you for all your help today my friend." She whispered, then she turned away, and walked over to Namdarin.

"I think I understand friend now." She whispered, then turned to the strange sounds behind her. Mander looked like he had fallen from his horse and was trying to hide in the grass. She looked at Stergin, who had a huge smile on his face.

"What's wrong with him?" she demanded.

"Well," replied Stergin, "We had been discussing the feelings of inadequacy caused by Branks current attire, the you went and did that to him." He waved a casual hand in Branks direction. "Now Mander feels like a tiny little worm and is doing a fine impression of such." Jayanne, looked from Stergin to Brank, to Mander, to Branks midriff, to Stergin, to Brank, to Mander.

"You do know that you people are completely crazy, don't you?" She asked softly, a wide smile on her face.

"Jayanne," said Jangor, "they are fully aware just how crazy is the world they live in. Mander, get up, the sight of a naked man is not going to burn your eyes out, and I am certain that your ego will recover as soon as an acceptable woman comes along. Get those branches propped up against the pyre." He walked over to Jayanne and spoke quietly.

"You are playing a dangerous game with these men, you do understand?"

"They aren't men, they are friends, admittedly friends with penises, but friends all the same. Am I wrong?"

"No and yes, they are friends, but if you push them too far, they may just return to their primal nature, that would be bad."

"I understand, I am just getting used to the idea that males can be friends."

"These men are more than friends, they are brothers, brothers in arms."

"I think I know how you mean, they are almost like sisters." she smiled.

"They may be a little perturbed to be described so, but if that helps you deal with your feelings for them, then so be it." Jangor smiled and turned away, to supervise the final stacking of the pyre. Once this was finished, he turned to Jayanne. She and Brank were returning from the river, where they had washed of most of the stains caused by the heavy work they had been doing. Branks embarrassment had reduced to more normal dimensions, at least normal for him.

"The pyre is finished, are you going to say some words for these people?" he asked.

"Not quite finished," she replied, "how many bottles of your magic incendiary do you have?"

"There are only two left."

"They'll do, I want this pyre to burn fast and hot, and most of the wood is at least damp."

"Mander, go fetch the bottles, we do still have them, don't we?" Called Jangor.

Mander simply nodded and went over to the pack horses, rummaged in a pack and returned to Jayanne with a bottle in each hand, he handled them gingerly, as if they were in some way dangerous. Jayanne took the bottle off him one at a time, and scattered the contents liberally over the large pile of wood. Finally she handed the empty bottles back to Mander, he seemed even more unhappy about handling them, especially when empty.

"Does anyone know the funeral words for these people?" she asked.

"We don't even know which god they followed." Said Jangor.

"We are sure about one of them." Said Gregor, he was unsure how the Zandaar funeral service would go down with Namdarin.

"I am sure I can come up with something that won't upset too many." said Granger.

"Fine by me." Namdarin said, looking at Gregor.

"I have no problem," replied Gregor, "these innocents deserve a decent burial, and for some a funeral pyre is more normal than anything else."

"If I return to the religion of my childhood," said Granger, "I will use the funeral prayers I learned then, and I will add some references for Xeron and Algoron, so long as no one has any objections?"

There were no replies from those around him, so he went on. "Jayanne, Brank, do you wish to get dressed in more funeral attire before we proceed?"

"We are dressed as we came into this world," Jayanne said loudly, "and as these children left this world, we shall stay as we are, until our business here is concluded." Brank came and stood next to her, then took her hand in his.

"We stand as parents for these poor children, even though we couldn't be here when they needed us the most." His words caused more than one eye to weep.

Granger indicated to Gregor that he should stand next to him, then he started to speak, this in a language that none of those present could understand, after a short time he switched to the language they all used.

"We have no names for the souls taken here, we have no heritage to call on for them, we know no gods that they followed, hear me oh gods, if these are your lost children then claim them as such, if there are none to claim them, then I ask that Xeron and

Algoron take care of them in the afterlife, lead them onto new planes, to begin again, in a place where they can find some happiness." He looked across at Gregor, then struck his staff against the ground, a blue flame leapt from the top, Gregor did the same, the hot blue flames were then turned down towards the pyre, the oil caught fire with a rush that blew a column of white smoke upwards, slowly a mushroom cloud formed above the pyre, as they watched a face formed in the cloud, an old bearded face, he smiled down upon the living and the dead. A huge spectral hand reached down into the fire, and then withdrew, the open palm held many small figures, a man, a naked woman, two naked children, some soldiers and one dressed entirely in black. With a second surge the fire leapt up into the sky, tearing the cloud and its figures to shreds as it climbed ever higher, for a few seconds it raged thus, then slowly it settled down to a more normal level, the heat lessened and the roaring subsided. The hot white smoke was replaced by oily black tendrils and an odour of burning meat.

"Well that was interesting." Gregor laughed.

"What do you mean?" Asked Granger.

"I'm fairly sure, someone is going to very upset by what happened here today."

"You're going to have to explain in simple words for us." Jangor growled.

"Well," laughed Gregor, "it's not something a member of my faith should ever even think, let alone voice, but I do believe I just saw Xeron, or an image of him, and he reached down and collected the souls of those that died here. We are told that Xeron doesn't exist, and yet he appears to have come here, at your bidding Granger, then he took away the bound soul of a priest of Zandaar. Zandaar's going to be mightily put out by that, his rage is going to be unmeasurable. He so hates to lose followers while they are alive, but after they are dead, they should be his forever. His anger is going to be monumental." Gregor roared with laughter.

"How can you find the anger of your god to be funny?" Demanded Jangor.

"It's not, it's really not, but it just feels so crazy, Zandaar goes to such lengths to ensure that people never leave the faith, or worship another god, or even think about another god, and after that priest dies, Xeron just snatches him up and steals him away. It just so wonderful."

"The real question," says Namdarin, "is whether he is going to take some sort of direct action, is that at all likely?"

"No." Gregor smiled. "The deed is done, and Xeron has gone, to wherever it is he currently resides, anyway Zandaar won't move far from his power centre, he knows we are coming to him, all he has to do is wait."

"That makes me feel so much better." muttered Namdarin. Jangor turned to Jayanne saying. "The day is only half done, do we stay here, or move on?"

"Everything that needed doing here has been done, just wait while I get cleaned up a bit and dressed, then we can leave, I don't think I could stay here now, this place is too depressing."

"Agreed." said Jangor, "Mander, Andel, get the horses ready, we'll be back on the road in a little while, Namdarin, which way?"

"More south than west, but not much." Namdarin's eyes lost focus, his head fell slowly forwards, for what seemed like a long time, then he looked up again. "I feel no horses at all in range, and with such a large local herd the range is quite long, I'd never noticed that before."

"We've never had this many horses before." Muttered Mander, fighting to get a tether around one of the more recalcitrant pack animals. Namdarin turned to watch a much cleaner Jayanne walking back from the river, she was arm in arm with a now clean and smiling Brank. Namdarin's thoughts turned to the impressive looking pair. 'Mander may have been right, he could definitely have someone's eye out with that thing.' He laughed loudly as Jayanne came into his arms and kissed him.

"What are you laughing at?" She asked quietly.

"Ask me again when we are alone." He whispered. "Get dressed wench." He laughed much louder. She simply smiled and collected her clothes. Jangor came over while the two were dressing.

"That woman is crazy." He said to Namdarin.

"But don't you love her for it?"

"Certainly, she could cause problems, you know that?"

"Yes, that's one of things I'm working on."

"So I see, earlier she talked of friends with penises and sisters."

"That's good." Namdarin smiled.

"Perhaps, somehow I don't see Kern as a sister, do you?"

"No but if Jayanne can think of him that way, it may help her to get over her hatred of all men."

"Not all, you are most certainly not in the hated for all time camp."

"I'd hope not."

"Did you get any impression of horses at all, we need to lighten our load of animals, they are starting to become a problem."

"We could just turn them loose."

"I can't do that, I've spent my entire life making a crust were ever I can, there's a serious value to these things, I just can't bring myself to leave them for someone else to capture."

"How full is the war chest?"

"Brim, we now have enough gold to buy a small village, or a large farm."

"So what do you need the gold from the horses for?"

"Could you leave Arndrol behind?"

"Obviously not, but he's my friend, these spare horses mean nothing to you."

"No, but they represent lots of gold, it's the gold that means more to me."

"What about that bay filly that Jayanne claimed?"

"That has to be the most beautiful horse I have seen in years."

"Careful, you'll make Arndrol jealous, and what about the gold you could get for that one?"

"Now you are just making things difficult, I can't ever begrudge a member of the team anything they need, hell, we'd all give our very lives for the other people in the group, that's part of who we are. I believe that Jayanne would do the same."

"She would, but that horse is now hers, not yours." Namdarin smiled.

"You expect logic from me where my team are involved. Dream on." Laughed Jangor,

"So just turning them loose is never going to be an option?"

"No, we'll continue south and see if we can find a village, or a small farming hamlet nearby, we could do to report the death of the wine merchant and his family as well. Someone will be missing them."

"I suggest we don't do that."

"Why?"

"The involvement of local law enforcement is never a good idea, they can be a serious pain. They expect explanations, reports, statements, and probably courts. We can do without that."

Jangor thought for a moment before answering.

"The only connection we have to them is the horses and the gold, the horses could be recognised, but the gold is just local currency."

"Here's a question." Namdarin spoke slowly. "Why does a wine merchant have so many bottles of wine and so much gold? One or the other, not both. Another thought, why bottles, not casks?"

"I've no idea, maybe he had a customer in mind that prefers bottles to casks, but then the strongbox should be empty. There's definitely something a little strange there. We'll probably never know."

Jayanne and Brank now dressed were the last to mount their horses.

"Kern, south and move out, moderate pace, we can make a few more miles today before we have to camp. Namdarin keep your ears open let's not be surprised again." Shouted Jangor, Kern led the column back onto the road, such as it was."

CHAPTER FIFTY-SEVEN

Kevana woke in the pre-dawn light, to the warmth and comfort of his friend in his arms, a smile shaped his lips, as he released his hold, and slowly backed away. He managed to crawl from the tent without waking Alverana. Pulling on his outer clothes as he stamped in the frosty grass, the boots came last, as he moved away to where Petrovana was standing watch, the younger man handed him a steaming cup of tea as he approached.

"It got cold during the night." Mumbled Petrovana, as Kevana nodded his thanks.

"Looks like winter is finally starting to catch us up, again." Kevana sneered.

"So long as it doesn't get as cold as it was, I don't really care."

"Too many good men died in that cold."

"We must be far enough south by now, frosty mornings and cool days, surely that's as bad as it's going to get?"

"It is not unknown for Zandaarkoon itself to see a thick coating of snow."

"That's right, look on the bright side."

"It is rare I know, but it does happen. We need to be getting everyone up very soon, I would like to be on the road before the sun comes up."

"Wouldn't it be better to wait until the searches have passed us by, that way Worandana doesn't fall off his horse?"

Kevana looked at Petrovana with raised eyebrows for a moment before Petrovana continued. "I know, I'd laugh like a madman if he fell off, I don't like him, but I don't want him to die, at least not actively."

"Not actively? So you'd be passive and let someone kill him?"

"No," sighed Petrovana, "but then you already know that, he's still a brother."

"What about the hounds?"

"If they draw swords on me, they'd better be ready for the next life."

"Agreed. I'd actually like to test my skills against theirs."

"I'm fairly sure that Worandana could best all their magicians, but we'd be hard pressed to beat their soldiers, we're shorthanded."

"There is one thing that goes in our favour, if nothing else, we are used to opposition, they, are not."

"You could be right, they don't generally get to hunt down bandits and such, we do."

"They don't fight in any of the major battles either, they are Zandaar's stick to beat us with."

"We'll hand them their heads."

"I'd prefer it not to come to that."

"Me too." Laughed Petrovana. "I'll start waking the others." He wandered slowly off to the tents to do just that, before long there were many groans and grunts of waking men, Petrovana returned to the fire, soon the smell of bacon and frying bread filled the air, good though this was it didn't seem to improve the feelings of the men. Tense eyes kept turning east, the gradual lightening of the sky darkening their moods. Worandana captured Kevana's eyes with a glance, and with a nod told him that they needed to talk somewhere where the others couldn't hear them. The two walked slowly away with their breakfast, Alverana stared hard for a moment, then the tiniest of gestures from Kevana calmed him. Once they were far enough away from the camp Worandana spoke in a hoarse whisper.

"I've been thinking."

"That's a surprise." Smiled Kevana sarcastically.

"I'm old, I don't sleep well."

"I had noticed that, you know, especially on the downwind side."

"No need to be nasty."

"Please, oh great one, share your thoughts with this mere jester."

"Idiot," sighed Worandana, "I think we can build on Gorgana's idea. I may even just steal his entire idea and increase the power of it."

"Enough for us to take him on, and win?"

"No, well, let's say unlikely, his base is now tried and tested, he's going to be very secure within that construct, I don't think we can take his power far enough to break him."

"So what do you plan?"

"When the searchers come looking we give them something to find, the green goddess is just a great image, it will do fine, when the searchers find her, we'll be right in the centre of our power, they'll be days of travel away, and extended, over extended most likely, she slaps them hard with a surge of power, enough to shake them but not break their circle. Then she tells them to stop peeking into her world, I was thinking about that glade where the tigers are. It should be interesting if they send the hounds there."

"You know very well that cats and dogs don't get along." Laughed Kevana. "Can you do this? It sounds a little complex, even for you."

"Not really, just a little out of the ordinary."

"So how would this work? You understand we only get the one chance to fail?"

"I know the risks, and I believe I can keep them within acceptable levels, as to how. Simple circle, low rate and low power, we won't need much, the headman of the circle feeds me every pulse or every other, randomly so that my power doesn't have that characteristic pulse. When I make contact, I suck as much of their power as I can, just to give me the extra edge, I'll use imagery, and fear rather than power, I'll distract their primary character, and break their circle, they are sure to be using circles this far out."

"Old man you are starting to sound excited by all this, are you getting carried away by your own enthusiasm?"

"No, I just want to teach them a lesson they won't forget any time soon." His grin seemed too large for his face.

"We don't have long to set this up, dawn is coming quick."

"It's simple really, the only hard parts are the feeder out of the circle, and my imagination."

"Fine." Kevana shook his head. "Let's get this done." He marched back into camp, watching the preparations for departure. Worandana on his heels.

"Listen up people," he called, "Worandana has an idea how to beat the searchers, and make them leave us alone, we'll have a circle feeding round, I'll be the only one facing outwards, I'll feed power to Worandana, we don't need massive surges, just a steady and smooth power feed for the old man, this is his idea, mine is that once the searchers are in contact with Worandana we push that rate and the power up as high and as fast as we can, it's not going to be monumental, we have too many inexperienced men in the group. I'm sorry my friends, but you don't have our practise or co-ordination, the rest of us have been together a long time, you will get better, but it's going to take a while. Everyone clear?"

"I have only one change." Said Worandana.

"Go on?" Kevana asked with a frown.

"Kirukana not you as the interface between the circle and me."

"Why?" Snarled Kevana.

"He's a more skilled cleric than you, he can handle higher loads, and if a backlash comes our way, then you are going to need someone really stubborn to hold them out of our circle and stop it collapsing. If that happens, mount up and ride like hell. Do you understand?" Worandana cast a worried glance at the eastern sky.

"Yes, form up circle facing inwards." He shouted. They all gathered into a circle, holding hands, all facing inwards, Worandana moved a few, changing the balance of the circle, to smooth the power flow out as best he could, standing at the eastern edge was Kirukana facing outwards.

"Fine, you crazy old man," said Kirukana, "how do I feed you when my hands are already full?"

"I have an idea about that," Worandana smiled, "now don't panic." He stepped slowly forwards until he was right in front of Kirukana, his belly touching the younger man, then his hands reached up, and took Kirukana by the head, hands above the ears, palms and fingers flat against the skull, he pulled Kirukana's head down until their foreheads were touching, Kirukana felt a contact far more intimate than he was either used to, or prepared for, he pulled back, but found he couldn't actually move.

"Don't panic," Whispered Worandana, "Just relax, feel the power and the sharing, breathe and relax, this sort of connection can carry so much more power."

"So why is it prohibited?" muttered Kirukana.

"I'll explain later, get the power flowing." Kirukana did as he was told, he started the power flowing in the circle, it came back to him, much larger than it set off, and he passed this straight on to Worandana, same with the next few cycles. Worandana borrowed the image of Gorgana's mother, but shifted the colour to red, and the core of her power to be that of fire, the fire of a burning mountain. Gradually the image grew in strength, her hair became plumes of hot smoke, steam roiled from her hands. 'Randomly now, but nothing too hot.' Thought Worandana at Kirukana, the clerics eyes flashed open and suddenly frightened, but he didn't stop the circle working, round the power went, three times building gradually before he passed it on to Worandana, this surge fixed the female fire figure, her eyes pools of hot white fire. Worandana took the next surge of power and turned it into a wall of fire surrounding himself and his friends. The next surge he held within himself, and the next, with the one after that he reached into the mental plane, he felt a presence approaching.

'They come.' he thought to Kirukana, pulling the fire tighter around his friends, he felt the mind approaching, he animated the fire figure, focusing hard to make her movements as natural as possible and the colours of the fires realistic.

"Who are you coming into my realm?" She howled, the figure slowly coalesced, its form thickening into a man shape, perhaps not an exact representation of the man in question, more an image of how he sees himself.

"Who are you woman? You're not the one I am looking for." Worandana reached out one fiery hand and took the figure by the throat.

"This is my realm, you have been flitting around for days and I don't like it." The fist tensed and the fire burned hotter, helped along by another surge from Kirukana, the figure in black was now expending a great deal of power to counteract the heat of the hand at its throat. Worandana was taking that power, and the energy from Kirukana, strengthening himself all the more.

"I am Axorana, I am looking for a renegade of my order, he has committed great offences against our god. Have you seen him within your realm?" His voice shaking with the tension.

"I have seen some of your ilk, though not normally as many as now, your incursions are becoming a nuisance. You should stay away from my home."

"Where is your home? Then we can avoid it." Axorana's power was beginning to fade, his image started to degrade. Worandana sent an image of the clearing where they had seen the cats, and a huge firepit, giving the impression that there was a volcano there.

"You stay away from my home, and we will have no problem, if you continue these invasions of my places, then there will be some consequences, do we understand each other?"

"I agree, we will stay away from your home, can you agree to the deaths of the heretics? The only thing our god requires is the blue bladed sword that they are carrying. Will you collect it for us?"

"If they invade my home in a physical way, I will kill them, but if you want some sword you can get it yourselves, I have no interest in such things."

"How will we know if you have killed them?"

"How will I know which of them to kill? Your black robes flit hither and yon, seemingly without reason. Hurry up little man your power is failing."

"I can call you again, but I need a name to call, who are you?"

"I have many names, some call me the Trickster."

"I shall call you again, at sunrise tomorrow, will that be acceptable?"

"Not really, but if it must be, then tomorrow." Axorana's figure flashed then faded out completely. Worandana held the fire shrouded figure for a while longer, so that he could be sure the other had left, then he released the simulacrum, and returned to the plane of the living. All around him his friends were staggering with fatigue, they each looked like they had given everything they had. Kirukana turned to Worandana, a scowl on his face.

"What?" demanded Worandana.

"Did you really just set Axorana up to take on Gyara?"

"It could be that he'll try to contact Gyara."

"And you sent him to a place where you know those tigers are?"

"That too, I'm hoping he'll send the hounds there, it will be interesting to find out how they perform against real predators. Anyway, how do you know all this? Was there any chance that Axorana may have felt your presence?"

"None, your fire was a very good shield, and very much one way."

"Kevana, did you feel any of this going on?" Asked Worandana.

"We got nothing, only Kirukana's demands for more power, you almost killed us all."

"You're tired, that is all."

"Explain." Snapped Kevana.

"Our glorious leader," interrupted Kirukana, "managed to convince Axorana, who was leading the search, that he was a female figure wreathed in fire, and that she is known as the trickster, he gave the location as the clearing where we met the tigers, and put a fire pit in there as well. I know he said it was possible to lie with the mind, but I never imagined he could do it so comprehensively."

"I had no choice." muttered Worandana, "he asked the god like creature that he had just met to kill us all. All they want is the sword. I really hope he goes after Gyara tomorrow. But in the meantime we need to put some distance between ourselves and this place, just in case he got some hint of our location."

"Just how tired was he before he broke the connection?" Kirukana's question surprised them all.

"He was hanging on but barely, taking power from his circle at every revolution, not allowing any build up at all, but he needed it all, and they had precious little left to give."

"Will he go looking for Gyara, or will he have enough of your alter ego to focus on you?"

"I can't be sure, but I wasn't broadcasting much of anything beyond the image. Every iota of contact I used to drain power from him, and his circle."

"I wasn't aware that was even possible."

"Nor was I." Laughed Worandana.

"Enough chatter." Interrupted Kevana. "We need to get moving, before they regroup and come looking for us."

"I agree we need to move." Said Worandana. "But I don't think they'll even be walking, let alone regrouping for quite a while yet, I drained them, and I do mean drained. I don't believe that Axorana will wake up before noon. But they have other groups who have power left still, so we need to get moving."

"Right." Yelled Kevana, "I want this camp packed and us on the road in five minutes. Move it!"

All the men rushed to do his bidding, they all wanted to be moving before any possible search came their way again, they didn't relish the idea of another meeting like the one they had just endured. Petrovana came up on a slumped Strenoana, he prodded him with a booted foot.

"Get moving, we need to be on the road."

"I'm too tired to even move."

"Then you die."

"What?" Strenoana looked up suddenly frightened.

"If we leave you behind, and the searchers come looking, you'll tell them everything before you die. Kevana won't let that happen. Get ready to ride, you can rest once we have some miles between us and this place. Can I be any clearer?"

"No." Strenoana hauled himself slowly to his feet and looked sourly at Petrovana. "I'm not used to this sort of work. I can't believe how tiring it is."

"It does take some getting used to. Keep at it, it will get better, in the meantime move your backside." Petrovana laughed, as Strenoana moved off to help with the preparations for departure. In very short order the whole troop were mounting up, ready to leave, even Strenoana was hauling himself up into his saddle.

"Direction?" Demanded Kevana, looking at Worandana.

"South then east, heading for Angorak, the current destination hasn't changed."

Kevana glanced at Alverana, and together they set off almost directly south, pushing hard as the horses were fully rested, not that the same could be said for the riders. In only a few minutes it was clear that the riders were recovering, the mental strain of the morning was fading as the physical effort took over the demands on their bodies. Riding hard for the early part of the morning they covered a lot of ground, about mid-morning Kevana slowed the pace down to give the horses a rest, and Alverana turned the direction a little more easterly. It was just after noon when they were thinking about stopping for a meal, they came upon some cultivated fields, the valley ahead of them gradually became more and more cultivated, then round the bend in the river appeared the village, a large collection of houses, not enough to be a town, but certainly a large village, there were at least seventy dwellings by Kevana's estimation, no tower to indicate a monastery, for which Kevana was suddenly grateful. Alverana dropped the pace to a walk before they reached the outskirts of the houses, the road was wide enough to them to ride three abreast and still have a cart pass the other way, one such cart driver made no pretence of indifference, he stared quite openly at the riders, as his cart rolled slowly passed them.

"We seem to be making quite an impression." Muttered Alverana.

"It just that they're not sure who we are." Replied Kevana gently.

"Is that a large inn I see ahead?"

"It could be, we'll make for it, see if we can get some beds for the night, that will give us some time to get new clothes."

"I thought you wanted to get to Angorak as soon as possible?"

"Yes, but we need our new identities first, I had a nasty

thought as we came into this village, what if there had been one of our monasteries here? We'd have most likely been in serious trouble. Any established force could cause us some real problems."

"You really believe that our brothers are our enemies?"

"From what Worandana says Axorana has made that so, they are all out to kill us."

"With any luck Axorana will go looking for Gyara in the morning, and that will be the end of him."

"What are the chances of him actually finding her?"

"Slim, he's going to be focused in a given direction, so she's not likely to hear him, he's not a believer, so she'll probably just ignore him."

"I thought gods could see and hear everything?"

"If so, why are the hounds still looking for us?"

"Damn, this is getting all too complicated, I'm a soldier, give me some heads to lop off and I'll be so much happier."

"We have some heads to take, but we don't seem to be able to catch up with them."

"Thanks for reminding me." Kevana smiled. "I think that is an inn ahead. You and I will enquire inside." He turned to Worandana behind him. "You hold the rest outside, stand ready there is no saying what will happen."

Kevana pulled up alongside the hitching rail and dropped to the ground, looping his reins around the rail, as he stepped towards the entrance, he knew that Alverana was only half a pace behind. The veranda across the front of the building was little more than a covered walkway, no seating, no tables, he paused for a moment to check his sword, then stepped in through the open doorway into the darkness of the interior.

The inside of the inn was much the same as others to be found everywhere, there was a huge fireplace on one wall, with a small wood fire burning gently, just enough to take any chill off the room, but not too much to make the place actually warm, the dancing yellow flames definitely added something to the feeling of warmth in the room. There were three customers in the bar, two old men sitting at a table, their conversation obviously stopped by the arrival of the two strangers. Kevana nodded in their direction as an acknowledgement of their presence, the third customer was well into his cups, slumped at a table a beer mug gripped firmly in one hand, though he seemed to be asleep. The bar ran along the back of the room, any exit that side meant going over the bar,

Kevana thought that this was a very bad idea, but he said nothing about it, he walked up to the bar where a man stood slowly wiping a mug with a rag, it was really too grubby to be called a towel.

"Good afternoon gentlemen, how can I help you today?"

"We're looking for a night's rest for twelve and stabling for horses, we have horses to spare, and would like to trade them for supplies?"

"I am certain we can come to some form of accommodation." Said the Barman, "They call me Joe, and you are?"

"I'm Kevan, and this is Avler." said Kevana slowly. Joe smiled and looked slowly from one to the other.

"Other than your grubby over-shirts, everything else about you fairly screams Zandaar, would you be the ones we have been warned about?" Kevana's hand settled on his sword hilt. "Relax gentlemen, whatever your true names are, our village is too small to have a resident presence of your people, and the tales they tell of you are far too fanciful to be believed. Your disguise may work at a distance, but up close there is no doubt as to your identities, perhaps we can do something about that while you are in our little town. How many are you?"

"How many are there supposed to be of us?"

"Numbers are unclear, though you are said to be guilty of all manners of savagery and crimes against, well, just about everyone, including your own god. I think the only thing you aren't guilty of is raping goats, but that's most likely down to the lack of imagination of your accusers, they just don't have my flair for the lurid."

"So, we are only accused?"

"The impression I got is that accused is enough, any trial is going to be by combat."

"I think I can deal with that." Smiled Kevana.

"I believe the odds will be somewhere in the range of ten to one, against."

"I don't think that is exactly true to the conventions of trial by combat."

"I don't think they care about the conventions, they want you dead and the blue sword in their hands. You're not carrying it, do you have it?"

"No," snorted Kevana, "that's probably the worst part about all this, we don't actually have the damned sword, the people that found it took it, and they are going to use it to kill Zandaar, or so I think."

"Gentlemen, as a former commander of a city guard, I recognise you both as military, not religious, I ask that you both put your hands flat on the bar, I have a question to ask, and I need the extra heartbeat it will take for your hands to get back to your swords." Kevana and Alverana looked at one another, then Kevana slowly placed his hands as requested, Alverana followed suit.

"That makes me feel a little better." said Joe as his hands fell below the bar, completely out of sight. "Given your current position with your brethren, would it be a bad thing if this other group were successful?" Kevana and Alverana twitched, their shoulders dropping as their hands started to rise. Kevana blew out a long breath and placed his hands firmly on the bar.

"What weapon have you got under the bar?" he asked slowly. Joe's hands came up and placed a four-foot-long wooden club on the bar. Kevana looked at it and frowned, Alverana did the same for a moment then he started to laugh loudly.

"What's funny?" demanded Kevana, poking Alverana in the ribs with a stiffened finger.

"Joe wanted time," spluttered Alverana slowly getting his laughing under control, "but not for him, for us, look at that thing, he swings that on us and it is firewood, and he knows it, he wanted you to think before you drew sword on him."

"The question is still not answered?" Said Joe.

"I don't think it can be," replied Kevana, "but it will be held in mind, I may answer that one at a later date." Behind them the doorway darkened briefly as someone passed through it.

"Now, that one is a cleric." Muttered Joe.

"What's taking so long?" Demanded Worandana. "Are you two getting drunk on your own again?"

"We have important matters to discuss." Said Kevana, without looking back. "We are twelve."

"We have beds enough and more and stabling for twenty horses."

"Have you a yard or a paddock? We've got more than twenty horses."

"We have a yard inside the walls, and a relatively secure paddock outside, I'd unload them if they are carrying anything of value though."

"Now the price?" Asked Kevana.

"How does three horses sound?"

"Including food and drink?"

"Make that six, and I get to choose."

"Five, and you can choose any of the pack animals."

"Agreed." Joe reached forwards a hand to seal the deal, the two shook.

"Now," smiled Kevana, "Do you have a seamstress in this town somewhere?"

"Once you're settled in, I'll take you to old mother Handard, she does most of the dress making around here."

"We'll want something quick and simple, I'm thinking colourful capes, something that won't foul a sword."

"I'm sure she can manage, though speed is not normally her way."

"We need to be moving by the morning, so she's going to have a heavy night." He turned to Worandana, "Get the men moving we're staying here, he has stables and bed for us all," he turned back to the barman Joe, "Entrance around the back?"

"Aren't they always?" He turned to one of the two doors behind the bar, "Helen," he called, "Come watch the bar." A woman's head came around the door and nodded, the rest of her came into view. "Helen my dear," he went on, "there are a group of men of this ilk," he sneered in Kevana's direction, "they have a tab, for food and drink tonight and breakfast for tomorrow." He turned to Kevana. "If your men drink too much, I'll have to charge you an extra horse."

"There'll be precious little drinking going on tonight." Interrupted Worandana. Joe leaned towards Kevana and spoke in a stage whisper.

"See, I told you he was a cleric." Kevana smiled, Worandana did not. "Follow me gentlemen." Called Joe in a loud voice, a huge smile for Worandana as he passed.

It was some time later when Kevana and Joe returned to the bar, they found the men drinking beer slowly, and waiting for the evening meal to be served.

"How are we doing for gold?" He asked Worandana.

"We're doing all right I suppose, how are you doing?"

"Strange place this, the people know we have to be going in the morning so the price of clothing is sort of high, I can understand that because they are going to be working through the night, but the value of horses is almost nothing, we might be better taking them on to a busier town. The best price I've been offered is from the butcher, and that's not really worth taking, I've told him he can have five, that just about pays for the capes that are being made. Alverana will select the worst of the lot in the morning. We are going to look quite gaudy when we leave here tomorrow morning. That seamstress appears to be unloading some old stock that she's had around for years, but it's colourful so it will do."

"What do you mean by gaudy?" asked Kirukana.

"I don't really know how to explain this, I think the effect is somewhere between the browns and blues of a pheasant, and the glowing eyespots of a peacock." Kevana laughed aloud, many of the others joined in.

"I'm not at all happy about all this frivolity, our black clothing represents the simplicity of our faith, our adherence to the doctrines."

"Have no fear my friend," Kevana smiled, "as soon as anyone gets close enough to see your face, they will know who you are." He turned to the group in general. "Remember, these disguises will only work at a distance, our own people will recognise the rest of our equipment, and even our faces, but they may just give us the heartbeats advantage we need to stay alive. How's the beer here?"

"You my friend are quite presumptuous given our very short acquaintance." Laughed Joe, "The beer is good, the wine better, and the prices ridiculously low."

"We'll see about that in the morning, I'm still a little confused as to why you are being so helpful to a band of renegade churchmen?"

"We recently met a group of not so renegade churchmen, they knew themselves to be the best of their kind, they wanted supplies and would only pay in promissory notes, which have to be taken to a monastery to be honoured."

"Sounds to me like you met the hounds of Zandaar, they believe themselves to be the best, you should have told them gold or starve."

"Such was suggested, they said they'd burn the whole village to the ground, so we accepted their terms."

"Who holds these notes?"

"I do, I'm the most travelled person in the village, and I sometimes do go south, there is one of your monasteries that way, about three days ride."

Kevana turned to Worandana.

"Pay the man for his notes, we can cash them easier than he can."

"That will leave us dreadfully low on funds."

"We'll still have horses to sell, and maybe we'll chance upon the hounds, and collect their gold from their cold, dead hands."

"I'd rather not have to face them. But you are right about the notes, some abbots are loathe to pay expenses incurred by any not of their staff, they can get quite rude about it. They generally declare the papers forgeries and refuse to pay up. Sadly not all churchmen are as honest as they should be." Joe looked from one to the other, somewhat aghast.

"Joe," said Kevana, "fetch your notes, Worandana get the gold." Joe went behind the bar and disappeared into the back for a moment, while Worandana waved a quick hand signal to Apostana, who produced a heavy leather pouch from his belt, and passed it to the older man.

Joe came from behind the bar and passed three pieces of paper to Kevana. He read them carefully.

"Where they supplying a battalion?"

"No, a group about the same size as yours."

"Prices must be high here sometimes?"

"Prices fluctuate depending on how much the buyer irritates the seller, these pompous asses were really irritating."

"These amount to forty gold pieces, Worandana pay the man." Worandana looked hard at Kevana but didn't actually question him.

"Can you read what it says here?" Kevana asked Joe.

"Yes, it says pay the barer an amount when presented at a monastery."

"What about the section at the bottom?"

"He said that was a code to ensure these documents weren't forgeries."

Kevana passed the notes to Worandana, who looked at them briefly, then whispered one word. "Bastards."

"What is wrong?" demanded Joe.

"The code," said Kevana, "is written in a long dead language, that all Zandaars learn, in this particular case it tells the abbot to kill the barer and disappear the body. I agree with Worandana, not all churchmen are as honest as they should be."

"I also agree with Worandana," said Joe, "bastards." He looked slowly from one to the other, a deep frown on his face. It was a short while before he spoke softly.

"These notes are worthless, but still I have forty gold in my hands, why is this?"

"I believe," answered Kevana, after a moments glance to Worandana, who gave him the nod to proceed, "that churchmen should be totally honest in all their dealings, we should be the essence of all that is right, within the bounds of our faith, our dealings with outsiders should be above reproach. I shall present these papers to the council when we next meet and explain to them the errors of this sort of casual murder. We can't expect people to believe in us, if we behave in such a high-handed manner."

"Is that going to be before you butcher them all or after?" Asked Worandana.

"You have a point. I'll present them to the new council, not the one that declared us heretics, hopefully they will see things my way, if they don't then the next council might."

"If you plan on burning the council members, as appears to be common practice these days, then you're going to have to make some sort of deal with the elves for some forests, the men elected to the council not always the brightest, it may take more than a few re-elections to get the message across." Laughed Worandana.

"I'm thinking of a return to the fundaments of our faith, kneeling in front of a nice big block of wood, and a single stroke of a sword. Fires though pretty are wasteful and slow, I'm of an age where I really don't have time to waste on frivolities."

"An axe is more customary." Interjected Kirukana.

"I agree, but I have a sword not an axe."

"Unless it's done properly a sword can get messy, multiple strikes, sometimes the head doesn't come off clean, it's distressing for the soon to be departed." Laughed Alverana.

"Are you volunteering to be the axeman then?" Asked Kevana.

"Not as such, but if needed I can lend a hand or two, always better two handed."

"Suddenly I get a picture of a blue bladed longsword taking the heads of the council, and I'm in no way distressed by it."

"It does have a certain poetry." Laughed Worandana, then his head snapped around to the windows of the bar.

"How long till sunset?" He asked loudly.

"Not long," replied Joe, "not enough time for you to have another beer, but maybe enough for Alverana." He laughed. Worandana nodded.

"Anyone else feel a ripple in the other plane?"

"I felt something, but it was so small and fast I wasn't really sure." said Apostana, none of the other sensitives spoke up. Worandana thought for a moment, then called sharply. "Circle, now, just like this mornings, that ripple could have been searches launching, big ones. I want power and I want it fast." The locals were startled by the actions of the brothers, tables where pushed out of the way and their circle formed in only moments, Worandana took his place facing Kirukana. Then he spoke to the people.

"If there any sensitives present then you may see things that aren't real, you may hear things that aren't real, these things cannot in any way harm you, I ask that you remain as calm as you can and don't panic, now please relax." He took Kirukana's head in his hands and touched foreheads as they had in the morning. The first rush of power Worandana used to recreate the glade and the fire pit, the next only a moment later he used to build the female figure, fire and smoke all around. He hoped the attackers would arrive soon, it was quite strenuous holding this illusion, he didn't have to wait long, Axorana appeared, across the fire pit from the woman, the position of his hands almost made Worandana laugh, he was facing the inside of a circle, without speaking Axorana hurled a bolt of energy at the woman, she caught his power on her fire wreathed hands, and simply absorbed it. She threw back her head and howled with laughter.

"Is that the best you can do? The great and good of Zandaar. You gentlemen have lost your fire, you've lost your way, and soon you will lose your lives. Not necessarily at my hand, the auguries say that many of you will die before this thing is finished, the manner of your deaths is unclear, but it is certain." While the woman was speaking, Worandana watched the energy levels in Axorana rise with every pulse from his circle, he timed his counterattack to match the next pulse, the woman hurled a huge bolt of power straight at Axorana, with a howl the image of Axorana vanished. Worandana held the images for a few moments, waiting for a return, Axorana didn't come back, so he broke the contact with the circle and let the images fade.

"Did you kill him?" asked Kevana.

"I don't think so he was making too much noise as his circle collapsed, we may have harmed the weakest in the circle, it certainly fell apart quickly."

"What was all that about the auguries?" demanded Kirukana.

"I just had to keep him listening, I knew he would be building power while I was jabbering, his circle had a high rate, but not really much in the way of power, I had to get the timing right, but the trickster wasn't wrong, they have lost the fire. Forty years ago, with those sort of energy levels, they'd still be novices. Seems that standards are dropping even quicker than I thought."

"Did you kill any of them?" Kirukana was getting even more distressed.

"I can't say for sure, we might have killed one or injured a few, from the feel of things they don't seem to have much in the way of power handling abilities. They certainly don't deserve to be attacking the likes of us."

"But you could have killed some members of the council."

"We, you mean, we, and don't forget these are the men who set the hounds on us. They intend to kill us all, I'm not going down without a fight, and neither are you, get used to the idea."

"That's easy to say, I've been following these people all my life."

"And now they want to end that."

"That doesn't make rebellion any easier."

"Rebel not heretic?"

"Yes, definitely."

"Call yourself what you will, they still want us dead. The real question is why?"

"They think we have the sword. Are you finally losing your mind, old man?" asked Kevana.

"I'm going to explain a few things to them, I'm going to talk to Axorana right now, while he's still reeling from his contact with our trickster. Circle as before, only this time I want it really hot. I have enough of his pattern to go straight to him, this might be fun." The circle formed much slower this time, taking on the council directly was not what they wanted to do.

"Our new circle pattern will hide everyone but me from Axorana's view, he's in for a real surprise."

"Are you certain that he won't be able to see any of us?"

"Not completely, but he's going to be too busy to be looking for anyone else, form up and get the power building." Worandana paced the room slowly, as he watched the power build in the circle, each man in the circle glowed briefly as the power passed through him, the transfers were fast and the energy levels were high, as he stepped up to Kirukana he whispered, "Random." Then he took the next surge and launched into the other plane, using the mental pattern of Axorana he focused straight on the leader of the council, he established contact with such a ferocity that Axorana was momentarily stunned and he fell to the ground.

"Axorana." he yelled, driving the thought deep into the man's brain. "Wake up fool."

"Who are you to call me fool?"

"I am Worandana. Why are you trying to kill me and mine?"

"How do I know you are Worandana, all I see is white light?"

"That is all you will see, I ask again, why are you trying to kill me and mine? If you make me ask again, I'll fry your mind and talk to your successor."

"You have the sword and you plan to kill Zandaar with it."

"Wrong, and well, wrong. A man called Namdarin has the sword, he's a man who cannot die, and he is marching to Zandaarkoon to stick the sword in Zandaar's guts until the lights go out in Zandaar's eyes. Do you know why he is so set on this course?"

"I've never heard of him, who is he?"

"Just some simple farmer from the west, we burned his house down with his family inside it, now he's gonna do the same to ours. We don't have the sword, he does, call your damned dogs off, or we'll be forced to kill them all." Axorana paused before he asked.

"What do you know of the trickster?"

"We met her, she has something going on in these events, but as always with Gyara it is unclear."

"I just had a meeting with her, she set one of my men on fire, fried the brains of two more, and a further two have hands so badly burned we may have to amputate."

"Well I lost one, only one, Helvana died when she demonstrated her power. At least two of your men should have been holding hands better, a good grip transfers the power better, we all know that. We came up against one of your hunting parties only a couple of days ago, they all died bar one, he'll live if he's careful and lucky. We have no wish to kill any more of our brothers, their blood will be on your hands, and we will expect you to pay that price when we meet. Will you call the dogs off?"

"I can't, Zandaar himself sent them, his instructions were very vague, find and kill Kevana, Worandana, and any in their party, bring back the sword."

"We don't have the damned sword, and the party that do have it would eat the hounds for breakfast, now that is something I'd really like to see. You can't stop the hounds, but they are going the wrong way anyway, but will you call off the brothers?"

"I cannot, I have an instruction from Zandaar."

"You're a political animal find some interpretation that keeps our brothers alive, if you don't then you will certainly die when we get to Zandaarkoon, or perhaps even before, you do understand that I could have fried your brain as soon as I made contact?"

"I could do the same to you."

"No, actually you can't, you can't even find me, let alone identify me at distance, if you burn the world with black fire, then you might just get me, but I wouldn't count on that. The only way to be certain is a knife in the back, and you don't have the balls for even that. Call off the brethren, or the next time we meet, you die. I am Worandana high priest of the Zandaar, my word is my bond." Worandana broke the link with such brutality that Axorana fell to the ground again.

CHAPTER FIFTY-EIGHT

It was two days later as they were making camp for the night that Namdarin finally gave then the news they had been hoping for.

"I can sense horses." He said to Jangor. "We should meet them tomorrow, most likely in the afternoon."

"What sort of location can we expect to find?"

"Many horses in a small area, most likely a small village, or perhaps a garrison."

"A monastery?" Asked Gregor.

"No, I don't think so. It's too spread out, monasteries have stables, with all the horses together."

"A garrison would be the same as a monastery?"

"Not that I have seen, garrisons from my experience generally have the stables spread out. Tactically it's a good idea, stables have been known to catch fire."

"How many horses?" Jangor asked, nodding.

"Quite a lot, but it can be difficult to tell, horses don't actually count the way we do, I only get a feel for the numbers, when they are within sight of each other they have a better feel for the numbers, but it is only a feel. Horses are strange."

"Says the man who talks to them." Laughed Mander.

"At least we'll be able to unload some of these horses." Andel smiled.

"That will be a good thing." Said Jangor.

"At least one group of horses," Namdarin spoke softly, "appear to be in a field or large paddock, so it can't be a monastery, or a garrison, this is a village or a town at the most."

"Let's just hope that they are friendly." Mumbled Mander.

"The way our luck is running they are most likely to be cannibals." Andel laughed.

"That's right, look on the bright side." Stergin smiled.

"Fine." Said Jangor. "Usual watches, get some sleep, if we can get an early start, we might even find out about this village in time to get some lunch."

As the people retired to their respective tents Kern walked out of the camp, near to the picket line, but not close enough to disturb the horses, Wolf at his hip, he sat down to start the first watch of the night, listening to the sound of people preparing for bed. He was surprised when Brank came out of his tent, a blanket wrapped around his body, he stood by the fire for a moment before he walked slowly over to where Kern was sitting.

"Mind if I join you two, for some reason I can't seem to settle?"

"Of course, what is disturbing you?"

"I just can't get the brain to go to sleep, every time I close my eyes, I see pictures of raped and murdered children."

"That is understandable, those were some very bad sights to see, but we dealt with the perpetrators, and gave the dead a decent funeral, Xeron took care of them. We did everything that anyone could have expected of us."

"I understand all that, but I fear for my reaction should I see its like again."

"I know that my reaction will be exactly the same, rage, I do wonder how much pain I will be inflicting on those robbers, should I catch them alive."

"I worry that I'll either break down or become even worse than they are. I don't want to do that."

"No sane person would, I can't believe that those robbers were actually sane, there has to be some madness in them for them to do those things."

"I agree with you on that point at least, they have to be mad, but what caused it?"

"Perhaps simple greed, or the fact that they have been working outside any normal laws for far too long. Maybe a slow and steady decline in moral values, or a gradual erosion of the normal inhibitions. There is no way to know. We'll find out if we meet their like again, someone will talk to us."

"Whether they want to or not?"

"Definitely, we need to find out what causes this sort of madness, then we can hunt it down, and destroy it."

"I'm ready for some of that." Muttered Brank, as the two settled down to watch the night close in.

Namdarin and Jayanne were settled down in their tent, her head against his left shoulder, his right arm across her naked belly.

"How are you getting along with the idea of your new friends?" He asked quietly.

"It's different, but I begin to get the feeling that they are more than just men."

"They are men and much more, they are brothers in arms, this is the code they live and die by."

"I have been watching them carefully for the last couple of days, I've never really noticed it before, but now I see how they all work as a team, each knows where the others are and what they are doing. Is this part of their training?"

"Oh yes, it's a large part of the soldiers training, each depends on the others, sometimes they think and move like one large animal, the best armies that ever were had that sort of instinctive reaction to the world around them. These men are the best warriors I have seen in many a year. Jangor is the glue that keeps them all together. He's a very impressive man."

"I've noticed, even when he's standing next to Brank, he's still feels like a big man."

"But Brank takes big to an entirely new place." Laughed Namdarin.

"He's definitely built like a wall, solid, you know what I mean." She whispered.

"You have more experience of his hardness than I have."

She pulled her head away from his shoulder and looked into his eyes, now far enough away to come into sharp focus, after a moment she replied gently.

"Are you jealous?"

"Yes, no, and no, yes, I don't know. Sometimes I think he may be better for you than I am, he's more your age, he'll be a good protector, and damn him to hell, he's huge. Judging by Laura's reactions he's a good lover." Namdarin's voice trailed off.

"Are you saying you don't want me anymore?"

"Of course not."

"But you'd rather I was with him?" Her voice shook with emotion.

"No, by all the gods, no." His arm tightened across her ribs, he felt her heart pounding in her chest and the harshness of her breathing. "It's just that your life means more to me than you know, as this quest gets nearer to its end, I begin to realise how much your survival means to me, if everyone else dies in this, you must live. My life is already forfeit, or so it feels to me, I can think of no one better to look after you once I am gone."

"If your life is over, then so is mine, such I have sworn in my heart of hearts, you have showed me how to live and how to love, and together we will learn how to die. Perhaps I should go and challenge him, let Algoron decide."

"Could you do that?"

"No," she barked, "he is as a sister to me, I couldn't harm him, and you damned well know it." A small smile softened her face.

"Nor could I." His smile bigger, his large right hand reached up and pulled her face slowly to his, the kiss burned hot and long. His hand slid slowly down her body, over her large breasts and down her belly, as it entered the hair on her mound her legs opened slightly, the hand moved down to cup her completely.

It was fully dark when Namdarin heard a voice softly calling his name. It was Brank.

"Come on Namdarin, your turn for the watch."

"I'll be out in a minute or two." Muttered the older man, hoping that he wouldn't wake the tired Jayanne, he rolled slowly out of the warm and damp blankets, snatched up his clothes and made his way outside, the cold of the night chilled him quickly, as he watched Brank crawl into his tent, across the fire. Dressing quickly against the chill of the night, Namdarin moved slowly away from the camp, so that the dying embers of the fire wouldn't disturb his night vision. Slowly as his eyes became accustomed the starlight began to pick out more than just shapes and shade, not enough light for colours to come out, but enough to see by, the dark of a nearby copse stood out ominously against the mountain side behind, the rock formations almost glowing in the subdued light. Wolf came out of the dark, his eyes glowing yellow, he dropped down beside Namdarin.

"You found anything interesting to do tonight?" Asked Namdarin, the canine just looked at him, Namdarin smiled, then chuckled softly, thinking of an observer in the night seeing a man holding a conversation with a wolf. He reached out and ruffled the wolf's ears, and his mind turned to the task ahead. Currently his plan was simple, walk up to Zandaar and stick the sword in him. Anything else would have to be ad-libbed in the moment.

"It's not much of a plan, is it?" He asked of the wolf, not really expecting any answer.

"You'll need to think of something better than that." Came a distant voice on the wind, like the rustling of dried leaves in the winter.

"Who's there?" Muttered Namdarin looking around, Wolf

looked at him, then lowered his head to rest on his forepaws, if not to sleep, at least he had no sense of alertness. Namdarin looked round, there was open ground all around, no one could have got close enough to whisper so quietly and still be heard. He launched his mind and rushed into the consciousness of the horses, he merged so fast with them that all of them spooked a little, no horses close by, only the distant ones sleeping now in the village. 'Am I going mad?' he thought to himself.

"Madness is like so many things, relative." A dry laugh filled his mind.

'Now I'm starting to worry.'

"Insanity is not the most important thing for you to be thinking about right now." Amusement so clear in the distant voice.

'Well, who are you?'

"That also is of no importance."

'So what is important to you?'

"Not me, you. You need to think about things you already know, and things you have heard recently. Old facts and new, that fit together in a certain way."

'You'll need to give me more information than that.'

"I can't there are rules, as you well know."

'Sadly Zandaar doesn't play by anyone's rules but his own.'

"There will be a price for him to pay for those breaches, but you'll not have to pay, because I'll not tell you anything that you don't already know."

'You tell me I already know everything that I need, but won't give me any hints as to how to put this information together?'

"Sadly that is correct, but I do know this, and I can tell you this, you will come into the full knowledge by the time you really need it. I would like to say that you have nothing to fear, but I can't, there are still many ways this can go wrong, right up to the very last moment. You need to trust yourself and your friends. Together you will find a way." The voice faded and Namdarin knew that whoever this was, was gone.

"Now that was strange." He said to Wolf, who only looked up for a moment before going back to sleep. Namdarin's thoughts turned inwards again, looking for any hint at the knowledge that would help him to defeat Zandaar when the time came. There was nothing for him to find, or so he thought as he chased the ideas round and round in circles inside his head. One thing that just kept on coming to the fore, was the words that Grinderosch had spoken as he died, 'Something moves in the darkness, this way it comes.'

"I wonder what it can be, this terror that comes?" He asked of Wolf, barely an ear twitch by way of a response. Namdarin became distracted by the thoughts chasing circles in his mind, so he slowly stood, and walked away from the camp, for a little way then started a slow patrol, looking for something to distract him from the turmoil within. As he passed the picket lines, Arndrol stamped himself awake, and watched as his friend passed by, slowly his head dropped and he returned to that restful state that all horses specialise in, asleep, but only an instant from full wakefulness. Namdarin's slow and very quiet walk brought him within sight of a small group of fallow deer, three does and two kids, he looked carefully around expecting a buck to be somewhere near, no sign. Suddenly something spooked the deer, and they vanished in a flourish of flashing white tails. Namdarin looked around, he knew it wasn't him that had frightened them, then he saw the great yellow eyes of wolf, the scent of the great predator had reached the deer and put them to flight. Wolf came padding over to stand beside the man, together they listened to the sound of the small hooves of the deer as they raced off to safety.

"Not hungry enough to chase them?" He asked. Wolf sat and yawned hugely in the darkness, Namdarin wondered briefly how his jaws could open that wide, without his head falling into two parts. He laughed for a moment before continuing his patrol, approaching a small gully a growl from Wolf alerted him to some sort of danger, though he couldn't identify it yet, then out of the gloom of the gully bottom came a wide bustling shape, akin to an ambulating rug.

"Don't mess with that wolf, it's almost as tough and angry as you." He laughed, getting hold of a large handful of the wolfs mane. "It's a badger, they can be very dangerous, they don't see too well, but their sense of smell is great, they tend to be bad tempered, so leave it alone." A second badger appeared, shorter but wider.

"Time to leave wolf." Namdarin pulled Wolf away from the foraging pair, hoping that the smell of people would keep them away from the camp, but you can't always be sure of badgers, they can be more than a little belligerent. Continuing their patrol, they found nothing else of any interest, other than the passing of time. Wolf caught an unwary rat and swallowed it in two bites. The horses were quiet at their pickets, nothing big enough to disturb them had been near. Namdarin returned to his seat on the small rise, and stroked Wolf as he settled down alongside.

"Sometimes, you know," said the man, "the worst part of night watch is the fact that nothing happens."

Wolf just looked up at him.

"Well, strange voices, and badgers. Almost nothing." He smiled and settled in for another hours quiet watching. Together they watched one of the minor moons set, the temperature continued to drop steadily as their watch progressed, the grass became covered in dew that sparkled in the light of the major moon, when it found its way between the intermittent cloud cover. Namdarin was just thinking of waking someone else to take the last of the night, when Mander came into view, he walked slowly over to Namdarin.

"Anything exciting?" He asked.

"Nothing worth talking about, some badgers over that way, but nothing else."

"I'll take over, for a while at least, you know what Jangor is like for taking the last watch."

"I'll get a little sleep. See you in a little while." Namdarin walked over to his tent, and quickly vanished inside. He stripped off his clothes and slipped into bed behind Jayanne, pressing himself up against the furnace of her heat, gradually his mind settled down into a trance like state, he decided it was time to practice the dream war techniques that his enemies were so adept at, his mind reached out tendrils of thought feeling around for dreams to invade, he soon entered a dream, a man was walking through a narrow cave into a small library, this was obviously Granger, he was accompanied by a tall woman, with red hair, though to Namdarin she didn't look too much like Jayanne, even though he knew that was the only person it could have been. The man's eyes focused on the curve of her breasts, and they became bigger and more prominent, the nipples standing hard against the cloth of her thin shirt. His gaze turned to the narrowness of her waist and the flare of her hips; these were both enhanced as he watched. The man was rummaging through books on the rickety table, but his mind was focused on the triangle of hair at the junction of her thighs, he couldn't actually see it, but he knew it was red and luxurious, and as he thought of it it almost glowed with redness and warmth. As he picked on a page from one of the books, he noticed that the crotch of her pants shone with a deep amber light. Namdarin felt a surge of jealousy, but that was followed rapidly by guilt, this was a friend's dream, and he really shouldn't be here. Unheard words were exchanged between the woman and the man, his staff sent a stream of blue light into the axe, and a surge of white energy shot upwards from the axe, Namdarin's dream presence followed it, upwards into the dark it streamed, out past the moons it raced, on into the darkness it flowed, a tremendous outpouring, until it vanished into a solid darkness, the darkness heaved and twitched, it roiled and turned, it was black against black, but it's darkness had a different texture than the space it was in, it's huge shape slowly resolved in front of Namdarin's eyes, it became like a bat, a central body, with two large leathery wings, there it's resemblance to a flying mouse ended, even without anything to judge it's size against, Namdarin knew it was huge, so enormous that no wings could ever have carried it's weight in air, not without some magic to drive them. It turned towards the energy surge, as the bright shaft stuttered and died. It's eye's dim red coals in the dark, it caught sight of Namdarin's glowing nimbus, the man turned and fled, back the way he had come, in a heartbeat he returned to the centre of Granger's dream and broke out of it with a hot surge of his own power. He woke shaking with the cold, and reached out to the hilt of his sword, letting a portion of its energy heat him, and settle his shaking nerves.

Jayanne's naked form pushed backwards against him, adding to his personal warmth in a way that he found very distracting. He settled down slowly as if to go to sleep, knowing that dawn would be coming fairly soon, just as he reached the boundaries of sleep, he heard quiet voices. He couldn't quite make out what they were saying, though his name was mentioned at least once. He ignored them and let sleep take him. It seemed to be only moments later that Jangor's not so quiet voice shattered all their dreams and pulled them back into the land of the living.

While they were eating Granger came to talk to Namdarin.

"Did I feel you in my dream last night?"

"Yes." Namdarin looked down, trying not to feel guilty.

"Did you find anything important there?"

"Why do you ask?"

"Because something pulled me into that dream, it felt like it was important, so I went along with it, it was from the time in my cave, when I forced the axe to tell me who it was. It took a tremendous amount of power."

"And I now know where that power went."

"That must be important, please tell me."

"It was something dark and sleeping in the spaces between the stars, that bolt of energy woke it, it turned towards me, it was like a bat, only far bigger, huge wings, all of it midnight black, except for the eyes, small and glowing like the dying coals of a fire."

"Oh my, that doesn't sound good at all."

"Worse still, I felt it's hunger, a deep and ravening cavern of a hunger. It's coming this way to feed."

"That's what Grinderosch meant. Something moves in the darkness. I may know something about this thing, I think it was called Glard, it was banished many years ago, by the old gods, perhaps it now knows that they are almost gone, and want to try out the new gods."

"Do you think they have the power to banish this Glard creature?"

"No, they don't have that sort of strength. We're going to have to deal with Glard as well as Zandaar."

"I'm not at all sure I like that idea, we have enough to do with killing one god. What is this Glard anyway?"

"No one knows what Glard is, it's thought to be from that time before time, it's so old, the tale goes that it came with its all-encompassing hunger for life, and the old gods banded together to banish it. This is a story so old that it comes down through time as a fairy-tale sort of thing. Glard is the essence of the monster under the bed, something to frighten children with, not something that turns up every day."

"So why now?"

"You could look on this as a good sign, once Glard is here, and all the old gods, then in some way they can all come to an end and leave us here to get on with our lives without their interference."

"Alternatively," muttered Namdarin, "Glard swallows all life, and only Gyara walks away."

"That could be what Gyara is hoping for, but if we woke Glard, then how can the Zandaars be involved in making the end come so that Gyara can leave?"

"There is something else that must be done to release Gyara, and either group can do it. I have no idea what it is. I believe that only Gyara knows, and she also knows that if she tells us, then we'll avoid doing it at any cost."

"Just to recap," smiled Namdarin, "we have to kill one god, so the others can leave, and kill or banish a creature from the time before the gods, and stop Gyara from ending all life so she can leave, am I correct?"

"Pretty much." Nodded Granger.

"This day just keeps on getting better. And another thing, your dream self was looking very lustfully at Jayanne."

"Hey, it was my dream you invaded, and I'm old, not dead." He smiled. Granger walked slowly away to help with the dismantling of the camp. It wasn't very long before they were back on the road, Kern setting a good pace, Namdarin directing then towards the horses grouped in the village or town.

It was only just afternoon when they started riding through the sort of cultivated fields that normally surround villages and towns. The field boundaries quickly guided them to the roads that the people used every day. They came over a small rise in the road, and ahead of them they saw a large open valley, the river glinting in the afternoon sun, heading in a roughly southward direction, though it meandered across a wide flood plain, much of this had been converted to rice paddies, there were people working in them, harvesting the rice at this time of year was an arduous task at best, but the wind was enough to keep the worst of the biting insects at bay. On the sides of the fields where the people were working there were torches burning smokily, such that the smoke blew across the fields, presumably some effort to keep the mosquitoes away, how well it worked Namdarin wondered but couldn't guess. Jangor hauled hard on his reins and stopped the entire column.

"Listen up." He called. "We want to make the best impression we can going into this town, let's try and look like real soldiers for a change. Front rank, Namdarin, Jayanne, Granger, second myself, Brank and Gregor, third, Kern and Stergin, then the pack horses, finally Mander and Andel. Yes gentlemen you get the shit end of the stick again, no bitching. I want a fast rolling trot, not too fast to frighten them, but not slow enough to give them too much time to organise. Questions?" He paused for barely a heartbeat, before going on. "I thought not. Move out." Namdarin heeled Arndrol and set the pace, Jayanne fell in to his right and Granger to his left, Jangor dropped in behind Namdarin, with Brank to his left and Gregor to his right. He didn't bother to glance backwards because he knew that his instructions would be followed to the letter. As they approached the first buildings of the village. Jangor spoke up above the sounds of the horses.

"I see a green area in the centre, we'll form up there to camp and meet our hosts, magicians, if you can spare a little of your blue fire, just to let these strangers know who they are dealing with, that would be appreciated." Immediately small blue fires appeared at the end of each upright staff. Jangor smiled softly to himself, he thought for a moment or two about how much easier these people made his life, sometimes blank shields entering a new village had a very rough time. Then he thought about how dangerous his life was now, and in addition actually exciting. They rode down what Jangor took to be main street, and he laughed loudly. Each house they passed, that fronted the street had a walled or fenced garden behind, the walls simply to mark out people's property, not enough to be defensive in any way. Namdarin led them round the green once, and then they formed up beside the lake to make camp. They had barely dismounted when people came running across the green towards them. They were armed, but no swords were drawn, there were quite a few of them, and more were arriving steadily. A large man in the lead, who was struggling to run, but having no problem staying at the front of the obviously fitter and younger men.

"Who are you people and what do you want here?" He shouted as he stumbled to a stop only yards from Namdarin.

"We are travellers, passing through, looking to trade for supplies, and in the morning, we will be gone. Is there some problem here we can help you with?" Jangor said pushing his way to the fore. Brank and Kern stood with him.

"I am Brass elected headman here. You are?" A snigger from behind Brass brought a sharp stare, when Brass looked back at Jangor, the soldier smiled.

"I am Jangor, these are my friends, we mean you and yours no harm, we wish to trade and move on."

"Why have you brought a wolf into our town?"

"You have nothing to fear from Wolf, he's very well behaved. You don't mind us camping on your green, do you? There must be a tavern in a town this size, we could do with some food we haven't cooked ourselves?"

"I have only your word for the behaviour of that animal."

"My word is considered good in many places, you just haven't met me before."

"If you vouch for the behaviour of your men and that animal, then I suppose you can stay."

"Woman." Called a new voice from behind Brass, as a man pushed through the crowd. "Why are you riding my wife's horse?" The tension in the crowd rose quite considerably. Jayanne passed her reins to Namdarin, swung her leg over the horse and slid to the ground. Namdarin hit the ground only a second later, he passed her reins to Arndrol to hold. As Jayanne walked slowly towards the man wolf paced alongside her left hip, Namdarin only half a stride behind her. She faced the man and spoke calmly.

"If she was your wife, who was the wine merchant?"

"My brother, and what do you mean was?"

"The children?"

"Mine, what do you mean was?"

"You know exactly what I mean. We came upon them a couple of days ago, we spent half a day consigning their bodies to the fire, we didn't know who they were or where they were from, we assumed they were a family, so we burned them along with the retainers that had been travelling with them and those of the robbers that they had killed before they were taken. Xeron himself came to collect their souls, they are in good hands."

"How do we know you didn't just kill them for their horses?"

"Why was the wine merchant travelling with a cart full of bottled wine, and a strongbox full of gold?"

"My wife wanted one of those fancy elven horses, my brother has contacts in Breewood, elves prefer their wine in bottles to casks, he was hoping to make a deal for a horse."

"Who else knew of his mission?" Demanded Jayanne.

"No one, only Brass, he advised me which roads they should use, as there are brigands up in the hills."

Jayanne turned to Brass.

"What of these so-called robbers?" Brass said loudly.

"Dead to a man." Whispered Jayanne. "Some worse than dead." Brass seemed more than a little shaken.

"All dead." He muttered, shaking his head in disbelief.

"Not true." Shouted a voice from the back of the crowd. "Brass's cousin came home this morning riding a half dead horse." Jayanne looked at Brass, he seemed even more shaken than ever. Jayanne fell to her knees and threw an arm over Wolfs shoulder.

"Remember the fire, remember the dead, remember the smells of the killers, one of them is here, find him and hold him." She released the canine and he started to force his way through the crowd, it didn't take Wolf long to identify the man, he was the one running like all the demons from hell were on his heels. He wasn't too far wrong, he made it almost to the edge of the green before Wolf hit him in the back, and knocked him to the ground, then wolf took him by the throat, and almost dared him to move. The deep growl was more than enough to keep the others away, none came to the man's defence. Jayanne pushed her way slowly through the crowd and walked over to the fallen man. Namdarin, Granger and Jangor came with her. She stood over the man.

"Good job Wolf." she stroked his mane, but didn't tell him to let go, she turned to the prone man.

"Your choices are simple, tell us why and you get a clean death at the jaws of Wolf, don't tell us and the axe takes your soul."

"I can't speak with this wolf at my throat." The man whispered.

"Then die." Jayanne's reply was flat and without any emotion.

"We were sent to kill them and bring half the gold back here for Brass. No survivors was the only instruction."

"Did you kill them?"

"No, that black magician started hurling fire and lightning around and I fell to the ground and hid."

"So, who took pleasure in the rape and torture of children?"

"Not I, I had a go on the woman, but not the children, I couldn't do that."

"But you didn't stop them, did you?"

"No, they'd have killed me."

"You didn't even speak out against them, did you?"

"No." He whispered.

"Where the children and the woman still alive when they were impaled on the swords?"

"Yes."

"Have you made your peace with your gods?"

"Yes."

"Wolf kill him." Her quiet words were the exact opposite of wolf's actions, with a snap of the jaw and a twist of the heavy shoulders the man's head came clean away. Wolf sat back on his haunches, blood dripping from his chin, and howled. This song was joined by every dog in the village, from the largest of the hunting hounds to the tiniest lap dog, it took considerable time for the dogs to settle down again.

Jayanne walked back through the crowd, though they separated to give her space, and the wolf walking at her hip. By the time she got back to the centre Brass had accumulated five men, they stood around him with swords drawn. The crowd of villagers fell back quite a way, more than enough to give the newcomers space to do battle on the men.

"You men." Called Jayanne. "You have chosen to stand with the child slaughterer, your lives are forfeit, but they are for the people of this place to take, not me. Brass on the other hand will give his soul to Algoron today." Silence fell on the crowd, nothing moved, the five swordsmen stood ready to take on any that approached. From somewhere in the crowd a single bow thrummed, an arrow took one of the men in the leg, and he staggered but did not fall. Another arrow flew into the five men, and another, slowly the bowmen came to the front of the crowd, making their shooting easier. More arrows buried themselves in the bodies of the men.

"Remember Brass is mine." Called Jayanne, these bowmen were hunters, they didn't miss. The last of the swordsmen fell when Brass could no longer hold him up as a shield against the arrows. The bows were all lowered.

"I have family all over this land, they will hunt you down and kill you all." Yelled Brass.

"People of this village." Jayanne shouted. "Remember today, the day you stood together against the bullies and rapists and child killers. Brass you are wrong, you may have family all across this land, but it is me that is doing the hunting and I will kill them all."

She walked into the cleared space the axe swinging nonchalantly in her right hand, Brass bent and picked up two swords, both far too long for him to wield in any effective way, but he was such a swordsman that he didn't understand that. He swung a huge overhand blow at Jayanne's head, she caught it on the flat of the blade, and the sword leapt from Brass's hand and spun away, the other sword was in his left hand and he couldn't even lift it. She stepped in close and swung the axe in on an upward trajectory, it caught him low in the gut, and cut upwards through his huge belly, separating into to hemispheres that slowly split apart, blue and pink intestines flowing outwards, to tangle around his feet, there was little blood as the axe drank it all, it was jammed in his ribcage, not high enough to stop his heart, the axe was hungry it wanted it all. The dreadful sound of its feeding filled the green, as it sucked the life, the blood, and finally the soul from the former headman. A dried-up husk of sticks and skin fell into the steaming pile of intestines. She turned towards the villagers, wolf came running up to her, and he placed his front paws on her shoulders then gripped her jaw in his teeth, for a moment before he fell back to the ground, Namdarin Jangor and Brank were moving in quickly in case things became dangerous. Only one of the villagers had the bravery to walk into that empty space, his neighbours were aghast, gasps and muttering voices were heard behind him, Wolf growled, Brank turned, his hand on his sword hilt, the man stopped, the crowd fell silent again, not even breathing.

Jayanne waved him forwards, Wolf watched, Brank watched the crowd, dreading to see the tip of a tensed bow above the heads of the people. The only bows visible were the longbows fashionable all over, and they were so low that they must have their other end resting on the ground. The man arrived in front of Jayanne.

"I am Steel. Did the killers of my family die like this?" he glanced down at the remains on the ground.

"Some." She answered, "Wolf got a couple, Brank and Kern got some, they didn't all get the full treatment, I was rushed, and there were many of them."

"You attacked many men because they killed my family?"

"No. They attacked us without any provocation, or warning, I was angry, very angry."

"But you killed them all?"

"Yes, I said angry, they killed my horse, but that didn't stop me. How did that one get away, there were no horses around, we captured them all."

"Ah, that particular man has a problem, he can't ride horses, they don't like him, mules, on the other hand are not so sensitive."

"That explains something, I am sorry that we weren't there to protect your family when they needed us."

"I wasn't there either. Not that I'd have been much use against armed robbers."

"Your village did well today, they stood together, and that is all it takes sometimes. I need a bath, Brass suggested there may be an inn?"

"There is such an establishment, but it belongs to Brass, belonged I should say."

"It is yours now, I have no need of such a thing, I don't believe that any will complain about the new management."

"His family may turn up to claim the place."

"If they do, explain to them what he did, and how he and his men died. I'm fairly sure the opposition will fade away if they have any sense at all."

"There is something I want to know and don't want to know at the same time."

"How your family died?" Steel nodded.

"Take my word for it you don't want to know. Rest assured they died in agony and fear, but they are at peace now. All those involved are now dead."

"That will have to be enough for me then, it seems I have an inn of sorts, and I'm sure it has a bath house fit for a lady such as yourself."

"I am getting a little bored of being called a lady by men who are frightened of me."

"All men are frightened of you, at least the ones who have met you." Steel smiled and took her arm to walk her across the green into the village.

"Why Steel?" she asked.

"Mother wanted me to be a blacksmith, but I have much more aptitude for the growing of vines and the brewing of wine. My brother was a trader, a real dealer, for some reason people just loved to deal with him, and he always made plenty of profit. His last trip he was carrying two years profits and most of this year's best wine. And now I am alone." His voice cracked, as he thought of his wife and children.

"You have a new business to run, and new challenges to face, you're not too old to start again."

"I don't think I can face that, the prospect of losing them all over again, that's even more painful than I feel right now."

"They are with Xeron now, I watched him reach down and gather them up. They can feel no more pain, other than their separation from you. And that will pass in due time, once you go to join them."

They stepped off the green into what passed for main street, only a few buildings down the street stood what could only be the local inn. A large veranda with tables and chairs. Jayanne pointed at the sign board that hung on one corner of the veranda.

"That's a little unusual for an inn, that is more often for a very different business." Three large balls hanging from a crosspiece.

"Yes." said Steel. "Normally a pawnbroker's sign, and that is most likely where Brass made his money, he wasn't exactly scrupulous, but he always had cash for people with problems and collateral to put up for it. If I can find all his records, I'm going to make a few people very happy around here. He did have a tendency of charging just more interest than people can repay within the time allotted. Though my own business has taken somewhat of a hit."

"I'm sure you will recover, and I'll have a word with Jangor, I'm sure he'll release a good portion of your gold from our war fund."

"That would be great, though to be truthful I have no call on it now."

"Let's go inside and explain things to your staff." She crossed the veranda and strode in through the front door.

Both Steel and Wolf a step behind her.

"Who's in charge here." She shouted.

"While Brass is away, I am, what's it to you?" Snarled a large man behind the bar. Wolf growled, low and loud.

"You need to be more polite, you're upsetting my friend here and that never goes well. Am I clear?" The doorway behind her suddenly went dark, but she already knew who was there. Brank, flanked by Namdarin and Jangor.

"I don't care about your friends, this is Brasses place, and what he says goes."

"That would be a was." She smiled, Steel laughed softly, Wolf still growled.

"What you mean was? And take that damned hound out of here or I'll turn it into a rug." Wolf's growl stopped, and he looked up at Jayanne, her green eyes caught his yellow ones.

"Number one." Her voice like ice, without looking up. "Brass is dead. Number two, Wolf. Hold." Her eyes left the wolfs and went straight to the barman, Wolf cleared the bar in a single bound, knocked the man to the ground, stood on his chest snarling. The man was frozen in fear. Jayanne leaned over the bar and looked down into his wide brown eyes.

"If you move he'll take your head, it won't be the first one in this town today." Wolf's jaws snapped shut with a resounding clack so close to the man's nose that he felt the wolfs hairy lips.

"I understand." He mumbled.

"We uncovered one of Brasses more unpleasant schemes today, so I challenged him to single combat, he lost, he died. By right of conquest all his goods are now mine, I have gifted them to Steel, he who lost most to Brasses confederates. Your choices are limited today, and for a very short time today, your best option is to tell us everything you know about Brasses nefarious activities, and prove that you had no part in them, then you can stay and prove yourself to be a model citizen, second tell us everything and prove that you were coerced into taking part, then you leave today and never return, in all other circumstances you die, am I clear?"

"I for one wouldn't miss him too much." said a voice from the doorway, the locals were starting to return from the spectacle on the green. "Nor I, he's a bit of a mean bastard. There are more of Brasses lackies around you know." said a third.

"Well you can deal with those yourselves, but this one, he disrespected Wolf." Jayanne snarled.

"I can't believe that anyone would disrespect such a

magnificent glorious killer." Said the first voice.

"He's truly beautiful, but not long on patience." Replied voice two. Jayanne glanced at them, and they smiled, but came no closer, effectively blocking the door.

"I'm very sorry I upset your wolf, he's a wonderful animal, and he's slobbering all over my neck." The barman quaked without moving any more than absolutely necessary.

"He's looking for lunch." Said voice one, a glance from Jayanne made the man smile.

"He holds my note." Said the barman. "I borrowed money for doctors for mother, now I work for Brass for free, he just keeps paying the doctor bills, while she lives, he owns me, when she dies, so does he."

"Too late he's dead, I thought I told you that."

"I won't believe that until I see his corpse for myself, I've made that promise to myself so many times, I won't give it up until I know for sure."

"His corpse isn't much to look at, barely recognisable really." Said voice one.

"Except for that huge pile of guts." Said voice two.

"You two really aren't helping you know." She said to the men by the door.

"I know," replied the first, "but we're having fun." She turned back to the barman.

"Wolf let him up, you, go view the corpse. You two." She turned to the men by the door again. "Be useful, take him there bring him back, if he runs tell me, Wolf hasn't had a good run for a few days." The barman came around the end of the bar with Wolf right behind him.

"Is he really dead?" He asked.

"Very." She replied tersely.

"He runs a large band of robbers nearby you know?"

"That would be another was. Wolf killed the last of them on the green today."

"You killed them all?"

"I was angry, Wolf got a couple, Brank and Kern the same. But yes, I killed most of them."

"Steel's family?"

"They were dead when we found them, you knew?"

"I heard, but who was I going to tell?"

"View your corpse, we have things to talk about." The barman nodded and walked towards the door, where the two men waited for him.

"Brank, guard the door we have things to talk about, only the barman gets back in, keep those comedians out if they come back." Brank nodded and stood just inside the door with his arms folded across his chest. A glare was enough to keep most away.

CHAPTER FIFTY-NINE

Axorana struggled slowly to his feet, his second helped him and asked.

"What happened?"

"I've just been contacted by Worandana, directly, right here into our home, he attacked me here, that is not acceptable. We need to call the brethren off them, I want to know where they are, and only where they are. Worandana says they don't have the sword, some farmer from the west has it."

"My lord, the searchers are all out, they won't return until they are out of energy."

"Once they return, I want every troop commander contacted in person, and told to back the hell off Worandana, is that clear?"

"That may not be possible, they'll all be very tired." The second put an arm around Axorana and helped him walk back into his inner sanctum, the smell of burning flesh had almost dissipated.

"I don't care how tired they are, they get there asses out there and warn the brothers. I don't believe that I can stress this enough, I got half my first team incapacitated by the damned trickster, then I'm attacked in my own hallway, by one of my own men, and he tells me that if he has to kill any more of his brothers then he's going to hold me responsible and kill me for it. So, you get the word out, if searchers have to die here, I don't care. This Worandana is completely crazy, he says they've already killed one of our hunting parties, he says the hounds are looking in the wrong place, and that he is the high priest of Zandaar. He's mad, and he's coming to kill me."

"Don't worry my lord, we'll get the word out, but how can he know all these things?"

"I have no idea, the only thing I can be sure of is that he knows more than we do, he even identified himself as the high priest of Zandaar."

"How can that be?"

"I have no idea, get me some protection, I want heavy barriers up around this building immediately, he's not getting inside again."

"If you put the barriers up, then we can't get out, we need to know what is going on out there."

"Right, barriers around my chambers, and you can escort me there right now."

"Of course, my lord, I shall keep you informed as to the progress of the call off, it's going to take all night because there are a lot of groups out there. Why don't we just counterattack Worandana, you have his pattern now?"

"I cannot believe that he would leave himself open like that, the bastard knows far too much."

"I thought it was impossible to hide one's pattern, it is ones identity."

"That is what is taught, but I am certain that Worandana knows far more than we do, a long way beyond the standard texts. The feeling that I get is that to pursue that pattern would lead one into a blind alley with no escape, no I'll not follow him there."

"Is he really the high priest of Zandaar?"

"I believe that Zandaar himself once called him such, it was quite a few years ago, but he had performed some great service, I can't remember what, but Zandaar was impressed."

"Is he that good?"

"Oh yes, and much more, he works outside the standard texts, he knows much that is discouraged, if not actually forbidden, worse than that he knows many things that would be forbidden if we knew about them."

"So, he is a heretic, and should be denounced as such."

"You go find him and lay the charges against him. His people will eat the likes of you for breakfast. His soldiers will step over your corpse in a heartbeat. No, he may be a heretic, but no one will challenge him. Unless you want to do that?"

"No, I think I'll let Zandaar take care of them when they get here."

"If they get here, we have no authority to recall the hounds, they'll keep on hunting them, or die in the attempt."

"I shall make it as you request, I'll arrange for priests skilled in blocking to surround your chambers and I'll make sure that word gets out to the hunting parties, before the night is over, I do suggest that you don't ask anything of the searchers tomorrow."

"Fine, just make sure I am protected."

"What did Axorana have to say for himself?" asked Kevana, as the circle dispersed, and the tired monks took whatever seats they could find.

"They believe we have the sword and plan to kill Zandaar with it."

"Did you manage to disavow them of this belief?"

"I think so, he explained that he'd had a meeting with Gyara and had one man set on fire, two more with their brains fried, and two more with serious burns to their hands. I told him that Gyara only killed one of mine. I think he was impressed. He said that he would call off the brethren, I don't believe he'll recall them, just rescind the kill on sight command, he'll still want to know where we are, he can't stop the hounds though."

"We'll still need our disguises, those few moments that the hounds are unsure will help us enormously."

"Agreed. I'm really surprised how much damage we did to his group." Worandana grinned.

"We seemed to have found a very efficient way of doing battle, but don't forget, a bad grip can cause all sorts of strange resonances in a circle. Did you get any side thoughts as to how much of his party was damaged?"

"I have no idea, but it felt like a large portion, there was something in the back of his mind about needing a lot more people. He was turned inwards as well."

"So, he can't trust his group enough to be turned outwards in the direction he is travelling. With more people he'll trust them even less, this seriously affects the efficiency of the group."

"Hang on." Interrupted Kirukana. "You were turned inwards, I was the one turned away from the circle."

"I had no circle, nor any strong hands to hold on to. As far as Axorana was concerned I was talking to him with my own power. He was frightened, personally he carries so little power that he'd barely be able to reach the other plane. There was a time when the leaders were chosen for their strength, and skill. Now they seem to simply be politicians, they don't engender trust, they rule by fear, which is no way to strengthen a team of people."

"And you don't?" Laughed Kirukana.

"I suppose my team are a little afraid of me, but they do know they can trust me to die alongside them, could you trust Axorana in that way?"

"I wouldn't trust that man to stand behind me." Snapped Kirukana.

"What would happen if a man like him tagged himself onto this group?"

"He'd never do that, he'd have to bring so many guards that nothing would get done. If he came on his own, then he'd have one of those riding accidents you have threatened me with."

"Yes, but you have learned such a lot, you've come a long way."

"I can't say that I have enjoyed the process."

"I think you are a much better person because of it, you've learned to think for yourself, not just follow the dogma. I'm not saying there is anything wrong with dogma, it's good for keeping people in line, but not good for us that have to walk outside the lines. Do you understand?"

"I understand far more than is comfortable."

"Sometimes comfort is not a survival trait."

"Enough." Interrupted Kevana. "What are we going to do now?"

"Simple," smiled Worandana, "we carry on as planned, head for Angorak, find the thieves, kill them and take the sword back to Axorana, you can decide what to do then."

"If I decide to kill that fool, then what?"

"We'll have no problems with Axorana, or his guards, but the response from the others, may take a while, but it will come."

"Any response will be weak and disorganised. We'll be ready for them, I foresee no problems we can't deal with."

"I agree," said Kirukana, "the other factions will be too frightened to take any direct action, they'll just make peaceful noises, while planning to stab you in the back. You will notice that in the council chamber only one chair has a solid back." He laughed loudly.

"I have no intention of taking a seat on the damned council." Snapped Kevana.

"You think they'll give you a choice? They can't afford for you not to be leader, you've just killed the leader, no one will take that seat again, not and risk your wrath. Their choices are elect you or kill you, the second may take them a little time to arrange. Deniability is important."

"I have no deniability, I'll even have witnesses." Snarled Kevana.

"Agreed, but Axorana tried to kill you, and us, worst of all he failed. The others need deniability to protect their families should they fail."

"Why should their families be in danger?" Kevana frowned.

"You really are naïve when it comes to politics, aren't you?" Kirukana smiled.

"Careful," said Worandana, "he's setting himself up as your advisor."

Kevana frowned at his old friend.

"The power behind the throne." Worandana went on. "With a nice figurehead to take the blame when it all turns to shit." He laughed loudly.

"Perhaps I should cut his throat now." Muttered Kevana.

"That won't do any good. We still have a long way to go before we need to make those decisions, until then, we pick up our disguises and leave first thing in the morning."

"What in all the hells have you lot been up to?" Said Joe loudly. It was only then that the Zandaars noticed that the rest of the room was very quiet. Worandana looked around at all the faces, some a little surprised, some a little frightened, and a very few almost shocked.

"Ah." said Worandana. "Apologies, this is not something we generally do around the uninitiated. We have been communicating with our home monastery in Zandaarkoon. As I did say you may have seen some things, but you were in no danger. What did you see?"

"I saw a woman made of fire." Called out one man.

"That was the image I was projecting." Answered Worandana. "Anyone else?"

"I saw the woman in a glade, and a man dressed in black." Said a woman.

"The man in black is the leader of the council."

"You're not on the best of terms with him, are you?" She asked.

"Let's say that relations are a little strained right now." Worandana smiled.

"He's trying to kill you." She grinned.

"He was, he's going to call off the hunters, or most of them. Anyone else?"

"I didn't see any of those things, just a bright light travelling around the circle, a strange light that cast no shadows." Said a young man from his seat by the furthest wall.

"Now that really is interesting." Worandana looked at Kirukana, and saw as expected a wide-eyed stare, Worandana's eyebrows raised in question, Kirukana shrugged by way of answer. Worandana continued. "Those that saw the images, you people have a sensitivity to the other plane, this is a place different from our own, but close by, or even in the same place, but somehow separate. It's both complex and simple, basically a person has the sensitivity, or they don't." He turned to the young man. "You have something more, if you can see the power in our circle, then you have the latent power to be one of us, and in your current untrained state, you will probably be one of the more powerful ones. I suggest that you visit a monastery and apply to become one of us."

"Thank you for the offer, but somehow I don't think that your life is for me. You are currently running for your lives, from people who can kill you at a distance." He shook his head. "Not for me I think." He smiled and raised his mug of beer by way of acknowledgement.

"With your sort of abilities, you could go far."

"I'll stay here, this is the life I was born for, this one will do for me."

"Have you no ambition?"

"Yes, I plan to raise a family, in relatively peaceful circumstances, I intend on living to a ripe old age, with my children and grandchildren around me. All I need right now is a wife." He laughed loudly, and his friends joined in.

"I admit," said Worandana, "our way of life isn't for everyone, but there are wonders to behold in this world, wonders that won't come walking through your small town."

"There is nothing more wonderful than the love of a good woman, or the adoration of a child. Where do these things fit in your life old man?"

"Of women I know little and children less, but my life has been full."

"But you have no one to pass this on to, you leave no legacy for the following generations, all you have is for today."

"I have passed much on to my students, there is knowledge that comes from me, and still it exists, no matter how the council try to restrict it."

"But how many of your students still live? How many still practise what you have taught them?"

"That's an interesting thought."

"Not many." Answered Kirukana.

"What do you mean?" Snapped Worandana.

"So many of the things you taught are now so seriously frowned upon that no one admits to the practices, especially when the council members are around."

"Some must still believe?"

"Not openly. Sadly, your followers are all here today."

"How many are dead?"

"I'd rather not say." Kirukana, looked for support from the others and found nothing. Worandana glanced at Kevana. With a swirl of long robes Kevana spun in towards Kirukana, his belt knife drawn under the cover of the sweeping robe, when he stopped, the robe fell and the knife appeared pointed into Kirukana's belly, the point facing upwards, and shaking with the tension in Kevana's arm, the simple relaxation of the restraining muscles would send it upwards into Kirukana, death in less than a single heartbeat.

"Hey," shouted Joe, "we'll have no blood shed here tonight." A stout cudgel came up from below the bar, Alverana's sword flashed from its scabbard and fell on the staff.

"This is our business, stay out of it." Whispered Alverana. The staff dropped to the bar, but Joe didn't release it. The other customers in the bar showed no intention of getting involved, they just wanted to watch the action unfold. Joe shook his head slowly.

"Speak." Yelled Worandana, so loudly that everyone in the bar twitched, even Kevana, a small trickle of blood appeared at the point of his knife. Kirukana looked down but didn't move.

"Remember you forced me to tell you." He spoke slowly and paused waiting for permission to continue. Worandana nodded. "Fine. None, not a one, the ones that aren't dead are lost and in hiding, they hide so deep that no one will ever find them. Their power is broken, your life's work is destroyed by fire and fear. I am sorry, but the power of the council is complete." Worandana slumped, his thoughts turned to all the bright minds he had taught in all his years, to the lively faces, and the intense hopes, the sharp brains, and the talent that he had stretched to its limits and beyond. With a groan he fell to his knees, his head bowed.

"Speak." Muttered Kevana. "Does he live or die?" The silence in the room filled all the minds there, none moved, breathing was restricted to the shallowest and quietest that could be managed. Slowly the hunched figure of Worandana raised its right arm, the hand reached up fingers stretched to their limits, palm toward Kirukana, the robe fell under its own weight, exposing a thin and wiry forearm. Slowly the fingers clenched into a fist, a fist that vanished into a dark ball, the blackness of night, even in the brightness of the lamps, a globe of purest night enclosed the hand of the old man.

The young man with the sight spoke in the merest whisper, just one word. "Shit." He didn't move, he dared not. Slowly the kneeling figure raised its head, the hood fell backwards, his black eyes clearly visible to all, no whites, no irises, only pupils, black as night and empty as death. Slowly the old man's chest filled to its limit and his mouth opened. A howl straight from the depths of hell came forth, the arm snapped forwards, a stream of hot power shot from the hand into the ground, flags shattered, straw flared into nothingness, and the soil beneath started to smoke and glow, in only a moment, long before the howl finished the power faded to nothing. Worandana slumped again.

"Live or die?" Whispered Kevana. Worandana looked up again, his eyes more their normal colours.

"Is there a difference?" Asked Worandana. Slowly he raised both arms and shook them, so the sleeves of his robe fell down exposing his old arms for all to see, he spread them wide, and then with a smooth motion that belied his advanced years he rose to his feet. He stepped towards Kirukana, arms held wide, hands open, Kevana backed out of the way. Another step, almost within arm's reach now.

"You will learn something now." He spoke purposefully. One more short step and his hands snapped forwards gripping Kirukana's head and pulling them both together. Kirukana's right hand snapped to his belt knife and drew it, the scraping of the blade was unmistakeable, the shriek of the blade filled the room, as it started its upward journey, the two foreheads came into contact, Kevana's knife was flashing in to take Kirukana's life. A soundless concussion filled the room, a quiet detonation filled everyone's minds, Kevana stumbled mid strike, Kirukana's knife clattered to the floor, amongst the shattered flags. A moment later Worandana stepped away, Kirukana's turn to fall to his knees. Kevana recovered himself and swung towards Kirukana.

"No." Whispered Worandana, somehow the quiet word carried more power than the loudest yell. "Never again." Worandana smiled at Kevana. "Never again." Kirukana looked up from his place on the floor.

"What in all the gods have you done to me old man?"

"All the gods?"

"Yes, all of them."

"I have showed you the way. I was hoping for enough disciples to be able to take over the council and teach all the brothers the way to true power. You destroyed that hope, now we will together burn the whole council to ash. Stand up brother."

"What have you done?" Demanded Kevana.

"You know that I have been collecting the old magics, no one has ever been aware just how much of the old power I have collected."

"That is not true." Interrupted Kirukana. "The council knew what you were doing two years ago, one of your trainees was denounced as a heretic, and in an attempt to save himself from the fire, he gave you up, and most of your network. Obviously, it didn't save his life, his death just became a little more private, and somewhat quicker. The rest were hunted down and quietly killed off. There may be a few left but not many."

"And now I have a new one, stolen from under their noses."

"I could still side with them."

"Only until I am dead, then they'd kill you in a heartbeat, they'd not allow someone so powerful to live."

"I could train them." Kirukana mumbled.

"Could you?" Laughed Worandana. Kirukana looked up and shook his head.

"Their brains would explode, they have neither the strength, nor the imagination to deal with this, I'm not sure that I do."

"Up until now I have been keeping this very secret, only the trusted few, and you tell me that they are all dead. So now there is just you."

"What about your friends here?"

"Only Gorgana was close to learning about it. Only he chose to leave us, before I had chance to teach him."

"He was probably worried that he would be declared heretic and killed. After all he knows nearly as much as you."

"Don't be ridiculous, he is as a child compared to me, as are you."

"Why have we never seen this power before?" Asked Kevana.

"It needed to be secret, at least until I had control of the council, the need for secrecy has passed, with all my friends, now I think I'm just going to burn them down."

"I am sorry, there is a queue here, I get first strike."

"Fine, I'll be a second or so behind you, together we'll kill them all."

"And then what?" Asked Kirukana.

"That part we haven't really thought about." Laughed Kevana.

"I bet you haven't considered the repairs to my floor, either?" Demanded Joe.

"Apologies," said Worandana, "I needed something to get his attention." He nodded in the direction of Kirukana. Then he brought both hands together as if they were holding a ball, within the confines of his hands a darkness formed, a small, swirling patch of midnight that grew rapidly, until it filled the hands. With a nonchalant flick of the wrist Worandana dropped the ball onto the broken flagstones, it settled into a black puddle, with small ripples flowing across it, first one way then another, gradually the ripples settled out completely, and the black liquid appeared to sink through the surface of the now repaired flags. Worandana slumped a little. Then sighed.

"Mending is always more difficult than breaking."

"Old man." Called a voice, Worandana looked round into the wide eyes of the very same young man. "You need to be very careful of that dark power, it has a hunger that can never be sated."

"I am aware that it is hungry, but it is manageable to a great extent, though it can get slippery occasionally, one just has to maintain a close focus on it."

"One day it will slip your control and eat you."

"I have confidence in my abilities, I have nothing to fear. What do you know of this power?"

"Only what I see, a deep hunger, one that can never be filled. Please don't use it around here. I'd rather not die of your stupidity."

"I'm sure that won't happen."

"I am not that sure."

"So why are you still here?"

"It will make no difference how far away we are, that force will eat the world."

"You worry too much." Laughed Worandana.

"Believe what you will, old man."

Worandana smiled and turned back to Kevana.

"Will this be of any use against Axorana?" The younger soldier asked.

"We'll find out next time he calls. I'll have a different robe and a different voice, I'll need very little of your power, just myself and Kirukana will face him and his circle. He's in for a serious surprise, if his recent meetings weren't enough."

"Does this power have a name?"

"If it did, it has been lost to time, I can find no record of a name, only a sequence of syllables, that make a pattern of thought in the mind, this summons the power, more accurately, creates a link to it, so that it can be called upon. It doesn't actually exist in this plane, so it never passes through the person wielding it, hence there are none of the usual limitations. No risk of burn out, the only risk is being too close to the point of use. I believe it is possible to summon a bolt of energy to destroy the council chamber, even from this far away. Though such energy expended here would kill us all."

"Then what would happen to the open link?" Demanded the young sensitive.

"I have no idea, it should shut down, once the mind that had opened it died."

"Remember the lightning stone," said Alverana, "if Anya hadn't taken it over, it would most likely have made a real mess before it ran out of power."

"So, it could be that an arrow to the back of your head, while you are wielding that power, and the whole world vanishes into that blackness?" Asked the young man.

"I'd never looked at it that way," Worandana paused, "I'll check out the records when we get back to Zandaarkoon."

"It could be too late by then." Observed Kevana.

"Possibly, but what choice do we have? Even our own are out to kill us."

"Then let's make that as difficult a task as we can. Joe," he called, "any chance of some food and beer?"

"If you are going to stop hurling black fire around and sit nicely like civilised people?"

"I am fairly sure we can manage that, it's full dark outside now, all our brothers will be sleeping or too tired to attack us now. Some good wine would be appreciated as well?"

"I have wine, but I wouldn't say it was good, it's passable at best."

"He'll drink it anyway." Laughed Petrovana. "I have to admit that I have seen him reject a bottle of wine once, but maybe that was an empty one." A laugh passed around the people in the bar, especially amongst the locals. A little laughter makes everything seem better. The Zandaars re-arranged the tables, and formed them into two parallel benches, so that all could be seated in a small enough area, leaving more than enough room for the local residents and even for some more to come in. Quickly Joe and a serving girl started bringing out the food and drink for them, plates of meat, potatoes, and vegetables. Jugs of beer, and wine. Joe dropped a jug of wine heavily beside Kevana, along with a tray of wooden goblets. Kevana frowned a question up at Joe, Joe shrugged and turned away. Kevana glared at his back as he went into the kitchen for more food. Alverana laughed softly to himself.

"What are you sniggering at?" Snarled Kevana.

"The look on your face, you are such a snob."

"What do you mean?"

"Wine comes in barrels as well as bottles. It's always cheaper and sometimes better."

"Wine keeps better in bottles, when it goes off in a barrel, there's a lot more of the bad wine to drink before you can open a new barrel."

"Or you could bottle it, cover the bottles in dust and cobwebs, then sell them to snobs like you at ridiculous prices, quoting things like, one of the greatest wines of the area, the best this vineyard has to offer, a classic from a great vintner." Alverana laughed and dropped a heavy hand on Kevana's wrist.

"Well," mumbled Kevana, "your beer isn't much better. Many are snobbish about that, as you well know."

"Beer is for the working man, it's a good, honest beverage, it's supposed to be drunk in quantity. It's even less well lived as your wine, it can go off in a heartbeat, so drink it fast and brew some more. Why do you think so many fields are planted with barley?"

"Barley is for whiskey, not beer."

"Beer first, then whiskey when you've got an excess and the time to distil it."

This argument continued as it usually did, until the food was all eaten, and the beer and wine drunk, the plates were cleared, and more beer and another jug of wine appeared at the table.

"What do you think of my rough and ready country wine?" Asked Joe, poking Kevana gently with one callused finger.

"It's surprisingly good, it would probably be even better served in glass, not wood."

"Glass is too fragile and far too expensive around here. Perhaps once the farmers have gone home to bed, we'll share a glass or two."

"They do seem to get a little rowdy." said Kevana glancing over at two of the locals sitting opposite each other at a small table, arm wrestling.

"Oh, they're just having their usual argument, they always settle it that way, they're so closely matched that the result changes regularly."

"What exactly are they deciding?"

"Whose bull has the longest penis."

"Really?"

"Oh yes. It's of vital importance to both of them. They're both getting old, and their bulls they inherited from their fathers. The bulls are even older than they are, I think they'll die quite soon."

"I still don't see the importance of the current competition."

"There is a tradition in these parts, that when a prized bull dies, it's penis is preserved and turned into a walking stick, much prized are these canes. So, you can see that the length could seriously affect the function of the cane." Joe laughed loudly at the look on Kevana's face.

"This is a joke surely?"

"No, fact."

"You're making fun of a poor sap from the city, aren't you?"

"No. It's true, though I think one of those farmers is going a little far with his claims, he's expecting to make a crook such as shepherds use, any bull would be permanently tripping over the thing."

Kevana looked to Alverana for support.

"He's joking, right?"

"Actually." Answered Alverana slowly, "I've heard of it before, it's not just round here, I have heard of something called a 'Bulls wazzle stick.' A rather strange shaped walking stick, from what I remember, I was much younger then and wasn't interested enough to ask questions about some knobbly cane."

"Knobbly is the right word." Laughed Joe. Looking round the contest was over, the locals paid no more attention than normal, the crowd started to thin as the farmers went home, early starts for most of them. "I'll go and get you a bottle of the good wine, how does that sound?"

"That sounds good to me." Said Kevana, he looked around the room, most of the Zandaars were sitting quietly, drinking slowly, talking in soft voices, other than Worandana and Kirukana, they had retired to a dimly lit corner, sitting in small chairs facing each other, foreheads touching, there was an aura of power around them, a slight crackling of electricity filled the air, Kevana shrugged and turned back to the table as Joe presented a bottle of wine.

"That bottle looks far too clean, and it has no label, how do you know what's in it?" Asked Kevana, smiling.

"I know." Replied the barman, producing a corkscrew and opening the bottle, he gently placed the bottle on the table then produced two glasses from the pockets of his jacket, polished them with a flourish using the cloth stuck in his belt. He half-filled both glasses and took one for himself. "Tell me what you think."

Kevana picked up the other glass, held it up to the soft yellowish light of the lantern above his head, swirled it around, he held the glass to his nose and inhaled a lung full of the smell, he took a small sip and sucked some air through it, inhaling even more of the fragrance. He finally swallowed the sip and sighed.

"That's much better, that's quite a good wine, crisp and fruity, I like it."

Joe laughed briefly before speaking.

"It's the same wine, poured from a jug into a bottle only a moment ago. You my friend are simply a snob." Alverana laughed out loud, taking Kevana's left hand in his own.

"I don't care what you say." Said Kevana, loudly. "Wine tastes better served from a bottle and in a glass." He shrugged Alverana's hand from his, only to have it return in a moment. He glared into Alverana's eyes, but only for a short time, the laughter there was contagious. Soon he smiled and looked up at Joe. "It's better in a glass." He re-iterated.

"I'll not argue with that statement." Smiled Joe. "Glasses are precious around here, they have to be brought a long way, there is no one nearby that makes them."

"I understand that, anyway, this is a good wine."

"I'm glad you approve." Said Joe, turning away to talk to another of his few remaining regular customers. Long before Kevana finished his bottle of wine, the Zandaars were the only ones left in the bar. Worandana and Kirukana left their huddled corner and returned to the table where the rest were still sitting. Kirukana looked more than a little shaken, his face more pale than normal, his generally challenging eyes turned distinctly downwards.

"Kirukana, have you learned something useful today?" Asked Kevana. The younger man looked up suddenly, stared briefly, before responding.

"Useful? Perhaps. Frightening? Certainly. I can't believe that this has been kept so secret for so long."

"Do you think it is as dangerous as that young man felt?"

"It could quite easily be, power always comes at some sort of price, for us it has always been the energy we carry within us, this black power comes from outside, and I can't tell where. It's quite disturbing."

"Is it perhaps even a little heretical?" Smiled Kevana.

"Oh, it's that, and so much more. This power comes from somewhere other than Zandaar, which is totally contrary to the teachings." He turned to Worandana, "Does the council know of this power?"

"What do you think?" Worandana turned the question to Kirukana.

"They know that your disciples had some power, but they didn't know exactly what it was, only that it threatened them. I think they didn't truly believe in it, but they couldn't take the chance. Even if they read the documents in their own archives, the hidden archives. I think they'd disregard it as insane. They'd certainly never take the time to go and visit Maurid, they don't have the necessary thirst for knowledge." He paused briefly.

"I don't believe I am going to say this." Muttered Kirukana. "I've always thought of the members of the council as visionaries, looking to the future of the faithful. The more I learn, the less they seem to be. They now look like self-serving fools, they are each fighting to be the biggest fish in a pond that they keep making smaller. I think we should explain things to them."

"Well done." Said Kevana, a huge smile on his face. "Worandana strikes again, another council lackey turned into a heretic. It's surprising what a little power can do."

"This is no little power." Said Kirukana. "This is actually much bigger than they can ever imagine."

"They do tend to be a little short on imagination." Laughed Worandana.

"They have no difficulty imagining new things to be labelled as heretical. There was a council member a few years ago, I forget his name, he decided that keeping dogs in the house should be classed as heresy, his reasoning being that dogs are used for hunting, and they are the symbol of some of the old hunting gods, so anyone keeping dogs must be supporting one of the old gods, and therefore a heretic."

"That's ridiculous." Laughed Alverana.

"Agreed." Smiled Kirukana. "He really didn't think it through properly, he became quite vocal about it, both in the chamber and in public. He accused one of the council members of supporting an old god, and explained the rites, and rituals by which this support gave him power over some people and animals. Just knowing these rituals exist is considered heretical, but actually describing them in detail, now that was stupid, he continued his denunciations even as the fire consumed his feet. A very special sort of stupid, but looking back, not too unusual. I've never really questioned the members of the council, but now they all seem to be more than a little stupid, if not actually crazy."

"I agree with you," grinned Worandana, "the only thing of any importance to the council is power, their power over the people, and I think they believe themselves to be more than the servant of Zandaar, I think they see him as their personal source of power, and not something they should be sharing with the rest of us."

"Enough politics for now." Interrupted Kevana. "You can explain all this to them if we get to meet them, and that is by no means certain, they are going to put obstacles in our way. They may have agreed to rescind the kill on sight command, but I for one wouldn't trust them if they said the sun was going to come up tomorrow."

"May I make am observation?" Asked Joe quietly.

"Please do." Said Kevana.

"You're all priests of Zandaar, but it doesn't seem to be very brotherly to me?"

"You've noticed, this sort of infighting doesn't happen too often, but it does happen." Answered Worandana. "According to our records it seems to happen every couple of hundred years, the council splits into two or more factions and eventually one faction takes control and normally kills all the others, not terribly brotherly you are right."

"How can you take this sort of thing so calmly?"

"Who says we are calm?" Snarled Kevana.

"That's true." Laughed Petrovana. "Kevana has a serious need to chop heads, and Worandana wants to boil them in their own oils, it's going to get really messy before it is over."

"I don't know much about the current council but rendering them down for their oil sounds like a plan to me." Laughed Worandana.

"You'll get plenty of oil," said Kirukana, "if they have to run away, they'll not get far."

"Are they out of condition?"

"No, not that, they are in condition, you know, like barrels ready to roll down a hill."

"So not the healthiest of people?" Asked Alverana.

"Definitely not."

"We could just wait for them to die, it can't take all that long." Grinned Alverana.

"No." Said Kevana. "They set the dogs on us, they die by my hand."

"See Joe." Said Worandana. "That's how it both starts and ends. We are one faction, and the other is the council, the city guard, the army of Zandaar, and worse still, the hounds. I am sorry to say that they don't stand a chance."

"I am fairly sure that you people are crazy, you should be running for your lives."

"We can't." Said Kevana gruffly. "We have been given a task by our god, and by that god we are going to perform it. If the council get in my way, I will end them. Same goes for all the others, eventually we will have a reckoning with Zandaar."

"Now I am sure that you are crazy. Though I do wish you all the luck in the world, I can't help but side with the underdog, you do understand that you have no chance at all of coming out of this alive?"

"We may not have much of a chance, but we've been through many difficult situations and always prevailed." Said Worandana.

"That may not be true this time." Mumbled Kirukana.

"Possibly," snapped Kevana, "but we will go down fighting, fighting for what is right, and fighting with our honour intact."

"As I said, crazy." Joe turned away and walked slowly into the kitchen, to get another bottle of wine for Kevana, with every intention of drinking at least some of it himself.

He returned to the bar to hear Kevana declaring an early night for everyone.

"But I've brought another bottle of wine." He said.

"Fine, we'll drink that one and then call it bedtime, we do need to be up early in the morning, I want to be on the road before the sun comes up."

"That won't be a problem, my neighbour has a crazy cockerel, it has been known to crow at moonrise, it will wake you up in plenty of time." Joe poured the wine into both their glasses and sat down. "Don't worry we'll have you on the road before sun up. Have you a long way to go?"

"Yes, first we have to cross the river, have you any idea where the easiest crossing is?"

"You have a few choices, head east, you get to the crossing upstream of Angorak, somewhat south and you get to the Angorak crossing, this is going to be busy and heavily policed, if you get my meaning. Further south and you will reach the crossing south of Angorak, not so busy, not so often watched. The choices are yours."

"We'd much rather not be observed, you understand?"

"Of course I do, south of Angorak is a tiny crossing, though the barges that make the crossing are much dependant on the wind, if it's blowing the wrong way, they won't even attempt it. They end up too far down stream, and it can be a nightmare getting back up against the flow. North of Angorak, that's a raft and rope affair, small but reliable, no more than three horses at a time, and it takes a while, not a place to be caught separated by the river."

"So let me sum this up, the north crossing is dangerous if our enemies know we are there, the Angorak crossing is dangerous, because they will know we are there, and the southern crossing is dangerous because it could take days to get across."

"That's about right."

"Worandana, can we rely on our disguises to get us past the guards on the gate at Angorak?"

"Probably not, they'll know who we are as soon as they see the horses and the gear, there may even be some there that know our faces."

"What about the northern crossing?"

"It's a good day's ride north, they'll probably not bother with it too much, they'll be watching the city crossing and the southern one, that one is a more direct route to Zandaarkoon."

"I agree, we take the northern crossing and ride into the city through the north gate, it does have a north gate?"

"I think so, from memory there are two on the river, where the docks are, one in the south wall, two on the east road, and one on the north side, though I have to admit the last map I saw of the city was very old, things could very well have changed."

"Could we just ride south along the river?"

"There is a road that side, but it will be heavily policed, not somewhere we really want to be."

"What about the roads through the city, how big a police presence could we expect?"

"I have no idea, but it's not going to be the city guard that will be our problem, it's going to be our own brothers, they could make it very difficult for us to get to Zandaarkoon."

"Great, you don't believe that Axorana has called them off?"

"Oh, he'll rescind the kill on sight, but we can expect a heavy escort as soon as they find us."

"Fine, north crossing, then south through the city, we'll wait on the south side for our enemies to come to us." Snarled Kevana, dashing down the last of his wine. "Time for bed, we have to be up early." He pushed his chair backwards, and stood up, glancing around the room, catching each person's eyes, for an instant, just enough to express his anger.

"You heard the man." Said Alverana. "Early to bed, early to rise. Move it." He scuffed his chair back and climbed slowly to his feet, tapping Petrovana on the shoulder as he did so, with a nod the smaller man started to get up. In only moments all of them were moving towards the stairs leading up to the rooms.

"Good night, Joe." Said Kevana. "Don't forget we need to be on the road real early."

"Don't worry about that, I'll make sure you are up in plenty of time to leave us."

"Somehow I get the impression that you'll be glad to see the back of us?"

"I feel that you people are dangerous to everyone around you."

"That is probably true, though it's not something we can do much about. We have done nothing wrong, but still they have sent out a kill on sight instruction. Anyway, thanks for all your help." Kevana, nodded to Joe and walked towards the stairs, he wasn't the last to go up, but there was only one behind him.

CHAPTER SIXTY

"Steel, are there any serving staff here as a rule?" Demanded Jayanne.

"There's usually a couple of girls around. Service." He yelled.

Two frightened faces looked round the edge of the kitchen door.

"Come here girls." Said Jayanne, slowly they did as they were commanded, but neither would look into her eyes. "Look at me." She snapped, both faces turned upwards.

"There are going to be some changes around here, we need a little privacy for a while, I want you to serve people waiting on the veranda, drink only, not food, it takes too much time, Jangor's paying."

"Woman you're going to break me."

"Shut up, I haven't even started on you yet." She turned back to the serving girls.

"As I was saying, Jangor is paying, I am sure that some of your neighbours are going to try to take advantage of my commanders' largess, you'll know who they are before they attempt it. When they do, explain to them that Wolf still hasn't eaten today. I'm sure they'll not want an expensive bottle of wine anymore, and a mug of nice ale will do fine. Now hold out your hands. Wolf meet two new friends." Both girls giggled at the soft touch of his tongue as it washed across their palms.

"Now if you slap your right hand against your hip, wolf will come to you. In case they need a little more convincing. Everything clear?"

"Yes." Said the blonde, the dark-haired girl simply nodded.

"Good, go to it. Wolf door." Wolf followed the girls to the door and sat beside Brank.

"Jangor," said Jayanne, "we need to talk about the gold we just captured." Jangor looked at Namdarin for assistance, Namdarin perched on the edge of a table and smiled.

"What do you want to do with it?" he asked looking back at Jayanne.

"It belonged to Steel and his family, I think we should give him some of it back, how about a half?"

"How about three quarters?" Asked Jangor. Steel looked confused.

"Two thirds." Said Jayanne.

"Deal." Said Jangor. He spat in his right hand and held it out. Jayanne did the same, and they gripped hands.

"Woman, you are going to break me." He said.

"You want to live forever?" She countered loudly.

"No." He muttered, turning to glare at Namdarin.

"It's not my fault." Said Namdarin, "You've trained her as much as I have." He laughed.

"What just happened?" Asked Steel.

"Well," replied Jayanne, "we just decided to return some of the gold you lost, it won't replace your family, but it might make things a little easier."

"What am I going to do without them?"

"You'll find a way to carry on, perhaps even make a whole new life for yourself."

"I have her family to inform, that's not going to be easy."

"She has a big family?"

"Yes."

"Maybe she has a lonely sister, who can help you get over things?"

"She has two lonely sisters, but they are lonely for a reason, they are utter harridans."

"There may be someone closer to home?"

"I don't think I'm ready for all that again. I still need time to weep, I know it's going to happen soon, the headlong rush that is today, since you arrived, it has to fade out soon and then I'll really feel it."

"You're probably right there." The barman returned at this point, he was allowed in but the two with him were firmly told to wait outside. As he was walking slowly over to Jayanne, Wolf vanished from his post and went out onto the veranda, Jayanne smiled to herself.

"Your name?" Asked the barman.

"I am Jayanne, these are Namdarin, Jangor, and the mountain at the door is Brank, Wolf you met."

"I am Nigel, and I am afraid I may have embarrassed myself, when I saw the remains of Brass, I took a leaf out of Wolf's book."

"I don't understand." She said as Wolf returned to his station at the door.

"Wolves, and canines have a very simple philosophy, if you can't eat it, or mate with it, then pee on it and walk away."

"And you did just that?"

"Yes, I apologise to any undertakers that get lumbered with the task of dealing with that corpse."

"Be best to just build a bonfire on it and burn it to ash." Laughed Jangor. The blonde serving girl came into through the door, and approached Jayanne, she stood staring at the ground.

"Look up and speak girl." said Jayanne.

"Wolf is a good friend to have, the men are all afraid of him."

"He's very good for that, but you shouldn't need the men to be afraid of you."

"I know, can you tell me who has taken over from Brass?"

"This man here, he is called Steel, he is taking over all of Brasses businesses." The girl looked Steel up and down before speaking.

"You are not as fat as Brass, and a little younger."

"Thank you for that, I think." Said Steel with a gentle smile.

"I shall be your bed companion for tonight, the other girl tomorrow, Sundays are special, we both share your bed." Steels jaw fell open, he was struck speechless. For a while he could find no words.

"Are we not acceptable?" She asked in a whisper.

"How old are you?" He asked finally.

"I am nearly fifteen."

"How long has this arrangement been going on?"

"Almost two years now. Our families owe a great deal of money."

"Let me make this very clear for you and your friend, there will be no more bedroom duties for either of you, you have no need to worry about your family and their debts, I shall be having words with them later, they may even survive. But no matter what happens you will always have a home here under my roof." He hugged her tight, with tears in his eyes. He held her by the shoulders at arm's length and spoke slowly.

"Don't worry about anything, I'll make everything all right, now back to work." He smiled and turned her around with a gentle push towards the door. Once she was through the door, he spoke again.

"Anyone else feel like a pissing party?" There were many nods around the room, he turned to Nigel.

"Did you know?"

"I knew they shared his bed, I didn't know they'd been coerced by their families."

"I wouldn't say that was the action of a true family, would you?"

"I'd say they aren't fit to have children, especially not daughters." Said Nigel.

"I agree." Said Steel.

"It looks to me like someone just acquired two teenage daughters." Said Jayanne. "They're damaged but not broken, they'll need some serious care, and some real training, but I'm sure your up to the job."

"This morning I had a son, a daughter and a wife, now I've got two daughters and Nigel the barman. This is a very strange day. Nigel, have you any idea where Brass kept his important papers, and money?"

"Strong room in the cellar, the keys will be in his pocket, and you're never going to break that door."

"I don't need to break the door, only the lock," said Steel. "lead on."

"Wolf fetch Granger." Called Jayanne. Wolf vanished through the door and there were shouts of alarm from outside.

"We'll wait for Granger, there may be traps that require his skills." Said Jayanne. Steel nodded, then turned to Nigel.

"You've been effectively running this place, haven't you?"

"Brass never did anything when he could trick someone else into doing it."

"I begin to realise the nature of that monster, so I ask that you continue to work for me in a similar capacity, and I will pay you one third of the profits, on a weekly basis, until we get things stable, then we will renegotiate, is that acceptable?"

"That should give me enough to pay mothers bills and enough to live on as well. I accept, though I do have a couple of recommendations that need to be implemented immediately."

"Recommend away." Steel smiled.

"No free drinks for Brasses cronies, and no more discounts for his favoured."

"He still has cronies left?"

"A few that your new friends haven't killed, and quite a few favoured ones."

"I have a counter proposal. End discounts yes, but cronies pay a quarter more than anyone else, and anyone buying them drinks goes in the crony price bracket."

"That sounds very fair to me, some of them have been drinking here for free for years."

Is this acceptable to you?" He asked.

"You mean." Said Beth's father, looking from Beth, to his wife, to Steel and back to Beth. "You mean."

"Daddy," said Beth, "he said that's what you wanted, to pay off your debt, he said."

"You mean." Said Beth's father, looking her up and down, "whore." he muttered.

"He said, daddy, he said." Beth cried.

"You didn't know?" Asked Steel.

"Of course not." Snapped the old man. "You can keep her." He snatched his wife's hand and set off towards the door.

"He said it was for you daddy." Howled Beth.

"Whore." Muttered the old man. Brank and Jangor showed no signs of getting out of their way. Steel swept Beth up in his arms and looked over her shoulder at Brank.

"Brank," he said, "I wish it was possible to beat some sense into these people, but I feel it is already too late. I tell you two what I told Crystals parents, if you enter my property again I'll take a whip to your hides, now get out." Brank and Jangor stood aside to let the two leave. Only when they were out of the door did the father yell one more time. "Whore."

"Wolf." Said Jayanne. "Chase." With a flurry of skittering claws Wolf set off after the parents.

"Will he hurt them?" Asked Steel.

"Probably not," answered Jayanne, "he'll most likely just chase them home, but to be frank, I really don't care." Steel looked down onto the head of Beth, her face was buried against his chest.

"I've had enough of these people for one day, bar's closed. Nigel go and check on your mother, then can you come back? There are bound to be things that need doing, and I have no idea what they are."

"Half an hour to get her to bed and I'll be back, don't worry about it, they'll all be back again tomorrow, where the hell else are they going to get a drink in this town?"

"Crystal." Yelled Steel. The blonde came running.

"I'm closing up early tonight, it's been a long and hard day for all of us, please start kicking the customers off the veranda, if any are reluctant, I'm sure Brank can explain things to them."

"I'll explain," said Jangor, "Brank will pour their beer over them, and seeing as I'm paying for it, I should get to drink it. They'll not object with Brank standing behind me." He laughed and stood to one side as he waved Crystal through the door. He followed her

"That will do for a start, it's probably going to take more than a few days to sort through all his papers, once we have a clearer idea as to the state of the finances for this place, we'll come up with something better." Wolf returned, yapped and took his post beside Brank. The dark-haired serving girl came in with a tray full of empty mugs, she walked over to Steel.

"I hear that you have released us from some of our duties, how are my family going to pay their debt?" she asked.

"Their debt was to Brass not me, I don't take such liberties with little girls, I'll talk to your family later, in the mean time you will be paid in money or goods for the work you do here, once things are settled, we'll talk some more."

"Crystal is right, you're not as fat, and a lot younger." She smiled briefly, "Who is Jangor? The villagers want to know who's paying for their beer."

"I am, and I want to make it clear, I was volunteered to pay, it was not my idea."

"They say thank you." She looked him up and down slowly. "You're not too old either." Then she turned to the bar and started filling mugs from one of the jugs. Jangor waited until she went back outside before speaking.

"She should be playing with dolls, or sewing pretty clothes, not propositioning old men." He raised his arm. "Any one for a pissing party?" Arms around the room raised.

"At this rate the bastard is never going to burn." Laughed Steel.

"Who's not going to burn?" Asked Granger from the doorway.

"Don't ask," said Jangor, "we have a door for you to open, can you do it."

"I can try."

"Nigel, show us the strong room." Said Steel. They all followed Nigel towards the door to the cellars.

"Brank, you're on your own up here, can you cope?" Said Jangor.

"Me and Wolf can cope with these people, easy."

"Good."

Down the narrow steps into the cellar Nigel led the way. The cellar was deep and cool, half way along on one side there was a small black door, it was only four feet high, and three wide.

"That's his strong room." Nigel said.

"Have you ever seen the door open?" Asked Granger.

"No, he makes sure this room is empty, and the door locked on the inside, before he opens the strong room."

"This is very unusual." Granger explained. "The door is iron. It opens outwards, with the hinges concealed on the inside, the lock plate." He pointed at one edge of the door. "Is from a three key sea chest, any two keys will open the chest, the shipper has one, the captain has one, and the receiver has one. You never see this sort of thing on land, now that would be an almost never. The lock catch plate is buried in the stonework, someone put a great deal of effort into making this, it could take days to break into this room."

"I suppose I'll have to go and get the keys from Brass's pockets." Mutter Steel.

"That seems like an awful lot of effort just to open a door." Granger laughed.

"Can you open it?" Asked Steel.

"I can break the lock in a few heartbeats, opening it may take a little longer."

"If you open it, will it still be operable?"

"Yes, with the keys."

"Then please sir, open the damned lock for us." Said Steel.

Granger nodded, then placed the end of his staff against the lock plate. Jagged worms of blue fire started to creep along the length of the staff, the oil lamps in the cellar began to die, everything around started to get cold and dark.

"Granger, we'll freeze to death at this rate." Said Jangor. The lamps brightened a little and the all-pervading cold became a little less, not much, just a little. The lock plate gave some small groaning sounds that were barely audible over the crackling of blue fire from the staff. After a minute or so Granger lowered his staff.

"Can't you open it?" Asked Steel. Granger examined the outer surface of the door and found a slightly more polished area near the bottom in the middle. He gave it a hefty kick, the door boomed and then swung slowly outwards.

"It's got no handle, even with the keys in the lock it's not going to give enough purchase to overcome the friction in the old hinges, a swift kick and it bounces open, Brass has been kicking it in the same place for a long time. The top key is almost a full circle with a notch and levers on the inside, the bottom key is flat, only works one way up and has three levers on each side, the centre lock is broken, which is perhaps why it is here and not still in a sea chest."

"Do I want to know how you know all this?" Asked Jangor.

"I pick up this knowledge as I travel, any day you don't learn something is a day you've wasted."

"Let's have a look inside." said Nigel. "I've always been curious about his hoard."

Granger swung the door wide and stepped back. Kevin took down an oil lamp from its hook on a joist and crouched to enter the small door.

"Oh my." he said from the inside. Steel followed him in a moment later. Once inside he lit the lamps hanging from the rafters and said. "You better all come in here, you're not going to believe it."

The room they found was much larger than they expected, there was plenty of space for them all to stand in it, and even a couple of wooden chairs, Granger sat in one, and Jangor the one nearest to the desk. Steel checked a couple of the chests along the longest wall.

"Jangor," he said, "I think you can forget about our deal for the gold, I no longer have any need of it."

"I'm an honourable man, my word is my bond, you get your gold, like it or no." Snapped Jangor.

"How about another deal then? For the funeral services you provided for my family, and the hunting down and disposal of their killers, all their killers, I offer a sack of gold, how does that sound?"

"That sounds like a fair price."

"Let's say this sack is the same as the one you owe me?"

"Sounds good."

"Then we don't actually need to go to the trouble of exchanging sacks of gold, do we?"

"I suppose not."

Steel held out his hand for Jangor to shake, the old soldier took it, saying, "I think you are going to do well here."

"With this sort of start I don't see how I can fail in my lifetime. I don't understand."

"What don't you understand?" Asked Granger.

"Well, look at all this wealth, how could Brass have accumulated so much, and more to the point, why?"

"Why is easy," replied the old magician, "people measure their own worth in different ways, some by the number of children they have, some by the number of friends they have, some by the power they have over others, and some like Brass are like the dragons, they only count the gold they hold in their hands. How he managed this astounding feat is another matter entirely, though I do have an idea. He doesn't pay any of his staff, they all work for free, presumably he doesn't pay any of his suppliers, they are under the same sort of duress as his staff, any coin that comes across his bar, comes straight down here. His roving band of robbers presumably pay a percentage on their take, for the information he provides. He's probably got a network of informants around the area, passing on important information from time to time. You'll have to watch out for them, they could be dangerous."

"His bookkeeping is impressive," said Jangor looking up from the desk, "his ledgers are good and his handwriting exquisite. It looks like his records are well organised and complete. Did he spend a lot of time down here?"

"Generally most of the morning, he'd lock himself away in here." Said Nigel.

"If his records are as good as his bookkeeping, then you should be able to find out who he was blackmailing, who owed him money, it may take a while, but you should be able to unravel it all. You could have this whole village in your hand just like he did." Jangor looked straight at Steel as he said this.

"You can't believe I would do that, surely."

"It's got to be tempting."

"It might be, but not to me, he's been screwing this whole region for how long? No one really knows, I may find out from his ledgers, but what has he actually achieved? A pile of gold, it sits here in sacks doing nothing, how much better would this place have been if this gold had been put to work for the people that live here, not just buried in this hole in the ground. No, things are changing, and for the better. The really sad part about all this, most of this gold has come into this town through me, my wine is the only product that is sold out of this town, other than his takings from the robbers, most of this is mine."

"Yes but you've been paying your bills he hasn't, I'm sure that some of the farmers hereabout ship their produce out of town as well."

"I suppose, but their product is cheap, a whole cart full of wheat makes as much as a small cask of my wine."

"So has Brass tried to take over your business in the past?"

"A time or two he's offered loans to help me through a bad patch, but I've always managed without his help."

"Think about these bad patches, could they have been engineered by someone really sneaky, because the man Brass was definitely that?"

"One year was a blight that made all the grapes small and sour. One year the yeast just died. All of it, even my back up cultures, yeast is very important."

"How do these things happen?"

"Blight is a disease, it's passed by contact or in bird droppings when the birds have eaten infected grapes, I did get a request from a grower some distance away, he wanted to buy my grapes as he had blight as well. But he was too far away for my grapes to have caught the same blight."

"I'm not a sneaky man," said Jangor, "take blighted grapes, wash them in some water, sprinkle said water on good vines, are the good vines now blighted?"

"That is possibly a way to do it, come to think of it, the spread was incredibly fast, like whole slopes were infected at once. I had enough profit and wine stored to survive a year without production, Cut the vines right back and pray, we had grapes the next year, and they were some of the best ever."

"Interesting," said Jangor, "Yeast death?"

"Perhaps some contaminant introduced to the fermenting tanks, but the seed cultures are kept separate, though in the same building."

"How did you recover from that one?"

"One of my workers reminded me of a particularly warm patch, one particular fermenting vat was going really fast and blew off one of the planks that made up the top, there was such a mess, red wine froth went everywhere. We cleaned up most of it. He pointed out a purple stain on one of the really high beams, dried wine froth, contains dried yeast. Seed cultures were restarted from those, and later dried yeast stored safely. The dead batches were recovered by heating and acidifying with lemons, not the best wine I've ever made, but saleable, after a fashion."

"Would either of these events put you out of business?"

"Both easily could have, but Brass would have been there with a loan to help me over the bad times."

"Five years and your business would have been his."

"If I thought for one moment that he had a hand in any of my problems I'd have killed him on the spot." Snarled Steel.

"Well that's no longer a problem." Laughed Jangor.

"So," said Steel, "my new business here is safe, given Nigel's help, and the barmaids, my wine business is safer than ever, all I need is a salesman, there is only one serious issue now."

"And that is?" Asked Jangor.

"I have no family to share it with." Steel burst into tears and fell to the ground. Jayanne bent over, grabbed him by the shoulders, and pulled him to his feet, she held him in her arms, and spoke softly to him.

"You don't have time for this just now, one of Brasses remaining cronies is probably planning to get you removed even as we speak, you need to be strong for a little while longer, you need to take this shit hole town over and make it yours. There will be plenty of time for grief later, but right now you need to be strong enough to make this a better place."

He dashed the tears from his eyes and glared at her.

"Bitch you just called my home town a shit hole."

"With Brass in control what was it?"

"Right now, I could easily hate you. Sadly you are right, we still have work to do, and I will get my own back on you for these words."

"You can let go of me anytime you like."

"Fine." He released his arms from around her waist. "Let's get upstairs and see just how drunk my new friends are getting. Nigel, can you watch the cellar door and keep the girls supplied with beer, after all Jangor is paying."

"You got it boss." Said Nigel. They trooped up the stairs, and back into the bar.

"Brank," said Jangor loudly. "Any problems?"

"Nothing that me and Wolf couldn't cope with, the local doctor's going to be a bit busy today though."

"Why?"

"A couple of hooligans decided that Wolf wasn't a threat, and nor was I. We proved them wrong."

"How serious?" Asked Jayanne.

"Cuts and bruises, all limbs intact." Laughed Brank. "They walked away, well crawled the first part, then Wolf let them stand up, and run, you should have heard him laughing, did you know wolves can laugh?"

"Any problems since that?" Asked Jangor.

"Nothing at all, they've been good as gold, they're just waiting to see what happens."

"Jayanne," Steel asked, "Can you do me a favour?"

"Of course."

"Please come outside with me, and take down that sign of Brasses, and then go and get me the keys to that damned strong room, somehow my position is weakened by those keys being elsewhere."

"Not a problem, I'll take Wolf, that should lower the tension a little."

"I'll talk to the gathered worthies while you are gone."

"I'm going to miss the good bits." She laughed.

"I'm sure you'll be back in time for some enforcement." Chuckled Steel.

"Let's make a show of this." Said Jangor. Jayanne looked back at him and smiled.

"I hate that smile." Whispered Jangor. Jayanne walked out of the door and spoke loudly.

"Wolf with me, Jangor guard the door."

"See." Whispered Jangor, as he stepped up beside Brank. Jayanne was crossing the veranda with Wolf at her hip when Steel called out.

"Lady Jayanne, could you please take down that cursed sign of Brasses?" Her reply was a nod, then as she stepped off the veranda, with a casual backhanded blow from the axe she took the support post at the level of the veranda rail. Then carried on walking without a backwards glance, she cared not where the post and the sign landed, luckily into the street.

"Right." Said Steel in a loud voice. "There are going to be some changes around here. I have taken over all of Brasses businesses, as gifted to me by the lady Jayanne who bested him in single combat, I'd personally like to thank the bowmen who helped out, I'm so glad you didn't kill Brass, she'd have been mightily displeased, and that is something I never want to see. As some of you are lucky enough not to know Brass was a very bad man, not only was he blackmailing some of you, he held loans for some of you, and threats over others. Please be assured that though I have taken over his businesses I will not continue his nefarious activities, any loans are his and not mine, there will be no interest payments that people can't afford any more. Any dubious secrets that he held, I may find in his records, will never be made public by me, unless someone has been harmed by illegal activities. Just to make something clear, illegal activities are anything that I think is wrong. I am imposing a new pricing policy here, I need a name for my inn, I'm looking for suggestions, anyway policy. Some of Brasses cronies, well any of them really, will not be drinking here for free, any of his favoured ones, will not be getting their discounts. Favoured will be paying standard prices, cronies will be paying one quarter above standard prices, they've been drinking here for free for far too long. Be aware people anyone buying drinks, or food for cronies at standard prices will be added to the crony list, they've had it far too good for far too long, and I don't require their illegal services. If anyone wants to open an inn to compete with mine then please feel free to do exactly that, I will not resort to any of Brasses tactics, I will simply compete on price and service. Service, now that is something I need to be clear about, as you should be aware, Brass and his band of roving robbers killed my family, all of them, in the most disgraceful manner. They were travelling with wine and gold, his robbers attacked them, raped them, killed them. Not just the females, they raped the boy child as well, before they killed him. My new family is here, the serving staff at my inn are now my family, I'll not lose them again, if any offend them I'll hurt, if any harm them I will kill, in a heartbeat, family is more important to me than ever, so be warned. Oh, here comes the lady Jayanne, looks like she has something for me." He glanced at Jangor in the doorway, Jangor nodded, he stepped back to allow Namdarin, and Granger out onto the veranda. Jayanne was walking towards the inn, Wolf snapping at the heels of an old man he was herding towards the inn.

"Jayanne." Called Steel. "What do you bring for me?"

"He was after the same thing we are, so I brought him to you." She said, as Wolf guided the man up the veranda steps. "Give him what you took from Brasses corpse." The old man reached out with a bunch of keys in his hand. Steel looked at Jayanne, she smiled. Steel took a mug of beer from a man sitting nearby, the man tensed, but said nothing, after all he hadn't paid for it. Steel poured the beer over the keys, before he took them from the old man.

"Why did you want these keys?" he asked.

"Brass holds promissory notes that I can't afford to pay, I thought to take them from his vault."

"If you'd stayed here with the rest of these freeloaders, you'd have found out that any debts to Brass are now over. Don't worry old man, everything will be sorted out shortly. Now people of this place, we have something important to decide, our headman has been killed. We need to elect someone new, someone with the vision, someone with the power to make things better, I believe that someone is me. I think we have enough voting members here, can I get a seconder."

A man raised his hand and called "Second."

"Fine," said Steel, "I accept your kind nomination, we need to put this to the vote. All those in favour of the motion raise your hands now." He pointed at Wolf, who growled loudly. A forest of hands were raised, Steel didn't bother to count them. "All against raise your hands now." One hand went up, to be quickly pulled down by a neighbour.

"Carried unanimously." Called Steel. "As your newly elected headman, my first action is to suggest that our town be renamed after our greatest benefactor, she who freed us from the evil yoke of the wicked Brass, I propose that this place be called Jayanne from this day forward. Any against please raise your hands now." No hands were raised even momentarily. Steel turned towards Jayanne and spoke slowly and clearly.

"From this day forwards, this place shall be known as Jayanne, and that Jayanne shall have board and lodging paid and entertainment for her party free of charge as long as she shall live. Are there any that say nay to these conditions?" No hands rose.

"Carried." said Steel. He looked across at Jayanne, stuck his tongue out and grinned.

"Now I have a town named after me, just what I need." Laughed Jayanne loudly.

"I think I shall rename this inn as well, it shall be called the Axe. For obvious reasons. I have just a couple more things to take care of before we re-open for business. Crystal, please bring your parents inside, we have things to talk about." He looked round briefly, then caught the eyes of the other girl. "Beth, please bring Brank a beer, standing guard is thirsty work."

"Milk will do nicely for me, thank you." Brank smiled at Beth as she passed.

"Only babes drink milk." Said a voice from the veranda.

"I'd prefer it that you didn't actually break anybody." Said Jangor, giving Brank enough room to go onto the veranda. Crystal escorted two people into the bar, where Steel was waiting.

"Hello," said Steel. "I'm sure you heard what I said earlier, any debts you had to Brass died with him, so there is no reason for your daughter to work in servitude any more, if she wants to continue working here, then I have no problem with that, I'll pay her an appropriate wage, once I work out what that is, it's difficult because no one round here seems to work for a living, all they do is work for Brass. It may take me a while, but I will sort out something equitable for all. She could even come back to live with you and just come to work like a normal person. What do you think?" The two adults standing beside him at the bar exchanged glances for a moment then the father spoke.

"But what about the payments?"

"I have told you, you own me nothing, so I require no payments."

"You miss the point entirely, Brass paid us for the services of our daughter. We earned twenty gold pieces a week for her labours."

"Crystal, did you know about these payments?" Crystal shook her head, too shocked to speak.

"Sir," said Steel as calmly as he could, "were you aware of the nature of her services, bar, kitchen, and bed?"

"Of course, will you continue to pay the twenty gold a week for her services?"

"I need to be clear on this matter," said Steel slowly, "you knew that she was to share the bed of Brass, and you would receive twenty gold per week, and this has been going on since she was thirteen years old, is this correct?"

"Yes, will you continue with the current arrangement?" Steel sighed deeply, he turned to Crystal.

"I had thought that the evil in this town came entirely from Brass, but it seems his corruption has spread much further. Please rest assured you will always have a place here, I cannot in all conscience expect you to return to a family that would prostitute your body at the age of thirteen to an animal like Brass. My own daughter was thirteen when she was raped and murdered by Brasses associates. Crystal, my dear." He took both of her hands in his. "Would you do me the service of staying here under my roof, until such time as I can find you a decent husband, one that meets my approval, I have to admit that the chances of finding such a thing in this town have just taken a serious drop. I feel that we may have to look further afield, will you stay?"

"Do you think you can find me a husband?" She asked quietly.

"With your beauty, and your skills, I see no reason why any man wouldn't be glad to marry you."

"I will stay until you find one that I like, if not I'll just stay, if that is all right with you?"

"More than acceptable terms for me."

"And what about us?" Asked the father. "How will we survive?"

"I have to admit," Steel spoke coldly, "your survival is of utter indifference to me, if I had dogs I would set them on you." He turned to Nigel. "Perhaps we should invest in some dogs?" Nigel smiled. Steel turned back to Crystal's parents. "You will get off my property immediately, if you ever set foot on it again, I shall take a whip to you." He turned to Nigel. "Do we have a whip?"

"I dare say something could be improvised from a length of rope or two." Laughed Nigel.

"Get out before I rip the hide from your backs." Yelled Steel. He turned back to Crystal as the two hurried from the bar. He opened his arms wide and she fell into them, he held her close while she cried.

"Have no fear, I'll look after you from now on." He whispered into her soft blonde hair. After a brief time, Steel swept the tears from her eyes with his thumbs and held her face in his strong hands.

"You'll be fine, don't worry." He muttered.

There was a commotion by the door, Jangor turned back to the door he should have been watching, he pulled his sword with his left hand and buried it to the hilt in the belly of the man who was trying to get past him.

"Jangor." Snapped Namdarin, Jangor looked at Namdarin and wiped the tears from his face with his right hand. "Even I know," Namdarin continued, "even I know you're supposed to jab them with the pointy end."

Jangor looked down at the man on the ground gasping for breath. A hand the size of a ham grabbed the man by the collar, and threw him across the veranda into the street.

"Somehow that seemed un-necessary, anyway he's left now." Jangor laughed as Brank took up station alongside, together they sealed the doorway completely. Steel turned back to Crystal.

"Somehow I don't think it's going to be boring here, do you?"

"Anything but." She smiled.

"Can you carry on?" He asked.

"No problem." She grinned, tossing her hair back.

"Good, send in Beth and her parents please, let's see what they have to say for themselves."

Crystal picked up her tray, squared her shoulders and walked over to the door, her smile was enough to make the two men stand aside. She walked out onto the veranda, had a quick glance around. She saw Beth and called.

"Steel would like to see you and your parents now." Beth looked a little disturbed as she took her parents into the bar, she had after all just seen Crystals parents leaving in some sort of hurry.

Steel turned to the new group of parents, wondering how it would go this time.

"As I have already made clear, any debts owed to Brass died with him, I would like Beth to continue to work for me as bar maid, kitchen and chamber maid, I will of course pay her for her time and services, I will expect none of the bedmate, services that Brass did.

out, with Brank on his heels. Crystal started collecting empty mugs.

"Ladies and gentlemen, Steel is closing the bar, it's been a hard day, he'd like you to put your beers down and then leave. He'll be open again tomorrow for business nearly as normal, but for tonight he's had enough." He looked around briefly, then spoke again, much louder, those that knew him, were aware he had more volume available, but in this audience, he really didn't need it. "I'm sorry, what part of 'put your beers down' was unclear?" He turned to Brank, "The thing I hate about veranda's like this one, there are no windows to break as people leave, I love the sound of breaking glass, oh, and the blood." He looked back and there was a logjam of people stuck in the exit. He smiled and set about helping Crystal collect the not so empty mugs. Jangor was emptying the mugs into a jug, presumably just for himself. When Crystal carried a tray full of empty mugs into the bar, she started unloading the tray next to where Steel was standing, he looked at her helplessly. Beth was still in his arms sobbing her heart out.

"How many beds do we have here?" He asked her, realising he'd never paid that much attention to the local bar, he considered his wines far too good for the people here.

"We can sleep eight, excluding your bed and ours."

"Namdarin how many in your party?"

"There are ten." He answered after a quick count up. "Oh, and Wolf"

"Nigel," said Steel, "can we rig a couple of beds on those benches?"

"We could but I wouldn't ask a friend to sleep there, I have a spare bed at my house, it's big enough for two, empty since my sister and her husband moved away."

"I'll take that." said Namdarin, "It's been a long time since I've slept in a real bed. What do you think Jayanne?"

"Sounds good to me."

"Stabling?" Asked Namdarin.

"Nigel?" Asked Steel.

"We have enough stalls for your riding horses and the pack animals can just mill around in the yard."

"I'll take Wolf and collect the rest of our people." Said Jayanne.

"Just leave the tents," said Jangor, "If anyone decides they don't like our tents, then Wolf will find them in the morning, anything of value comes here."

"I understand." Said Jayanne heading out of the door, with Wolf on her heels.

"You people are amazing." Said Steel.

"What do you mean?" Asked Namdarin.

"You achieve so much, so fast, and there's only half of you here."

"We are who we are, and we do what we do." Namdarin shrugged.

"You are special, very special."

"You're the one that is special, you have taken over the care of two teenage girls, and that is not something I would wish on anyone." Namdarin laughed, he looked pointedly at the one still clutched in Steels arms, still crying. Steel rolled his eyes for a moment, then pushed Beth away just a little so he could look into her eyes.

"Come on Beth, there is still much to do. Your parents have proved to be unworthy of you, though I don't think your mother agrees with your father, she may be able to talk him round. For me, you are all the family I have."

Beth looked up at him, her blue eyes, and her mouth formed three large circles.

"I am sorry, in my despair I had forgotten about your loss."

"There is nothing to forgive my dear, nothing to forgive," he smiled before going on, "can you do something for me?" he asked.

"What do you need?"

"I'm going to be staying here, I can't really leave just yet, and I'd rather not have to sleep on sheets that Brass has been sweating on." Beth pushed away and grinned.

"I'll go and fix that right now." She almost ran to the stairs that led to the upper floor.

"Keep them busy," said Namdarin, "busy with the mundanities of life, and they'll get over this far quicker."

"They may, but will I?"

"No. Vengeance may make you feel better, but Jayanne has already killed all those responsible, the only real vengeance available to you, is the final eradication of the influences of Brass on the people around here. If you can make this a happy place to live, then you will have your vengeance on Brass and all his cohorts."

"I'll try to do that," said Steel, "I'll try." Jayanne walked in through the back door to the bar.

"You really need to do something about the security of your back gate, it's far too easy to just push open."

"I'll sort that out sometime soon." Replied Steel.

"I wouldn't worry about it, Stergin and Andel are working on it now, they'll have it sorted before they come inside, but you better have some beer ready for them." She laughed aloud.

"I believe that Jangor has collected at least a jug full." Grinned Steel.

"Hey, that's my beer. Get your own." Said Jangor.

"I don't think that beer is something we are short of around here, but we do need to discuss the price of beer, Crystal, how many jugs does Jangor owe us for?"

"Only four, the customers were hoping for some good wine, but they tried to drink their beer slowly, and bet on the wine coming out later, they all lost the bet, you closed the bar."

"That's very good, can you show the guests where their beds are? Jayanne and Namdarin are sleeping at Nigel's house for the night."

"Certainly." Crystal grabbed Mander, and pulled him gently to the stairs, up to the upper floor. He followed her along the corridor all the way to the end, she opened the door of the last room.

"This will be Steel's room, you are not sleeping here." Mander frowned briefly, as she led him to the next room.

"This is the room that I share with Beth, you will not be sleeping here, if you seek to gain entry during the night, you will be singing soprano, is that clear?" Mander gulped and nodded. "Good, spread the word. The rest of the rooms on this floor are yours, two beds to a room, they're clean and comfortable. Make sure your friends understand the rules."

"Have no fear, I will make sure they understand, and to be honest, most of them are quite boring when it comes to night-time activities."

"Why do you think I picked you, to give the tour to?"

"I was hoping for a little encouragement, perhaps a little kiss or two, not a smack round the head with a rule book, but life is such, sometimes, maybe some other time?"

"Not likely, perhaps when Brass was in charge, if he felt you deserved some favour, I don't believe that Steel would ever even think such a thing."

"I don't know the man, so I'll bow to your experience of him."

"Actually, I don't know him that well, but he has always been an honourable man." Crystal left Mander to check out the rooms and returned to the ground floor.

"I don't suppose you have any food available?" Asked Jangor, of Steel.

"I've no idea. Nigel, have we any food?"

"Beef stew and yesterday's rolls, that do?"

"More than adequate." Jangor said, "it's not dark yet but the night is coming on, and we still have a lot to do tomorrow, I think a quick meal then early to bed." He looked around the room and found no objections. Beth came out of the kitchen with a tray full of bowls of stew, then she was followed by Crystal with a tray full of warmed rolls.

"These were supposed to be for tonight's customers, but seeing as this seems to be it, supper is served." She laughed. Very soon everyone was tucking into the rich stew, dipping rolls in the thick gravy, and drinking beer alongside.

"I have a serious question." Said Jangor.

"Please ask away." Steel replied.

"Who in this town have the spare cash to buy a few pack horses that we don't really need?"

"Judging by the grip that Brass had on the people here, I'd say the only one with spare gold is now me, I'll give you a decent price for them, I'll feed them to the people over the next few months."

"Have you supplies you can spare?" Asked Jangor.

"I'm sure we can come to some arrangement."

"Steel," Jayanne said, "would you like your wife's horse and saddle back?"

"No, my dear, you have more than earned the right to ride them, please accept them with my gratitude."

"Thank you, she's a good horse, and it's finally good to have a saddle not made for some man's fat ass." She laughed.

"I know what you mean." Said Steel, smiling. Their evening meal was over in fairly short order, everyone was hungry, it had been a trying day.

"Namdarin, Jayanne, would you like to come with me," said Nigel, "I'll show you to your beds. Someone lock the door after us." Kern followed them to the door and dropped the heavy bar on it after they had gone.

"Doors and windows?" asked Jangor.

"All secured," said Kern, "back gate not the best but it will do for tonight."

"Good, you get the first watch, we've made some upheavals in this town, someone may decide to take advantage. Bed, early start." He rose, and Mander led the way to their assigned rooms, in a matter of minutes the whole inn was quiet, with everyone in their respective beds.

Steel lay in his strange bed, for the first time in hours, he actually had time to think, the loss hit him hard, he cried for his dead wife and children, and his brother, he sobbed for the loss of everything that meant anything to him, the single candle on his bed side cabinet cast flickering shadows all around the room, he heard a small shuffling in the corridor outside his room, then the latch on the door slowly lifted, the door swung inwards a foot, Crystal stepped through, then Beth, Beth closed the door and made sure the latch was secure.

"Girls, you shouldn't be here, please go back to your room." He whispered, not wanting to wake the others.

"We have talked about this, at some length." Said Crystal, slowly dropping her nightshirt to the ground, Beth's only a heartbeat behind. "You have lost your family, ours have both rejected us, we see no reason why we should be lonely tonight. She crawled into his bed and faced him, she kissed him on the forehead as Beth crawled in behind him, carefully Crystal turned her back to Steel, and pressed back against him.

"Girls, this is wrong, and I'm sorry but I have no control over that." Crystal giggled softly, blew out the candle, reach behind to take his hand, she pulled this around her belly and settled back against him, Beth's hand wrapped itself around his stomach as she pulled herself up tight behind him. In the darkness of the night their tears soaked into his pillows, it was a while before sleep took the three, but eventually it did.

CHAPTER SIXTY-ONE

It was still dark when Joe woke Kevana, but Kevana didn't object, he rolled rapidly to his feet, leaving Alverana behind, but only for a moment or two, before the bigger man rolled to his feet, Joe raised an eyebrow but made no other comment.

"Breakfast will be served shortly. Sunrise is perhaps an hour away, is that early enough for you."

"Should be good enough, has the old woman delivered the cloaks yet?"

"No, I've sent one of the boys to see what she's up to."

"We'll chase her after we've had breakfast."

"I'll get back downstairs to get your food ready." Joe left the room, Kevana turned to his friend.

"You get the rest moving, we really don't have any time to waste." Alverana pulled his clothes on quickly and left Kevana to get dressed. Kevana performed a few stretching exercises before he got dressed, then packed his saddle bags ready for loading. By the time Alverana returned Kevana was ready to go down for breakfast.

"I'll only be a short while." Said Alverana, Kevana simply nodded as he left the room, Alverana shrugged, and started packing his things. As Alverana walked into the bar, he dumped his bags alongside Kevana's on one of the long benches along a wall. Then he sat on a high stool at the bar, alongside Kevana, he picked up a mug of beer that was waiting for him.

"You're in a bad mood this morning." He observed.

"I have a really bad feeling, and I don't know where it is coming from. I'm not angry at you, more the world in general."

"I know what you mean, our lives seemed to be so ordered, planned out to the last detail, right up to the moment we die in battle. Now everything is turned on its head, our brothers want to kill us, we have two crazy clerics with us, who have some contact with an ancient dark power, and then there is whatever is going on between the two of us."

"Another bunch of bastards that want to kill us, I can deal with that, not like it's something new. A pair of mad monks with black hands, I can deal with that, it is new, but I can deal with it. The rest I'm not sure about at all. I was a little harsh with you upstairs and that made me feel bad, why? I'm used to cursing soldiers, questioning their abilities, their parentage, even their manhood, in front of a whole platoon, or even a brigade, and I feel nothing. But I'm a little short with you and I feel sad for the pain I've caused you. Why?"

"We've known each other a long time, we've been together a long time, well, long in soldiering terms. We both care about each other, which is unusual, but not unheard of, these sorts of bonds often form between soldiers, you know, the heat of battle and all that. You feel that you were a little rude to me earlier, now I have a question, it doesn't actually require an answer, just a thought or two. What if someone else had talked to me like that?"

The two sat on their stools, facing the bar, mugs cradled in their hands, for a long moment. Before Kevana mumbled.

"I'd have had his head in a heartbeat."

"Likewise, so let's try not to overreact when our friends behave like soldiers, we don't have much in the way of allies right now, and we really can't afford to lose any more." He turned slowly to face Kevana, who was already looking straight at him, Alverana smiled.

"That's not going to be easy, you know how hot headed I can be." Grinned Kevana.

"Agreed, you need to be especially careful around Kirukana, he's tapped this dark power that Worandana has been hiding for so long, his world has been turned over far more than ours, he's lost everything that made the foundations of his life, while he comes to terms with that he's going to be very dangerous."

"And I'm not dangerous?"

"You're dangerous enough for me, but I have no knowledge of this black power at all, I've no idea how fast he can call it, or how tightly he can control it, so give Worandana a few days to get him trained and under proper control, or things could go badly for us all."

"I'm not used to that."

"What do you mean?"

"Well, it seems to me that you know about everything, your life has brought you into contact with all sorts of powers and peoples, gods and goddesses, you always know something, but not this time?"

"It is beyond my experience, I've never heard of this dark power, not even a hint as to its existence, but a thought just struck me."

"Go on."

"Gyara."

"I don't understand."

"Gyara said that both groups have the power to end life here, and release her from her servitude, what if this black power is what she is looking for?"

"That is a possibility, we need to talk to Worandana about this, could it be that he already knows?"

"I don't think so, he's so focused on using it to subjugate the council."

"I think he was planning on simply pushing them aside, and replacing them with his group of scholars, but now they are all dead, he's going to kill them all, then replace the council with something more manageable, could even be as small as three or five members."

"Which three?"

"Obviously himself, Kirukana, and you, for your military skills."

"Which five?"

"Add to that, perhaps a surviving councillor, if there is one, or an aid, and me for my knowledge of things he's never met."

"Beyond five."

"It's unlikely he would form a replacement council with more than five, but any additional members would simply be puppets for him to control. I don't believe he'd go that far, too much like hard work. Better to burn the council and start again with something more manageable."

"You're a soldier, how did you get to be such a politician?"

"I observe." Laughed Alverana.

"I'd noticed that actually." Kevana smiled.

"Joe." Called Alverana. "Where's breakfast, we've got a few hungry men here?" The rest were trooping down the stairs into the bar.

"I'll be with you in a moment or two." Came a distant voice from the back of the bar. Kevana waved to a table that had been set up for them, it was more than big enough for them all to sit at in comfort. There were small mugs of beer already filled on the table, wooden plates, knives and forks, the only thing missing was the food. Kevana and Alverana took seats at one end of the table, and Worandana, along with Kirukana, took seats at the other end. Joe and one of the serving girls came through from the back with huge platters, Joe balancing two, one full of sausages, the other bacon, the girl brought the warmed rolls, and butter, she placed her platter first then turned to help Joe with his.

"Gentlemen, please be seated, there is more beer to be had, and more bread warming, please enjoy your breakfast." Said Joe. The girl scurried back into the kitchen and came out with a large jug of beer for the monks, which she dropped onto the table with a little more force than was necessary. Joe raised his eyebrows by way of voiceless recrimination. She ducked her head and scampered into the back, to return in moments with two large pats of rich yellow butter. As they started to eat, what looked like a perambulating pile of colourful cloth came walking in the front door. Once the pile was fully inside, it turned towards an unoccupied table, only then was the boy carrying them visible. He dropped them carefully on the table and caught one that tried to slide off the top, he folded it gently and placed it back on the precarious looking mountain.

"Your cloaks gentlemen." He said as he disappeared into the back of the bar.

"Damn that's yellow." Said Alverana, laughing.

"I'm really unhappy about this," said Kirukana, "At least black gives us some camouflage at night, I think a blind man could see these in the dark."

"I actually have a good idea." Laughed Alverana.

"This has to be good." Smiled Petrovana. "Carry on, enlighten us."

"In garments like these we could masquerade as strolling players, presenting the works of the great bard, does anyone know 'Troilus and Cressida'?" Alverana laughed out loud.

"We are serious people, we wouldn't ever be players." Snapped Kirukana.

"Have you ever seen the works of the bard?" Asked Worandana.

"No, it's frivolous nonsense."

"Oh, my." Smiled Worandana, "You really need to see some of his works, they are so complex, there are tales within tales, meanings within meanings, and they all come with some sort of sting in the tail. They masquerade as entertainment, but quite often are educational. Much like the fairy tales told to children, these are fairy tales for adults. Watch or read them, you have something to learn. Kirukana, do you know why the works of the bard haven't been declared heretical?"

"I've no idea."

"Because they are considered by the council to be nonsense,

just as you have said, and they are anything but. I think that if there were enough groups of players, then our religion is doomed, the people will rise up and kill us all."

"You're joking."

"No, I'm not. The stories speak out against despots, tyrants, and religion. I am sorry to say that Zandaar fits all these categories."

"How can you say that about our living god?"

"Because it is true. Can't you see it? He controls everything we do, and everything we say, and everything we believe, I have been trying to assemble a force to replace the council, and perhaps change things for the better, but they have put an end to that plan, they have taken away my dream, now I can only take their dream and their power from them."

"Along with their lives?"

"If necessary, yes, I'll kill them all, and replace them, hopefully with something that will be better."

"Run by you?"

"Do you know anyone better?"

"How about Zandaar?"

"He's the one that has allowed things to get this bad, he should have taken better control of the council, but he hasn't, and now I'm not sure if they plan to kill him, or merely subjugate him. Whichever it is, they're the ones in charge, which is not going to be good for any of us. Can't you see that."

"You're saying that our god isn't fit to run our world?"

"I'm afraid so, he's lost control of the council, and they're going to make him pay for that lapse, probably with his life."

"How can they survive without the power of Zandaar to back them up?"

"I have no idea, but I am certain they have some plan for this."

"How can they maintain the threat of black fire? That comes directly from Zandaar, and no one else."

"That you know of, but perhaps they have some way to imitate the black fire."

"Could that be done?"

"Using their standard methods, I think not, I've felt the fire, from a safe distance, though it burns dark and hot, it is not self-sustaining, it needs to be fed, and controlled, or it will fade out and die."

"Perhaps they've found a way to make ordinary fire burn dark, or black?"

"That's more likely, perhaps we'll have to ask the last one, before he dies."

"What if he doesn't want to tell us?"

"From my experience, most people will tell you everything they know by the time their toes are on fire."

"You'd actually put a council member to the fire?"

"What have they done to all my friends?"

"I suppose, but we should give them the opportunity to talk first."

"But can we trust them to tell the whole truth, except in extremis?"

"Probably not," Kirukana shook his head slowly, "they won't believe until they are actually burning."

"So long as they believe the burning can be stopped, they'll talk."

"All this chatter is interesting," said Kevana, "but it's only slowing down breakfast, and delaying our departure, eat, then we can be travelling before they start searching for us."

"Sorry," said Worandana, "we can continue this discourse once we are on the road."

"I still don't see what the council can do without god to stand behind them." Muttered Kirukana.

"You'll be able to get your answers once we start chopping pieces off them." Snapped Kevana.

"You'd actually torture them?"

"You forget, they set the damned dogs on us." Kevana slammed his hand down on the table to emphasise the point.

"How can I forget that." Kirukana said loudly, "I spend half my time trying to look through trees, and behind rocks, waiting for that moment when the trap closes on us, and we all die."

"Don't fret." Smiled Kevana. "We have a few days before they can catch up with us, they are most likely still heading in the wrong direction, unless they're killing horses, they won't realise the deception for another day or two."

"Unless the deception was spotted immediately, and they turned back instantly."

"In that case, they could be knocking on the doors." Laughed Kevana, at that moment there was a loud pounding, like someone was indeed knocking on the door, all eyes turned to the door. Only Alverana's laughter gave him away, that and the jumping of the beer mugs on the table.

"Someday my friend," said Kevana, "your sense of humour is

going to get you in serious trouble." All eyes turned to Alverana as his hand came up from beneath the table, a huge grin on his face. "How long to sunrise?" He asked.

"Not long," said Joe, "the sky is lightening already, so I'd say not an hour, what is so important about sunrise?"

"That's when our brothers will start looking for us," said Worandana, "we need to be a moving target, which makes us more difficult to find."

"If they are that close, they can still see you at a gallop, why the urgency?"

"They'll be looking for us from Zandaarkoon and Angorak, and maybe a few other places as well."

"They can see that far?"

"It's not exactly seeing, but it's close, the thing is that they only have so much energy to use up, so they have to search fast, they may miss us completely in their haste to cover as much territory as they can."

"Worandana," interrupted Kirukana, "You are giving away the secrets of the brotherhood."

"And they are intent on our lives, if there is any way I can hurt them I will do it. If the whole world finds out that they can search for people and things over great distances, without leaving their castles, then so be it."

"You know that that is considered heresy?" Smiled Kirukana.

"By you?"

"Not as much as it used to. They set the dogs on us." He laughed loudly.

"So, you are ready to make them pay for that error of judgement?"

"Even with their lives. I can't believe that I've spent my life, following their dogma, because I now have no doubt that these petty rules don't come from Zandaar, somehow I don't see our god worrying about the colour of our underwear, do you?"

"I am fairly sure he has bigger things on his mind, and for some reason the sword is currently the biggest. It is my belief that he has set us on the trail of this weapon, because he doesn't want the council to get their hands on it."

"We'll find that out only if we get our hands on it first," Kevana said, firmly, "so eat up we need to be chasing the damned thing as soon as we can." He turned to Worandana. "Can this dark power be used for searches?"

"I've never tried it, endeavouring to keep it as secret as

possible. We can give it a try if you want?"

"I think we should wait until mid-morning, once all the searches have been done."

"Agreed, I wouldn't want to blunder into a search, that would definitely give the game away."

"But they already know about this power." Said Kirukana.

"They don't know what it can do."

"What can your acolytes have told them?"

"They really only knew about its existence, and the fact that it is far and away more powerful than their circles. They knew how to access it, and how to focus it to some extent, but basically that was it."

"So now the council have this power as well?"

"Unlikely."

"How can you say that?"

"It's simple, the council no longer have anyone with the skills necessary to reach this power, let alone do something useful with it."

"But they are the highest of our order."

"Only because they kill off anyone with real skill and power. They remain the highest on the ladder by pushing off anyone who could go past them and reach the top."

"So how have you managed to stay alive so long, don't they see that you threaten them?"

"They do now, until very recently they thought I was an old fool, who wanted only the knowledge, and that I had no hankering for the power that comes with a seat on the council."

"Well you don't, or has that changed?"

"No, I still don't want that sort of responsibility, which is not the way they see it, but if the only way I can survive is to kill them all, then that is their problem. I'm fairly sure I'll be up to the task, of leading the Brotherhood of Zandaar into a new and brighter existence, if I survive, of course."

"If any of us survive."

"Well I intend on surviving," said Kevana, "at least until I take the heads of the bastards that sent the dogs after us."

"I'm with you on that." Muttered Alverana.

"Great," said Kevana, "Eat up it's time to go, we need to get dressed in our fancy new cloaks, I'm having the red one, it will hide the blood stains of my enemies."

"I'll have the green." Said Alverana.

"Yellow." called Worandana.

So the calls went on, until only Kirukana was left.

"So, what am I left with?" He laughed.

"The last one is I believe, a very fetching cream with wide stripes of blue running through it."

"So, it's off-white with broad blue stripes, at least they're not arrows."

"Well now you mention it, some of them are more than a little pointy." Laughed Petrovana.

"Great," said Kirukana, "I'm the one that looks like a convict."

"At least you won't look like a Zandaar." Laughed Petrovana.

"Enough joviality." Said Kevana. "Let's get dressed and get out of here before the sun catches us stationary. Joe, thanks for all your help, and the great food, good wine, and wonderful company, now we must bid you farewell."

"Good luck on your quest gentlemen, I hope that you come back this way and tell us how it comes out. That's one of the problems with running an inn, everybody passes through with so many good stories to tell, but we never get to hear the endings, I hope that's not because they all end up dead."

"If we can get word to you, we will." Assured Kevana, as he led them all out of the bar.

In only a few minutes they were on the road eastwards out of the small town, heading towards the river, at a fast canter, the sky in front of them was blue with scattered clouds, the weather looked good for the day, the wind was soft and from the south, which usually gives fine weather this close to winter, it's the heavy wind from the north that brings the real wintery weather. The usual column formed as soon as they left the inn yard, Kevana and Alverana in front, Worandana and Kirukana in the second row. The road was wide enough and sufficiently smooth to give the horses no problems, even before the sun peeped over the horizon they felt the searches reach out for them, Kevana ignored the one that was howling his name, Kirukana reached a hand to Worandana, for his support when he heard his name called on the etheric wind, a flash of darkness passed between them, and the search rushed on by. The search that was calling to Worandana came sweeping towards them, Worandana's response was different again, he struck the leader with a surge of black power, enough to stop the search in its tracks, and scatter the consciousness of the head man.

"Damn." Shouted Worandana.

"What's the problem?" Asked Kevana.

"Axorana is smarter than I thought, or maybe just more cunning than I realised."

"Explain please."

"The search they sent for me, I was expecting Axorana to be leading it, he wasn't, it was someone else."

"Is he dead?"

"No, just stunned, as are all the rest of his circle, I was hoping to slap Axorana again, I want him to learn to leave us alone, maybe he can learn from someone else's pain."

"Do you think that is likely?"

"No, he's most likely standing over his fallen colleagues and crowing about his superior intelligence."

"Will they recover?"

"Most likely, but I don't think they'll come looking for me again, or any of us. Would you?"

"No."

"They may not get the choice," said Kirukana, "search or die."

"Would Axorana actually do that?" Demanded Worandana.

"I'd hope not, but he's really frightened of you, perhaps frightened enough to do almost anything."

"If he kills brothers just to get to me, then the bastard is going to die slow." Snarled Worandana.

"You better tell him so, or he'll do it again." Said Kirukana.

"When we stop for lunch, I'm going to break that bastard once and for all, and you're going to help me."

"No problem with that."

"I have an issue." Said Kevana.

"What?" Asked Worandana.

"Who will replace him? Could it be someone worse?"

"It may take them days to settle on a new leader, could be a fierce competition, perhaps even fatal." Said Kirukana.

"Is that a bad thing?" Asked Worandana.

"More brothers die. Here's another thought," said Kirukana, "he's a cunning bastard, by now he's realised that you can strike back, and strike hard, so where is he now?"

"He's looking for somewhere to hide, I have his mental pattern, he can't hide from me, not anywhere, there is nowhere out of my range."

"Perhaps, but maybe he's running into the temple, and heading for the catacombs, to reach him, you'd have to pass right through the space that Zandaar controls absolutely. Care to risk that."

"I think not, I'll just have to drag him out by his ears and cut his head off." Snarled Worandana.

"Sounds like a plan to me." Smiled Kevana. "Less chatter more speed, we need to be in Angorak before Namdarin and his group." Kevana laid his heels into his horse and kicked the pace up to a gallop, this caused the group to stretch out some as the other horses took a little while to pick up the speed. Alverana glanced back at the riders and laughed at the capes blowing in the wind created by their own speed.

"We look like a rainbow riding on the road." He shouted to Kevana.

"I just had a crazy thought." Laughed Alverana.

"Explain." Called Kevana.

"Who rides on rainbows?"

"I have no idea." frowned Kevana.

"All we need are some imitation horns for our horses."

"Still no idea."

"Unicorns ride on rainbows, and are supposed to be the friends of virgins, we're monks and theoretically we should be such."

"Have you been out in the sun too long, my friend?"

"No, but this mission is getting to be so surreal that the riding of unicorns seems almost mandatory at this point." Alverana laughed loudly, then focused on his horse the ground was getting a little too rough to not be paying full attention. Kevana just shook his head in dismay.

"Sometimes I worry about the sanity of this whole world." he muttered, then settled down to the task of riding a horse over rough ground at speed.

Kevana was woken from his concentration by a shout. He glanced back and saw one of his riders fall. He pulled hard left on the reins and turned back down the line, Alverana turned right and followed as the others reined their horses to a stop.

Kevana slipped from his horse beside the fallen man, he let the horse go its own way, knowing full well that someone else would chase it down for him. Davadana groaned as Kevana knelt beside him. Kevana placed a hand on the man's chest and pushed him into the ground.

"Don't move. Check that everything works. Hands and feet, can you feel them? Breathe slow and even you may have broken ribs."

"I am winded, that is all," said the fallen man, "hands and feet feel fine."

"That's good, now wiggle those fingers and toes."

"Yes, they wiggle, why?" Asked Davadana.
"Don't ask." Suggested Worandana.
"Ankles and wrists?" Said Kevana.
"They work."
"Knees, shoulders?"
"Fine."
"Neck, slow and gentle?"
"Neck fine, hurts like hell, but moves fine."
"Nothing sharp, or scrapes or grinds when it moves?"
"No sharp, no scrape, no grind, just pain in knee, hips and elbows, and left forearm hurts like a bitch."

Kevana looked down at Davadana for a long moment, then spoke softly with a tear in his eye.

"On your feet soldier, nothing broken, we have many miles to go." He turned away to where Petrovana was returning with his horse. Worandana helped Davadana to his feet.

"What did you mean, don't ask?" Asked Davadana.
"Are you sure you want to know?"
"I think so."

"Fine, you asked, if your fingers or toes don't work, then your back is damaged, and you can't ride, if you can't ride, you are dead, and he," Worandana nodded his head in Kevana's direction, "has to take your life."

"Would he actually do it?"

"Oh yes, he'd hate it, but he'd do it. He can't cure you, he can't take you with us, he can't leave you behind for some random predator, or worse still for thirst to take you, he can only relieve your pain in one way."

"I don't think I'm suited for command, I couldn't do that."

"None of us truly know what we are capable of until we are tested, now back on your horse, and hold on tighter." Worandana smiled, as Petrovana brought up Davadana's horse.

"Mount up. Move out." Yelled Kevana.

"See." Laughed Worandana, as he reached behind himself for the reins, he knew Kirukana was holding.

Kevana set a slightly slower pace as they turned a little north of east on their run to the river, he turned to Alverana.

"Do you know anything about the territory between here and the river?"

"Nothing, I don't even recall seeing any maps of the area, it's not been something of importance to me."

"Me neither." Kevana turned to Worandana. "You know

anything?"

"Not really, usual agricultural communities every ten to twelve miles, but other than that nothing of interest, Angorak is only a couple of days away, so no need for any monasteries, no major resources, they grow food and sell it in Angorak, generally a peaceful sort of existence."

"Until we come storming through. Any bandits or brigands in the area?"

"Nothing that I have heard about, but dressed up like popinjays we are likely to attract them, if they are around, why?"

"Why?" Howled Alverana, "Because my friend here is a barbarian, he is getting a little frustrated because he hasn't been able to kill anyone for a few days, he feels a need for swordplay and death, a dozen robbers would suit him down to the ground, some fancy sword work, heads and various body parts flying, he'd be happy as a pig in shit." Alverana threw back his head and roared with laughter.

"It's not like that at all." Mumbled Kevana.

"Oh, but it is exactly like that, you need that rush of battle, just to be sure you are still the fastest and the most brutal."

"Fine, believe what you want, I just want to be ready, in case we are attacked by blood thirsty bandits, I have an uncontrollable urge to protect your feeble old bodies."

"You are aware that most of us are younger than you?" Laughed Kirukana.

"Yes, but you move like librarians."

"As you can see gentlemen." Said Alverana. "The Kevana school of etiquette and good manners has totally failed in its first and only student."

"I'll have you know my manners are impeccable, I never pick my nose when any one is watching, and I always let the lady open the door for me." Kevana laughed, most of the others joined in.

A few hours later, the horses moving at a walk, they came to an open area of grassland, there were a few large trees, but none of the smaller ones that should normally be around the mature, if not ancient ones.

"Is this pasture land for cattle?" Ask Kevana, looking at Alverana.

"It could be, though there don't seem to be any droppings from cows or horses hereabouts."

"So, there should be a settlement around here somewhere, I'm seeing no smoke from fires, nor any roads, or even pathways through the grass."

Kevana raised a clenched fist and the column stopped. He turned in his saddle and looked to Worandana.

"This is a strange place; do you have any idea what it is?"

"Nothing that comes to mind, though it does look a lot like the grassland we encountered when we escaped the mountain, remember."

"Agreed, but that grass had evidence of cattle grazing, no cow pats here at all."

"Something else, sheep perhaps."

"I see no sheep droppings either." Said Alverana.

"This looks like someone's front lawn." Said Kevana. Alverana dropped from his saddle and plucked a handful of grass, then climbed back up onto his horse.

"Look, this grass hasn't been cropped by animals, it hasn't been cut by man, it grows this long and then stops." Each blade of grass was exactly the same length and had the unmistakeable point that meant that Alverana was right.

"Don't be ridiculous," said Kirukana, "no one can tell grass how to grow."

"Actually," spoke Worandana slowly, "there is someone, or perhaps a group of people, and I use the term people in its loosest possible sense, they can do just that, they are the ultimate gardeners." He paused for a moment then looked around. "How far inside their garden are we?"

"A few minutes, not as many as ten, I think." Muttered Alverana, looking around quickly.

"Perhaps they haven't noticed us yet, turn around and let's get out of their garden as quickly as we can." Worandana turned his horse and set off in the direction that had come, not at any speed, but a fast walk for the horse, the others turned and followed him.

"What is that crazy old man frightened of?" Asked Kevana, looking at Alverana.

"I have no idea, but if he wants to get out with the minimum of disturbance, then I'm with him, he's frightened of something, that's more than enough for me. Keep a good look out, there must be something dangerous here."

"I see nothing only grass and trees, it's not too important anyway I see the boundary just ahead, we're almost out, of whatever this is."

"We're not out yet, and I can feel something powerful

approaching."

About halfway between Worandana and the boundary a section of grass lifted up, like it was a trapdoor, turned over along one edge, and fell to the ground leaving grass roots and wriggling worms exposed to the light of day. Slowly a man shaped creature, came up out of the ground, as if he was climbing a stair, once he was up onto the grass he stood to his full height of three and a half feet, his green jacket and trousers unmarked by the soil he had climbed out of, his red hat was equally clean, as was his long white beard. He stood with his legs slightly parted and his small hands on his hips.

"Why have you invaded my garden?" Demanded the figure, his voice far deeper than any of them expected, it resonated like the rockfalls in the deepest caverns.

"We apologise, we weren't aware this was your garden, and as soon as we discovered our error we turned round to leave, before we caused you any disturbance."

"Why are you apologising to a gnome? Just take his head, and let's be on our way." Called Davadana laughing out loud.

"Silence fool." Snapped Worandana, never taking his eyes off the figure. "I am sorry Lord of the Gnomb, this idiot has no idea what he says."

"You trespass upon my land, murder my grass," his deep brown eyes flashed at Alverana, "and then insult me," the eyes snap to Davadana, "there must be payment for this insult."

"We came in peace, and meant no harm, we only wish to leave in peace. Rest assured that the fool will be punished most harshly." Worandana's voice as low and calm as he could make it.

"You are joking?" Called Davadana, Worandana didn't look round, he was trying to hold the eyes of the Gnomb.

"Your punishments are as nothing compared to mine."

"Lord, he is young and foolish, let us take care of our own please."

"No," said the Gnomb, "the rest can leave, but he is mine."

Alverana's hand reached out and snatched Kevana's wrist willing him to remain silent.

Davadana stood up in his stirrups, nocked an arrow, pulled and released, the arrow flew true, and struck the Gnomb in the eye, as Davadana had intended, the distance was small, and the target was not moving, so he couldn't really have missed. The arrow shattered into tiny fragments. The Gnomb's large white bushy eyebrows moved together and downwards, his frown darkened his whole face, something spooked Davadana's horse and it bucked him off, then it ran for the boundary like the devil himself was chasing it.

Davadana climbed to his feet nocking another arrow, then he looked down, his feet had been pulled together by the grass, and he started to scream as the grass grew quickly up his legs.

"Ride." Yelled Worandana, laying into his horse's flanks. The others followed rapidly, Alverana had to pull Kevana along to be sure he cleared the Gnomb's garden, in only a few heartbeats they were across the boundary, and Worandana reined in hard. They turned back to see the punishment of the Gnomb. Davadana's howling became less as his body slowly changed, his arms became branches, his torso, a trunk, his hair, moss on the trunk, as the branches spread and grew the leaves blossomed on the tree that used to be Davadana.

"We don't leave men behind to be turned into trees." Yelled Kevana directly into Worandana's face.

"There is nothing we could have done for him. You should be glad anyway."

"Why should I be glad, one of our men has been turned into a tree by a garden ornament, where is the glad in this?"

"If it hadn't been Davadana, it would have been the grass murderer to pay the price."

"Nobody killed any grass." Snarled Kevana.

"I did," mumbled Alverana, "that would have been me there."

"Are you sure there is nothing we could have done to save him?" Snapped Kevana.

"The power of the Gnomb is rooted in the earth, in the rocks, in the soil, in the plants, and in the air. I have no waterpower to hand, once we get back to Zandaarkoon I'll send the teams out and we'll fence this one in with rivers and lakes, canals and streams, over the years his power will fade, and he'll disappear."

"Could your new dark power not have overcome him?"

"I don't know, if I had tried, and the dark power didn't work, then he'd have a copse there, not just a single tree. Speaking of which, as that tree matures, and it is doing so quite quickly, the garden extends, and we'll be back in the same mess all over again, I suggest we ride north, and head around the territory of this Gnomb."

Kevana looked down and saw that the grass was indeed changing, he turned to Alverana and said "North and quickly." They all turned north and pushed the horses into as rapid a pace as the terrain would allow.

CHAPTER SIXTY-TWO

Namdarin woke to the sound of cockerels, and felt Jayanne pressed against his back, he could tell from her breathing that she was already awake.

"We need to get moving." He whispered.

"I know, but I like it here."

"So do I, but we have a long way to go yet."

"Fine, let's get back to the inn, and see what's for breakfast." She rolled away from him and started to pull her clothes on, he watched her for a while.

"You said move." She laughed, "So, move." He smiled and rolled out of the other side of the bed to start getting dressed.

"Do you think Steel is going to be able to make this town a better place?" He asked.

"I don't think he could make it any worse."

"That's fairly sure, it's going to take a strong will to turn all these people around."

"He doesn't need to turn them all, only a few, then the others will realise that there is actually a right way to do things, and they'll follow suit."

"You have far more faith in people than I do." He smiled and walked out of the door now fully dressed, Jayanne followed him closely. Down in the kitchen they found Nigel fixing breakfast for his mother, he was singing softly to himself.

"You sound sort of happy." Said Namdarin.

"I am, I can finally see things getting better around here."

"I hope so," said Jayanne, "people deserve a chance to live their lives without fear."

"We'll see how it turns out. Why don't you two get back to the inn, tell Steel I'll be there as soon as I have mother fed and installed at her loom, she likes to weave, even if she can't walk."

"We'll see you in a little while. Look after your mother." Said Jayanne, she touched Nigel softly on the arm, then walked to the door, with Namdarin behind her. Before her hand reached out for the door handle she stopped.

"Where's wolf?" She asked.

"Did he leave the inn with us?"

"I think so, but he's not here, we must have left him outside all night."

"He's a big boy, he can look after himself."

"I'm not worried about him, I'm worried about the locals."

"I'm sure he can't have eaten all of them." Laughed Namdarin.

"This town is a bad place, it's bound to have dogs running around loose."

"He'll be fine, I'm sure you are worrying unnecessarily."

"He's an innocent in this world, I worry about him."

"Fine, let's see if we can find him." Namdarin reached past her and opened the door, as he did, he saw Wolf sitting on the doorstep, staring up at them. Namdarin looked at Jayanne and smiled.

"See Wolf is fine, he's just sitting here waiting for us." Then he looked further out from the doorstep, in a circle about fifteen feet away were many dogs, some large, some small, they all seemed to be waiting for something. Jayanne reached down and stroked his head.

"Are these nasty dogs giving you a hard time?" She asked the wolf, he just looked up at her and let his long red tongue fall from his mouth. The axe of Algoron leapt into her hand with a flick of the wrist. "Have no fear my friend, I'll kill them all before they can harm you." She stepped through the door and walked slowly into the street, waiting for the dogs to make some form of attack, Namdarin followed her, his sword drawn and ready, Wolf took his usual place at her right hip. Together the three walked into the centre of the street, two prepared for battle, one just as relaxed as normal. The circle of dogs fell back in front of them, they turned towards the inn, as they started walking down the street, wolf held his position at her hip, the circle of dogs slowly formed up almost as an escort, some ranging to the side but the majority followed up behind them, there were none of the usual aggressive moves from the dogs, just a regular escort, almost as if they were pack mates.

"What is going on, why aren't they attacking?" She asked, looking around warily.

"Perhaps our friend has been elected pack leader for this group, at least until we leave."

"I wonder how he managed that?"

"I'd suggest that somewhere the old leader is lying with his throat ripped out, I don't see much in the way of blood on Wolf, but that could have been some time ago."

Jayanne started to relax as their escort slowly got closer, but still showed no sign of aggressive intent.

"This is very strange." She whispered, her hand resting on Wolf's wide head.

"I know what you mean, but they're not getting excited, just following. I'm almost getting to trust them."

"Almost, but not quite." She replied, as the main pack was only ten feet behind them, and those ranging to the sides were almost as close. They turned a corner into the street where the inn was, and saw Steel was already out on the veranda, he was doing something that they couldn't quite see yet. They walked towards the inn, the pack of dogs settled into formation behind them.

Once they were a little closer Namdarin called out. "Steel. What are you doing up so early?"

The man jumped, and turned to them, he had a paint brush in his hand.

"I'm fixing the sign, but I'm not sure how I'm going to fix it up on the post again yet."

"You wanted it down, so I took it down." Laughed Jayanne.

"Now I don't have the skills to put it back up." Smiled Steel.

"I'd suggest," said Namdarin "you drill the base, and the upright, insert a steel bar, then brace the outsides with wooden pieces fastened with rope or screws, that should be strong enough."

"That's for later in the day." Said Steel, "What's with the dog pack following you?"

"I've no idea, they were waiting for us when we left Nigel's house, they seem to have attached themselves to Wolf." Said Jayanne.

"Perhaps they'll all leave the newly christened village of Jayanne, when you do." Steel laughed, and held up his sign, which had a rough painting of an axe in white on it. "What do you think?"

"Looks fine to me." Said Namdarin. "I've seen far rougher signs than that outside inns."

"I'm not an artist, so I'm not upset by your opinion."

"Oh, you are an artist," said Namdarin, "I've tasted your wine, that is a work of art."

"Well, thank you, but it's not entirely down to me, I have a good team working for me and they do a sterling job."

"I have a question for you." Said Namdarin.

"Please ask away." Said Steel.

"I need to get to Zandaarkoon, do you know the way?"

"First you need to get to Angorak, it's no more than three days ride, south and a little west, then the main road south from there will take you straight into Zandaarkoon, but I'd actually advise against going there, the priesthood rules that place with an iron fist, they don't take too kindly to outsiders."

"I have no choice, I need to face them and their damned god, my intention is to kill him."

"Not a task to be taken lightly."

"I'll agree with that, but it is something I must do."

"Let's go inside and get some breakfast, the girls are already cooking. Have you thought that you could always stay? I'm sure the village could do with a new law-man."

"No, I have to go, those damned priests have got this coming, they have to learn that the world is not theirs to do with as they will."

"I understand, they do have a tendency to think they own the place."

"They already think they own it, and they actually intend to take it all. I'm going to make them think again."

"Well I can only wish you the best of luck with that, I've always found that religious folks can be the most stubborn."

"They'll get my message, without any doubt."

"Anyway, breakfast awaits." Steel waved his hand towards the door, then followed them inside.

Once they were inside and the door closed, Wolf wandered over to the fire and lay down in front of the hearth.

"Crystal." Called Steel. "What have we got for breakfast, for these fine gentlemen and lady?"

A voice came from the back of the bar.

"I don't know about fine, but we have bacon and mushrooms and warmed-over rolls, from last night." Crystal came into view, a huge smile on her face, she walked slowly up to Steel, pulled his head down and kissed him on the forehead. She turned to Namdarin and Jayanne, "Please take a seat, breakfast will be served as soon as it is ready." Namdarin nodded and escorted Jayanne to a small table in one corner, Wolf lifted his head briefly to be sure where they were.

"Don't you think they are fine people, they liberated you from your servitude to that wicked Brass?"

"For that I am grateful," she said, she held out her arms and turned slowly, "but where am I and what am I doing?"

"I see." Said Steel. "Almost nothing has changed, however, you can now walk out the door any time you choose, I'd rather that you didn't, because you really are too young to be making your own way in this wicked world. You could leave with these people, I'm sure they would train you, I can really see you as a sword maiden, you have the flashing eyes that would strike terror into the hearts of your enemies. I'd much prefer it if you stayed here and gave me the chance to find you a decent man to marry, one that meets your exacting requirements of course." He smiled, cocked his head to one side, and opened his arms wide. Crystal looked at him and laughingly walked into his arms and hugged him, he enfolded her in his arms and rocked her slowly from side to side. "Please tell me you'll stay." He whispered. Slowly she raised her head and looked up into his eyes.

"I'll stay, for now." She whispered, turning her head back down against his shoulder and smiling softly to herself. After a short time, she wriggled out of his arms and smiled at him, then she turned away. Crystal almost skipped into the kitchen, she seemed so happy. Steel looked round at the others and shrugged. There was some noise from the kitchen, heavy pots being moved, then Crystal reappeared.

"Breakfast will be only a few minutes." She said loudly, she smiled at Steel, and walked over to the table that Namdarin and Jayanne were sharing. She turned to Jayanne and asked. "May I have a word lady?" She turned to Namdarin and spoke sharply. "In private." Namdarin looked up at her and said. "Should I go somewhere else?" Crystals only response was a glare.

"I think I'll go somewhere else." He said getting up from his seat, he was only a step away when Crystal sat down, she turned to watch him and make sure he was out of earshot. She turned to Jayanne.

"Lady I'd like some advice if you don't mind, you are older than me and so must have much more experience of the world."

"Older?"

"That didn't come out exactly right, will you help me?"

"In any way that I can." Jayanne smiled.

"Well, this is difficult, so I guess I'll just tell it how it is. Last night, I really can't say this without causing offence to someone, this isn't easy. Last night, myself and Beth were a little, well more than a little frightened to have so many rough looking soldiers in the house, that Brank is huge."

"Yes, Brank is a large man, in more ways than you know, and none of us look too trustworthy." Jayanne grinned.

"Well, Beth and me, we had a long talk, not that long, but together we decided that the safest place for us wasn't in our room, so we decided that if anyone was going to look after us it was going to be Steel, after all he'd been so nice to us earlier, he promised to look after us. So, we went together to his room, we both got into his bed." Jayanne's face hardened at this point. "Relax, please and hear me out."

"What did he do to you?" Whispered Jayanne harshly.

"I wriggled in alongside him, Beth went to the other side, I turned my back to him and pressed up against him, I pulled his hand around me, and I felt Beth's hand come around his belly and between us both, I felt the hardness of his need against my back." She paused.

"And." Muttered Jayanne, her hand twitching on the haft of the axe.

"The three of us cried ourselves to sleep."

"That's all?"

"Yes, we cried like babies."

"And the point of this conversation."

"Oh yes. Do you think Steel is an honourable man?"

"Given what you've just told me, I'd say almost without doubt. Why?"

"Is he husband material?"

"For you?" Crystal nodded. "Well," continued Jayanne, "you have to understand that he has just lost his family and that his eldest child was only a year or two younger than you, but other than that, I'd say he is a good man, though crawling into his bed was not a terribly good move."

"I understand that, but you people are so fierce and scary."

"We'll be gone in a short time, are you sure you want to make this man marry you?"

"I think so, he's nice, and he smells nice too."

"If you are sure that's what you want, he seems to be a nice man, he has a prosperous business, and he's just inherited a lot of gold from Brass. There's too much metal going on around here, Brass, Steel and gold."

"The gold is of no importance, I can always get men to give me gold."

"If you want to be wifely material, that's something that has to stop, understand?"

"Yes, I know that, I think he'd be a good husband."

"If you want him to be yours, you'll have to go slow, and I mean slow, this is not going to happen in a week or a month, probably not even in a year. The next time it must be him that comes to your bed."

"Can't I just lay him on the floor and jump on him, I'm sure he'd be impressed with the skills I have acquired?"

"That would be the act of a whore, not a wife. You'll have to tempt him, a smile, a touch, a good morning kiss on the cheek, make that a ritual, something that happens every day. A goodnight kiss and hug, the same, make it a ritual. It's not going to be easy, because you'll remind him of his daughter. Give it some time, she will always be as he saw her last, you will grow older and become different from his memory of her. You must always be as clean as you can, and you should smell nice, find a perfume he likes and wear it all the time. When he knows you are standing behind him from your scent, then you'll know you're getting to him. He may never accept you as wife, but you could be together for many years."

"It's going to take a while." Crystal sighed. "Are you and Namdarin married?"

"No, I don't believe we ever will be, he saved my life, and we've been together ever since, we have become lovers, which is not something anyone who knows me would ever have bet on. I love him, he loves me, but married, that's not going to happen. I don't need it; all I need is him."

"I need Steel."

"No, you want him, maybe you'll have him, but need, that is something else." Crystal looked down at the table for a moment or two, then looked up into Jayanne's intense green eyes.

"Thank you for your help, I think that I'm going to get my man, maybe we'll not be married, but we'll be together." She rose slowly and went back into the kitchen. Namdarin returned to the table and asked.

"What was that all about?"

"Things are going to get a little rough around here."

"What do you mean?"

"Steel is going to be arranging husbands for those two girls, and Crystal has already decided who is going to marry her."

"Who's she chosen?"

"Steel."

"Should we tell him?"

"No, let him find out for himself, most likely after the trap has already snapped shut." She laughed loudly as Crystal came out of the kitchen carrying platters of bacon and warmed rolls. Crystal squeezed past Steel with a smile and a brush of the hip against his thigh. Jayanne giggled, and Namdarin smiled.

Moments later Crystal appeared from the kitchen with some scraps of meat and some boiled bones, she presented them to Wolf, he made short work of the scraps then started to break the bones open for the marrow that was inside.

"You are a beautiful animal." She whispered, reaching down and stroking his head slowly.

"How soon will you be leaving?" Asked Steel.

"As soon as breakfast is finished, I am sorry, we have a long way to go." Said Namdarin.

"We need to collect our tents, don't forget." Said Jangor.

"I haven't forgotten, it won't take us long to drop them and pack them away."

"Agreed, we can be on the road in less than an hour."

"It will be full daylight by then." Said Steel. "You should be able to leave town without any problems; I wish I could say the same for myself."

"I am certain that the people of this place will be happy to see the end of Brass."

"Most of them for sure, but not all. The ones that have been living off Brass are going to be a problem."

"The majority, the ones that Brass has been blackmailing and charging ridiculous interest to," said Jangor, "those are the ones that will be on your side, use them, there have to be many more of them, otherwise his whole business plan falls apart."

"He's been fleecing most of the people in this town for a long time, just to support himself and his 'friends', and to accumulate that pile of gold down there." Snorted Steel.

"That should make support for you even stronger." Said Jangor.

"You need to sort through all his documents and find out exactly what was going on," said Namdarin "there may be some people in serious need of help right now."

"That too is likely," said Steel, "I have a serious question for you people."

"Ask away." Smiled Jangor.

"Do you always cause such upheaval in the lives of people you meet?"

"Sometimes we simply turn them into dead people."

"I'm not entirely sure that wouldn't have been better."

"At least you are still breathing." Laughed Namdarin.

"And how much longer is that going to last?" Asked Steel.

"It better last a good time." Said Crystal. "I have plans."

"And what are those my dear?" Asked Steel.

"You may just find out, given enough time." She laughed and returned to the kitchen.

"Does anyone know what she is talking about?" He looked to the room in general, he failed to notice Jayanne tap Namdarin on the shin with her foot, just as he was breathing in. Her smile told Namdarin to be quiet.

"You know women," said Jangor, "always planning something." His smile did nothing to allay Steels fears.

"You people are crazy." He said loudly.

"This may surprise you," laughed Kern, "you are not the first to say that."

"Nor the last." Said Gregor. "There are bound to be more as we get closer to our destination."

"You one of them?" Asked Mander.

"Almost certainly." Laughed Gregor, stuffing the last of his bacon roll into his mouth.

"This is not helping me a lot." Said Steel.

"I wouldn't worry about it too much," laughed Jangor, "I think you are going to have plenty to keep you busy for the foreseeable future."

"I'm supposed to be looking forwards to my retirement, not taking on new businesses and new responsibilities."

"I'm sure you'll find plenty of people to help you along the way." Jangor's smile did little to calm Steel's nerves.

"What are you worrying about?" Asked Crystal, returning to the bar with another jug of beer.

"The future, for all of us." Crystal put the jug down next to Jangor, and stepped up close to Steel, she looked up into his wide blue eyes, smiled slowly, and pressed her chest against his arm.

"I'm sure you'll manage everything, it will all come out well for everyone, especially you." She held his eyes for a long moment, then turned slowly away, as she walked behind him Jayanne caught her eyes and her smile. Jayanne almost laughed aloud.

"Don't you think she's going a little fast for him?" Whispered Namdarin.

"I think she's going to work on him so fast that he'll never know what is happening until she has his baby in her arms."

"That's not really fair, is it?"

"No, but such is life, especially for young girls, abandoned by their parents."

"Will she be alright here, do you think?" His question caused her to raise her eyebrows.

"Considering she had been pimped out by her parents, I think she'll do very well now. Why? Were you thinking of taking her along with us?"

"Not with any seriousness, but I'd not want her life to get any worse."

"Since Brass died her life has become a lot better, I don't see it getting any worse for her any time soon, unless she came with us, then her life would be short and brutal."

"No, she couldn't come with us, but I don't know." His voice stumbled to a halt.

"I see," she smiled, "short and brutal is fine for me, but not for Crystal?"

"That's not what I mean, you are older and more experienced," her raised eyebrows caused him to stop again.

"Namdarin, my love, there are times when you should simply stop talking and kiss me." She leaned across the table and waited to be kissed, she didn't have to wait long. Once the kiss broke, she carried on. "You don't have to worry about the little girl, she can look after herself, and Steel will make sure nothing bad happens to her."

"Are you sure?" He muttered.

"Oh yes, and she'll make sure Steel doesn't do anything rash in the grief of losing his family, she'll hold his hand, or something until he stops weeping." She chuckled softly to herself.

"How can you be so sure?"

"By my reckoning she'll be married within the year, and with child very soon after." She laughed and tossed her hair backwards.

"We need to be on the road." Said Namdarin looking around.

"What's wrong?" She asked, her right hand straying close to the axe.

"I don't know, I just feel a sudden urgency, we have a long way to go, and I feel that we are running out of time." He stood and loudly turned to Jangor. "We need to be going, and I mean now."

"What's wrong?"

"I don't have any idea, I just know I need to be moving."

"Right." Jangor turned to the others. "Eat up, we're leaving. Thanks Steel, we wish you all the luck there is with your new ventures, and your new life." He stepped up to Steel and shook his hand firmly. The rest shook his hand as they left, some with bacon sandwiches in their jackets, Brank merely tapped him on the shoulder as he passed. Jayanne hugged him tightly for a moment, then kissed him on the cheek, "Good luck, you are a good man, and I am sure everything will come out right for you in the end." She whispered, then walked out of the bar. Crystal walked up to Steel and put her arm around his waist.

"What did she say?" She asked softly.

"She was just wishing me luck, she said that everything would come out right in the end, what did she mean?"

"I've no idea, perhaps she's some sort of seer."

"Do you think everything will turn out well?"

"I am certain, that we will all be just fine, all of us." She smiled for a moment, then squeezed him gently and went back into the kitchen.

In the yard, horses were saddled, loaded, and readied to leave. Nigel came in through the back gate, he struggled more than he usually did.

"Are you all leaving so early?" He asked.

"Yes," said Namdarin, "thanks for the bed, it was wonderful, but I feel we have to leave."

"Good luck, in everything that comes your way." Nigel reached out a hand to Namdarin and shook his hand, before stepping slowly past him and going into the bar. Jayanne smiled and tapped Namdarin on the elbow and looked up at him.

"Perhaps two weddings here."

"What do you mean?"

"Him and Beth."

"You think?"

"Maybe, only time will tell, he's another nice man, and she's had far more experience than a girl her age should have."

"You suddenly turning into a matchmaker?"

"No, just hoping for a better life for others." She smiled as she climbed onto her horse and turned towards the now open gate. Her horse balked at the collection of dogs in the alley behind the inn. Wolf walked to the front, and faced the pack, they slowly backed away, Wolf's tail rose and flew above his back like a flag, a grey and black hairy flag.

"To the green to collect the tents." Called Jangor. Namdarin and Jayanne led out, the others fell in quickly behind them. In almost no time at all the yard was empty, and somehow lonely. Steel walked to the gate and closed it.

Namdarin led the way through the village, or he would have, if he hadn't been following Wolf, their escort of dogs flanked them all the way to the green and surrounded them as they quickly dismantled what was left of their camp.

"Is it just me," said Granger, "or do these dogs make everyone else nervous?"

"They certainly make me nervous." Said Gregor. "I'm not letting go of my staff, I'm hot to burn the first group that attack."

"I'll take the second wave." Laughed Granger, "If there is one."

"I don't think we have anything to worry about," said Jayanne "these guys are just here to make sure Wolf leaves town." She laughed, pointing at the large canine, he was sitting proudly surveying all the others, almost grinning. She looked across the green, then spoke slowly.

"Am I mistaken, or is the pile that used to be Brass, considerably smaller than it was?"

"Looking at the way his guts are spread out," said Kern, "I think something has been lunching on him, probably one or more of these dogs."

"So why aren't they eating what's left?" Asked Jangor.

"Perhaps someone chased them off then marked it for his own." Laughed Kern, looking straight at Wolf. As if to prove the point a small dog from the outer edge of the escort made a slow move towards the obviously tempting sausages that used to belong to Brass. A resonant growl leapt from the throat of Wolf, the small dog dropped to the ground, it's belly in the grass, and it skittered away, towards the safety of the buildings.

"There you go." Laughed Kern. "Once Wolf leaves, there won't be much left for a funeral."

"I'm sure that will make some people happy around here." Called Jangor, "let's get moving before anything else happens here."

In very short order the tents were packed away and loaded, and the normal column of riders formed up.

"Kern." Commanded Jangor. "South and west, and pick the pace up, Namdarin seems to be in a hurry today." They moved off at a fair pace, their escort followed, but kept a safe distance, as they approached the edge of the village the dogs suddenly vanished. Keeping the newly risen sun over his left shoulder Kern pushed the pace up to a canter along a road that was in reasonable condition. Namdarin glanced at Jayanne and smiled, thinking, 'Another day nearer the end of this.'

CHAPTER SIXTY-THREE

They headed north, trying to turn east whenever they could, but for a considerable distance their path was blocked by the carefully manicured lawn of the Gnomb. As they travelled Kevana questioned Worandana about Gnomb.

"They are an old race, very few in number, but very powerful and very protective of their territories. No one knows much about them, they don't interact with the rest of the world, we simply fence them off with water and slowly they fade away. Once the Gnomb is gone the territory turns back to its natural ways quite quickly. It easy to tell that they have gone, but no one knows where they come from, or realistically if there is even more than one, it could be that Gnomb is actually a single entity, not a race. Sometimes we don't hear of them for years, and occasionally centuries."

"I don't really care who they are or where they come from the only question I have is why is a short man, with green jacket and trousers, a long white beard, bushy eyebrows and a red hat, why is this the ornament of choice in so many gardeners?" Demanded Kevana.

"As I said the ultimate gardener, perhaps some lore has leaked through into the general population and someone decided that this is the colourful little person to look after their gardens, luckily these people have never met one, we are now members of a very small group of people who have met Gnomb and survived."

"I'm still very unhappy about leaving a man behind to die."

"Perhaps you should look at it this way, he's not dead, he's most likely to live much longer than you will."

"That's pure sophistry, he's a tree, that is not living for a man, that is at best a living death, I only pray that he has no consciousness, please let him be entirely tree. For a mind to be trapped in that shape for the lifespan of an oak tree, is just unthinkable."

"The trees never come back to human form, they die quite quickly once the Gnomb has left."

"Please tell me that all those trees were not people?"

"I don't think so, it is said that the Gnomb pick acorns from their trees to plant, and nurture, they grow much as trees do, but slowly their garden extends. In the archives there is a tale, or a report, depending on how you look at it, of a Gnomb taking root on a small island, not one with a resident population, just a small place that sailors put in to fill water chests occasionally. A captain reported over a period of years that the place changed from a wilderness to a garden, the lawn came down to the edge of the shingle beaches, almost into the sea. On one visit he reported that a small figure was seen running towards them while they were filling their chests, they retreated to the safety of their boats. The figure is said to have been dancing and singing. Perhaps hopping from one foot to the other and shouting in rage, there was nowhere for his garden to extent, there was only saltwater all around. The next time the sailors visited, they were very wary when they approached, they stayed off the lawn, and filled their water chests standing in the stream. No figure was seen. Over the next few years the lawn gradually receded, and the wilderness returned."

"So, we just fence them in with water and wait from them to go away?"

"Yes, and it doesn't take a lot of water, a stream a hand wide and a hand deep will stop them expanding, stationary water a foot wide and a hand deep will do it."

"So, if we'd dug a trench around ourselves, and filled it with water, the damned thing wouldn't have been able to take Davadana?"

"I can't say, no one has ever attacked the lawn of a Gnomb and reported the fact. Their power is deeply rooted in the earth, I really wouldn't want to take it on, we fence them with water and wait for them to die."

"Perhaps a better method would be to burn his damned lawn, burn the soil, all the way to a tree and then cut it down? That would keep him in check, far better than waiting for him to die?"

"You saw how fast Davadana was turning into a mature oak tree, I think the grass would grow faster than we can burn the stuff."

"Has anyone actually tried it?"

"Not that appears in any of the records, and I'd not like to try it without a good water barrier in the way, there are no records that say the Gnomb is confined to his lawn, if he moves from one place to another, then he must be able to step outside, you saw what happened to the arrow, that one hit fair and square, if that had been a man, that arrow would have gone straight through his skull and probably not stopped until it landed on the grass."

"Are the Gnomb actually flesh and blood, like us?"

"No one knows, no one knows if they are male or female, or even if such a dichotomy exists for them, they are designated as male simply because of their beards, but they could be both or neither. They are a natural force, of that we are certain, they have great power, but other than that we try to avoid any interaction with them, it never goes well, as we have discovered."

"Why have I never heard of them?"

"They are so rare, that there may even be just the one, we have no idea. Zandaar has been of no help at all with the Gnomb. Questions have been asked, theories proffered, but it is as if Zandaar either can't admit the Gnomb exists, or a worse thought, won't."

"So, we just turn tail and run like frightened rabbits?"

"Today we had no choice, he'd have turned us all into trees in his orchard."

"I hate to run from a fight, it's not right, we should have taken the bastard on, and killed him."

"Or turned into oak, trying?"

"Perhaps, but it would have been a fitting end for warriors."

"We still have important battles to fight, a futile death serves no purpose."

"I suppose, but it galls me to leave a man behind."

"You're a warrior, you've done it before, you've even sent men to their death so that you could escape, don't give me that shit."

"I have sent a rear-guard to help a main force survive, that is very true, but they have always been volunteers."

"That's what you do, you turn sane men into martyrs, they will die for you. Davadana was our rear-guard."

"It still seems wrong to sacrifice him and run away."

"That is what happens when a force retreats, isn't it? They live to fight another day, when the ones they leave behind don't."

"I'm feeling emotional and you're spouting logic, please stop it." Kevana smiled slowly.

"Have you noticed something?"

"What?"

"While we've been talking, and riding, but mainly talking, our course is now almost due east, and judging by the slope of the ground, and the height of the mountains in the distance, I'd say we'll be at the river very early tomorrow, or even tonight if we push on through the dark."

"Travel at night, you're mad, what if we wander into that Gnomb's garden again? I'm not losing more men. No, we camp, and go on in the morning, do you take me for a fool?"

Worandana didn't reply he just smiled. Kevana shook his head and heeled his horse to catch up with Alverana.

Kevana woke to that warm feeling of being enfolded in his friends arms, he revelled in the luxury for a while, he focused on the warmth and security, feeling a heat rise in his blood, he wriggled back against the hardness of Alverana, he felt the steady rise and fall of the large chest behind him, slowly he turned over to face Alverana, he rested his head on the heavy bicep, and then looked up into Alverana's open eyes.

"You need a shave." Muttered Alverana, the stubble on

Kevana's cheek was rubbing against the naked skin, Kevana lifted his hand and stroked Alverana's cheek.

"You're not much better." He moved slowly forwards until their lips met, just a soft and gentle contact, held for no more than a few heartbeats. Kevana pulled back and sighed. "Time to get moving, we still need to get across that damned river." Alverana's heavy hand dropped onto Kevana's hip, and pulled them together for just a moment, the touch of their naked bodies caused him to sigh, and then nod.

"Let's move." He mumbled, then pushed away and rolled over. Kevana watched as his friend climbed slowly to his feet and start to get dressed. As Alverana pulled his trousers on he stared down at Kevana and raised his eyebrows. Kevana nodded and stood slowly. Moving with efficiency they dressed and started to pack their tent away, the bed rolls first, then they exited into the grim light of the burgeoning day. Low clouds, passing by quickly but no rain, nor any likelihood during the upcoming day. Crathen was already up, making tea, and breakfast.

"One of you can take over, just while I drop my tent." he said, Alverana nodded, and took over, while Kevana went to load their horses, he returned to the fire, and sat beside Alverana. Food and drinks were passed around as the people finished packing up, there was little conversation, the events of the day before weighing heavily on their minds.

"I've not seen so many long faces in quite a while." Said Worandana.

"Yesterday was not good for us." Growled Kevana.

"Now remind me, what's that question you soldiers always ask?"

"What do you mean old man?" Demanded Kevana, Alverana simply smiled.

"Now what is it?" Grinned Worandana.

"You're starting to irritate me." Snapped Kevana.

"Oh yes, I remember," Worandana paused before calling out, "Do you want to live forever?"

"No." Yelled Alverana, making most of the jump. He laughed loudly, some joined in. "We've left dead men behind before, on this particular mission a lot of them."

"Yes." Replied Kevana, "Davadana isn't exactly dead though, but still we left him behind."

"It's more than likely that he'll live far longer than we're going to."

"He's a tree, is that really living? Or is his consciousness trapped in there screaming?"

"That we can never know," Said Worandana, "no one has ever returned from that sort of transformation. I think he'll be happy as a tree, once he gets used to the idea."

"And until then he screams without a voice?"

"Perhaps, neither of us knew him that well, we are only guessing, and I ask again, do you want to live forever?"

"No." More called this time.

"Do you want to live forever?" Yelled Worandana.

"No." Almost the whole company, including Kevana.

"Good, now let's take this fight on to the place it needs to be, we are bound for Angorak, mount up and move out." Worandana spun away in a swirl of yellow, and stamped over to his horse, by the time he had hauled himself up into the saddle, the others were all following. "Alverana take point, east and set a good pace, I want to be across that river today."

The normal column formed up in moment, Alverana and Kevana at the front, a fast trot to start off.

"He's a bit of a bully, isn't he?" Observed Kevana.

"Just a little," laughed Alverana, "but only when he needs to be."

"I was a little surprised, I've never seen him act like that before."

"Nor me, but he certainly got things moving, much as you would have done."

"I did notice that, I should be happy about it, but somehow it sort of sticks in my throat."

"You've had a lot on your mind, let's pick up the pace, sunrise is not far off." They kicked the horses into a faster pace and glanced back to see that the rest were accelerating as well, though the column was getting a little strung out, he wasn't worried by the separation, because they'd catch up quickly if they met any problems. He concentrated on maintaining the highest speed he could with reasonable safety. The rolling hillsides made things easy for them, downhill would always take them to the river. Just after the sun appeared above the horizon Kevana had to make a choice, cross a small river, or follow it to the river. Crossing the river would slow them down, and he didn't want to do that this close to sunrise, the searchers would still be out looking for them, so he turned north, following the river, but not too close. They were so close to Angorak now that almost all of them felt the searchers, only Worandana,

Kirukana and Kevana, had to avoid contact with searchers who were looking for them specifically. A few minutes later Kevana reined in and slowed the pace to something a little more comfortable, no means easy, but one that didn't require such concentration. Worandana moved up the column, until he was alongside Kevana.

"Did you feel them looking for you?" Asked Worandana.

"Yes, but they are moving too fast to feel me, I was focused on the grass. Do you think it might be possible to track them on the etheric planc?"

"It may be, but I don't think it's worth the effort. We'll just let them sail on by, don't overlook the cunning of Axorana."

"He's going to be sending more soon, he'll give us a while to let our guard down, then he'll come looking for us."

"No, he'll send someone else, he's far too frightened of me, and rightly so."

"If he comes looking for me, I'll call you."

"Might be an idea to actually call him yourself, I could feed you enough power to reach him, where ever he is, you have no fear of Zandaar, you are simply following his instructions, if he feels you passing near, he'll not even contact you, his trust in you is complete, you are only a soldier, not an intellectual like me. It's us he fears."

"I might just give that a try, if they don't make contact, I'll go looking for Axorana about midday. That'll give me a little time to prepare, I'm not used to this sort of thing like you are."

"Agreed. Keep shying away from contact until then, if you can." Worandana nodded then fell back until he was alongside Kirukana again.

"How's Kevana doing?"

"He's doing fine right now."

"Does he know he's most likely to be their next target?"

"No, he hasn't worked that out yet."

"I thought you would have warned him?"

"That would only have made him worry more. Just be ready to lend him assistance if he needs it, whether he asks for it or not."

"I'm sure I'll be able to help him, how about you?"

"I guard the rest, there could be more than one attack. I don't trust that Axorana one little bit."

"I am fairly sure that our return home is going to interesting, at least for some of us."

"Perhaps. We can only hope that we survive."

"I'm sure we can beat him."

"But can we beat them all?"

"The great Worandana has doubts?"

"A little, I really don't want to have to kill too many of my brothers, they have been led astray by Axorana, and his cronies."

"Any that survive we will lead to the righteous path." Smiled Kirukana.

"Have you any idea how much you have changed?"

"I know, but I feel so much better about myself, it's something I never thought would actually happen, I didn't realise just how restricted my thinking was, how I was being controlled by others, I can now think for myself, I am not reliant on the judgement of others. And I have you the thank for that, Dare I say it, Kevana as well, his threats gave me the incentive to think, before I speak. It's surprising what a person can find inside themselves if only they give themselves the time to think."

"You still may end up dead, we are riding into a nest of vipers."

"I'm quite looking forwards to de-fanging a few snakes." Laughed Kirukana, Worandana joined in, their laughter became so loud that Kevana called back to them.

"What's so funny?"

"I just got the image of Kirukana pulling Axorana's teeth, one by one, until the screams drowned out the sounds of battle going on all around."

"Now that would be something to see." Yelled Kevana, joining in the laughter.

"See how far you have come." Said Worandana.

"Yes, but though things are much easier here, once we get to Zandaarkoon, then the whole city will be against us."

"Just because Axorana thinks the whole world sides with him, this doesn't make it true."

"You think more of the people will side with us?"

"There must be many that see the way Axorana has controlled everything and everyone."

"You think they'll join us, once they see someone standing up to him?"

"No, not really, they may avoid physically supporting him, but they're unlikely to actively join us until we've won."

"Can we actually win?"

"Who can tell. I'd say it's not going to be easy, but it is possible."

"To quote our colleagues. Do you want to live forever?"

Laughed Kirukana.

"I'd like to give it a damned good try." Laughed Worandana.

"You two seem to be having a fine old time." Called Kevana.

"We are just speculating about our life expectancy." Said Worandana.

"And what did you come up with?"

"Basically, everybody dies." Laughed Kirukana.

"And you are alright with that?"

"Do we have a choice?"

"Not really." Kevana turned back to the front, he glanced at Alverana and smiled. Slowly he leaned back in his saddle, causing his horse to slow first to a trot, then to a walk.

"Good," said Alverana, "the horses will need a rest before long, we may be asking them for some serious speed at some point, and it would be good if they weren't already exhausted." The rest of the group caught up quickly and settled down to the slower pace.

"Do you think the searches are all done by now?" Asked Petrovana.

"We are getting so close now," replied Worandana, "that they may even be able to simply feel us in the area."

"Let's hope they are still looking further afield for us." Said Kevana.

"Searchers." Whispered Alverana loudly, as he felt the approach on the etheric plane.

"Silence." Snapped Worandana reining in hard. They all stopped and stood as still as they could. Worandana took a deep breath and focused his mind on the grass beneath their feet, from the image of grass he slowly erased the feet off the horses, then their legs, and bodies, on to the riders, and their colourful cloaks. In his mind the grass became an empty field, this image he projected outwards, looking for the searchers, hoping to make them see the field as he wanted it to be. He felt the gentle fluttering of a contact, a searching mind was looking for some riders, though he didn't actually know who they were, or where. This was a mind of some power, it started to poke around the edges of Worandana's illusion, there was something there that didn't quite fit. As the searcher pecked away at the perimeter Worandana drew power from the distant darkness, suddenly the whole illusion collapsed like a bursting bubble, the searchers mind was filled with the recognition that he had found something, but only for an instant. Worandana hurled a mass of the dark power straight into the searching mind, there was a moment of clarity for the searcher, then utter darkness fell on that mind, the lights went out.

"Is he dead?" Whispered Kirukana.

"I don't think so," replied Worandana, breathing hard, "I think he'll wake up in a while, I'm not sure how much he will remember, he may have some idea where we are, but I don't think he'll know who we are."

"What will the rest of them think about his failure to reach us?"

"It could be that Axorana will have him killed for his failure."

"Is that really likely?" Demanded Kevana.

"I don't think so, Axorana already knows enough about failure." Laughed Worandana.

"He'd probably have to come out of hiding as well." Said Kirukana, smiling.

"Any signs of more searchers?" Asked Kevana.

Worandana closed his eyes for a moment, before responding.

"I'm sensing nothing, and I do mean nothing, the other plane is completely empty, as if everyone has suddenly left. It's very quiet, very, very quiet."

"That's a good thing." Said Kevana, the look on Worandana's face said otherwise. Kevana continued. "Let's ride on, we still have a job to do." He turned his horse and together with Alverana set off again in the direction they had been going, before the searcher had stopped them, they were only a few minutes down the road when Worandana pushed to the front of the column.

"We need to move." He called to Kevana.

"We are, what do you mean?"

"I mean we need to move faster, that searcher could wake up any time, I'd rather have some distance between the place we were and where we are now, and the faster we are moving the more difficult we are to find."

"You think he'll be searching again so soon?"

"No, but someone else may be, given his information."

"Don't you think you can beat the next one just as easily?"

"I'm fairly sure that together we can beat them all, but the closer we get the more likely it is that our opposition will die in that conflict. I'd much rather they didn't find us."

"Agreed, are we killing horses?" His frown showed how much he hated that idea.

"Until we have spares, I think not, but we certainly need to pick the pace up, and pick it up as high as we can."

Kevana nodded and waved at Alverana, the immediate increase in pace caused their column to spread out more than a little. Worandana looked back for a moment and yelled.

"Close up that line, I've no idea how far I can spread the defensive cover." The riders from the rear kicked hard to catch up, the column of two's became a column of three's greatly reducing its length, riding this close at such speed increased the dangers of collisions and falls, but speed was more important, even though Worandana wasn't exactly sure why. It seemed to him far too short a time when they had to slow to give the horses a chance to rest. Once they had slowed to a walk Worandana could feel how hard his horse was breathing, and how long it took for that breathing to slow down, he started to become anxious to set off again, this walking was too slow. Alverana showed no intention of speeding up for a considerable time. He waited until the horses had stopped sweating, and cooled down completely, then advised that they be allowed to drink, after that they walked some more.

"When can we speed up?" Demanded Worandana, finally losing patience.

"We can't ask them to run just yet," replied Alverana, "have you ever tried running with a belly full of wine?"

"I can't say that I have."

"Perhaps you should try it, it's not very comfortable at all, and they'll run a lot better once some of that water has been absorbed." It wasn't long before Alverana gave the command to speed up. Soon they were riding hard through the open woodland, until they came to a road, it was wide though not too well travelled, rutted with cart tracks, and the impressions of the wide hooves of heavy horses, Alverana turned eastwards, the sun to his right and at its height.

"Will we make the crossing before dark?" Called Worandana.

"I've no idea," replied Alverana, "but we are certainly getting closer."

"Will we stop for lunch?" Called Petrovana from his place near the back of the column.

"I'm getting hungry as well." Laughed Kirukana.

"When we find somewhere for the horses to drink and eat," said Alverana, "then we stop, if only briefly." it was only a few minutes later that a patch of inviting grassland appeared to their right, with a small pond. Alverana pulled off the road, and quickly dismounted.

"Walk them and let them cool down before you let them drink." He called to the others, these instructions not really necessary as they all knew the rules. Kevana passed his reins to Alverana, then took Worandana's reins and passed them to Kirukana. He guided Worandana away from the group for a private conversation, one or two looked inquisitively, but none approached.

"Why the sudden rush?" Asked Kevana.

"I'm not sure, but we need to cross the river early in the morning, we need to be at the crossing before first light, I have no idea why, but if we don't make that crossing, we'll be too late."

"How do you know this?"

"I have no idea, it's one of those feelings, you know the ones I mean, you must get them?"

"I'm not sure what you mean."

"How many times has your life been saved by the fact that you decided not to go around that particular corner just yet, you pause, and then a troop of enemy soldiers come riding by, they'd have been happy to ride down commander Kevana on their way out of town. How many times?"

"There have been a few, I admit, but I could give no good reason at the time."

"Exactly, I have the feeling that the pursuit is getting closer, I can feel the hot breath of fate behind me."

"What about ahead?"

"Nothing, just fear catching up from behind."

"You think the hounds have already turned to come after us?"

"That is the most likely reason for this fear, but with all the crazy things that have happened, I would like to limit it to something so mundane. They must be too far away by now to do us any harm. We'll be in Angorak long before they can get here."

"Let's hope so," snarled Kevana, "I have some serious words to say to them."

"Words?" laughed Worandana.

"Well, a song to sing for them." Smiled Kevana.

"You think we are strong enough?"

"With your dark magic, and my sword arm, how can we lose?"

"I wish I was as confident as you seem to be."

"Have no fear, we will certainly triumph, after all, we are simply following the will of god."

"But so are they."

"They are misguided, they have been led astray, we should lead them back to the true path." Kevana laughed again.

"That being the one we follow?"

"Of course."

"If they choose not to follow the same path as us?"

"Then it shall be as it always has been, they die."

"Don't you get tired of the killing?"

"They die, or we die, only by mortal combat can the path of righteousness be proved."

"You begin to sound like Axorana."

"I am only quoting from the book."

"That is perhaps the most frightening part of all this. All the people involve are following the word of god, and all are trying to kill each other to prove which is right. Somehow it just feels wrong."

"We are going to take the sword from Namdarin, perhaps his life as well. Take it home, shove it so far up Axorana that the point will come out of the top of his head, then give it to Zandaar as we have been commanded."

"Let's just hope it is as easy as you make it sound."

"I have confidence is our abilities, don't you?"

"I am by no means certain what we are going to be facing. Axorana, him I can beat in a moment, but Picarana, now that's a fish of a different sort."

"Who's he?"

"Cleric in command of the hounds."

"You know him?"

"Yes."

"Does he know you?"

"Yes, why?"

"Does he know you well enough to find you even if you are hiding?"

"Now that's something I hadn't considered, and perhaps, it's been a while, but he may know enough about me to reach me directly."

"We really don't need any surprises."

"What about Rikorana, have you had any dealings with him?"

"The name is familiar, but nothing else. Who is he?"

"The equivalent to you in the hounds."

"I've never met him, I've known his reputation, very skilled with a sword, and quite ruthless, somewhat of a sadist, he likes to hurt people."

"And you don't?"

"I don't do it for fun, he appears to."

"Can you beat him?"

"I can keep him busy until Alverana sticks a knife in his kidneys."

"Speaking of Alverana, things seem to be changing between

the two of you?"

"What do you mean?" Kevana almost whispered.

"You two have always been close, but you appear to be getting even closer."

"I don't understand."

"You may not be lovers yet, but that can't be far away, it's easy to see, for those with a certain sensitivity, a look here, a touch there, you've been together a long time, and through some serious problems in recent times. It's not surprising that you begin to depend on each other more than you used to."

"That sort of thing is forbidden." Muttered Kevana.

"Perhaps, but not uncommon, human beings are not designed to be alone, or celibate, no matter what our god says about these things."

"What will people think?"

"You really care?"

"I don't want to cause conflict within our group. Some will not look favourably on this, Alverana is staring at us even now."

"The only one who might object is Kirukana, and he's so far down the path to heresy that he may as well build his own fire. He'll recognise that as soon as the 'h' word reaches his lips. That should be fun."

"Do you think everyone will understand?"

"Of course, they will, and by the time you liberate a few heads, no one is going to argue." Laughed Worandana.

"I can't afford to lose any more men. We may have to go up against the hounds, and that's going to be hard."

"The hounds are too far away, any battle with them will be magical, they don't stand a chance."

"Good, let's grab some food, and some for the horses and be on our way, I don't want to cross the river in the dark, but I do want to be across as soon as we can in the morning." Kevana turned and stamped back to where the rest were waiting.

"Who's turn is it to cook?" He called as he approached the group.

"Yours." Laughed Alverana.

"Not happening," said Petrovana, loudly, "his food is only fit for pigs, I'll cook."

"I could be offended by that, you know." Said Kevana.

"Your choice, I'd rather have something edible." Laughed Petrovana, he strolled past Kevana and slapped him gently on the shoulder, smiling as he went to start the cooking. Alverana came over to Kevana and whispered.

"What were you and Worandana talking about?"

"Things and other things."

"You were talking about us, I could feel it."

"It was mentioned, relax, we'll talk more later, when everyone else is asleep. There is nothing to fear." Kevana walked slowly away, smiling to lessen Alverana's fears, he went to help Petrovana with the cooking. The role reversal made them both feel better, Kevana fetching wood, and peeling vegetables, while Petrovana did the actual cooking. In fairly short order food was ready, the horses were resting, cropping green grass as they chose, the men all sat around the small cooking fire to eat. Conversation was light and intermittent, most intent on their own thoughts, many looks were exchanged between Kevana and Alverana, but nothing was said. The meal over, Kevana spoke loudly.

"Let's get moving, I want to be across the river by the morning." He stood slowly and reached a hand down to help Alverana to his feet. Together they started to round up the horses, suddenly Alverana froze.

"Searchers." He called.

"Circle." Yelled Worandana. The men started forming up the circle that they had been using recently, Kirukana at the point, and Worandana on the outside. The circle was barely formed when Worandana's mind was flooded with an external presence.

"Worandana," said the presence, "It's been a while, you have certainly been causing us some problems."

"Picarana, your problems are nothing to do with us, we are simply following the instructions of Zandaar."

"As are we, only we lost two men to some damned tigers yesterday, and for some reason I believe that you are to blame. We know where you are, and we know where you are going, and we are coming to get you. Do you understand?"

"I think that I do. We lost a man to a Gnomb yesterday, so if you are coming this way, then I suggest you tread carefully."

"Gnomb is a fairy story, they don't exist, we are coming for you and yours, be ready."

"Why wait, strike now, what difficulty can we present to the great hounds of Zandaar?"

"The range is extreme, and you are protected by your brothers."

"I am alone, can you feel a circle around me? Can you feel the pulses of power?"

"No, you seem to be alone."

"I can feel your circle, I can feel the pulses of power that you are using to hold this contact open, do you really want to take me on." Worandana slowly pulled a large charge from Kirukana, bolstering his power levels, hoping that Picarana would attack, "Or are you afraid?" Worandana knew that Picarana could not turn down this challenge, everyone in his circle had heard it, he had to respond. Picarana took three cycles of power from his circle before he launched his attack, Worandana smiled inwardly, he took the bolt of energy that was supposed to kill him and many of those in his circle and dumped it into the darkness. He breathed in a charge from Kirukana and sent it to Picarana, not to kill him, just to show him that things were not going to go the way they usually did. While Picarana was reeling, Worandana spoke.

"You'll have to try harder if you want to kill me or mine, I can defend myself just as effectively as I can defend them. I think you'd better wait until you are much closer, and preferably standing behind me, you might stand a chance then." With this thought he broke the link, and stepped away from Kirukana, a huge smile on his face.

"Well," said Kirukana, "that didn't go as he expected." He laughed aloud.

"True." Smiled Worandana. "We better get moving before he gets his mind in order." He called. The men started mounting their horses and preparing for travel.

"Do you think he's going to attack again?" Asked Kevana.

"No, by now he's far too frightened. He's never had any lone man put up that much resistance to one of his circles. He's most likely to wait until he can actually see us before he tries again."

"How far away are they? Did they give you any impression?"

"Yes, like us they had paused for lunch, the thought that I got, was that they are killing horses to catch us up, they know that we sent them on a wild goose chase, and they are not happy about it, it cost them men, and time, now they are trying to make up the later."

"How far away are they?"

"Not as far as I would like. The feeling I get is that they are more than a day behind us but catching up all the time."

"You don't think they'll attack until they are much closer?"

"No, our next meeting with the hounds will be personal, very personal."

"I can deal with that; we'll be ready for them. Do you think they'll catch us up before the river?"

"I don't know, they might do, but I think they'll be on foot if they do."

"They could always steal horses along the way, after all, who's going to stand up to them?"

"True," Worandana paused, "let's get moving, if we can find the river crossing soon enough, we can cross today, and not wait for daylight tomorrow." Kevana nodded and indicated to Alverana to move out. Only an hour or so later they caught a flash of silver in the distance, the river, this gave them the impetus they need to push just a little bit harder, they all wanted the river between themselves and those following.

They came through a lightly wooded area and there before them was the river running in a deep gorge, it was about a hundred feet deep, and gave no indication that there was a path down to the water.

"Anyone know which way we should go?" Asked Kevana, loudly.

"North I think," said Petrovana, "I remember a journey down the river, it passes through a gorge, perhaps this on, and then opens out into a large lagoon, where the docks of Angorak are. So, the crossing must be north of this ridge."

"How long is the gorge?"

"Sorry I have no clear idea, I was travelling downstream, so the river did most of the work."

"Fine, north it is, move out." The last yelled, as he and Alverana set off along the edge of the gorge. The path they followed was little more than a deer trail, quite steep and narrow in places, Kevana didn't like the way their column got spread out, in the confines of the track, but there was little he could do about it, nor could they make any real speed, the terrain was too variable. Gradually the track tended downwards, as the gorge became shallower, and they were moving across the flood plain, open grass land, with slowly undulating hills, they pushed the pace faster, as the ground became easier. The horses started to tire again, to the extent that they were running down the hills and walking up them. They came over a shallow ridge and ahead was the river crossing, the barge was already on their side. It was a small barge, so it would certainly take more than one journey to get them all across. He thought about how they were going to get everyone across, there was no way the two main clerics could cover all sections of the party, there would be one group on this side of the river, one group on the other and one group crossing the river, additionally the pack horses would be a problem, as they galloped up to the crossing point, he worked things out slowly, he needed to ensure the maximum safety of his people. As they rode up to the barge, he rang the bell to bring the ferryman running. Today was going to be a big day for him, his grin was clear as he ran up to the man ringing the bell.

"We need to cross, all of us, and before sundown, can this be done?"

"Surely sir, it may be close but there should still be some light."

"No, I mean before sunset."

"Aye sir, that can be done, but you need to get boarded right now."

"Good, Worandana, Alverana, Apostana and Strenoana, you go first, take two of the pack horses with you. Ferryman, is there anything we can do to speed things up?"

"Some muscle to operate the winch would be helpful, it would certainly make the return easier."

"I am sorry," laughed Kevana, "Apostana, as the man with the widest and strongest shoulders you are volunteered to be second winch man. But that will leave us with only three on the other side after the first trip, Crathen you go with the first group seeing as Apostana is going to be shuttling backwards and forwards. Get loaded and get moving. Worandana pay the man."

"Don't you know anything?" Said Worandana. "The rule is, don't pay the ferryman, until he gets you to the other side." He laughed loudly. In very short order they were on the barge and the ferryman showed Apostana how the winch operated, and together they started to winch the barge across the river, from Kevana's point of view, the progress was painfully slow, the barge slowly moved away, then it started to come back, empty this time. Kevana had the next group ready as soon as the barge grounded on the bank. Fabrana, Briana and Astorana, boarded with pack animals in tow. And the winch was reversed, the barge started to move again. Kevana became aware just how far away Alverana was and he didn't like it, he was starting to get anxious. It seemed to be forever before the barge started its empty return, Kevana was painfully aware of the failing light, sunset can't be far away, and they needed to be together when it happened. The barge reached the shore and Kevana leapt aboard, followed by the others and the last of the pack horses. As soon as the barge started moving Kevana relieved Apostana and waved at Petrovana to replace the obviously tired ferryman, together they worked the winch as it had never before been pushed. The urgency of their need was not to be denied.

"Careful my lord," said the ferryman, "please don't break it, it's not used to working this hard."

"Judging by the way this mechanism is flexing, I'd say the weakest part is the cranking handles, and those can be replaced fairly easily, once we have made it to the other side. Relax, you have nothing to do until after we have left."

"How much more difficult would it be for the hounds to follow us, if they found this crossing destroyed?" Asked Kirukana.

"It might be worth it, if only we can be sure they are coming this way, they know where we are heading, and unlike us, they have no reason to hide who they are, they'll be taking the fastest route, they'll be crossing at the lagoon, more boats, and bigger ones too. They'll go that way."

"Please my lord, don't destroy my livelihood, this is all that I have to support my family." Said the ferryman, his voice quaking.

"Have no fear." Said Kevana. "I'll not do that, it would serve no purpose." He turned to Kirukana. "Any action on the etheric plane?"

"Nothing specific that I can feel, but there is a certain tension building, sunset is close."

"Can your dark magic be used to propel this bucket any faster?"

"Perhaps, but I don't know how, experimentation will be needed."

"We'll make do with simple brawn then, no trials that could actually sink us."

"There may actually be a way." Kirukana replied slowly.

"A safe way, a very safe way?" Asked Kevana.

"Give me a moment." Kirukana's eyes went blank, his hands were encased in the darkness, the ferryman mumbled prayers softly. Kirukana stepped jerkily towards the front of the barge. "That would work, not a great effect but every little helps I suppose."

"Explain." Snapped Kevana straining at the winch.

"I can pull myself towards the shore, if I brace myself against the boat, then I will be pulling the boat towards the shore, but only with the force that I can apply with my own body, it won't be a lot, but it could take some of the strain off you."

"Fine, do it."

Kirukana nodded and went to the front of the barge, sat down with his legs braced against the left-hand bow section, the rope for the winch was hissing out of the water only inches from his left shoulder, to wrap around the pulley, driven by his two friends. He reached out with the dark power, his whole arms turned black, very soon the strain in his legs was clear to seen, his knees were shaking, and his breath came is huge panting gulps. Some unseen force was pulling his arms towards the bank, and he was transferring that force to the barge. The rate that the pulley was turning increased but the load on it lessened, there was less risk of it breaking. Now there were three men powering the barge to its landing stage. Soon that staging was approaching at a startling speed.

"Slow down." Called the ferryman. "Slow down or we'll crash." Kirukana released his force and lay back on the deck panting.

"Slow." Said Kevana, as he and Petrovana did just that, the reduction in the driving force was such that the bow wave from the barge broke loose and washed up against the pier long before the barge arrived. The barge nudge gently against the pier and the ferryman breathed a huge sigh of relief, Apostana walked to the front where Kirukana was still lying on the deck, he reached a hand down and helped the man to his feet. The horses were collected, and the people started to dis-embark.

"Worandana." Called Kevana. "Pay the ferryman, we're on the other side now." He laughed. Worandana scowled but pulled his coin pouch from his belt.

"How much do we owe?" He asked the ferryman.

"Nothing lord."

"Why?"

"There was talk of destroying this crossing, to stop others following you, but that lord," he nodded in the direction of Kevana, "said not to do that. That is payment enough for me." The ferryman bowed low. Worandana shrugged and put is money pouch back in his belt.

"Worandana." Said Kevana. "If you don't pay the ferryman at all, have you any idea how much bad luck that can bring?" He laughed.

"Sometimes my friend," mumbled Worandana, "I could easily hate you." He took out his money purse and paid the ferryman five gold saying, "That should bring us enough good luck to keep us all alive."

"Sunset." Yelled Alverana. Kevana turned to the ferryman.

"Go home, and do it now, things could get very bad here and very quick." The ferryman just nodded and jumped aboard his craft, turning the crank on his own set of at a more normal pace to cross the river in the failing light. The monks in their colourful capes formed their circle, as normal Kirukana facing outwards, and

Worandana as the only character actually visible on the etheric plane, the others were hidden.

It was only a few moments after sunset that the searcher found him, at this range he didn't even attempt to hide.

"You are Worandana." Said the strange voice, and the strange face.

"I am, you are?" Replied Worandana, slowly gathering force needed to wipe the brothers mind completely.

"I'm not stupid enough to give you my name, there is power in a person's name."

"Your purpose, nameless one?" Worandana used the time to decide another course, one that didn't involve the death of a brother.

"I am to find you and report your location."

"So, where am I?"

"I headed north out of Angorak, you are only a short distance north, I was here in moments."

"Are you sure? Are you absolutely certain? Think what would happen if you reported my position incorrectly, some people are going to be mightily irritated with you."

"You are less than half a day's ride north of the city, of that I am certain."

"I'm actually much further north, look around me." Worandana sent the man a vision, it was of Anya standing over the lightening stone, a column of bright fire burning upwards, into the night sky, the only real difference was that the image of Anya was replaced by a man in a black robe, his black hood covering most of his face.

"This stone gives me the power to reach you where-ever you are in the world. Are you sure you want to report where I am?" Worandana didn't really need to kill this man, he only needed to cast doubt in his mind, then use the dark power to drain the energy from the monks circle, once he had enough of the man's mental signature, he did just that, he sucked the power out of the circle until the circle collapsed under its own weight. The searcher vanished. The power now passing slowly around Worandana's circle, he maintained his presence on the ethereal plane, In moments another searcher, this one out of Zandaarkoon, the same chatter, the same image, the same result. The circle was now carrying so much power that the weaker members were struggling to maintain the transfers, this is not how circles are supposed to work, they don't generally accumulate energy from outside. The next searcher that came upon Worandana made no attempt to communicate, nor even locate, he simple launched a savage bolt of energy, with only one purpose, the intention was to kill. Worandana absorbed the blast, held it for a moment, the returned it threefold. The target vanished in a flare of power and a scream of agony. Worandana held his circle together, and kept them cycling the energy, he started broadcasting his identity, challenging all to come and find him. They came, the ones that tried to communicate had their circles drained until they collapsed, their power added to Worandana's own, the ones that attacked died in a white-hot surge of power. Worandana's group were sweating and hurting, but the practise was improving their abilities, their power transfers were faster and hotter than ever before. If any of them had been able to look around them, then they would have observed the drop in ambient temperature, there was fog forming around their feet and they sucked the energy out of the air around them, not that they could spare the time to actually see. Worandana was just starting to relax when two circles attacked at the same time, this sort of co-ordination was unheard of, generally speaking, if one circle wasn't enough, then use a bigger circle. Worandana dealt with this in an equally unusual manner, he reflected one attack against the other circle, and disabled its prime character so that they vanished, the first attack he responded with a verbal message.

"When are you people going to learn to leave us alone?"

These words screamed so loud directly into the brain of the attacker, that he folded into unconsciousness, and his circle collapsed around him. A few more tried to contact Worandana but had their circles drained and they vanished, before, finally, a large circle sent a message.

"I am Adenthana, I am told by Axorana that you intend to kill our god, is this correct?" This came in so loud that Worandana almost stepped back from Kirukana.

"I am Worandana, it is not my intention to kill our god, Axorana has some other purpose in this."

"I am Adenthana, stop trying to drain my circle, we are fifty, and we have five pulses running around this circle, you cannot drain us. Axorana says you bring the sword to kill Zandaar."

"I'm Worandana, how many times do I have to say this? We do not have the damned sword, Namdarin has it. If the sword is needed to kill Zandaar, then Namdarin is the one with the intent, and no real surprise there, he has cause."

"I am Adenthana, who is this Namdarin and what is his cause?"

"I am Worandana, how many times do I have to report this?

Namdarin is a farmer, we burned his house, now he intends on burning ours. I have said this so many times, I am beginning to get very tired." At this point another circle attacked Worandana. With an impatient twitch Worandana sent a pulse of power that tore the circle apart. "I have killed enough brothers defending my life. Stop these pointless attacks, your circles cannot beat me, I stand here alone and beat your best. Stop these brothers dying."

"I am Adenthana, you really believe you can beat our best? You've not done so well with me."

"I am Worandana, you have fifty in your circle and I stand alone. Do you wish to stand alone against me?"

"I am Adenthana, your hands are empty, of this there is no doubt, we can feel that, but I don't believe that you are alone. You are using some technique as yet unknown to us. Your circle is hiding behind your skirts."

"I am Worandana, it is our intention to take the sword from Namdarin and bring it to Zandaarkoon, we will first meet with Axorana, then take the sword to Zandaar as we have been instructed by god."

"Will Axorana survive this meeting?" The sudden omission of the initial announcement made Worandana smile to himself.

"That very much depends on his ability to grovel, let's just say that he has made no friends here."

"He is not known for his grovelling."

"Then he'll die, like so many he has sent against us."

"How many days away are you?"

"Directly, two or maybe three days, however we are intending on waiting for Namdarin at Angorak."

"Have you any idea how far away from Angorak is the man with the sword?"

"No. We cannot spend our energies on searching for the sword, or the man, because we are too busy defending ourselves from attacks."

"If I see to the ending of the attacks, can you find the sword and advise me of its location?"

"I can do that, but can I trust you to stop the attacks?"

"I am different from Axorana, he's a power-hungry fool. I can stop the attacks."

"What about the hounds, can you put them back on their leash?"

"No, they are Zandaar's alone. You will have to deal with them yourselves."

"Stop the attacks, with the rising of the sun I will find the sword and then contact you. Is this acceptable?"

"I agree."

"Good, be aware, if we are attacked again, then you will meet with us in Zandaarkoon, and you will grovel like Axorana."

"You have my word, I will stop the attacks, and once you have met with god, then we will talk."

"Until tomorrow."

"Tomorrow." Adenthana broke the link, it was Worandana's turn to be shocked by the ferocity of the separation.

"Well, that was different." Said Worandana.

"Very," said Kirukana, "do you know who he is?"

"Not a clue."

"He's the leader of the other major faction, Axorana's primary adversary."

"He wants to give the sword to Zandaar?"

"Correct, he follows the word directly."

"So, why hasn't he dealt with Axorana."

"Axorana has too many friends, too many followers, the balance between the factions is very close, all-out battle would cause far too many deaths, neither can risk a serious confrontation. They just keep on bickering about minor points, hoping the matter will sort itself out, before it comes to war."

"Too bad for them." Snapped Kevana. "War is riding their way, it's names are Kevana and Worandana."

"This is going to get very bloody." Replied Kirukana.

"Never mind that just yet." Said Worandana. "Sensitives, anyone feeling anyone looking our way." He looked at the men he knew to be sensitive, each shook their heads.

"Good." Worandana smiled. "Circle and get charging, I'm going to find that damned sword, it can't be that far away by now." He paused and focused his own mind as the circle formed, Kirukana facing outwards as was the normal method for them now. Worandana waited for a while for the circle to build up a good size charge, then he stepped in and took it on the next cycle, adding some of his own black power, he launched onto the ethereal plane, the blue sword his target, spreading his influence rapidly eastwards, north and south as well, pushing hard he covered ground rapidly, and passed the city in moments, reaching out into the countryside, towards the mountains to the east, towards the great forests northwards, and the open seas to the south. Long before the range was going to be a problem, he found the signature of the sword, bright and blue, the black pommel now green, it was sitting quietly in a tent, it was hot with stolen power, it had recently killed, and taken energy from the dying. Casting carefully around, Worandana found many people, far more than were in Namdarin's group, there were soldiers, and fighters, there were men tied. He considered contacting them directly, but with no seriousness, he knew that the members of Namdarin's group could defend themselves more than adequately. 'I wish I had some like them,' he thought, 'but their very independence means they would never follow me and mine.' One last look around, there wasn't much in the way of sleeping going on, so he returned to his body, that first shuddering breath told everyone that he was back, the circle stopped its cycling, and the broke up. Each man tired to some major degree.

"Well, what did you find?" Demanded Kevana.

"They are on their way to Angorak, a much bigger group now, they picked up some more soldiers."

"How far out of Angorak are they?"

"Perhaps a day, but definitely not more, perhaps a lot less if they rise early and push hard. They are currently camped for the night."

"Are they closer than us?"

"I'd say not."

"So, we can rest for the night, and set off early without the need to rush, we only need to catch them on the south side of the city."

"I suggest we don't dally, we don't want to be chasing them on the road south, if they get ahead of us, they're going to be difficult to catch."

"We could always chase them." Suggested Kirukana.

"What do you mean?" Asked Kevana.

"We let them get ahead of us, then harry them all the way to the walls of Zandaarkoon. That way they have no time to make any plans to invade the city, they can't sneak in, we chase them all the way to the gates, then smash them against the walls." Alverana looked at Kirukana and smiled, nodding slowly, he approved of this plan.

"That's good," said Kevana, "except that I need the sword in my hand before we get to Zandaarkoon. I don't want to be fighting the city guard for possession."

"If the city guard have the sword then it is Axorana's" Laughed Kirukana.

"Then we take it before they get there." Said Kevana. "We set out before sunrise, and we ride hard."

"Agreed." Said Worandana. "Quick camp, light meal, then sleep. Alverana you can wake us before dawn. Kirukana and I will stand watch, the dark power will keep going, everyone else rest."

"If you're staying up all night, why do you need Alverana to wake you?" Asked Kevana.

"We will be here, we will be watching, we will be guarding, but we will be communing with the dark power, I have a need to know more about it, seeing as there is no longer any worry about being discovered. Someone moving around in the camp will be enough to bring us home, and Alverana has the best time sense here."

"Agreed," said Kevana, he glanced around, "here's good enough to camp, I don't think the ferryman will come back this way any time soon, at least not until he is sure we have left."

"Strenoana, Astorana, and Pertovana," said Worandana, "get to fire and food, the rest get the tents up and ready. Quick meal and then sleep." He turned to Kirukana. "We don't need a tent, nor food, water would be good though." He glanced over his shoulder at Petrovana, who ran to the river to fill a water-skin for the clerics. He returned quickly the heavy bag sloshing around as he moved, he passed it to Worandana with a bow, then returned to his duties as fire starter. Worandana took a huge draft from the skin, then passed it to Kirukana who followed suit. Kirukana dropped the water-skin, to the ground, then they walked together a short distance from the camp that was growing quickly around them. They sat on the ground, legs crossed facing each other, their knees almost touching, Worandana held his hands out, Kirukana took them in his, together they closed their eyes and bowed their heads, silence descended around them, it was clear they were not to be disturbed until morning. A short time later, the tents all erected, the horses picketed, and the fire settled.

"Damn," mumbled Kevana, "those two are crazy." Looking over at the two clerics, who hadn't moved a single muscle since they sat down.

"What is crazy these days?" Asked Alverana.

"I'm not entirely sure." He took two bowls of broth from Astorana, passing one to Alverana. Sipping the rich soup, they watched as night darkened around them, the cloudy sky hid the stars from view, but equally ensured that the night wouldn't get too cold. They were sitting in front of the tent they shared.

"Do you believe they can keep watch in their current state?" Asked Alverana.

"If he says so, then I believe him." Said Kevana.

'You can be sure of that.' Worandana's voice echoed through both their brains.

"Now that is creepy." Muttered Alverana.

"Damned truth. The real question is did they hear voice or thought?" Whispered Kevana.

'Voice.' This time Kirukana.

'Like we would tell you if we were reading your thoughts.' The humour in Worandana's thought was unmistakable. Kevana shivered at that thought, then passed their empty bowls to Astorana.

"Bedtime," he called, "we have a lot to do tomorrow, and much distance to cover." He stood and reached a hand down to Alverana, who took it and climbed to his feet, before the two went into their tent.

"They look happy together." Muttered Petrovana.

'Keep your prejudices to yourself.' Worandana's thought rattled Petrovana's jaw.

"Can't a man even talk to himself without being interrupted?" He asked. A gentle laugh echoed through his mind.

CHAPTER SIXTY-FOUR

The next day, as the sun was approaching its zenith, not that they could see it through the clouds and the miserable drizzling rain, Namdarin suddenly called out.

"Jangor, horses in that woodland over there." He nodded his head, rather than waving an arm.

"Many?"

"I make it about fifteen."

"What are they doing?"

"They seem to be simply watching."

"The road in general or us in particular?"

"The horses are watching the grass grow and wondering how good it will taste. The riders, who can tell?"

"Sometimes I wish you could reach their minds as well."

"Are you sure about that?" Asked Granger, smiling.

"No, I'm not, but it could be a useful talent." Jangor paused for a moment. "No big moves, but prepare for battle, let's be ready for them if they mean us harm." He twitched his sword in its scabbard, and the others did the same, Wolf sensed the change in posture and moved in closer to Namdarin.

"They're moving," said Namdarin, "Not in a hurry but they should be visible some time very soon." As he finished speaking the riders appeared from the wood, they rapidly formed up into a column of twos. All were wearing similar clothes, red and blue mainly.

"These guys are professionals." Said Jangor, he saw the formation had four pike men at the front, six swordsmen in the centre, and four bowmen to the rear, and one man out of the formation, obviously the officer in charge. They came down from the copse in a smooth flowing formation, even the horses seemed to be matching strides. As this formation reached the road and turned to face Namdarin, it subtly changed, again without a missed step, four pike men formed the centre, with the swords behind, bowmen each side of the advancing line, the officer centred at the front. Jangor pushed to the front, taking Kern with him. Then he stopped their formation and waited for the soldiers to approach. Jangor didn't look back, he made a point of holding the eyes of the officer, as the approaching troop slowed to a walk and finally to a stop, before any words were spoken the officer turned briefly to check the positions of his men, at that point Jangor smiled, that smile was broad when the officer looked back at him.

"Good morning." Said Jangor. "How is your day going?" The smile returned.

"Good day." Replied the officer. "Who are you, what are you doing and where do you go?"

"I am Jangor. You?"

"My name is of no importance," said the officer gruffly, "we are protecting the roads from bandits and such, what is you purpose here?"

Jangor breathed in slowly and nodded slightly, Namdarin moved into place beside Jangor, and Jayanne fell into Kern's left, Wolf unsure which of his friends to stay with sat beside Jayanne.

"We are simple travellers, we have horses to sell, as you saw from your concealment within those trees." Another nod and Granger moved beside Jayanne, with Gregor taking up position on Namdarin's left, both staffs crackled briefly with blue fire.

"How can you prove you aren't the highway men we are looking for?" The officer again checked to make sure his pikes were close enough, he looked up to the heavy teardrop shaped heads, and breathed again knowing that if the pikes came down to point forwards, he would be protected by them.

"What band of highway robbers has a woman and two priests with them? We are simply travellers with some horses to sell, we travel south for Angorak."

The officer looked slowly at them all, emboldened by the extended silence, Wolf stepped forwards, and approached the line ahead of him. The horses noticed him for the first time, perhaps a shift in the wind brought his scent to them, they shied away and had to be pulled back into line, as soon as the line was again straight a pike fell to point straight at Wolf. Wolf's mane fluffed up to its full size, and a deep growl boomed from his chest, again the horses twitched, and tried to pull away. Arndrol stamped, hard on the ground and spit out his bit.

"You." Shouted Jayanne, with a short glance at the officer. "Tell your man to put up his weapon, he is frightening my wolf."

"Did I mention a Wolf?" Asked Jangor, getting the officers attention again. Jayanne threw her reins in Kerns direction, and slid from her horse, she stepped forwards and stood beside Wolf. Jangor turned to face her slowly, knowing that the officer would be following his moves. "Lady, I am sure I have pointed out that foot soldiers don't take on mounted lancers."

"If he attacks Wolf," she replied, not taking her eyes of the mounted man, "I'm going to shove that pole so far up his ass, he'll be sitting ten feet up in the air."

Jangor turned back to the officer. "She means it, please tell your man to put up his weapon, I am fairly sure we are not the group you are looking for." The officer thought for a few moments then waved to the man to put up his pike.

"We are looking for a larger group than yours, perhaps as many as thirty, our instructions are to verify their size and location and report back, so a proper force can be sent out to deal with them. We've heard no tales of women or wolves from the survivors."

"That's good." Said Jangor. "No need for any of us to die today." He smiled at the officer.

"I wouldn't be too sure about that." Said Namdarin. Jangor turned to him and saw that he was stringing his longbow.

"Well?"

"Many horses, and I do mean many, coming fast and over that ridge." He nodded in the direction the soldiers had come from. Jangor stood up in his stirrups, and looked around, there was nowhere near enough, that could be considered defensible, he resumed his seat, and spoke to the officer. "Draw your sword, there's going to be work for it very soon." The officer slowly drew his sword, as Jangor drew his breath. His next words were spoken with all the power of his parade ground voice.

"You men, reform that line, on the road facing up that slope, pikes in the centre, but tighter, bows on the ends, magicians, charge hard, get behind that line and protect them, short burns only, preserve what power you can. Mander, Stergin, Andel, protect the line, Jayanne mount up, work for your axe." A nod from the officer told the men to do as they had been instructed, they moved slowly at first, then riders appeared over the ridge, riding hard, and waving swords, now the soldiers started to follow the instructions with a little more enthusiasm. Arndrol froze as Namdarin stood up in the stirrups, the bowmen at the ends of the line were still waiting for the enemy to come with in their range when the bow of Morgandy started to thrum.

"Brank, Kern on Jayanne." Yelled Jangor. "I'm with Namdarin, you bowmen, pick your targets, if you shoot my people in the back, I'll be very cross." He turned to the officer. "Are these simple robbers?"

"They do leave survivors, but the women do have a very bad time. Why?"

"Time to earn your commission, you are with me, be ready to ride, if you're not with me, I'll kill you when I get back." He turned to see Namdarin shoot his last arrow and drop the bow on the ground. He caught Kerns eyes for a moment, as the bowmen started shooting. Then he yelled. "More damned rapists." The officer was completely unprepared for the speed of the action that followed. Jayanne set off up the hill, with Brank to her left and Kern to her right, Wolf at her feet, heading straight for the centre of the force coming down the slope. Namdarin and Jangor only an instant behind, heading more to the left, hoping to pull some of the enemy away from Jayanne, the office kicked his horse hard in an attempt to catch Namdarin, it was a vain hope, Arndrols massive strength was leaving Jangor and the officer behind, the sword of Xeron leapt into Namdarin's fist, the green jewel in the pommel glowed bright as the sword rose in the dull day, casting a sick hue over the attacking men, every time it fell it struck true, men died.

Jayanne tore through the centre, her axe flashing clean through every contact, Kern's strength to her right, his sword taking its fair share, to her left, the mass that was Brank, moving so fast with the skill of his elvish horse, and all around them Wolf casting fear amongst the enemy, ripping throats from horses and men alike. Three attacked her at once, Brank and Kern were not close enough to be of much help, having their own enemies to deal with, as the axe flashed down to take the life of the one in the middle she knew she was wide open to the other two, each of their heads flashed with a bright blue light, and their hands covered their eyes, giving Jayanne enough time for the stroke that took both heads in one pass, stealing enough energy to keep her going through the rapidly thinning crowd of warriors. Namdarin was moving along the rear of the attacking force, killing as he went, or simply knocking the men from the mounts for Jangor and the officer to deal with, though Arndrol did stamp the occasional one to death. Now they were chasing the attackers down the slope towards the very short line of pike men. More than half the attackers were dead when Namdarin saw two going back up the slope, they were going to escape. Jayanne was driving the others towards the pikes and killing them with abandon.

"Brank." He yelled. "On me, Wolf." He turned to Jangor and waved him towards Jayanne, with a nod, Jangor took the officer with him to aid Jayanne, Brank and his fleet-footed horse had no problem catching Namdarin as Arndrol pounded up the hill after the escapees, Wolf was much the same, soon the three were side by side as they crossed the ridge, it would have been difficult to follow the escaping men, if that ride up the hill hadn't slowed their horses to a walk. They were breathing so hard and sweating so much, they had nothing left, even Wolf on their tail couldn't make them go any faster. Arndrol rode them down in short order.

"Drop your weapons." Shouted Namdarin as he crossed in front of them. Wolf growled and the tired horses tried to turn away, Brank swept one of the men from his saddle with the flat of his sword, the other dropped his sword and slid to the ground.

"You can walk back to the others," growled Namdarin, "if Jayanne has been hurt in my absence, then you will die very slowly. You'll get to watch Wolf eating bits of you. Now walk." Namdarin and Brank stayed mounted as Wolf herded the men back over the hill, by the time they cleared the ridge the battle was over, a very small group of men were tied up on the ground, a very small group. Jayanne was riding up the slope towards them, she stopped as soon as she saw them coming closer.

"Are these leaders or just too frightened to fight?" She asked as they came close enough.

"I haven't bothered to ask them, I thought we'd just turn them over to the officer and his men, they can drag them back to the city, at their own merry pace, for whatever punishment awaits them, robbers, killers, rapists, they'll probably die."

"Perhaps we should save the officer the trouble, and just kill them now?"

"We have powerful friends in the city, we will be safe there." Said one of the walking men.

"They're not very bright are they." Said Brank. Jayanne laughed aloud, before she looked down at the men.

"If Brank says you're not bright, then you really must be stupid, and he's not wrong. I have a standard response for rapists, I kill them, or I let my axe drink their souls, it's hungry right now, it didn't get much chance to feed, now a rapist tells me that he'll be safe once he gets to the city."

"Are you injured?" asked Namdarin, looking at all the blood on Jayanne.

"None of this is mine, they got close occasionally, but I think our wizards have come up with a new tactic, it's very effective."

"Tell me more, those are some intelligent men."

"Jangor told them to preserve what power they had, so rather than burning the whole heads of the enemy, they just burned them enough to blind them, a blind man can't really fight. They're getting quite good, perhaps they could practice some more on these here?"

"It must be very difficult to be a robber, when you can't see what you are stealing." Laughed Brank.

"In some cultures, thieves get to lose their hands." Said Namdarin. "I think eyes is probably a better way of ensuring they don't steal again." The looks he got from their captives only made him laugh harder.

As they came up to the group of tethered robbers, one of the prisoners decided to make a run for it, he dodged between the soldiers and ran along the road, he didn't get very far before Wolf snatched a leg out from under him, and he collapsed to the ground, blood fountaining from the wound in his leg. Jayanne rode up and dropped beside him, a quick glance told her he was not going to survive, so she buried the axe in his back, and allowed it to feed to its hearts content. She walked slowly back to the crowd of captives, leaving a dried-up bundle of sticks on the ground.

"Anyone else feel like running? My axe is still hungry." She laughed loudly and turned to the officer.

"What are you going to do about all those corpses?" She waved up the slope to the scattered remains.

"You people certainly leave a mess behind you." He said,

"Anyone injured?" Shouted Jangor. Both Kern and Brank admitted to a scratch or two, but nothing serious. One of the captives called out that he was injured and needed some assistance. Jangor stared at the man for a long moment, then called out.

"Jayanne, one of these animals doesn't think he's going to survive until they get to the city, can you put him out of his misery?"

"No problem." She replied, walking towards the complainant, the axe swinging casually from her right hand.

"I'll live." Said the man with a very quaky voice, and he tried to crawl away from the approaching woman, despite being heavily bound. Jayanne looked to Jangor, he nodded, she turned away. Namdarin rode over to her, slid from his horse and hugged her close, he looked round at Arndrol.

"Go round up the horses, Wolf help him." Arndrol tossed his head and set off to collect the loose horses, Wolf followed along. Jangor turned to the officer.

"Any injuries amongst your men?"

"One or two, all minor, which is astounding considering the odds against us. How can you people be so good at this sort of thing?"

"We've had practice, and we have a good team."

"I've never seen magic used so well, almost like seriously good bowmen, but without the need for arrows, how do they do that?"

"I'm not even sure that they know how, but they manage to surprise me every time they come to combat, they're almost as good an asset as Jayanne and Namdarin."

"What is it with her?"

"We recently came up against some robbers that tortured and raped children, mention rapists and she goes crazy, completely crazy."

"And him?" He nodded in the direction of Namdarin.

"His family were killed, he is the road to vengeance."

"You go with him?"

"He is an honourable man."

"Enough for you to ride the glory road?"

"Somehow we don't see it as that, we are certainly making some money, but I wouldn't say we were chasing glory as such."

"I see that you are rounding up the rider less horses."

"Yes, it's all right if we leave you enough for your prisoners, and take the rest with us?"

"I don't have a problem with that, but I don't think that stallion is going to give that easily." He pointed up the slope to where Arndrol was trying to separate the horses from the stallion, he was a large bay, with a long tail and mane.

"Arndrol will kill him if necessary, he's been told to collect the horses." While they watched Arndrol challenged the bay and rose up on his hind legs, to strike at the bays head, the bay rose up to meet the challenge, as their chests clashed a streak of grey rushed in from the long grass and slashed the hind legs of the bay with sharp teeth, the horse collapsed as his tendons failed, Arndrols heavy hooves dropped right onto the top of his head, with all the weight of the heavy horse behind them, the bay died in a moment.

"That is the sort of teamwork I never would have expected to see." Said the officer shaking his head, Arndrol and Wolf circled the now tightly packed herd of horses and claimed them for their own. When Arndrol stopped circling and walked slowly to where

Namdarin was waiting the horses all followed calmly, despite the fact the wolf was behind them, his jaws red with blood. Mander came forwards to gather the horses and separate enough for the surviving bandits.

"Do you want to question these men?" Asked Jangor. "It might go easier before we leave."

"That might be an idea. Which one do you suggest?"

"The surviving escapist."

"Why?"

"He's most likely one of the leaders."

"How can you tell? He might just have been very frightened, seeing Jayanne coming towards me would make me want to run."

"We'll see." Jangor turned and called. "Jayanne, would you care to lend us a hand here?" Jayanne nodded, and looked around for Wolf, he was cruising around the fallen, just checking to be sure they were dead. She caught his eyes and he immediately stopped and came running over to her, his usual greeting, paws on shoulders, and her jaw held in his briefly, before he licked her exposed neck, and dropped to the ground again. She stopped in front of Jangor.

"What do you need?" she asked.

"We need some information from these people."

"Have you asked any questions yet?"

"No, why?"

"Wolf's hungry, but not as hungry as my axe, it's suffering from a shortage of souls." She twitched her wrist and the haft slapped into her hand by way of emphasis. "How many do you actually need?"

"Well," said the officer, "I don't actually need any of them, heads will do, and much easier to transport."

"That makes things so simple." She said, she stepped up to the nearest captive, placed her foot on his chest and the axe against his throat. "What do we need to know?" The officer laughed softly.

"I don't know what you want, but that man there, he knows." He nodded in the direction of the man Jangor had indicated. Jangor smiled. Jayanne snapped her fingers and pointed at the man in question. Instantly Wolf jumped onto his chest and growled into his face. Slowly Jayanne let the axe sink into the man's neck, blood started to seep from the widening wound, only to be absorbed by the shining steel blade, the noise of the axe feeding grew as it swallowed the man's hot red blood, and then started to drink his soul, he groaned just the once, a desperate sound, gradually the life flowed from his body into the axe, and then into Jayanne. Soon the body was completely mummified.

"You've changed." Said Namdarin.

"What do you mean?" She replied, and she moved over to the man now trying to move his nose so that Wolf wouldn't bite it.

"I remember when you puked because I was torturing a Zandaar."

"That seems like so many years ago. Anyway, these are rapists. Are you ready to be sick yet?"

"I don't think so, I've seen Wolf kill before, and I've seen what that axe can do. Both have proved to be effective in the past. I'll be interested to hear what this man has to say."

"I'm sure we all will, speak fool and perhaps you can live a few more days." She looked down at him, and moved the axe up to his wrist, just so he could feel the coldness of the blade.

"Why should I tell you anything?"

"Because, if you don't you will die screaming."

"What is it you wish to know?"

"Firstly," said Jangor, "how did you know to attack this small group of soldiers with such a large force."

"The instructions were no survivors."

"From whom?" Snarled the officer.

"Gandar, you've been making noises that made things difficult for him, he wanted you out of the way for a while, to give him time to get other plans in place, before your people come looking for you."

"Gandar, why him? I've been speaking out against the damned robbers that have been making a nuisance of themselves around here."

"Well, he's the one been making the most money from us. He keeps the patrols running in the wrong direction. Except for yours of course."

"I believe I shall be having words with Gandar when we get back to Angorak."

"I think a sword in the belly would be better." Laughed Jayanne. She looked down again. "Who else is involved?"

"No one else of importance, only a few members of the priesthood."

"So," said Jangor, "who runs the city?"

"Nominally, there is a council, but Gandar controls most of them, so they do pretty much what he wants."

"You mean that Gandar is just getting rich off the whole city?"

"That's about right, he's not even very subtle about it."

"So why does he want this young man out of the way?"

"He's been stirring up trouble, his family is too powerful to be ignored."

"You're saying the Gandar wants my whole family out of the way?" Asked the officer.

"They are the most powerful group in the city other than his, with your disappearance, they'd have invested a great deal of time, effort and money, finding out what had happened to you. They'd most likely of ingratiated themselves to Gandar to the extent that he'd be able to control them. Then the whole city would be his."

"To what end?" Asked Jangor.

"I've no idea, I think he just wants the power over everyone."

"Is it true about your family?" Asked Jangor turning to the officer.

"I suppose, they are quite rich, they know everyone of importance, even Gandar, shall we say that his name isn't popular. There have been discussions about the removal of Gandar. It has been hard to find anyone with the skill to perform the task."

"Perhaps we should pay him a visit." Whispered Jayanne.

"You'd never get past his guards." Said the officer.

"They'd kill you before you got into the city." Laughed the man on the ground.

"I don't think so." Said the officer. "Look what these people did to your entire band? I can't claim that it was my men responsible for your defeat." He paused before turning to Jangor. "If you hadn't been here today, we'd all be dead, we couldn't have hoped to survive against such odds, they'd have just ridden straight through us. Thank you all." He bowed briefly.

"Your people are extraordinary," admitted the robber, "I've never seen their like, had I even thought that such a small force could be so effective, I'd have turned away, and waited for a better moment."

"There are times when numbers don't actually count for a great deal." Said Jangor. "We tore the heart out of your band, and she's going to tear the heart out of you, and feed on your soul."

"I thought you were going to take us back to Angorak?" He looked frightened.

"I am afraid friend," said the officer, looking directly at Jangor, "that he is correct, I need his testimony to bring charges against Gandar." Jangor smiled and looked at the recumbent man.

"You think that Gandar is going to let you live to testify against him? You're dead, whether we kill you or no." He laughed loudly.

"What about the rest of us?" Asked one of the other prisoners.

"I think that simple foot soldiers aren't much of a threat to Gandar, though you may know things that he doesn't want public." Jangor smiled. "I'm sure you'll find out when you get to Angorak."

"Which way are you going?" Asked the officer.

"We're heading for Zandaarkoon by way of Angorak, we've been told it's the easiest road to follow."

"That is correct, would you care to travel along with us, I for one would feel so much safer to have you and your people along with us."

"I have no problem with that, and I'm certain your prisoners would feel so much safer as well, knowing that Wolf could find them in the dark, and run them down in a moment." He smiled at the man lying on the floor. "Time for introductions. I am Jangor." He held out his hand.

"Greyham." Said the officer, shaking Jangor's hand firmly.

"Namdarin." Mumbled Jayanne, shakily. "Help me please." Namdarin stepped up to her instantly and whispered softly.

"What's wrong?"

"The axe, it's so hungry, it is desperate to kill him, it's already feeding slowly on the cut at his wrist."

"You have to be strong enough to keep it in control, you have already made it yours. Exert that control and stop it feeding."

"That is the problem, the energy it feeds me, it's hot, it's bright, and it feels so good, I want more of it, lot's more of it. You have no idea how good it feels."

"Jayanne, my love." He whispered, "You can't let this thing control you, it's up to you, you have to control it. Please my love be strong."

"I just want to let it lose, and let it drink his soul, so that I can feel that power again."

"The sword feeds me power as well, but I don't think it eats their souls, just their lives. So, it is different, but the strength it gives is just as real. Let this one live, at least for a little while, you never know, he may be stupid enough to run when he gets the chance."

Slowly Jayanne pulled the axe away from the man's wrist. The shallow wound bled a little but soon stopped.

"That was hard." She whispered, turning to Namdarin and hugging him to her, she rested her head against his shoulder,

"Greyham." Said Jangor. "Get these men mounted, and let's get on the road, there is still enough daylight, we can make more than a few miles before we have to camp, and I for one would like to get away from the stink all those corpses are going to create."

"Pay attention." Shouted Greyham. "You men can either ride in a saddle or tied across it, I don't particularly care which, if you chose the former and then misbehave, then I am afraid survivors will be tied across. Any questions?" There were no replies from the prisoners.

"I like your style." Said Jangor, "We're almost ready, Stergin, do we have much in the way of gold?"

"For such a successful band of robbers they seem to have very empty pockets." Replied Stergin, handing Jangor a small bag of coins. "Perhaps the value in this mission was on someone's head." He laughed nodding in the direction of Greyham.

"Get ready to ride." Called Jangor. "Andel, Mander you look to our collection of horses, Granger, Gregor, how are you two for power?" Namdarin and Jayanne walked to their horses and mounted, wolf at their feet.

"We are a little low," said Granger, "but I have a plan for a bit of a recharge." Together he and Gregor pointed their staffs at the pile of dead bodies, both staffs turned dark and small lights flashed up and down them. Jangor frowned but watched for a few moments it seemed that nothing was happening, then slowly the bodies became dusted in frost, mist rolled down the slope, in a few breaths the whole pile was white with a thick covering of frost. The two staffs rose and resumed a more normal colour.

"What did you just do?" Asked Greyham.

"We took the heat that was no longer needed, it's not a great deal of energy, but it's a start towards refilling that which we used in the battle." Said Granger.

"What would happen if you did that to someone that was still alive?"

"Perhaps it would be better if you didn't think about that." Smiled Gregor.

"Greyham," Said Jangor, "get your people ready to ride, and look to your prisoners, your responsibility not ours, the day moves on people." There was a scrambling, the prisoners were tied to their saddles in short order, and before long everyone was ready. "Greyham, you lead, Brank, Kern you're with him, the rest of Greyham's people, you surround the prisoners, prisoners your final warning, if you make a break for it, you will be run down in short order, Brank has the fastest horse you have ever seen, even carrying him, Namdarin is only a heartbeat behind, and Wolf will of course be there as well. Remember Jayanne is hungry for souls. Move out." The last at Jangor's full military volume. With Greyham showing the way and Kern setting the pace the column set off, bound for Angorak. They had covered many miles before the light started to fail, and Jangor decided it was time to make camp.

"Greyham." Called Jangor loudly, so that all could hear. "Your prisoners are your responsibility, if they disturb my sleep, then I'll kill them all. Are we clear?"

"Rest assured," replied Greyham with a smile, "they will behave themselves, my lord Jangor."

"Just Jangor, I've usually found lords to be unreliable."

"What about me?" Asked Namdarin.

"You aren't a lord anymore."

"I am still the lord of Namdaron, I may be the last member of that family, as such as am still Lord."

"Sorry Namdarin, I shall never see you as a lord, you are a fighter, perhaps a general."

"That's as maybe, but as Lord of Namdaron I shall see this thing through to the end."

"And I'll be there beside you."

"Thanks for that."

"Gentlemen," said Greyham, "I suggest that our teams share the sentry duty for the night, what do you say?"

"I'll agree to that." Said Jangor. "Kern will be first for us, as normal, he has a feel for the night, something that many don't have. Let's not forget that Wolf will be there as well."

"Agreed, my first man will meet Kern somewhere in the dark, after we have eaten. Two-hour watches at the most, is that agreed?"

"Yes," said Jangor, "Kern and Wolf will find your man, keep the fires as low as you can, we don't want to affect the watchmen's night vision." His vice dropped to a whisper. "Keep your prisoners under control, I really don't want to have kill them."

"I am sure they are currently pissing in their pants, if any of them start moving in the night, the others are going to be screaming to protect their own lives."

"That will be good, let's get what sleep we can, how far away is the city of Angorak?"

"If we set out early, and keep a good pace, then we should be there before noon, or just after."

"Good. Then it's only a day or two to Zandaarkoon." Said Namdarin.

The night passed uneventfully, wolf slept some with whoever was on guard, even though the light showers that wet everyone who didn't have a tent, those were mostly the prisoners, but they didn't complain not wishing to incur the wrath of Jangor. As normal for the old soldier he took the last watch of the night, he was waiting for the sky to lighten. Wolf appeared out of the gloom and sat beside Jangor.

"You have a good night?" Asked Jangor. Wolf just looked up at him and smiled, well for a wolf it was a smile.

"You want to wake them?" Wolf looked at the man then stood, filled his wide chest with air, threw his head back and howled, the loud resonance filled the camp and the surrounding area with the singing of the wolf. As he paused to breathe in, and answer came from the mountains to the east, weak and low, but it came none the less. People came running from tents and and dragging their clothes on.

"Glad to see you're all awake." Laughed Jangor. "Get moving, breakfast and on the road, the life of the freelance soldiers, one day soon we'll have a base and a lord to serve."

Groans were the only answers he got, but people were moving, even Greyham's troops were following the commands of Jangor, it was simply a matter soldiers following the instructions of anyone with the ability to issue them. Even the prisoners were lending a hand, under the watchful eye of Wolf.

The sun had barely shown above the mountains to the east, as they started to mount their horses, and set off, Kern and Brank bracketing Greyham, led the way. South and west through rapidly changing landscape, fields and roads becoming more common. The small hamlets that normally surround large cities became much more common, as they passed through, often there would be a group of gawkers standing and watching, sometimes small children would attempt to keep pace with the passing horses, the presence of Wolf made all the parents very nervous, often snatching the youngsters to safety. It was about midmorning that the plume of smoke generated by the city became visible, followed quite quickly by the huge walls.

"Kern." Said Greyham, "Follow the road to the south gate, I'll go have a quick chat with Jangor." He reined in and waved the others passed, he fell in alongside Jangor.

"We'll go in the south gate, my family are fairly close, we shouldn't have too many issues with Gandar or his followers, they are more in the centre and north of the city."

"What about the watchers on the wall?"

"They probably haven't recognised us yet, far too many of us, and they're too busy looking at Wolf cruising around."

"Let's hope that doesn't change until it's too late. Will we be safe from attack once we get inside?"

"You're worried?"

"Looking up at those walls, that's a big city. I don't mind taking on a few bandits, but a whole city, that's too much for even me."

"I'm fairly sure that your people could burn the whole place in a few minutes." Laughed Greyham, kicking his horse to get back to the front of the column.

As he moved to the front Kern was turning to the right, along the south wall, looking up and the huge tower, with many faces looking over. Kern's hand strayed to the hilt of his sword, as a shiver passed down his spine.

"Relax friend, everything will be fine. Only three streets back from the wall is the residence of my family, we'll be truly safe once we get there. Don't worry."

"I can't help it, this place frightens me, I have a bad feeling." He slowly raised his left arm his open hand high above his head. He clenched his fist. Greyham was surprised by the sudden sound of horses. Jangor came to the front rapidly, Jayanne, Namdarin, Granger, and Gregor, came forwards as well.

"What's wrong?" Demanded Jangor.

"Bad feeling." Said Kern.

"I feel it," said Jangor, "Granger, what do you feel?"

"Something bad, comes." Said the old man.

"What?"

The old man shrugged, clenched his fist on his staff, and looked up at the wall, as they passed it, the south gate was just ahead, with a small tower on each side, the sky above the city darkened.

"No." Shouted Gregor, pointing his staff upwards into the gathering gloom. Quickly a spinning column of darkness formed in the middle of the city, a twisting spiral of dark fire. Gregor kicked his horse hard and rode for the gate, Granger was only a moment behind, with the others following fast. Gregor slid from his horse as he arrived at the gate, and slapped it on the rump with his staff, then stood against one gate post. He waved Granger to the other.

"We're going to have to keep this gate free as long as we can, there are going to be a lot of people trying to leave."

"I don't understand." Shouted Granger over the increasing noise from the city.

"He's burning the whole city." Yelled Gregor, the fire was spreading out quickly, far faster than any fire should every spread naturally, nor was any natural fire this dark. "As soon as you see it, as soon as it is in range, start pulling energy out of it, the more you can take the less damage it can do, the fewer people it will kill." Granger just nodded and leant against the left-hand tower, waiting.

"Namdarin, Brank, guard Granger." Yelled Jangor over the howling from the city, "Kern, Jayanne, here with me, on Gregor." Then he turned. "Greyham, when people start running out of this gate, keep them moving, don't let them stop, we're going to need as much space as we can for survivors." He turned back to the look into the city, the wide road was starting to fill with running people, the city guard were scrambling down the long stairs from the battlements, in the distance he saw a swath of fire cross the road, turning people into torches, that ran briefly screaming, to fall into ashes. Gregor levelled his staff, Granger did the same, the affect seemed to be little, but Jangor could feel the heat rising by the moment. Blue sparks started to be shed from the end of Gregor's staff.

"Jayanne," he yelled, "Put your axe against his staff and let it feed." She frowned for a moment then did as he bid. He looked across the road and saw that Namdarin had already done the same thing. The blue bladed sword was already drinking deeply from the power in Granger's staff. Another wave of fire crossed the road, this time it struggled a little before it started to get hold of the buildings, the people still burn. Gregor leaned into his staff willing it to pull even more power, pushing it as hard as he could, his breath straining in his throat, his whole body shaking with the effort. Another wave of fire took some more of the road, the fire front was now only a hundred feet from the gate, the running survivors, were now very few. A strange opening appeared in the wave front of the fire, a group of riders came through at a gallop, horses struggling with their own fears, the riders rushed through the gate, each in a different coloured cloak.

CHAPTER SIXTY-FIVE

Alverana and Kevana stripped off and settled into their shared sleeping roll, Kevana turned his back to Alverana, and wriggled backwards until he felt Alverana's nakedness pressed against him, Alverana's arm came across his chest and held him tight. Kevana felt Alverana's heavy breath on the back of his neck, it made him shiver a little, but he didn't move away, he felt Alverana's excitement behind him, and his own growing urgency. Listening to the sounds of the camp as everyone went to their tents to sleep, Kevana started to relax, until he felt the feather like touch of Alverana's lips against his neck, his whole body tensed for a moment, then he leaned back against his friend, presenting more of his neck for kissing, as the two gradually relaxed together, Kevana put his hand on top of Alverana's and slowly pushed it down across his hairy belly, eventually down into the heavy thatch of hair above his manhood, there he paused for a long time, before he took his hand off Alverana's and slowly pushed it under the arm and round his back, to stroke Alverana's belly, slowly moving downwards, while Alverana made slow circles with his own, following Kevana's lead he moved downwards until his hand encircled Kevana's manhood, slowly they moved together, faster, each following the other, faster, until orgasm overcame them both. They caught their breath eventually and rested in each other's arms for a while before sleep took them. It was still full dark when Kevana woke, he moved a little, and felt Alverana wake behind him, he turned over slowly to face Alverana.

"Er." He whispered.

"Shh, words are not necessary." Alverana slowly turned over and pulled Kevana tight against his back. They returned to the darkness of sleep, their dreams soft and gentle, Alverana's dreams took him to the green forest that was his home and his strength. In the depth of the green wood he found Kevana sleeping with his back against a tree, resplendent in his nakedness. Alverana looked down at his own nudity, then watched as he slowly grew. For a moment he wondered how Kevana had ended up in his dream while he was so obviously asleep. Alverana shied away from the question, not wishing to disturb the situation, he saw his friend's chest rise and fall slowly with that regular pace that could only mean the deepest of sleep. Alverana approached his friend, placed one bare foot on each side of his thighs, then crouched down, once his face was almost level, he reached out and stroked Kevana's cheek softly. The eyes flashed open, and in an instant took in their surroundings. Kevana could see that he wasn't where he expected to be, so this must be someone's dreamscape. He felt more than a little strange to wake up in someone else's dream. 'Is this Alverana's dream?' He thought, looking into Alverana's eyes. He smiled slowly and reached out with both hands, the left one went to Alverana's neck and pulled his head in for a soft kiss, the right went to his hardening penis, to stroke and fondle it gently. Alverana broke the kiss and leaned backwards slightly, still looking into Kevana's eyes.

"This is strange." He whispered.
"Very, but nice none the less."
"Is this your dream?"
"I don't think so, yours?"

Alverana shook his head and looked around. Slowly he stood upright, looking carefully at the trees all about them. The light coming down through the high canopy was strange in that it had no defined source, it just seemed to stream downwards from a flat sky that he couldn't see. He was struggling to focus on the forest, the stimulation he was receiving was very distracting, the wood was missing something, it was sound, there was no rustling from the leaves, nor really any motion in the breeze he could feel on his face, there was no noise of birds or animals. As he looked upwards, he felt something warm and wet engulf him, a tongue swirled around the head of his manhood, and his vision became somewhat less, the trees became more like paintings on a wall, or a canvas, the darkness between them became more obvious, and closer than it was. The forest became two dimensional, pictures at an exhibition. The darkness from between the trees rushed in to cover them both. In that instant Alverana returned to the real world, his orgasm spending against his belly.

"That was weird." Muttered a twitching Kevana from behind him, his own spend spreading slowly over Alverana's back.

"Whose dreamscape was that?" Asked Alverana.

"I've no idea, but it sucked us both in."

"Perhaps not exactly the right word to use." Smiled Alverana.

"Maybe, but it seemed right at the time."

"That doesn't answer the question, who's dream world was that?"

"The best bet I can come up with, is those two damned clerics."

"You think so?"

"Who else has that sort of control and power?"

"I find it hard to believe."

"Everything they do is hard to believe." He wriggled hard against Alverana before continuing. "Sleep time, we need to be up early."

"I think I shall be having words with them in the morning."

"I have a feeling their new skills are going to be very important to us in the near future, we are likely to be coming up against some serious opposition, we need them."

"I understand that, I just don't like them messing in our lives."

"Didn't you enjoy the forest dream?" Asked Kevana.

"Of course," replied Alverana, his right hand reaching behind him to stroke Kevana's flank, "but that should be our dream not theirs."

"Good, let's get some sleep." Kevana smiled and settled against his friends back.

No more words were spoken, and sleep came quickly, but not for the clerics. Their wordless communications continued.

'Can we find the source of this power now?' Thought Kirukana.

'Yes, I think that one of us should go searching for the centre of this thing, and the other should act as anchor. What say you?'

'Agreed, I'll be anchor, you've had much more experience of this thing.'

'You need to be fixed in this time and place, hold on to the rest of the group as well, this will give you more stability.'

'I can feel the ground beneath me, and the people around me, the surprising thing is that Kevana and Alverana have such a solidity between them, when they are together.'

'And now we see why, there has always been an attraction between them, only now they know it.'

'I'm not entirely certain that the forest scenario was the way to go, but it definitely got them together.'

'There will be a price to pay in the morning for that one.' Worandana's thought carried with it a gentle laughter. 'At least

Kevana will be both calmer and more dangerous tomorrow.'

'What do you mean?'

'When they are together, he'll be more relaxed, but should anything threaten Alverana, then that berserker is less than a moment away.'

'What if the berserker comes out?'

'Stay far enough away and support him wherever you can. Get settled, I'm going to go find this power.' Worandana waited for Kirukana to give him the mental nod, then he launched into the night, feeling about for the intensity of the power, he followed the slightly higher density for a short time, though his body wasn't moving he felt the distance increasing at an alarming rate, calming himself with the solidity of his link to Kirukana, he moved faster and faster, through the darkness and cold. The distances became completely meaningless and his speed became ever greater. A sudden feeling of dread caused him to slow his progress, ahead his mind observed a black shape in the darkness, it shimmered almost purple against the dead black, a huge shape, almost without discernible shape, its edges seemed to writhe and wriggle. His reduced speed brought him closer and closer, suddenly the shape became more stable before his mind's eye, it was like a gigantic bat, membranous wings to either side, triangular shaped head pointing straight at the approaching presence. 'It's almost as if the act of observation fixed it's shape.' Thought Worandana, as the bat became clearer. Its small eyes focused on Worandana, unlike any bat he had ever seen, these eyes were triangular, and glowing red, they blinked slowly, three eyelids closed them, then re-opened. Below the hot pits of the eyes opened a huge mouth, again triangular, this a much hotter red, framed with teeth like columns of brilliant yellow fire. Worandana felt fear grip his heart, and a force start to drag him towards that burning maw. Using all the power he could muster he tried to pull away, his forward speed reduced but he wasn't able to stop. 'Kirukana.' He thought desperately, 'Help me.' Another force took hold of him, this one pulling him away from the bat shaped monster ahead. At first it has little effect, then it doubled, Worandana's approach started to slow, again the force doubled, and again, then a subtle change occurred, the new force completely encased Worandana, wrapping him in a field of energy, that broke the pull of the bat creature, and Worandana started to move away, returning to his own body at an incredible rate, racing through the dark, he was struggling to hold on to his own personality, the roaring of the blackness tore at the edges of his mind, trusting to the enveloping force of Kirukana's mind he let the darkness take him and he folded into himself, blocking out everything from around him.

Still linked together the two flashed into their own bodies, and each took that first deep breath, slowly they opened their eyes.

"What in all the hells was that thing?" Muttered Kirukana.

"I have no idea, but it is the source of this dark power, and it does appear to be hungry."

"And it's coming our way."

"Is this the power that will end life and free Gyara?" Asked Worandana.

"I've no idea, but I'd suggest it might even eat Gyara."

"I'd like to see that, she'd definitely be free of this place then."

"I don't think she's going to show herself, not until she has been freed. If that thing is coming this way, what are we going to do about it?" Asked Kirukana.

"I have no idea, it's certainly carrying a huge amount of power, we have been tapping it, looks like it can't stop us doing that."

"Perhaps this dark power is a worm."

"What do you mean?" Worandana frowned.

"Worm on a hook, we are the fish who have been caught, think about it. Any 'fish' that can tap this things power must have a source locally, perhaps one that this thing comes to harvest."

"You think it's going to harvest the whole world?"

"Could be."

"And I brought it here."

"Again, but it could be that there is someone else also calling on it's dark power, someone else has already started it coming this way. "

"Laying blame serves no purpose here," mumbled Worandana, "I think this thing is a bigger threat to all of us than the damned council, but I don't want to be dealing with this beast while the council are stabbing me in the back."

"I agree." Smiled Kirukana.

"So, we take the council out of the picture, then stop this dark power."

"You make it sound so simple."

"It may be just that, removed the council, have a quick chat with the beast, slap it on its nose, and send it away like a scolded dog." Laughed Worandana.

"I don't feel that it is going to be that easy."

"Agreed, now how about something closer to hand?"

"This power we are taking from the beast is better than sleep, what do you have in mind?"

"Let's find that damned sword." Muttered Worandana.

"Fine, do we need an anchor for this, or should we just link up and go looking?"

"Let's just send out a simple search, together, we can cover a lot of ground in a very short time, and we have a sort of idea where the sword will be."

"Form the link." Whispered Kirukana. Worandana formed the link between their minds, once he was sure it was stable enough, he thought. 'Launch.' Together their consciousness left their bodies and tore off into the night, heading first east, then south, in only a heartbeat they were over the city of Angorak, the smoke of all those minds packed into such a small space was clearly visible from a distance, especially given their current altitude.

'Notice how the people in the city generate a plume like heat or smoke,' thought Worandana, 'perhaps we can use that to locate other groups of people.'

'Probably, but there are going to be many groups, villages, camps, hamlets, we need to focus on the sword.' Replied Kirukana.

'Which way should we go first?' Asked Worandana.

'They're most likely coming from the elven forests to the north, so let's head that way, then sort of east.' Worandana's assent was declared by their rapid departure from the city, north then a little east, Worandana was feeling for the presence of the sword, his mind sweeping ahead of them, covering miles in a moment, only a short time later he found it, shining like a beacon, a blue flare that lit the darkness of the sky. Their joined mind rushed towards it, then at the very last moment Worandana stopped suddenly. Hanging a few hundred feet up in the air, half a mile away from the sword.

'Why here?' Asked Kirukana.

'Feel the power in that thing, it positively reeks of it, I can feel it distorting the space all around it, and it's not the biggest distortion in the area, right near it is another, bigger, much bigger, energy concentration.'

'What is it?'

'Given Crathen's descriptions, this is most likely the axe that the woman, Jayanne, carries. It's close by and even more powerful than the sword.'

'Crathen says it is a god's axe.' Thought Kirukana.

'I'd agree with him now that I can feel its power.'

'I can't see its power, only the distortion it creates. If we have to do battle against these, I'd be more frightened of the axe, it's rife with the power.'

'Yes, but it's very different from the power we are using, I wonder what it is, and were it gets this power.'

'When we meet these people,' thought Kirukana, 'you and I take on the axe wielder, and the rest can keep the swordsman at bay until we can take the sword from him.'

'I'll explain this to Kevana when we get back, there is a bigger problem.'

'What?'

'They are closer to the city than we are. If they have any sense of urgency at all they may just beat us to Angorak.'

'We have plenty of time before dawn, we'll get the others up early and ride hard all morning, we should beat them to Angorak.'

'Let's hope so, I don't fancy chasing them to Zandaarkoon. Let's head back to camp, I feel the need to charge up with some more of this black power.'

'Should we try to invade a few dreams, we could change the odds for when we finally meet?'

'I don't want to get that close, one of them almost killed Alverana by accident, no, they can dream their own dreams.' With this thought Worandana moved away from the camp, and headed back to their own, again the shock of entering their own bodies almost broke their linkage. Very soon they had their breathing back under control, gently Worandana released the linkage, and their minds became distinctly separated.

"That was harder than I expected." Mumbled Worandana.

"I'm certainly feeling more than a little tired." Smiled Kirukana.

"It definitely took something out of us, but we can now start taking energy from that dark bat thing."

"Do you think it has a name?"

"It must have a name, it has to know who it is, but what other people call it, who can tell?"

"If it is capable of consuming a whole world, then no one can survive to give it a name."

"Very true, we are going to have to work hard to defeat this thing, I hope that Zandaar can help us." Worandana sighed.

"Do you think that Gyara will help?"

"Unlikely, this thing is most likely to be what frees her from her servitude here."

"I still can't decide what sort of service she provides." Laughed Kirukana. Worandana's hands were surrounded by the darkness again, as he drew power from the dark bat shape, he started to feel much better, the tiredness just washed away in the surging darkness, Kirukana felt the same, but he was less comfortable about it.

"This power is wrong." Whispered Kirukana.

"It is power," said Worandana, "its righteousness comes from the way it is used. We use it for good, and to protect our own lives, how can that be wrong?"

"It just feels bad, our own power feels right because it comes entirely from within ourselves, this is something else."

"And so much more than anything we can generate internally, should we go and frighten Axorana some more? I have the urge to shake him up some more."

"Is that wise? Every time you meet him you give him the chance to learn how to counter this power of ours."

"He lacks any of the necessary skills to do that, and we have plenty of time to recharge before it is time to be back on the road."

"I'd like to have words with him, let's do it."

"Good. Link up with me and we'll go find him." Worandana linked his mind to Kirukana's, and together they launched into the etheric plane, leaving their bodies behind, Worandana set the pace high and raced down the river, southwards bound for Zandaarkoon. In minutes the river grew wide and slow, shallow and muddy, there were no channels for boats of any real size to use, which is why the docks at Angorak were so busy. Almost to the sea they flew, then turned east. The heat like plume that they had seen above Angorak was much smaller here, despite the population of the city being so much greater.

'Where is all the power from the minds of all these people?' Thought Kirukana.

'I've never noticed how low the energy is here, it's strange.' Replied Worandana, as he cast about looking for Axorana's signature, rapidly they closed in on the centre of the city, Worandana half expected there to be some watchers looking out for just this sort of invasion, but there was nothing. The plume of energy became visible as they moved towards the centre, the citadel of Zandaar was glowing with energy, and a stream of radiant particles rose from its domed roof.

'At least there is one centre with some power.' Thought Worandana, quietly.

'I'd rather not go there,' replied Kirukana, 'I'm frightened.'

'So am I, I can just feel Axorana below the citadel, he's in the catacombs. He's asleep but surrounded by watchers.'

'I can feel Zandaar, he is not sleeping, please let us leave.'

'Not yet, I have an idea.' In a flash they sped over to a library building only a short distance away, through the upper story windows, and down the stairwells, through the empty hallways, and down into the cellars.

'Where are we going?' Asked Kirukana.

'A little-known pathway, quiet now, we are close.' Worandana slowed as they crossed the dusty cellar, long unused. He went straight up to the wall at the end, and paused, shifting gradually and carefully he pulled them both through the stone wall, it turned out to be only a single layer of bricks.

'That's a lot easier in physical form, the door release is disguised as a rock in the wall.' His mind as quiet as he could make it. They wafted along the corridor, then eased through another wall, into the crypt beneath the citadel. Along tight corridors with the coffins of the dead all around them, they eventually came to a room where a man slept, surrounded by eight men, each one watching carefully, though they were looking in the wrong place. Worandana felt out the edges of Axorana's dream, it was the typical dream of a powerful man, far more powerful in his dream than in the real world, he was holding court and handing out instructions to all those who bowed before him, in the background was a large chained figure, who could only have been Zandaar. Kirukana felt Worandana's smile, twisting the dreamscape he caused a darkness to appear in the middle of the chamber, and from that darkness he and Kirukana stepped into the harsh light of Axorana's dream. Their robes not the bright colours they now wore, but the darkest of black.

"Axorana, what are you doing?" Called Worandana.

"Who are you? What do you want here? Speak quickly before I have you killed." Snappped Axorana.

"I am Worandana, and this is Kirukana." Worandana turned to the image of Kirukana, together they threw back their hoods to reveal their identities.

"Have you called off the brothers?" Demanded Kirukana.

"How did you get here?"

"Answer the question," yelled Worandana, "while you still can."

"Guards." Shouted Axorana. "Kill these fools." Sure enough guards started to approach from the entrances of the chamber, but none of them made it very far into the room, they simply faded away. Axorana watched as the guards faded from view. Then he jumped up from his throne and a cocked crossbow appeared in his hands. As he pointed it at Worandana and raised it to aim, it turned into a snake that coiled around his arms, causing him to scream and drop it.

"Have you called off the brothers?" Yelled Kirukana, the words took on a physical form, a wave of air that pushed Axorana back into his throne, fear now etched into his eyes. Worandana approached the dais upon which the throne was placed, as he did all the presences in the chamber faded from view, all bar one, the chained figure was freed in an instant, leaving Axorana alone to face the two, in front, and the one behind.

"I have sent instructions that you are not to be attacked, followed but not threatened, reports tell me that you are still north of Angorak, how can you be here, in what must be my dream?"

"That is a small thing," whispered Worandana, "know this we are coming, we may be a day or two away, but we will meet soon." Then he thought at Kirukana. 'Link hands, cover ourselves in the darkness, and then project upwards out of this dream.' As he thought it, that is what happened, their departure tore Axorana's dream to shreds and he woke screaming. Worandana led them out the way they had come, swiftly, before Axorana could stop his screaming and make some form of sense, it was possible that the guards could follow them, but only if they actually leapt onto the other plane and saw them there. Slowing down for the second wall Worandana knew they were not going to be followed, it seemed the guards were having a serious problem believing what Axorana was yelling at them. Up through the library they travelled, and out into the open sky, then northwards, accelerating all the time, over Angorak Worandana started to slow things down, and they both returned to their bodies in the same instant. They both struggled for a while with breathing as was normal for one of these excursions, slowly they settled down, Worandana smiled.

"That was fun."

"Are you sure about that? They are going to be running around like a nest full of angry wasps."

"They'll be stinging everything in sight, oh my, that's going to be entertaining for the next couple of days." He laughed loudly, then continued. "How are you for energy, I've spent quite a bit getting back here."

"I'm the same. We need to recharge."

"Agreed, we'll rest for a couple of hours then get the rest moving, early start, we don't want the sword to get past Angorak before we get there."

"Fine, let's just relax." Smiled Kirukana, closing his eyes, and letting his head fall forwards. It wasn't more than a minute before Worandana followed suit, the darkness of the camp spread quiet and deep, almost as if everyone was dead. In the darkness a lone otter came snuffling up from the river, hoping to find something to eat amongst the smell of human, it snuffled around for a while, but finding nothing worth eating, he made his way back to the river to hunt for some fish, or perhaps a tasty snake like eel. His passing spooked the horses a little, but only enough for them to stamp their feet to help him on his way. He stood upright on his hindquarters briefly and looked around, before dropping nose first into the river with barely a splash.

Worandana lifted his head and let his hood fall backwards, looking to the east he found that the night was nearly done, the eastern sky was lightening, but only just, sunrise was hours away, but definitely approaching. Worandana smiled to himself, looking for a dream to invade, he found one, Crathen was dreaming of Jayanne again, her soft red hair all around him as they rolled together in an embrace of love. Worandana reached inside and twisted things just a little, her long red hair turned into long thin snakes which started to tighten around him.

A blood curdling scream filled the camp, waking everyone up, Alverana and Kevana were the first moving, they rolled out of their tent swords in hand, and rushed to Crathen's tent, just as the scream choked itself down, as the man ran out of air, Kevana yanked the flap open and Alverana looked in, sword to the fore, Crathen took a deep and shuddering breath, then opened his eyes.

"Bastard." He shouted. "Which of you did that?" From the edge of the camp came the laughter of Worandana.

"What did you do, old man?" Demanded Kevana.

"I just twisted his dream a bit." Laughed Worandana.

"Damn it, that's what Namdarin did to me." Yelled Crathen, slowly levering himself to his hands and knees, before crawling out of his tent, he pushed Alverana's sword aside, snatched his own from its scabbard and barged Alverana out of the way as he left the tent, swinging the sword slowly he stalked towards the two clerics, anger filled his eyes.

"Crathen." Yelled Kevana. "Stop. You will not hurt him." Kevana strode after him. Crathen stopped, turned to face the rapidly approaching Kevana, he paused. Looked down at himself, light trousers and shirt, his normal sleeping attire, then he looked at the old soldier stepping smoothly towards him, sword ready, naked, not even shoes. Crathen lowered his sword and laughed loudly.

"How dare you laugh at me?" Yelled Kevana.

"I am sorry, but you look so funny, standing there waving a sword, and waving a," he looked downwards, "well, a sword." Alverana stepped up and slowly pulled Kevana's sword arm down, then crossed in front of him.

"I am sorry Alverana, but you're not much better." He turned to Worandana. "Why did you do this old man?"

"It wasn't intended to cause any harm, it was simply a joke, just to get everyone out of bed, because we have some news that you need."

"What do you know, old man." Called Kevana.

"The sword is close, very close, we need to be moving early and pushing hard if we are going to get to Angorak before it. If Namdarin pushes hard he can get there ahead of us, and we don't want that. So, we can take advantage of this early arousal and get on the road early today."

"I really don't like being every bodies wake up call." Snarled Crathen.

"Well, seeing as you are partly dressed," said Kevana, "you can start breakfast." He turned to Worandana. "How close old man?"

"Very, more than half a day, but not much, and if they decide to hurry not even half a day."

"Let's hope they don't see a reason to hurry. Did they know you were there when you visited them last night?"

"No, we stayed well back, the sword is definitely still with them, and carrying quite a charge of energy."

"How many in their group?"

"I didn't actually get close enough to count, but certainly more than when Crathen left them."

"Is Gorgana still with them?"

"I have no idea, I'd have had to get far too close to be sure I'd found him, and I wasn't going to do that."

"Frightened, old man?"

"Only of spooking them, if I can find him, then he can find me."

"Do you think he'd attack you?"

"Not necessarily, but currently I'd relish the opportunity to pit my power against his."

"Do you think you would win?"

"I have no idea, his power seems to be so much more than a lone man could ever carry, and mine is even more so."

"Together we could almost certainly beat him." Interrupted

Kirukana.

"I wouldn't count on that." Laughed Worandana.

"Our meeting is going to be interesting." Growled Kevana.

"Let's just hope enough of us survive." Grinned Worandana.

"You're sounding remarkably happy considering you've had no sleep."

"We've had some relaxation, and some fun. Travelled a fair bit, and had some more fun, it's been a busy night, but we've enjoyed it."

"Was the forest dreamscape yours?" Whispered Kevana having first looked around, with a nod he indicated that they should move away for a little privacy, Worandana followed, and answered in a whisper.

"Oh yes, that was ours. Did you enjoy it?"

"Sometimes that sort of coercion is bad."

"But you enjoyed it?"

"Yes, damn you, I enjoyed it."

"I'm sorry to interfere, but I think you two needed a little push, and the opportunity may never present itself again."

"I haven't had chance to discuss this with Alverana yet, someone woke us with all the screaming."

"I'm fairly sure he'll be fine with it all." Smiled Worandana quietly.

"I'm not so certain."

"The opportunity was presented, that is all, either of you could have broken away with almost no effort, but you chose not to."

"You don't have to keep belabouring the topic."

"Let's get some food and get back on the road. Miles to go before we sleep."

"Are you ever going to sleep again?"

"Of that I am in no way sure, but the mind tends to lose itself if it doesn't get enough sleep, so I'd say I'll be sleeping sometime, maybe not until this thing is over." He turned and walked back towards the camp where food was almost ready, a quick glance showed him that the sky was lightening even more, dawn would not be too far away. Kevana followed, and a quick glance at Alverana, and a small smile, told his friend that they had nothing to worry about.

It didn't take long for their breakfast to be completed, nor for the stripping of the camp, the sky was still dark to the west as they started to mount their horses.

"Right." Called Kevana, getting everyone's attention. "Our

clerical brothers didn't actually spend the entire night meddling in peoples dreams, they actually collected some useful information, it seems our quarry is approaching Angorak, they are still some distance away, but not all that much, we need to get to the city, and through it as quickly as we can, so today's pace is going to be quite fast, I will have absolutely no tolerance for anyone that falls behind." He turned to Alverana. "Move out." Alverana turned his horse towards the roadway, and started off, at a walk, which changed into a trot as soon as they left the soft verge and joined the hard ground of the road, Kevana was alongside him and together they pushed the pace even more, not quite a canter, but as close as a horse can get. A glance over his shoulder showed that all were keeping up. 'It's early yet.' He thought.

"How long to sunrise?" He called the question to Alverana.

"Perhaps half an hour, not much more."

Kevana turned in his saddle, calling out backwards to Worandana.

"Do you want to stop and defend, or ride through sunrise?"

"Ride on, if anyone gets too close, then we'll slap them till they go away." He cast his eyes momentarily in the direction of Kirukana to show that he was included in this plan.

"We'll ride hard through sunrise, make it more difficult for them." He faced forwards after glancing up at the eastern sky.

"We are getting so close that moving has little effect, if any." Called Worandana from behind, Kevana simply nodded. As they travelled the road became more and more busy, they passed carts bound for the city, loaded with food stuffs and other produce, the occasional wheeled cage with animals in it, small groups of cattle that served to slow them down quite considerably. Soon the predawn filled the sky and Kevana sped up, a rolling canter as they pounded along the road, the noise of their approach actually made things easier, the carts and groups of animals simply moved to the side of the road so that they could pass, their capes flowing in the wind of their passing. When the searchers finally found them, they came from a completely un-expected direction, from the west. Kevana felt the first tendrils of contact, then braced his mind to defend himself, before he had gathered his mind he was surrounded, but not by the invaders, Worandana's power shrouded him, the probe from the searcher hit this and was thrown back.

"Who disturbs our journey?" Demanded Worandana, sending a heavy probe of his own.

"I am Picarana. Co-leader of the Hounds of Zandaar, you are

the heretic Worandana."

"I am no heretic, we pursue the sword, as we were instructed, we shall bring the sword to Zandaar."

"I believe you had a different task, the sword was Kevana's job."

"The monastery I was investigating was destroyed by the man now carrying the sword, our tasks came together."

"We are to take you to Zandaarkoon for judgement, alternatively just your heads, should the whole bodies be a little too difficult."

"Join with us, we are heading to Zandaarkoon, once we have the sword of course."

"Our instructions do not allow for that."

"Then be aware, we will continue to defend ourselves, we will not be shaken from our avowed holy tasks, we shall take the sword from the thief, and we shall bring it to Zandaarkoon, to present to our god, if you attempt to prevent this you shall surely die."

"You threaten me?"

"We follow the will of god, if you try to stop us, then god will certainly kill you all."

"You have already killed enough of us."

"We haven't killed any of you, we only defend ourselves when attacked."

"We went looking for your fire woman, and lost three good men to those damned cats, and we found no fiery woman."

"The woman was a construct to ensure that you were looking in the wrong direction. We passed that way and lost no one, nor did we kill any of the tigers."

"We lost three men and killed the big male, the rest all vanished into the forest. Now we come looking for you."

"I am aware of that, you'd better hurry, we're not far from Zandaarkoon, even now."

"You have not yet passed Angorak, we shall be there shortly."

"How many horses have you killed and how many do you have left?"

"You actually think I'd tell you?"

"Of course not, but it was worth a try. We are moving quite quickly, so you'd better start killing horses again, or you're never going to catch us."

"We're not actually that far behind you, and we will be running quickly once it gets to be light enough."

"We're already on the road, as you can tell, perhaps we'll see you in a day or two."

"I shall take great pleasure in feeding your carcass to the pigs." The snarl in Picarana's thought was unmistakable.

"Picarana I wait patiently for our meeting, perhaps in your next dream." Worandana broke the connection.

"Kevana." He called. "Pick the pace up, the hounds are only a short distance behind us, they are maybe an hour or two from the river, and killing horses."

"When will they catch us?"

"Most likely not before we get to Angorak, I did ask how many horses they had left, Picarana refused to answer, but he couldn't help thinking about them. They have no spares left and the horses they are riding are just about done. They'll have to commandeer some horses very soon."

"You could read his mind?"

"It wasn't too difficult, the thought was very prominent, it is very important to them that they catch us before we get to Zandaarkoon, catch us and kill us. That was the instruction they have been given."

"Did you mine that from his mind as well?"

"Yes, he was so conscious of these instructions that he couldn't stop thinking about them."

"Did he get any extraneous information from you?" Demanded Kevana.

"Of course not, I have far better control than he does, I've had a lot more practice at hiding things than they have."

"That's a good thing." Laughed Kirukana.

"Indeed." Smiled Worandana.

"How far to Angorak?" Called Kevana.

"If you want to maintain some life in these horses," interrupted Alverana, "We need to slow down some."

"Another couple of miles, then we'll slow down, can they cope with that?"

"They'll be fine, but they will need to walk for a while."

"While we are walking, the hounds are closing in."

"I understand." Said Alverana. "We'll only rest as much as we have to, we'll be in Angorak before noon, or maybe just a touch after. We'll be well ahead of the hounds. Perhaps we can lose them in the city."

"That's unlikely," said Worandana, "They know us well enough to find us at that sort of range."

"But they'll still have to form a circle which they can't do while they're riding." Said Kirukana.

"They were riding when I was talking to Picarana." Said Worandana.

"That is very difficult to do."

"They've had a lot of practice. They've been together a lot of years. The circle was small, and not too powerful, pulsing very fast though."

"Can they compete with our dark power though?" Asked Kirukana.

"Certainly not," laughed Worandana, "and together we outclass them utterly."

"So why are we running?" Asked Alverana.

"I'd like them to tire themselves some more, we'll face them south of the city."

"What if Namdarin is already there?" Asked Kevana.

"That could get interesting, we need to get rid of the dogs first, then face the sword and the axe."

"Let's not forget Gorgana." Said Kirukana.

"Him I want to fry personally." Snapped Worandana.

"The sun is now fully up, and I have felt no searches other than the hounds, can we slow down a bit now?" Asked Alverana.

"Fine." Smiled Kevana. "Walk." He called backwards down the line, as he reined in his horse and dropped the pace to a walk, not as slow as the horses wanted to go, but slow enough. Even at a walking pace they were going faster than the heavily loaded carts rolling slowly towards the city. Alverana was curious about this, so he slowed down and waved Kevana on, he dropped in alongside one of the cart drivers.

"Good morning." He said.

"Aye."

"Aren't you a little late going into the city?"

"Nah."

"Don't you fellows usually get into the city as soon as the gates open?"

"Not needed here at Angorak."

"Why?"

"Too many people in the city, not enough farms hereabouts."

"So, you can turn up whenever you want, and still have a market?"

"That's the right of it." Grinned the driver.

"A fine life for you then?"

"Right, still graft to grow the food though."

"What you hauling today?"

"Taters."

"Good luck with your taters." Said Alverana, as he kicked his horse to catch up with the rest, he dropped in alongside Kevana, and settled down to a walk.

"You find out what you wanted?"

"Yes, when this is all over, I want to set up a farm around here somewhere."

"Why?"

"They don't have to work too hard."

"What do you mean?"

"There aren't enough farms to provide food for the city, so prices must stay high no matter what time of day you turn up at the market."

"You're planning to leave the church?"

"That's a possibility, it's just so stressful."

"At the moment I agree with you, here's an idea, once this mission is over, we steal a horse load of gold, and run for the hills, then come back here, and buy up a couple of farms, we can live out our lives in peace and quiet."

"Sounds good to me." Alverana smiled at his friend, then looked back at the line of horses, their ears were pricked up, and their heads were twitching in the morning light. He looked back at Kevana. "Time to move again." Kevana stood in his stirrups and turned to his right, looking back at the others.

"Pick it up." He called. "Move on." Then he dropped back into his saddle and kicked his black stallion hard in the ribs, the first surge took him to a canter, and the second to a gallop, he glanced to his left to see Alverana alongside smiling broadly. Alverana flashed a glance backwards, the rest were getting moving, but it would be a while before they were anything near catching up. Kevana slowed to a canter, not wishing to kill the horses just yet, the rest caught up much quicker with the sudden drop in speed. Soon they were pounding along the road passing carts and loaded horses every few minutes, the road became wider and the surface harder with every mile they got closer to the city gates. After a few miles Kevana reined in again, slowing down to rest the horses.

"Are you sure?" Asked Alverana.

"We can't afford to have dead horses under us, we may need that rush if the damned hounds have found themselves some good horses." He turned in his saddle, looked at Worandana. "Can you find them?"

"I could, but that might give them an idea how far ahead we

are."

"I can almost feel them breathing down my neck."

"Now you are being paranoid, they hadn't even crossed the river when they searched for us this morning."

"Would we have to stop while you search?"

"It's very difficult to search while moving."

"How long would we have to stop?"

"Only a few minutes." Muttered Worandana, obviously unhappy.

"Next time we stop to water the horses, then you can check on them." Kevana looked pointedly at Alverana, the intent easily clear to all, make this stop soon. Alverana stood up in his stirrups and pointed to a large lake only a hundred yards off the road. Kevana smiled and pulled off the road, Worandana just scowled at the back of Alverana's head.

They arrived at the lakes shore, a small gravel beach gave them plenty of places for the horses to drink. Kevana turned to Worandana.

"Find them." A quiet instruction.

Kirukana and Worandana separated themselves from the rest, and sat facing each other, holding hands, slowly their heads fell forwards, as if in sleep. No words passed between them, but each knew what they needed to do. Only a few seconds passed, while they were accumulating the dark power, then Worandana set off on his search, flashing back along the road, not in a smooth fashion, but in a series of steps, long steps, quick steps, so quick there was barely a pause at the end of each stride. He was still quite a way from the river when he came upon the priests dressed in black, they were pushing their horses hard. Worandana observed them for a moment, they weren't moving as fast as they could have pushed fresh horses, they were trotting slowly, and the leaders were cursing the pace. They failed to see that they were being observed, Worandana was glad that they were so preoccupied with their progress. Picarana suddenly looked around, Worandana was sure he felt something.

"We are observed." He called, all the members of the group looked around. "Someone on the etheric plane. I bet it is Worandana he's checking up on us."

"So now he knows exactly where we are." Said Broudana.

"Most likely."

"Can you kill him?"

"That is not an easy thing to do at the best of times."

"Can you?"

"No, he's rife with power and hiding from me."

"Damn." Broudana snarled as his angry eyes swept the area all around. He hadn't been able to find any horses for them to commandeer all day only heavy draft animals, far too slow to be of use. He knew that he couldn't push the horses any harder, they'd start to die in only a few miles, it just wasn't worth being on foot. He ground his teeth and turned to Picarana.

"Find some way to discourage them, make them go back to their group."

"It's most likely only Worandana."

"I don't understand how he can search all on his own, how can he carry enough power?"

"I have no idea, but take my word for it, he's powerful."

"I don't care, send him back."

"Circle." Called Picarana. knowing that his team didn't actually need to form a circle, power started moving amongst the group, each member knew their place in the circle, knew where the power was coming from and were to pass it off to. In a very short time, he had enough energy to pierce the veil separating the planes. Picarana stepped through the barrier, and only feet from him was the dark clad monk.

"Why are you here?" Demanded Picarana.

"I just watch."

"Please leave us be, we shall be catching up soon, then we can talk in person."

"That will be an interesting conversation."

"Only for one of us."

"Win or lose, it will be interesting."

"Perhaps, will you leave?"

"I now know what I came for."

"What did you come for?"

"I was tasked with finding you, I have done that."

"You know that we are coming for you?"

"Yes, you heard the command to leave us alone?"

"Yes, but not from a source that means anything to us. We still come to kill you and take the sword."

"We don't have the sword, but we may have before you catch up."

"You will die when we find you."

"Not really hiding, though we are currently resting our horses, we have a couple of hours before we need to get moving again."

Worandana laughed and turned away, in a flash he was gone, jumping back along the road, in huge steps, a few minutes later he was back at the lake, he stepped back into his body, the gasp of his first breath had all turning to look at him.

"Well?" Snapped Kevana.

"They are a couple of hours behind and their horses are nearly dead, they've been trying all morning to pick up some fresh mounts, if we save our horses, they'll still not catch us before we get to Angorak."

"We need to be through the city before they catch us."

"That shouldn't be a problem. The word has been sent out that we are not to be attacked. Adenthana kept his word."

"So, they aren't going to attack us?"

"No, they still intend to kill us all and take the sword."

"Why?"

"They don't recognise the authority of Adenthana, or anyone else, only Zandaar commands them."

"So Zandaar wants us dead?"

"That could be the truth."

"What other explanation is there?"

"Perhaps this is just another of his challenges?"

"Challenges?"

"Perhaps he's looking for a new group to be the hounds?"

"You think if we kill the hounds, then we get their jobs?"

"Maybe."

"Either way, we have to kill them. I'm fine with that." He turned to Alverana. "Are the horses rested enough?"

"If you don't expect them to gallop for a while, they'll keep going."

"Great." He filled his lungs and let loose the parade ground bellow. "Mount up, let's get moving, no matter how slow we move the hounds aren't going to catch us, so long as we are moving." He hauled himself up onto his horse and set off at a slow walk towards the road, knowing that the rest would soon follow. Turning towards Angorak he glanced back, just to make sure. Heading towards Angorak at a steady walking pace, the horses were gradually recovering from the effort they had expended in the morning. Less than an hour later Kevana suddenly tensed up, Alverana's left hand fell on his sword arm and he smiled to tell his friend to relax, the reason for Kevana's worry was coming towards them at a rapid trot. Four black clothed men, long capes flowing in the wind caused by their passing. Between them they had twenty empty mounts.

Alverana waited until they were out of earshot before he spoke softly.

"Those are fresh horses, probably for the hounds."

"Once they get fresh mounts, they'll be pushing hard to catch us. We need to pick up the pace."

"No great rush just yet, let the horses rest a little longer."

"Fine, it'll be an hour or two before those horses get to the hounds, then they'll be another hour at least before they get here."

"Give them an hour then they'll be a lot better."

"How long to get to the city?"

"Probably only a couple of hours from here."

"We need to lose them in the city."

"We can manage that, it's quite a busy place, if what I remember is correct."

"Have you ever been there?"

"No." Kevana smiled.

"Well, Zandaarkoon is a large city, but it is actually well spread out. It's a nice place, and very calm and pretty. Angorak is none of those things, it's small, packed and sweaty."

"So, we could easily vanish amongst all those people?"

"Yes, but they can still find us, they know Worandana's signature, and Kirukana much the same."

"Time to pick the pace up." Snapped Kevana, laying heels to his horse's ribs.

The sun was almost at its height when the walls of the city came into view, a dark scar on the horizon to start with that grew rapidly, the traffic on the road became more of a problem as they neared the walls, more and more wagons and carts joined the widening road as they neared the walls, empty carts leaving the city became more common as they got closer. Very soon they were riding in single file between the carts, being spread out like this was worrying Kevana, as he approached the gates the bored guard of the city watch paid him no attention at all, they trooped through the constriction of the gateway and into the courtyard beyond, crossing the open space into the northern thoroughfare they passed as the traffic lessened dramatically, as the carts turned left and right towards their respective market places. Along with the reduction of business traffic came an increase in the number of black robed monks on the road. Kevana and the others all did their best to avoid eye contact with any of these, they really didn't need to be discovered as they approached the centre of the city, the main monastery appeared ahead of them. Worandana pulled alongside

Kevana and nudged him to speed up. A glance and a smile did little to improve Kevana's nervousness.

"Relax." Whispered Worandana. "Your stress is so high it's starting to attract attention, I can feel it in the air all around us." Kevana looked hard at his old friend for a moment, then blew a long slow breath, followed quickly by another. The tension dropped out of the air as he relaxed. "Better." Mumbled Worandana. As they passed the eastern gate of the monastery, the tall black wall to their left, the gate guard was walking slowly in the sun, obviously with little to do. He turned towards them as they were only a few yards away, his gaze swept them all then suddenly snapped back to Worandana, a deep frown clouded the guards face.

"Hey." Shouted the guard. "You're Worandana, you have to surrender, you are to be held for questioning." As he turned to go back through the gate Kevana's sword appeared at his throat.

"Silence." Whispered Kevana gruffly. The guard froze.

"Are you planning on killing him?" Asked Worandana.

"I'm not sure, perhaps I'll just knock him out and throw him over one of the horses, just until we get out of town."

"Either way it's going to get messy."

"I thought the capture instruction had been cancelled?"

"The hunters have been called off, but lowly guards on the gates, who can tell when the word will filter down to them? Have you decided yet?" Demanded Worandana.

"Not yet." Smiled Kevana.

"You need to make your mind up, and soon." Said Kirukana, looking upwards and pointing. All eyes turned skywards, though the sun wasn't actually visible through the high level but light cloud cover, but it was visibly getting darker as they watched. Worandana looked around, rapidly.

"Kevana, forget him. We need to ride, and ride hard." He turned to the guard. "Which gate is closest?" The man just stared at him. "Which?" Yelled Worandana. The man looked towards the south gate, and that was enough. Worandana turned towards the south and heeled his horse. "Kirukana, you take the back position, everyone else keep up and keep tight, loose the pack horses, they'll slow us down." As the horses started to speed up Worandana rode down a guard that was approaching from the main road. He held his right hand above his head, suddenly encase to the elbow in the darkest of midnight. He shouted over his shoulder.

"Kirukana, open the path to the dark power, and open it as wide as you can, we are going to have to send lots of power its way. I'm going to need both hands for this. Alverana take my horse." Worandana tossed his reins in the direction of the larger man, knowing that he would do as was required. Kirukana called the same to Petrovana, in moments both had arms covered in dark power, held aloft. Alverana was pulling Worandana's horse as fast as he could, he could feel the urgency in the air around them, and the descending darkness from above. He looked at Kevana, a question on his brow, but not on his lips.

"Black fire." Called Kevana, "And a big one, a very big one."

"What's he burning?"

"From the looks of it, could be the whole world." Called Kevana, above the rising noise coming from the sky, a loudening crackling that was almost painful in its volume. They were all struggling to keep the horses moving, the noise and the darkness was almost too much for them, finally kicking the horses into a gallop, staggering and shaking but a gallop none the less. Gradually the sheer habit of the gallop got the horses into some sort of order, they were travelling at speed, in a herd, as they have done for a hundred generations. Worandana's blackened arms, held high, seemed to pull towards Kirukana's at the end of the column, a faint web of darkness joined them together, and somehow kept the black fire at bay, Amongst the screams of the dying, and the roar of the burning they worked their way through the devastation to the south gate. Ahead the gate came into view, somehow clear of fire, people staggering through the opening into bright sunlight of the outer court, simply a flat area where no grass grew. Worandana led them all through into the light. Once Kirukana's horse passed through the gateway, they both fell to the ground, exhausted beyond their ability to stay awake. As Worandana turned in his saddle, he saw the force holding the gate open fail, and the black fire dropped to the ground, burning everything within the wall. His own darkness descended.

CHAPTER SIXTY-SIX

The rider's horses staggered to a halt as they cleared the gate, two men fell from their saddles, obviously unconscious. Gregor turned to face them as the fire rushed up to the gate, there it stopped a twisting mass of burning black. He recognized them and cursed softly under his breath.

"Kevana." He called. "Stand your men down, they have been through enough today, they have no need to die today. Namdarin please don't kill these Zandaars, they could be of use to us."

Namdarin turned towards the horsemen, his sword in his hand, Jayanne stood to his left, Jangor to his right, Brank and Kern joined the line, Granger took his station at one end, Gregor at the other. Kevana glanced down at Worandana's motionless figure on the ground, Kevana's sword scraped from its scabbard as he turned to face the line. Greyham and his men moved in behind them. Kevana walked his panting horse slowly towards the line, Alverana to his left and Petrovana to his right. He felt quite confident facing enemies on foot. Wolf strutted slowly to the centre of the line, sat between Namdarin and Jayanne, threw back his head and howled long and loud. The horses were nervous despite their tiredness.

"I've been hunting you for a long time, and lost many friends in the course of this hunt, why should you live?" Called Kevana.

"Your people burned my house with black fire, you killed everyone I loved, why should you live?" Replied Namdarin, a glance over his shoulder made Kevana look into the black fire he had only just survived himself.

"That sword belongs to my god, I will take it to him." Growled Kevana.

"The sword belongs to Xeron and I intend on taking it to your god and ending him." Shouted Namdarin.

Kevana's black horse stepped forwards at some unseen command. Kevana's face flashed brilliant blue for a moment.

"If you attack, then I will blind you and you will die." Called Gregor. Kevana looked down at the motionless clerics, they had saved them from the fire only for them to die like animals.

"Gorgana you used to be one of us. Why have you turned against us?"

"I am Gregor again, and I turned away from you before Kirukana could declare me heretic and have me killed."

"You have no idea how funny that sounds. Things have changed quite considerably since you left. You really need to talk to the damned clerics if they ever wake up."

"I don't care, they'll kill me anyway." Said Gregor.

"You have no idea how wrong you are." He looked down again as Worandana groaned loudly and rolled slowly to his feet, he turned towards the gate and his arms blackened with power again, his steps became steadier as he drew on the darkness, he singled Gregor out with a glare before he spoke.

"Why have you sided with these criminals?"

"They are not criminals, they are good people, excitable yes, but good people none the less. Can you see it old man?"

"You could have been a good acolyte, what happened to you?"

"I knew that following you would kill me eventually, probably quite quickly, I ask again, can you see it old man?"

"You could have been alongside me in the struggle with the council. See what fool?"

"The fire, the black fire, it burns, it still burns, he has burned the entire city, and still it burns. Where is this power coming from?"

Worandana took a step backwards, looked carefully all around, the fire did indeed still burn, hot and high above the walls the black flames roared. He reached out with a tendril of darkness and shook Kirukana to wakefulness. The younger man groaned as he rose. Worandana looked at the frightened faces of the survivors, they numbered more than a hundred, all shocked, all shaken and all crying, amongst them a young mother sat cross legged on the ground, her shirt open and a baby at her breast, she rocked slowly backwards and forwards as the babe nursed, tears flowing freely down her cheeks.

"Yes." Called Gregor. "These people live because we held the gate, we kept the fire away so that some could escape. Could you have made those last hundred yards without our aid?"

"Arrgh." Yelled Kevana, even Worandana turned to face him. "This meeting was supposed to be a battle royal, an orgy of blood and broken bodies. Ending with me holding that damned sword and victorious." His shoulders slumped, and his head dropped forwards. Jangor snapped his fingers to get Gregor's attention. "Name?" He whispered. Gregor's answer was a frown for a moment until he understood. "Kevana." He replied softly.

"Kevana." Called Jangor. The monk looked up. "That moment is passed. There is no momentum towards battle right now, and I believe that even Namdarin's blood lust has been sated for a while by that monument to death behind us." He turned to Gregor. "What is the importance of the fact that the fire still burns?"

"Black fire, isn't like ordinary fire, it doesn't feed itself, it needs to be fed, he's still feeding this one, so where is that power coming from?"

"I have another question." Called Jangor, turning to Kevana. "We were outside the city, along with the sword, where were you when your god set fire to the place?"

"We were in the centre." Muttered Kevana.

"We were more than in the centre." Said Kirukana. "We had just been spotted by a guard at the gate of the monastery, he knew us, and called for us to surrender. Then the fire came." Worandana turned to face the younger cleric.

"Are you suggesting that Zandaar burned the whole city just to kill us?"

"That is a possibility, he didn't try to get the sword or the man carrying it, he burned the city, and it is still burning." All the Zandaars looked into the fire, still reaching high above the city walls, a plume of smoke filled the sky above, the steady roar of the flames stuttered, for a moment, then died, the flames flickered out of existence. A sudden blanket of silence fell across the city. Smoke continued to rise, then red flames started to grow, dirty black smoke rose slowly into the sky as small pockets of fire burned what the black flames had missed.

"Well." Said Jangor, his voice suddenly loud against the quietness. "We may not be friends, but can we at least agree not to go to war just now?" He turned to Namdarin, who nodded and turned the sword, so the point rested on the hard ground, he rested his wrists on the cross piece and waited calmly for the others to relax. Slowly the tension drained out of the air, Worandana shed the dark power from his hands and turned to Kevana. Kevana nodded and returned his sword to its scabbard before he slid from his saddle. Alverana only an instant behind him, reins were handed to Petrovana, who had no intention of dismounting until the situation became clearer. Granger and Gregor stood straight with their staves upright in their hands, each darkened for a moment then returned to their more normal colouration, is seems they were as full of power as they could be. Gregor glanced at Granger with raised brows, the look was answered with a shrug. Kevana walked slowly until he was standing in front of Jangor, Alverana beside him, Kern and Brank flanking Jangor.

"I am called Jangor, sort of military commander of this group."

"Sort of?" Asked Kevana.

"Well, it's difficult to put a traditional chain of command with a group such as this. Yours can't be much better?"

"It has its moments, those clerics can be awkward to deal with."

"Our magicians much the same, though they are useful. They saved all these people and yourselves as well."

"I find it hard to believe that anyone would even consider challenging black fire."

"Those two will challenge anything and everything, they were a great help when we took on the elven undead king, and his bodyguard."

"You tried to kill the undead?"

"And we succeeded, the basic plan was mine, but without them to help us, we'd not have beaten all those undead."

"Our own magicians can be useful." He turned to Worandana, the old cleric was staring at Gregor, but had not said anything as yet, he was still trying to work out what to say. "Worandana, what is happening in Zandaarkoon, does Axorana know anything about this?" Worandana nodded and turned to Kirukana, they stood facing each other and held hands, stillness took them.

"It may take them a while to find the man they are looking for, but they'll have a report for us soon."

"Ours don't do that sort of thing, Namdarin goes wandering occasionally."

"Yes, he tore apart one of Crathen's dreams and nearly killed Alverana in the process." Kevana's hand reached out almost unconsciously to ensure that his friend was still next to him.

"Speaking of Crathen," said Jangor very quietly, "he looks like he is going to approach Jayanne, would you be terribly upset if she kills him?" Kevana frowned, and checked Crathen's location, he was indeed moving forwards. He thought for a moment before replying.

"Not overly, he doesn't really fit too well with us, he has no talent, he's not a skilled warrior, he'd be no loss."

"He is under your command."

"True, not by my choice, more by Gorgana's."

"He's yours now, like it or no."

"Gorgana is right, you are good people." He turned and called loudly. "Crathen, I'd advise against asking any questions unless you are prepared for answers you won't like." He turned back to Jangor. "Good enough?"

"He'll stop and think but only for a while. She's getting more and more unpredictable, that damned axe is more dangerous than you can know." There was a muffled cry, they both turned in time to see the two clerics fall to their knees. Kevana stepped up to them quickly.

"Speak." He snapped, then noticed Jangor at his shoulder, looking round, Brank and Kern appeared to be dancing with Alverana, trying to get close to Jangor, to protect him. Jangor waved them off.

"Well?" Asked Jangor.

Worandana looked up slowly, tears clear in his eyes, Kirukana slumped to the ground, his shoulders shaking with his sobs.

"They're dead." Whispered Worandana.

"Axorana and his guard?" Asked Kevana.

"No." Worandana's frightened glance flashed all around as everyone looked to him for the news.

"Who's dead?" Muttered Jangor.

"Truth, old man, truth." Kevana's shaky voice giving the impression that he really didn't want the truth but would accept nothing less.

"They're dead, they're all dead, to get the power to burn Angorak Zandaar drained every living thing in Zandaarkoon, and much in the surrounding area, the only living thing in Zandaarkoon now is Zandaar himself."

"Is this the truth?" Asked Kevana.

"They're all dead, everyone is dead." Worandana slumped to the ground alongside Kirukana. Jangor looked into Kevana's eyes, knowing that the decision had to come from him.

"What are we going to do now?" Asked Petrovana. Kevana glanced at him and muttered.

"Silence fool." He turned slowly back to Jangor, their eyes met and held. Jangor knew that the decision had to be made, but he did nothing to hurry it, no words were exchanged, no thoughts, nor expressions, but as commanders they both knew the decision that had to be made.

"Damn." Muttered Kevana. He prodded Worandana with a toe. "Get up old man, there is work to do. Find the damned hounds, I'm going to end them first."

"First, what is second?" Asked Kirukana.

Kevana turned his back on the clerics, he looked straight at Namdarin.

"Can you kill Zandaar?" He called.

"Xeron believes that we have everything we need to end him, not sure if that means dead, but I think he'll be forced to leave."

"Well, right now, he has drained every resource he had in Zandaarkoon, to burn Angorak, with us in it." Kevana threw back his head and screamed to the heavens. "You missed fool, and now you're going to pay." He looked back at Namdarin. "He's most likely the weakest he has been in years, and no resources to tap, the word will be out, monasteries will be emptying, monks will be riding as hard as they can to clean up his mess and replenish his power. We need to get there first."

"You plan to kill our god?" Kirukana's voice stuttered with fear even as he uttered the words.

"He killed everyone in Zandaarkoon to burn everyone in Angorak, and us with them, damned right I plan to kill him." He turned to Worandana. "Can he kill another city to replenish himself?" Worandana's jaw fell open as the thoughts rushed through his mind. The look on his face gave the news long before his words did.

"Yes, I believe there is a way, it's complicated and would involve an awful lot of believers, we'd have to surround the city in question and build a standing wave in a circle around it, Zandaar could then tap the life force of the people inside the circle."

"How fast can this be set up?"

"It would take days if not weeks, brethren riding in en-mass is most likely the way he would go."

"How about draining small towns, or villages?"

"That would take less brothers, and be quicker to set up, but the return would be so much less. Not really worth the effort."

"Fine. Find those damned hounds." Kevana turned to the rest of his group. "Listen up." He called loudly. "I'm going to take that man to Zandaarkoon," he waved his hand in the general direction of Namdarin, "if it takes two hands to shove that blue sword up Zandaars ass, then one of those hands will be mine. Anyone not fully committed to this cause, mount up and ride now." His glare jumped from face to face waiting for the ones that would leave, he was surprised that none did. His angry glare finally fell on Namdarin's cold blue eyes. Namdarin nodded. Kevana walked slowly forwards until he was standing close enough to put his hand on the hilt of the blue sword, Jayanne was fidgeting, Wolf crouched, as if to pounce.

"Namdarin. Will you come with me and end the one that used to be my god? I think that we could be good together."

"I have had a problem with a man dressed in red before." Namdarin's voice was soft and smooth.

"I remember that he was a minstrel, if I were to sing for my supper, then I'd starve. The only song I know is the song of steel, will you sing this one with me?"

"How can I be sure that you will not betray me?" Asked Namdarin. Kevana reached out for Alverana's arm and stopped him before his sword was drawn.

"You say this is the sword of a god?"

"Xeron." Smiled Namdarin.

"If I swore to Xeron on this sword, would that be enough?"

"No," Shouted Gregor, "not on that damned sword it twists your words and takes things far too seriously." Kevana stared at Gregor for a moment then reached for the hilt of the sword.

"Enough." Said Namdarin slowly. "No more will be bound to this sword, your word as a warrior will be enough for me."

"Upon my word and my life," said Kevana, "I will be by your side until Zandaar is no more."

"Good enough for me," said Namdarin, "will your men follow your word?"

"If they want to live, they will." He paused, and smiled, then shouted. "Do you want to live forever?"

"Hell no." Came the answer from both sides. "Looks like we are brothers in arms." Said Kevana, he reached his right arm forwards, Namdarin reached similarly, hands gripped wrists briefly.

"I don't believe it." Shouted Gregor. "I have feared this moment since I made that jump, and here you two are playing like happy kittens, I don't believe it." He turned away and wandered a little way off.

"I don't believe it either." Said Crathen. "There was supposed to be murder and mayhem, and I would be here to pick up the pieces and console the survivors." His eyes locked onto Jayanne's green ones. He missed entirely the glance exchanged between Kevana and Petrovana, the latter slid from his saddle and scooped an arm around Crathen and guided him slowly away from further trouble. Kevana turned to Jayanne and smiled.

"Lady, I believe you to be formidable in your own right, I hope to prove my worth by your side in battle."

"Thank you, but I have more than enough bodyguards already." Her left hand reached down to stroke the head of Wolf.

"A fine animal indeed, I bet that he strikes fear into any that you face."

"I seem to have Kern on one side and Brank on the other as well. So I have a surfeit of bodyguards. I suggest you look to your own life, it's going to be taxed harshly before this is over."

"Of that there is no doubt lady." Kevana bowed and turned away, as he heard the sudden intake of breath from the clerics.

"Where are those hounds?"

"Coming south through the dockyards even now." Said Worandana, then he turned to the officer standing a respectful distance behind them. "Are you the ranking official of the city?"

"I have no idea, why?"

"There are small groups of survivors by each of the gates, and a large group on the docks, they are all in need of leadership. I suggest you gather them all together and start looking after them, though I would advise against going through the docks until we have dealt with the hounds."

"How close?" Snapped Kevana.

"Minutes only. They are angry, really angry. Picarana blames us for the burning of the city, they are going to ride straight into the attack."

"Namdarin." Called Jangor, "How close?" Namdarin's eyes closed for a moment, then opened, he caught Jangor's gaze and whistled.

"Mount up." Yelled Jangor, as Arndrol came up at a gallop. "Greyham, keep your people out of this, get your civilians to safety, magicians as last time, but expect resistance from their clerics. Kevana will they attack as a line, or a group?"

"These are supposedly the best of the best, they are supreme in their arrogance. They attack individually."

"Then they'll die fast and alone. Kern, Brank, on Jayanne, Kevana care to join me as escort for Namdarin?"

"Of course, Alverana on me, the rest targets of opportunity, clerics I expect extreme interference from you." Worandana merely nodded, his arms already black with power.

"We stand, let's try to look like we are waiting to die." Yelled Jangor, as the sound of hoof beats preceded the oncoming warriors. Around the curve of the city wall they came, as soon as they were in sight there was a subtle change to their arrangement, the clerics fell back into an almost circular formation, Picarana came to the front of the cleric group, but before he built up a charge Worandana got a clear view of the legs of a horse, a bolt of blackness tangled the legs of the horse and it went down, rolling forwards end over end, its rider crushed under the weight, and the horse killed judging by the flexion of its neck. Kevana stood nervously, looking at the approaching force, and worrying, he turned to Jangor.

"What is the signal to attack?"

"You'll know it when it happens, just try to keep up with Namdarin and keep any strays off him. Watch and learn." Jangor smiled then looked forwards again, waiting. The approaching horses started to select targets, Picarana and his group heading towards Worandana, Broudana and his escort heading straight for Kevana, the rest somewhat more fluid. Jangor waved a hand at Kevana, and pointed at the rump of Namdarin's horse, Arndrol was breathing heavily, flushing oxygen into his blood, then the rump dropped, the huge muscles tensed, hooves tipped forwards driving their points deep into the hard ground, with a sudden surge he leapt forwards, Kevana and Jangor kicked their horses into action, a full length behind before they got moving. Namdarin veered to the left, as Jayanne took off to slightly right of centre, this opened a wide gap in their line, but they weren't in any way worried by this, Greyham was there to protect the non-combatants, most of these in the dry ditch by the wall. Greyham stood on the flat ground, sword nonchalantly hanging in his hand, he was confident that he would not be needed, though he set his men to guarding the civilians. Kevana rode with his sword in his hand, and his left hand on the reins, he was worried by the fact that Namdarin was riding with his hands free and the blue sword still on his back, closing faster and faster at a full gallop Kevana was wishing for a long lance and full armour. In a moment the collision was upon them, Namdarin's sword appeared in his clenched fists and swept Broudana's number two from his saddle in two discrete parts, the two lines passed through each other, Kevana had little time to pay any attention to the others, he was turning to face Broudana, only to find Namdarin in his way, he switched sides and found himself on the same side of the big grey as Jangor, both slashed the same man from his saddle, Kevana turned again to see Broudana's sword come flashing downwards towards Alverana's exposed head, with a scream he heeled his horse knowing that he was going to be too late to help his friend, the blue sword appeared and Broudana's steel shattered against it, then Namdarin turned the blade and plunged it straight through the centre of Broudana's body, lifting him bodily from the saddle, and dropping him to the grass to be trampled beneath the milling horses, Kevana rushed to Alverana's side, and saw a fragment of Broudana's sword embedded in his friends chest, Kevana pulled Alverana from the melee and pointed him in the direction of Greyham, then turned back, his eyes red with pain and anger, in moments he was back at Namdarin's side, slashing at any black cloak that came within range, and one or two that were out of reach. Jayanne was carving her way methodically through the Zandaars, every stroke of her axe was another dead monk, some just dead, others drained first, they died screaming, they all died screaming, Wolf weaved through the whole mess, spreading panic amongst the horses and riders alike, his muzzle reddened with blood, his tail flowing in the wind. Somewhat separate was the battle of the clerics, Picarana's circle was destroyed every time it formed, he was reduced to one on one combat with Worandana and Kirukana, he was barely able to block their magical thrusts, and he was soon knocked from his horse as his fellows dropped to the ground around him, they joined into a solid circle, one that could not be distracted, their transfer rate was phenomenal, and their power level was something Worandana didn't expect, they were strong, very, very strong. They also had an advantage, Worandana wanted a survivor, they did not. The circle of Picarana achieved a level of coordination that Worandana had never seen before, they were acting as a single entity, generating power and throwing it out at Worandana and Kirukana, the dark power made a good shield but they couldn't assemble any sort of counter attack, they were entirely on the defensive, Worandana spent a few seconds sending a thought to Gregor, a plea for assistance, then another attack took all his attention, a black barrier took the next blast from the conglomeration that was Picarana and his men. Again and again the black shield absorbed the power, though it passed precious little on to Worandana, both men were weakening under the onslaught, Picarana could feel victory coming his way, all that training was paying off. Worandana saw Gregor ride up to the circle, rather than attacking it, he stood close for a long moment, Worandana's mind screaming for him to help them, slowly Gregor raised his staff and placed it against the head of one of the monks, Worandana breathed easier knowing this was going to be over soon, but Gregor didn't attack the monk, he didn't kill him, or even attempt to add power to the cycling entity, instead he pulled a pulse of energy from the ring as it passed, then another, and another, not consecutive pulses, but randomly, in moments the whole balance of the circle was upset, it started to oscillate, the oscillations amplified, as Gregor rode away carrying quite a charge from the circle it suddenly fell apart, three of the five simply exploded, burned to a crisp in a heartbeat, one slumped to the ground, his mind torn apart by the forces released in the dissolution of the cycling power, Picarana collapsed unconscious, stunned by the way Gregor had torn his construct apart. Gregor rode back towards the battle and used the stolen power to throw a man from his horse, he fell to the ground in front of Wolf, who ripped out his throat in passing. The sounds of battle were decreasing rapidly, as more and more of the combatants died, suddenly Jangor's voice boomed out over the noise.

"We need a survivor or two, we need information, don't kill them all."

"I think you may be just a little too late with that." Laughed Kevana, easing his sword from the belly of a black clad monk, who gurgled and died, falling from his horse. Namdarin held his sword aloft and called back.

"I got one that's not dead, well not yet, with care he may survive." Kevana rode up to Namdarin.

"I've seen worse, he'll live, but only if he wants to. That arm's a wreck, it needs to be removed before it dies and infects the rest of his body, and preferably before he bleeds to death."

"Granger." Yelled Jangor. "Come here and stop this man bleeding to death."

"I'd prefer that our own are seen to first." Snapped Kevana, he rode off to where Alverana was waiting, the sword shard still buried in his chest.

"How are you doing?" He asked as he slid from his saddle.

"It hurts, but it's not serious, I'll wait until Worandana is available to do the healing, then I'll take the blade out. I'll be fine in a day or two."

"I can't lose you now."

"I understand, how long do you think Worandana is going to be? This is quite painful."

"I'll go and chase him, the damned hounds can die for me." He leapt up into his saddle and wheeled his horse to run down Worandana, wherever he was. A quick scan of the battlefield showed Worandana's yellow cloak bent over a black robed shape on the ground. In only moments Kevana was there.

"Leave that bastard, Alverana needs your services."

"This is Picarana, we need to know what he knows, but he's not woken up yet, Gregor tore his circle apart while it was running at full speed, just look at them." He waved a hand to indicate the corpses all around. Will Alverana die in the next few minutes? If not, then he can wait."

"I don't want him to wait, I want him well now."

"Sorry, I need to look after Picarana for a while, go to your friend and hold his hand, I will be there as soon as I can."

"I will do as you suggest, but just now I feel a serious urge to take this head, and fix him permanently."

"Once we have his information then you can have his head, if that makes you feel better."

"Not much, Alverana is in pain now."

"Go to him. I'll be along presently."

Kevana gave Picarana a none too gentle kick in the ribs before he stamped off. Once he was gone the fallen monk opened his eyes.

"Will you really give him my head?"

"No, but the thought will keep him quiet for a while. What do you know that can be of use to us?"

"What do you need to know?"

"What has Zandaar done?"

"He's burned Angorak, and used the whole population of Zandaarkoon to fuel it. No one knows why, but he has called everyone to come to Zandaarkoon as fast as they can. But obviously you were not told this."

"No, I believe he burned Angorak just to get us, the real question is why?"

"You are heretics and must be killed before you get to Zandaarkoon."

"We are not heretics, or perhaps were not, until today, now we are going to go to Zandaarkoon and kill him. What do you think about that?"

"Every faithful soldier of god will stand in your way, and attempt to kill you. You cannot possibly win, you will all die."

"Ask yourself the question, why?"

"Why, what?"

"Why did god burn two cities?"

"I have no idea, but he is our god and his will is all that counts."

"I think he did it to kill us, why would he do that?"

"I have no idea." Picarana's answer was just a moment too slow.

"You are lying to me, I don't like that."

"Believe what you wish, I can tell you nothing else."

"Perhaps we'll just start taking parts of you away until you tell us what we want to know." Sneered Worandana.

"I have a better idea." Whispered Namdarin.

"Can you make him tell the truth?" Said Worandana looking over his shoulder at Namdarin.

"It may be that I have a way to force the truth, we shall see. Hold him here." Namdarin whistled Arndrol, then rode off to where the pack horses were. A short time later he came back to where Worandana was waiting with Picarana, a deep frown on his face. Namdarin turned to Picarana.

"You do understand that we don't really need you to survive this, in fact I would be extremely happy if you were to die in absolute agony?"

"I understand but I will not help you and these heretics."

"You don't have to. Just open your mouth." Picarana shook his head, Namdarin took his belt knife and pushed the point downwards against Picarana's chin, through the thin skin and against the bone, Picarana had no choice but to open his mouth, Namdarin pushed a flashing crystal into it. Then the knife passed around the chin and pressed against the throat. Worandana frowned up at Namdarin.

"How strong is your mind?" Asked Namdarin.

"I think I'm the stronger of the two of us. Why?"

"When you put this crystal in your mouth your minds will be in contact, communication directly mind to mind." Namdarin's strong hands pushed the crystal into Picarana's mouth and held the back of his head at the same time. Worandana took hold of the other clerics wrists, and twisted them to stop them moving.

"I just put it in my mouth and then talk to him?"

"No." Laughed Namdarin. "It's something new you will have to work out for yourself."

"No hints?"

"Sorry, I worked it out by pure chance, and I was talking to an animal, that barely had a mind to talk of, we communicated in pictures, he got the message, he was a large white bear like animal."

"You set the damned snow demon on us?"

"That would indeed be me."

"That cost us a horse but not a man."

"You were lucky."

"I'm going to have to see what this feels like. Hold him." Namdarin's hands clench on Picarana's head. Worandana gingerly put the crystal up to his mouth and placed it slowly on his tongue. There was a moment of disorientation, for a heartbeat he was struggling to get the crystal out of his mouth, and then he wasn't, he was watching himself held tightly in a vice like grip, focusing his thoughts his vision returned to his own view. He glanced up at Namdarin.

"This is strange."

"Oh it's that."

"How did it work for you?"

"We both wanted to communicate, I don't think he's going to want to." Namdarin's grip didn't change.

"Let's see if he can do anything to resist me." Worandana smiled into Picarana's eyes.

Worandana gathered his mind into himself and then reached outwards towards Picarana, he hit Picarana's mind and bounced, there was a heavy barrier in the way, it was visualised as a stone wall, the stones were such a tight fit that there was no mortar between them, irregular patterns and colours, Worandana's probe skated around the surface, he could almost sense Picarana smiling behind his wall, feeling that smile, he tracked it slowly, focusing on that impression of a smile, he followed it, not through the wall, not over the wall, but just on a different wavelength, his mind swarmed through and overcame all the defences that Picarana had erected, Picarana's mind was completely overcome by Worandana's ego, every memory open, every thought laid bare, every good deed, and every bad, all utterly visible to the invading presence. Picarana had no way to keep Worandana out of the deepest recesses of his psyche. Nor was Worandana in any way subtle in his activities, this was all new to him, and he was taking advantage of everything that he could find. After what seems like a lifetime of rummaging through the monks mind he departed, there was no barrier for him to force through on the way out, he returned to his own mind and pulled the crystal from his mouth. Slowly he looked up at Namdarin and nodded. Namdarin released the cleric, pulled the crystal from his mouth and wiped it on the black cloak. He held his hand out to Worandana for the other crystal, Worandana dropped the second stone into his open palm.

"That was different." Said Worandana.

"But did you find out what you wanted?"

"That and so much more, his whole life was open to me, I could have spent a lifetime in there, just poking through his memories."

"Did you find what you wanted?"

"Oh yes. Zandaar has called in all the monasteries within three days, they are going to be riding hard, we could face some serious opposition before we get to Zandaarkoon."

"Then we better get moving, don't you think."

"Agreed, but what do we do with him?"

"Is he worth saving?"

"No, he's a seriously bad person, he has a fascination for raping little boys, and I do mean little."

"Would you care how he dies?" Asked Namdarin.

"Not really."

Namdarin looked down at Picarana.

"Can you run rapist?" Picarana looked confused, both Namdarin and Worandana released their holds on him, Picarana eased himself to his feet. Namdarin smiled and shouted. "Wolf." Picarana set off towards the river as wolf came running up to Namdarin, who pointed and said "Catch." Wolf ran, as only wolf can, three strides to full speed, then three more to hit the man in the back, throwing him to the ground, Wolf stopped and returned, to stand on the man's back, his weight not really enough to hold the man down, but the fight had gone completely out of Picarana. Namdarin walked slowly to where Wolf was holding his prey. As he got close, he looked around and called loudly.

"Jayanne, how hungry is your axe? We have a soul for it, a very black soul, but a soul none the less." Picarana started to struggle now, Wolf had to grab him by the arm to hold him in place.

"The axe is always hungry, and I love the power it gives, but no, I'm not killing a man lying on the ground."

"No problem." Called Namdarin, the blue sword appeared in his hand, Picarana froze under the baleful green light of the mindstone, Namdarin's sword rose, and then paused. He stared at Picarana for a moment, then lowered the sword so the point rested on the ground.

"Granger." He called. The elderly magician turned towards Namdarin.

"I'm busy, we have injured."

"Please come here, I have a question for you." Granger shrugged and walked slowly towards the green light of the sword.

"What do you want?" He asked somewhat shortly.

"Yesterday I asked about what would happen if you harvested the energy of a living man, how about this one here?"

"He's not dying."

"Oh, he is, either by the sword or another way."

"Why would you want me to kill him?"

"I want to see what it feels like." Namdarin showed the crystals in his hand.

"That's sick, you do know that?"

"Perhaps, but I need to know."

"Fine, get ready." Namdarin put one crystal in his own mouth, and placed the other against Picarana's forehead. "Wolf, go to Jayanne." Wolf released Picarana's arm and wandered off. Namdarin closed his eyes for a moment, then looked up at Granger, he nodded.

"Are you sure?" Asked Granger. Namdarin only nodded more firmly.

There was a look of fear in Picarana's eyes as Granger lowered his staff.

"What are you doing?" Asked Worandana.

"I'm going to kill this man, and Namdarin is going to feel it from within his mind, while it happens, do you think he is sick as well?"

"Certainly, how can you be sure he will survive?"

"Even if he dies, he'll be back in a little while."

"That is real? I've heard it said, but never really believed it, I thought it was some sort of chicanery."

"Oh, it's real, I've seen it happen. Shall I proceed, this was your brother?"

"He may have been, but no longer, and to be honest, if you don't kill him, then Kevana is going to slice him up into small pieces, he'll take a while to die."

Granger nodded and levelled his staff again. The staff darkened, Picarana's breathing caught for a moment, then slowed, and slowed, and stopped. Frost started to appear on his face as Namdarin removed the crystal from the forehead, he slumped to the ground, breathing hard.

"Did you find out what you wanted to know?" Demanded Granger.

"I think so." Said Namdarin softly. "I think so. I've definitely been there, into the cold and the dark, it's frightening to watch it happen."

"Did you think you were going to get pulled in?"

"No, it never felt like that, without actually testing how death by the sword feels, I'd say that to die by that sort of cold is though frightening, completely painless, almost peaceful."

"Care to try it yourself?" Smiled Granger, levelling the staff again.

"No thank you, it gives me the shivers." The two looked at each other for a moment or two, then Namdarin rose to his feet.

"I suppose I'd better go and see to our injured." Mumbled Worandana, not really knowing what to say. Namdarin walked alongside him for a while, but only because Jayanne was in that direction. He walked slowly up to her and opened his arms, she stepped into the circle and he held her close, pressing her body to his, she leaned her head into his shoulder, she was shaking.

"What's wrong?" He whispered.

"I so wanted to kill that man, just to steal his energy and his soul, you have no idea how hard it was to turn down your offer, please don't make that sort of offer again, I don't like who the axe is turning me into."

"While you can still turn it down, then you are still your own person, you can leave the power un-used, I know it is difficult, but you still can, I'm not sure that I could."

"How much longer do I have to carry this thing?" She trembled in his arms.

"We could be as close as a day or two, or you could leave it behind, if that is your wish?"

"No I couldn't, it's power is too useful to us, without it we may not be victorious."

"I hope to beat Zandaar, but I'm not sure survival was in my original plan."

"What about now?"

"I hope that we can all survive, but that is unlikely. Was anyone hurt in this latest skirmish?"

"None of ours, the Zandaars lost one and have another one injured. It was a surprisingly easy battle."

"That is something else," he mumbled, "battle should never be easy, we should be doing everything we can to avoid it, but we don't."

"We couldn't have avoided this one, they didn't even pause, they simply attacked, without the warnings we got the outcome would have been very different."

"I agree. We need to get things sorted out here and move on. It seems Zandaars are going to be running into the city as fast as they possibly can."

"Let's go and talk to Greyham first." She released her grip from around his neck, and he let go of her waist, but captured her hand immediately, they turned to where Greyham was with his people, they caught up with Worandana. The old cleric was looking down at Alverana, the sword fragment still firmly wedged in his shoulder.

"I'm too tired for this, I'll get the men to set up a circle it won't take long."

"You need a circle for power?"

"Yes, I don't trust this black power for healing."

"Let's see if we can find you something." Namdarin spoke softly before turning to where Granger was walking slowly to his horse, as if preparing to leave. "Granger." He called, "We have need of your skills, we have an injured man." He turned back to Worandana. "Granger will have enough energy to heal, he'll be able to help." Jayanne glanced at Granger, he had stopped walking, but he wasn't coming to assist. She nudged Namdarin in the ribs, and nodded in the direction of Granger. Namdarin turned, then walked towards the old magician.

"What's the problem?" he asked once he was close enough.

"You want me to kill one of these Zandaars then save the next, what is going on here?"

"The one needed to die, we couldn't have left him behind, and I saw an opportunity to be certain of something that had been worrying me. The other one," he nodded in the direction of the injured man, "he is now one of us. He needs our help, I don't think he'd trust Gregor, too much has passed between them, but a kind old man like you, you he'd trust."

"What were you so desperate to find out?"

"I wanted to find out if I really die."

"And do you?"

"Oh, yes. It feels exactly the same, but for me the pain comes back, and the screaming."

"And what will you do when these Zandaars turn against you?"

"I don't think they can, their god tried to kill them. They have nowhere else to go, they can't run, they can't hide, they have to ride into the monsters lair and kill it."

"This could be a ruse, once they have enough of their brothers around us, then they'll turn and kill us in our sleep."

"No, when I was inside Picarana's mind, his hatred of me, was beyond measure. Even so, it paled into insignificance compared to his hatred of Worandana, he knew that Worandana had to die, as did Kevana. Picarana knew that they were his replacements, they had to die, by any means possible. Worandana knows this as well, and as soon as he gets the chance, he's going to explain it to Kevana. These are all ex-Zandaars."

"Are you sure of this?"

"I have seen the truth of it."

"Fine then. Be aware if they turn against us, I will burn you before they can kill me." Granger turned towards Worandana and stamped off. Namdarin was smiling, he knew that the threat was empty, Granger could no more do that, than he could kill Jayanne. He was right on Grangers heels when he arrived at the place where Alverana was lying on the ground, his head cradled on Kevana's thighs.

"Heal him now." Whispered Kevana a tear in his eye.

"Are you ready to help us?" Asked Worandana looking up and Granger.

"What do you need?"

"A slow feed of power, into this hand." He held up his left hand. "I'll channel this into Alverana and hopefully heal his injuries."

"You expect this charlatan to help?" Snapped Kevana. Granger looked down into his eyes, his raised brow asked a question without words. Kevana looked down. "I'm sorry, you've always been a charlatan." He looked up again, tears flowing freely down his face. "Please help my friend."

"Have no fear." Said Granger softly. "Between us, he'll be good as new in no time at all." He turned to Worandana. "How much power can you handle?"

"Start slow, I'm not used to this."

Granger placed on heel of his staff in Worandana's hand.

"Grip it firmly, if the power has to jump a gap it may just burn you." Worandana looked into Granger's eyes and nodded. Granger opened the pathway to the core of energy in the staff and fed it slowly and smoothly to Worandana. The clerics eyes snapped wide open, he stared up at Granger.

"Too much?" Whispered Granger. Worandana shook his head.

"Too smooth." He paused, breathing deeply twice before he went on. "Later. For now a little more." Granger smiled and increased the power flow. Worandana shivered briefly, then reached out with his empty right hand, he placed it gently on the end of the steel shard. Alverana twitched and grunted.

"Hold him still, this is going to hurt." Whispered Worandana, Kevana's strong hands gripped Alverana's shoulders and pressed them down. Alverana looked up, pain clear in his eyes. Worandana smiled to reassure him, then closed his eyes. Reaching into the cold steel with his mind, he felt out it's jagged edges. Into the soft tissues of the man's shoulder, as slowly and as smoothly as he could he withdrew the sharp steel, he focused on the damaged muscles, pulled them together, patched the veins together, then decided that the steel was causing more damage as he pulled it out, so he blurred the edges, rounded them, softened them. The sharp edges in his own hand got the same treatment, gradually the flat blade reformed, it became more like a rod, as the edges pulled back from the flesh Worandana held the flesh together and made it whole, as if it had never been separated. Gradually the steel came out of the wound, the wound closed, almost as if it had never been. Alverana breathed long and slow.

"Oh my." Said Kirukana. "Looks like you've just made yourself a tool for healing, sort of poetic really." Worandana looked down at the steel fragment in his hand, the part that fit into his hand now did exactly that, it was moulded to the shape of his palm, from there on it was slowly tapering to a point, a soft and rounded point. "You know what that looks like?" Laughed Kirukana.

"Yes I do." Worandana smiled and released Grangers staff. Worandana rose slowly to his feet and he looked down at the steel bar in his right hand, however he stared at it, no name sprung to his mind other than wand. He looked at Grangers smiling face.

"I'm supposed to be the charlatan and witch."

"Well," grinned Worandana, "looks like I'm a fully-fledged member of the witch club, wand and all." He flourished the item for all to see. Then turned to Granger.

"I hope I didn't take too much of your power to heal Alverana."

Granger smiled, struck the heel of his staff against the ground, a hot blue flame leapt from the tip and tore up into the sky, roaring for five heartbeats before he quenched it, it left a green strip on everyone's retinas.

"That burn was ten times the power you took, and I've probably got another twenty of those before I'm getting close to out of power. Both Gregor and I took a huge amount of energy from the black fire to keep the gateway clear for those that could make it through. Be aware Gregor's staff carries more than mine and can deliver it at much higher rates. That staff was well designed and built."

"The design was mine, the staff was mine." Said Worandana. "Built by a smith, one you have met, I can't remember his name."

"His name was Garin." Said Gregor.

"So it was. Good smith, an artist really, I don't suppose I can have my staff back?"

Gregor shook his head and gripped the staff more determinedly.

"No matter," laughed Worandana, "it's more yours than mine now."

"I can tell you something important about your new wand." Said Granger.

"Go on." Muttered Worandana.

"It's steel, and now doubly forged steel, it can take any load you can send through it, not something that can be said about my wooden staff. If I'm using a lot of power, then I have to use some more to make sure that the staff doesn't fall apart, it sort of puts a limit on the amount of power I can use at any one time. Gregor does not have that problem, the metal work on that staff can carry almost any load."

"It's a bit small though."

"Even so. More important than anything, it was forged by you, using the magic that you understand. I very much doubt that you'll ever be able to overload the thing."

"I can't say that I actually forged it," said Worandana, "it was created as a by-product of helping Alverana."

"Then perhaps it will help him again."

"Enough fairy tales." Snapped Kevana. "We need to be on the road, Namdarin." Namdarin turned. "We have no supplies, the pack animals were left behind, they were too slow to keep up. Do you have enough to share?"

"Not really, and even less because we have to share with all these homeless people." He looked around at the people gathered by the wall.

"I hadn't even thought of them."

"I suppose someone else looks after the poor people?"

"That has always been the case, or they look after themselves."

"No longer true, now we have to look after others, wherever we can, these especially, seeing as your god made them all homeless, took their families and everything they had. I sort of understand their situation."

"I suppose you do, but we still need to get to Zandaarkoon before the brothers start arriving."

"We'll set off as soon as we can. Let's go and talk to Greyham." They walked over to where the young officer was trying to console some people.

"Greyham," said Namdarin, "how are you doing?"

"Ask me in a few days."

"We don't have a few days, we need to be moving on."

"You've done everything you can here, have you?" He snapped. Namdarin tensed, his knees flexed as if in readiness for battle.

"I'm sorry Namdarin." Greyham went on. "I'm not having a good day."

"At least you're not falling apart like some of them." Namdarin waved casually at the survivors.

"Do I have a choice?"

"Not really, someone has to keep things together."

"When I have a moment, I'll mourn the loss of my entire family, and my city, and my wife." His voice caught in his throat, his hand fell to his sword hilt and his eyes locked onto Kevana's.

"I am sorry for what has happened, but this was not our doing." Said Kevana clearly. Alverana started moving towards them.

"It was your god, he burned our city." Greyham's voice rose a little.

"He burned his own city as well." Said Kevana, as Alverana moved in alongside him.

"Is that supposed to make me feel better?" Greyham's voice climbed a little more.

"Greyham my friend." Said Namdarin gently. "Don't make the mistake of dying today, you have people who need you, not something I had when Zandaar burned my house." Greyham turned to Namdarin and stared into his cold blue eyes for a long moment.

"You think you don't have people to look after? Think again. You've even got the damned Zandaars that look to you."

"You may be right there, but there is a good chance that we are going to die in the next couple of days, know this, if I have to spend my life to end Zandaar, then I will."

"I have to admit." Said Greyham slowly. "The death of Zandaar is most devoutly to be wished for, however, I don't feel the same about you, I'd be very upset if the lovely Jayanne didn't survive."

"If we do, then we shall certainly be coming back this way."

"It would be good to see you all again."

"You have a lot of work to do in the meantime, you'll have to look after all your people, and there will be more coming to light over the next few hours and days. You'll need to find places for them to sleep, and more important, you'll have a lot of unhappy farmers here-about, think about it. Not only has Zandaar destroyed your city, he's burned his own. There is no one left alive there. In one afternoon he's destroyed the economy of the whole area. That is going to take some real work to re-build. And you're going to have to do it."

"Thanks, no pressure then." Greyham looked around, more than a little disturbed. "I suppose I'd better wish you goodbye and get on with things. Don't forget to come back if you can."

"If we survive then you'll certainly see us." He stepped forwards and offered his hand to shake, Greyham hesitated for a moment then took it.

"Good luck." Said Greyham. "I'd suggest that Zandaar has lost more than a few followers in this area," he turned to Kevana, "You need to leave and quickly, it's only a matter of time before someone decides it's all your fault."

"I understand." Said Kevana. "I'm sorry for what has happened here, and if you will allow, we will return to help what is left of your people."

"I am certain that any help you can give would be great fully received, but don't come back wearing black."

"I'll never wear black again." Replied Kevana firmly. He nodded and turned away, Namdarin followed.

"You lost a man in this latest battle?" Asked Namdarin.

"Yes, Astorana, a new addition to our band."

"Do you want to bury him properly?"

"No, that would take too much time, we really need to be getting into Zandaarkoon before the brothers start arriving."

"How soon will that be?"

"I've no idea, but not much more than a day, some may even be there before nightfall."

"So, we could be facing a force holding the city walls?"

"Not likely, they'll be in the centre, either protecting Zandaar, or feeding him."

"Which would be better for us?"

"To be there first."

"Is that in any way possible?"

"I don't think so, perhaps one of the wizards will know a way?"

"Let's ask them." Together they walked over to where Granger and Gregor were talking quietly.

"Granger." Said Namdarin as they approached. "Is there any way to transport us to the middle of Zandaarkoon quickly?"

"There may be a way," interrupted Gregor, "after all, I've already done something similar."

"Could you move all of us, without the power of the lightning stone?" Gregor thought for a moment before replying.

"Not likely, it took an awful lot of energy just to exchange the two of us, and with nothing to exchange holding the balance would be far more difficult, when I switched places with Crathen, there was a certain balance that made the transfer easier."

"What about this new dark power of Worandana's?"

"I've no idea how it works, or how to tune to it. I had a serious incentive last time."

"Perhaps Worandana could help?" Asked Kevana. He turned to where Worandana was looking at the plume of dark smoke rising from the ruins of the city.

"Worandana." He called as the four of them neared. Worandana's gaze locked onto Kevana's.

"What?" He asked, a little tersely.

"Could your new dark power provide the energy needed to move all of us to Zandaarkoon?" Worandana's head twitched as if the suggestion actually hurt, he stared at the ground briefly, then up at the column of smoke. Finally he looked back at Kevana and held his eyes for a long moment before speaking.

"I don't think so, you saw how much power Gorgana used just to swap places with Crathen. To move all of us would take far more power than we can summon, no it's just not feasible, we are going to have to ride there."

"Then we better get started as soon as we can. The brothers are going to start arriving long before we get there." Said Kevana.

"How soon do you think they are going to start arriving?" Asked Namdarin.

"That depends on just how many he killed to burn Angorak, the nearest place with any concentration of brothers is the retirement home, it's half a day from the city wall, these are old and infirm, but many are still active, and the brothers that look after them are anything but old. They'll be at the wall today, perhaps just after sundown."

"The old and the children." Said Worandana.

"Children?" Asked Namdarin.

"The novices get to look after the elderly while earning their qualification to the priesthood, during this time they learn the basic mysteries and the warrior skills, they have enthusiasm and youth, but little skill."

"Babes." Whispered Namdarin.

"Indeed," replied Kevana, "but enough to foul your sword arm while an oldster stabs you in the back."

"I hate those sorts of battles," said Namdarin, "I've never been involved in one, and have no real wish to do so now."

"Are you going to turn away from your chosen path?" Asked Worandana. Namdarin looked into the old eyes for a long moment before answering slowly.

"No. I cannot, my house was burned, as was your city behind us, we need to end your god, and that is what we do, or die trying. What say you?" Worandana breathed slowly, a few times, before he spoke.

"We are with you, Zandaar has become a monster, the world needs to be rid of him, he has done a lot for us, but he has killed too many this day, two cities, I can't really believe that I am saying this, but there is no doubt in my mind, our god has gone mad."

"I agree," said Kevana quietly, "he has been all powerful for so long, that the thought that his life could be over is too much for him to understand, after all death is only for us mortals, gods don't die."

"I'm not entirely sure that death is what Xeron is suggesting," Namdarin spoke gently, "he said that it is time for the old gods to move on, and Zandaar has refused, I got the impression that he tricked the others into leaving, and then stayed himself."

"That's no real surprise." Laughed Worandana. "He's always been a slippery customer, certainly not the most trustworthy of deities."

"How long have you suspected this?" Demanded Kevana.

"Most of my life, I have studied the histories don't forget. I've seen so many of his sneaky plans that always seem to go his way, as far as I can tell, he's never had a plan go badly for him, almost any time the dice have rolled they've fallen in his favour."

"Until today?" Asked Namdarin.

"No, I think the reversal started the day he burned your house. The luck seems to be entirely yours now."

"What do you mean, I've been killed more than once?"

"And still you are here, fighting on, one more bloody day."

"I don't see that I have a choice, I have the sword and the mindstone, I have given my word to Xeron, I cannot back down."

"You also have a new family."

"What do you mean?" Snapped Namdarin.

"Look around, you have a family, and it just grew again. You cannot fight for anything else, it's not gods you fight for, it is family, both lost and found." Smiled Worandana.

"You may be right." Whispered Namdarin. "Let's get this thing finished, one way or the other." He turned away and called out. "Mount up, we're moving on." He whistled, and Arndrol trotted up, Namdarin swarmed up into the saddle, he looked down at the two men. "You coming?" They both smiled and ran towards their horses. Jangor mounted his horse and rode over to Greyham.

"You need to look after your people. Once the fires go out, your home town is going to be a target for looters, you better get in their first. Good luck, we may be back." He turned the horse and shouted. "Mount up, we are leaving." Everyone was already scrambling onto their horses and preparing to set off. Jayanne barged her bay through the crowd until she was alongside Namdarin, her left hand rested for a short time on his right leg, she smiled up at him. Kern formed up to their left and Brank to their right. Jangor fell in behind, with Granger to his right, Kevana fell in beside Jangor, and Worandana alongside Granger. Jangor looked backwards and saw that the column was forming up nicely.

"Move out." He called, then much quieter, "Namdarin, how are the horses?"

If took Namdarin only a short time to reply.

"Ours are in far better condition than theirs, that run through the fire really did them in, we need to walk for a while until they recover a bit."

"Walk it is then." Said Jangor.

"Alverana?" Asked Kevana.

"He's right, that run has taken a lot out of them, but they'll get better for a little walk." Was the reply. Kevana looked at Jangor and smiled.

"Namdarin." Said Jangor looking straight at Kevana. "Any others around?" There was silence for a while then Namdarin spoke up.

"There are a lot of horses that I can reach, all to the south, and all being driven hard, they're all going to the same place, and that is where we are bound." Jangor, still looking straight into Kevana's eyes, raised his eyebrows and smiled. Kevana glanced backwards and said. "Alverana?"

His friend just smiled and shrugged.

"How does he do that?" Asked Kevana.

"It's something to do with the herd mind of the horses, they are in some sort of communication with each other and he gets into their heads. It's quite a useful skill when one is being pursued."

"So we could never have surprised you?"

"We have been surprised, once, and very recently, so that's not happening any time soon."

"What happened?"

"Short, Namdarin took an arrow to the heart and died, again. Jayanne was unhappy. She set off after the men that did it, I sent Brank and Kern to guard her, Wolf was already at her horses' feet. Between them they killed them all. One escaped, but wolf dealt with him later, there were more than twenty corpses on that field, you've seen how that axe feeds? Well she fed that power back into Namdarin and brought him back. It usually takes hours for him to live again."

"I still find it very hard to believe."

"I've seen it more than once now, it is real." Kevana fell silent for a while, then finally spoke at little more than a whisper.

"Even if we had surprised you, we'd all have died?"

"If you came from behind those trees," Jangor nodded to his left, "cloaked in black, even at a full gallop Namdarin would have emptied that quiver of long arrows, that bow never misses, and then you'd have to face that blue bladed longsword, the green light of the mindstone makes his enemies pause, they freeze and wait for the death stroke. So, yes. Add to that, Jayanne and Wolf, you've seen what they can do."

"So what purpose do you serve here?" Kevana smiled.

"I'm not exactly certain. Perhaps by some act of bravery and death I give them the impetus to reach the limit of their powers, I've not seen them act in true concert, they would have to be impressive. To end the tyranny of the gods, I'd not hesitate for an instant."

"So why do your largest warriors protect the woman?"

"Namdarin took up a war against a god when the god and his followers burned his house and his family, and everyone he loved. Now he loves her, if she dies, he will hold the sword of Xeron in one hand and the axe of Algoron in the other, his wrath will destroy the world. And I will ride into that conflagration at his back, will you?"

"My world has been torn apart enough recently, mainly because of him, if the world's going to die, then I want to be there to see it." Kevana shook his head, before going on at a whisper. "You want to live forever?"

"Hell no." Replied Jangor with a smile.

The road south was wide and smooth, no major hills or rivers to cross, one or two shallow fords across small streams, all of which were properly paved, this road obviously gets a lot of use. The afternoon passed peacefully, as the sun sank slowly, the major moon rose, and its slightly red tinted light started to take dominance of the sky.

"Horses." Said Namdarin.

"Heading this way?" Demanded Jangor.

"No, they are running for the road, looks like a large party intending to stop us or slow us down."

"How far?"

"Not far, maybe a mile, or less."

"We can deal with them before we lose the light." He turned in his saddle and raised his voice. "Prepare for battle, it looks like they are setting up a roadblock. We'll walk until we see them."

Kevana turned to Jangor.

"He's a bit vague about the distance?"

"Horses are vague about distances, they don't measure them the same way we do."

"Is there some strategy for this battle?"

"Not really. Do you want to see that sword working?"

"Why not?"

"Fine, Jayanne will ride straight at them, flanked by Brank and Kern, Namdarin will ride straight at them flanked by me and you, everyone else is just mopping up the stragglers."

"That's not much of a strategy, I think I've seen it before somewhere." Kevana laughed, Jangor shrugged, then looked forwards for a moment then turned to Granger.

"Conserve your power, don't get too low, we may need it later for any of our injured." Granger simply nodded, his staff as dark as night, and the air around him cold. Jangor glanced backwards and saw that Gregor was charging in the same way but there was a plume of fog falling slowly from his staff as it soaked up the heat from the air.

Jangor felt the tension rising quickly all around him. He was getting a little nervous, so he asked Namdarin.

"How close now?"

"They are stopped across the road, just around the next bend, be ready." The green gem in the sword hilt flashed momentarily, then settled down to a soft glow. Jangor nudged Kevana.

"Be ready, that big horse of his has one hell of a take-off, when the rump drops start kicking and you may just keep up." They slowly rounded the next turn in the road, and ahead of them was an open area, basically flat, with the occasional drainage ditch, this was after all farming land, in the fields the ground would be soft, on the roadway itself more than hard enough for any horse to travel at maximum speeds. Arrayed across the road was a large group of black robed brothers. With a single sweep of the eyes Jangor knew everything that he needed. He turned in his saddle.

"Magicians, take out those archers, I want them blind if not dead." Granger and Gregor split off to the sides to get clear vision of their targets, long before they were within range of the bows the archers started to fall from their horses, as the last of the six bowmen pulled his bow, Gregor's staff flashed blue and the archers head disappeared in a white flash, his corpse slowly rolled out of the saddle and fell into the muddy ditch, while his colleagues were still staring at him, Jangor spotted Namdarin drop his reins, he nudged Kevana hard as Arndrol settled for that first thrust. Together they watched the huge muscles tense then release, the race was on. Kevana kicking hard into his black stallions' ribs, slapping the reins against his neck, trying desperately to catch the surging grey. A whole length opened up before he got the stallion moving, the long sleek legs started to catch up with the heavier grey, along the centre of the road ran Wolf, his toothy smile and his following flag of a tail send waves of fear amongst the horses, Jayanne to the right, axe in her right hand, the two edged blade somehow bigger than it was, the haft longer and thicker, the shining steel unchanged, though it radiated a hunger that filled the air like fear. The line of black robes adjusted to strengthen the points of impact they knew were coming. Namdarin used the sheer mass and power of his heavy horse to crash through the assembled monks, the green stone flashed brilliantly in the low sunlight, the momentary pauses caused by this mind deadening light meant that three heads flew from bodies in a single sweep, Jangor and Kevana pushed through the same opening in the line, each taking a life on the way, together the three turned as the line was still bracing to face the attack of the others, Namdarin cut towards the centre turning hard right, this lost him some forwards momentum, but he knew Arndrol could still kick up to full speed before he hit the back of the line. Jayanne didn't simply crash the line as had Namdarin she turned hard right, reaching across her body the axe took two men in a single swipe, separating one into two discrete parts and the other chopped almost through, the silver of the axe unblemished by the blood that poured from the bodies, Kern was struggling as her turn had put him very close to the line of enemy riders, though the line was now falling apart as she passed, some trying to chase after her, others trying to run away, he slashed at a few in passing, though he didn't actually score any serious hits, Brank had a much easier ride, he was simply riding alongside her. She reached the end of the line and sliced a blind archer, who was still mounted, though had no idea where he was, or where he was going. The axe caved in is chest and sucked the life and soul from his body, the empty husk fell to the ground and she moved left to attack the line as it came towards her, Wolf flashed in and snapped at the legs of the first horseman, causing the horse to shy away and as the rider struggled to maintain is seat, Brank's heavy sword took him in the shoulder and pitched him to the ground where Wolf made short work of his throat. Wolf ran on before the approaching horses could trample him, Jayanne rode straight at the attackers, a forehand slash took a horse's head and the rider in the chest, he died slowly as the axe fed again, Jayanne's eyes lit up with the stolen energy, Kern's wide strokes kept the enemies away from him and Jayanne, one follow through sliced the reins of one of the monks, the suddenly freed horse pushed forwards as hard as it could, passing between Kern and Jayanne, Kern struggled to foul the monks sword as it came round towards Jayanne, the axe flashed into the monks chest on a backhanded slash, ribs cracked and crackled as they caved in, the man groaned as the horse slid forwards underneath him, he hung briefly on the blade as he passed over the rump of his horse, his body fell to the ground in a clatter of broken sticks, Jayanne voiced a wordless howl, that was answered shortly by Wolf as he came back in to harass the horses some more, he grabbed a horses nose in his strong jaws, and pulled the horses head down, the sudden stop and ducking of the mounts head caused the rider to pitch forwards in his saddle, as he fought to recover his seat, Branks sword took him in the neck and almost severed his head, he continued his forward motion until he landed in a heap on the ground, almost on Wolfs back. Jayanne looked into the frightened eyes of the next man, behind him she saw the flash of the green stone, as the mindsword fell and took another life. The man in front of Jayanne sawed hard on his reins, turning left and away from the battle, kicking hard his only thought was escape, the last three of his brothers turned with him and kicked their horses hard. Namdarin paused then yelled.

"Magicians. I want live prisoners." His cry echoed across the battlefield, the four moved into open space, two staffs flashed with hot power and two horses fell, two sent bars of black force that threw riders from their saddles. Namdarin rode slowly over to where the men lay on the ground, one had his leg trapped under the saddle of a fallen horse, the horses head a mass of burned flesh. Two more were simply sitting on the ground waiting to die, the last was already dead, he didn't survive the fall from his horse. Namdarin looked down at the man trapped, his heavy boot pushing hard against the saddle of his dead horse, his hand grasping for the fallen sword a foot beyond his reach, his grunts and groans filled the air as he tried so hard to escape from beneath the horse.

"He is no-one." Said Namdarin. "Kill him." Jayanne nodded, and dropped from her horse, she walked slowly towards the trapped man, the axe swinging slowly in her hand.

"Lady." Called Kevana as he slid from his saddle. "I beg your indulgence, let me end his life."

"Why?" She snarled.

"Though the brotherhood think me as heretic at least, apostate at worst, I would rather not have a man die by that axe, when a cleaner death is available, please lady let me kill him." For a long breath her cold green eyes bored into his wide brown ones, he didn't shy away, though her gaze was so hot that his eyes itched to be looking somewhere else. Slowly she nodded and turned away. Kevana breathed a huge sigh and walked to the trapped soldier, he was no cleric, just a low ranking warrior. Kevana knelt beside the man.

"Make your peace with your god." He whispered.

"Fuck you. Zandaar will burn you in the deepest hell for all eternity."

"To burn in hell one must have a soul, yours is bound for the heaven that Zandaar has prepared for you, that axe would have taken your soul and fed it to her. Sadly I no longer believe in Zandaar as you do, perhaps my vision is the truth, perhaps not, my dice is cast, your life the same. Please speak the prayer of death, you have little time left, Namdarin will brook no more delays. Please speak with me the prayer of ascension." Kevana spoke the lines of the prayer, before he had finished the man was speaking with him, as the prayer ended with the name of god Kevana plunged his sword straight into the man's heart, he died with a sigh, and a single blood laden cough. Kevana stood slowly, a single tear on his cheek. He walked towards the other two survivors, a flick of the wrist shed the blood from his sword.

"These two are higher ranking clerics." He said to Namdarin.

"Which one is the highest?" Kevana pointed the sword at the one sitting to the left.

"I'll tell you nothing and curse you to the hottest of all the hells." Snarled the cowering monk, not taking his eyes off Kevana's sword.

"You will tell me everything I need to know, you will give up your entire knowledge before you die. And die you must, I cannot leave any of your kind behind me, I'm walking into the lair of the demon, I can't have you sneaking up behind me with a blade in your hand."

"I'll tell you nothing." The monk's tone was less confident now. Namdarin took the crystals from his saddle bag, and whispered a few words to Arndrol, and a small hand signal to Wolf. Both left the battlefield with a joint purpose but in opposite directions. Namdarin walked over to the ranking monk and pushed him backwards until he was lying on his back. The other monk moved to intervene, but the sight of Kevana's sword coming towards him stopped him, then the cold edge of the axe touched the exposed skin on the back of his neck, icy cold filled his mind and body. Namdarin forced the prone monks mouth open and pushed a crystal in as far as it would go without blocking the airway. Looking down into the frightened eyes he spoke slowly.

"Your mind will be mine, every thought and memory, all that is you will be mine to read as an open book. The more you struggle the more it will hurt." Namdarin put the other crystal slowly into his own mouth, as the connection between the crystals was made, and the pathway between the minds opened Namdarin swamped that passageway with all the hatred and pain in his heart, any feeble defences that the monk had were flattened in a moment as the wave of thought tore through his mind, shredding any cogent structures, and almost shattering the very ego that held it all together. Desperately the monk tried to hold onto simply who he was, as Namdarin's consciousness ripped through his own, back to his childhood and through every day up until this very one. It turned out that he had been an abbot of a nearby training school, all the best had been sent here to block the road to Zandaarkoon, the students departed to Zandaarkoon with equal speed, they should be there before the sun comes up, a few hours' sleep and they'll be manning the walls and the gates. 'You think that you could stop us? After Zandaar burned Zandaarkoon and Angorak and failed?' Thought Namdarin straight into the monk's mind.

'We were only expected to slow you down.'

'You didn't even manage that, we were going to be stopping for the night very soon anyway. You understand now just how feeble your defences are. I go to kill your god, but that shouldn't bother you too much because you will already be dead.'

'Together with our god we will find a way to stop you.'

'Somehow I doubt that. I have the backing of all the old gods. I have enough hatred to burn the world.'

'There is a way to stop you, and we will find it.'

'You're out of time.' Namdarin broke the link and stepped backwards.

"What is that magic?" Muttered the monk, spitting out the crystal.

"It is a magic of the first gods, the ones that were here when the world was new." Said Granger. "From a time before even Zandaar." Namdarin passed the crystal in his hand to Worandana with a question on his face. Worandana looked at it for a long moment before taking it, he didn't want to miss out on some new, or even old magic. Slowly he knelt on the fallen monk's chest and picked up the crystal, forcing it back into the monk's mouth. He paused for a moment before a thought came to the fore of his mind, a slow smile spread across his face, and he dropped the second crystal on the ground, he reached for his belt knife and cut a shallow wound into the palm of his left hand, he let the blood pool briefly before he placed that injury against the crystal in the monks mouth. In a rush he invaded the monks mind, there was no resistance at all, into the deepest corners of the mind, the parts even hidden from the monk himself, the deliberately forgotten memories, memories of love and hate, of pleasure and pain, of joy and sadness. These came rushing out of the darkness, and into the burning light of the man's mind, terrible destruction they wrecked there, these had been hidden away for many reasons, mostly for the sanity of the man. His mind dissolved in the roiling turmoil of forgotten memories. Worandana withdrew quickly before the mind fell apart completely, taking enough energy to heal himself and quite a bit more. Worandana rose as seizures gripped the body of the monk, teeth shattered on the crystal, bloody foam filled the mouth, stuttering breaths rushed through the nose before it too was filled with blood, slowly the man died. Worandana reached down and retrieved the crystal from the now slack jaw, he wiped the blood off on the man's black cloak, picked up the second from where he had dropped it, and handed them both back to Namdarin.

"What did you do and why?" Asked Namdarin, with a smile.

"I thought of the lightning stone and how blood is the power that opens the way, so I tried it on this crystal, it worked far better than I expected, I took his whole mind in a moment, all of it, I released those memories better kept hidden, his sanity failed, and he died. I am sorry, but I don't think he had anything more to give us. We both know everything that he did."

"Agreed." Said Namdarin with a smile. "That just leaves us with one spare Zandaar." They both looked at the last monk. The monk's eyes flashed from one to the other, seeing only death in their gaze.

"You don't have to kill me, I'll ride north until the horse dies, then run until this is all over."

"You are far too high a rank," said Worandana, "Zandaar knows who you are, and you'll tell him everything you know."

"I don't know anything, other than the fact that everyone bar me is dead. Killed in battle or murdered in cold blood." He glanced to his right at the slowly cooling corpse. Namdarin tensed and the sword leapt into his hand, the green jewel flashed and the monk froze.

"You want cold blood, ask the people of Angorak, or those now dead in Zandaarkoon."

"Will one more corpse advance your cause? Zandaar already knows where you are, he knew where all these were until you killed them. The thing I don't really understand is why he is so afraid of you."

"He knows we come to kill him, and he knows we have the power to do just that." Snapped Worandana.

"No, I feel that there is something else going on here, but I have no true idea what."

"What do you mean?"

"This latest episode of insanity serves no real purpose, he obviously missed his target, you are all still alive."

"Not all." Said Kevana.

"I'd say sorry, but all my friends are dead, I may soon join them. I can't believe that Zandaar missed the sword carrier when he burned Angorak, it makes no sense."

"Sense," sneered Worandana, "what sense? Namdarin wasn't in the city, we were. Make sense of that." The monk looked from face to face and saw only truth in their eyes.

"Give me a moment to think about this, it's strange." The monk closed his eyes for a while, a time that soon became far to long for the impatience of Namdarin. The mindstone flashed with every rush of irritation.

"Give him a moment longer." Whispered Worandana.

"All I see is a black robed killer that needs to die."

"He may know something that could be of use to us, please give him a moment." Worandana begged. The monk looked up and opened his eyes wide.

"Oh my. It is well known amongst the council that the sword can kill Zandaar, but he doesn't fear the sword, he is afraid of something you bring to this battle. What have the rainbow heretics brought with them? Some knowledge or power, some weapon or force?"

"Heretics?" Snapped Kirukana.

"Sorry, I meant no insult, only a description of how you look to me. What do you have that frightens a god so?"

"You have seen the dark power we carry, and you have seen what it can do." Said Kirukana, his hands darkened, encased in the hunger from the dark.

"Yes, I heard of this, it is quite impressive, but not something that Zandaar is unaware of. No there has to be something else. I can't feel anything strange about you, your colourful crystals aren't going to be of much use as Zandaar has no true physical form, the sword is useful, perhaps as a channel, but it isn't enough on its own. You have something else."

Jayanne snatched the haft of the axe into her hand and swung it towards the monk's head.

"That is more like it." Said the monk looking at the axe hanging in front of his eyes. "This is more powerful than the sword, but still not enough, it was outside Angorak. No, it must be something the rainbow, er, warriors have. I really can't feel what it is. If you don't know what it is then you cannot defeat Zandaar."

"This man is fishing." Said Kevana. "He spreads uncertainty amongst us and hopes to find something to tell Zandaar before he dies. We have the sword of Xeron, the mindstone of the elven king, the axe of Algoron, we have the power of the outer darkness, we have magicians of great might, we have the word of Gyara," that name caused the monks head to snap round and his eyes to open wider than ever. Kevana shouted. "Jayanne kill him now." The axe swung into the monk's chest and fed on his heart and soul, Jayanne screamed with the sudden surge of energy.

"Jayanne." Called Namdarin as he wrapped her in his arms.

"I'm fine," she whispered, "he was carrying an awful lot of power, almost as much as the sleeping willow, he was more than some simple monk."

"He was the abbot of a local training mission, advanced training, so he must have had some skill." Said Worandana. "So these must have been the best of the teachers, not really warriors as such, but skilled none the less. The question is did he get the information out to anyone else?" He turned to Jayanne.

"I didn't feel anything other than a massive surge of power, I felt no other presences at all. Just a man terrified to die." She turned out of Namdarin's arms and looked down at the desiccated corpse at her feet. "Now what?" She asked.

"We camp, for the night. Then head south in the morning." Said Jangor.

"Let's at least get away from all this death." Suggested Kevana.

"Agreed. Granger, Gregor, chill these corpses so they'll not get too ripe before we leave. Kern camp site?"

"Over there." Replied Kern, pointing to the east. "That notch in the trees indicates a stream, and there should be somewhere near it fit to camp for at least one night."

"We are a little short of the necessary supplies for camping." Observed Kevana.

"I wouldn't worry about that, we seem to have a herd of horses coming this way." Laughed Jangor. Looking to the south Arndrol was leading a group of horses with wolf keeping them close, herding them like a sheep dog. "They should have all the supplies you need, I see some pack animals as well as saddle horses."

"Those two seem to work very well together."

"You have no idea how good a team they make, perhaps you'll get to see sometime soon. The sun is almost down so let's see if we can get a camp set up before it gets dark." Jangor turned to Namdarin. "Horses?" Namdarin nodded and walked over to Arndrol, placed his head against the long skull of the horse, together they settled briefly, breathing slowly, unmoving. Namdarin looked up.

"Thank you, my friend." He whispered to the horse, as he ruffled the long white mane.

"Nothing nearby, only indistinct groups at long range, moving together, but nothing coming this way. We'll be safe well into tomorrow." Namdarin turned and followed Kern, with Arndrol behind him, Wolf fell in alongside him, leaving the humans to finish up collecting the horses, Jayanne caught him up, horse on a rein behind her, sure enough they walked up a short rise onto an open area, more than big enough for a camp site.

"Kevana." Said Jangor looking around. "Your people should find enough tents and such amongst the pack horses, and probably supplies as well. This close to enemy territory I want two men on watch at all time, one of ours and one of yours. Kern will take the first watch and I will take the last before dawn. Food will be served around a communal fire, we need this group to be properly integrated before tomorrow."

"Agreed, tomorrow we go to war against a city." Kevana shook his head slowly, he really didn't like the idea.

"Luckily we have some people who know the layout of the city, so it should be easy."

"Let us hope so." Kevana shrugged and turned away.

CHAPTER SIXTY-SEVEN

The camp took shape quickly, Kevana and his people finding most of what they needed amongst the pack horses that had been captured. Tents were erected slower than normal, but they were going up. Kevana made a few subtle hand signals, and two of his men left their tent assembling duties. They approached the fire that was already roaring strongly.

"We have some salted beef and some dried fruit, would that help?" Asked Petrovana.

"We could do with some vegetables." Replied Mander.

"I'll go and check some more of the pack horses." Said Fabrana turning away.

"I never for a moment thought that I would be here making food with you people." Said Petrovana.

"Nor did we." Said Mander.

"It's weird, but somehow it feels right." Smiled Petrovana, as Fabrana returned not quite at a run.

"All I could find is a few carrots." He showed them to Mander.

"They'll do, we could do with some bread to go with this stew, but I don't suppose it'll make a lot of difference, we probably don't have long left to live." Laughed Mander.

"Do you want to live forever?" Shouted Petrovana.

"Hell No!" Came the response from all around.

"Looks like we have much in common." Said Stergin.

"We're all soldiers." Said Fabrana.

"Well most of us." Smiled Mander.

"Those clerics are just different." Said Petrovana.

"Magicians are no better." Laughed Stergin, he paused for a moment, then continued quietly. "I want to ask a question, but I don't want to upset anyone, can you be calm?"

"Go ahead," said Petrovana, "we're all soldiers here."

"How come you've moved away from your god?" Petrovana stared at Stergin for a long breath, before responding.

"Brave question."

"It needs to be asked, and the air needs to cleared between us."

"I understand," said Petrovana, "we were given the honour of collecting that sword. We weren't actually expecting the call, so many groups have been given that duty and never had the call. You killed the tree and then we hit the road. Then we started to die, that cold was something I have never experienced before. Anyway, that is by the by. We've been chasing you for a while now, and four days ago we found that our brotherhood were searching for us, with instructions to kill on sight. You can understand that this upset us a little. Later Worandana cleared things up, so they were only searching for us. Except of course for the hounds, they were always going to kill us, they had some other plan. Then as we came through the centre of Angorak, Zandaar set the whole place on fire, and killed everyone in Zandaarkoon to do it. This sort of gives one a reason for a new religion, or better still none at all. Kevana intends on explaining all this to Zandaar, and we are going with him."

"You understand that Namdarin intend to kill him?"

"Yes, Kevana wants to explain first."

"That may be a little difficult, I'm fairly sure he's not going to want to listen." Laughed Stergin.

"Kevana will just have to talk him to death." Smiled Petrovana.

"Now that sounds like a plan." Said Alverana as he walked up behind them.

Short introductions were made, then Alverana continued. "The light is almost gone, how long before the food is ready?"

"Shouldn't be long." Said Mander. "Just waiting for the carrots to be cooked through, it's not much but it is fuel."

"You'd have to go a long way to make the worst food we've ever eaten." Laughed Alverana, he turned to Petrovana. "You remember that place in the east, I can't even think of its name. We were fighting and dying, there were hundreds of us, fighting off a hoard of horsemen. The food was some sort of thin gruel, well the place had been cut off from any supplies for weeks, it was truly vile. But we fought almost as hard for that bowl of slop as we did against those damned horsemen."

"It was called Rothgar, and it was special." Replied Petrovana. "It controlled a river crossing and the only pass through the mountains. The horsemen needed it to gain access to all the lands along the river. We held it, and we beat them."

"We didn't beat them, we survived, winter beat them. If they'd started that attack in spring, they'd have won. But picking the tail end of summer to launch something like that, that was stupid."

"They weren't exactly bright, but damn they were fierce." Laughed Petrovana.

"Have you ever had to fight sheep?" Asked Mander

"What?" Said Alverana. "Short guys, four legs, big woolly coats?"

"Yes, that's em."

"I wouldn't have thought they would be too hard to deal with." Laughed Petrovana, looking very confused.

"Imagine." Smiled Mander "Three thousand of those woolly backs driven straight at your platoon of twenty-five men. Only one in thirty of those brainless fur balls is actually a hound, trained to kill anything that attacks the herd." He paused to let the idea sink in. "We had lost five men before we realised what was actually in amongst the sheep. Wolf sized dogs that were just waiting for an opportunity to attack."

"I've never heard of the like." Said Alverana.

"You'll find them if you head west, those shepherds are serious people. I'd suggest you leave them be."

"I have a question." Said Petrovana diffidently.

"Ask, we're all soldiers here."

"Soon after we found the sword gone, we came across a battle site. Was it you that killed all those huge wolves?"

"It was." Said Stergin. "Now that was a battle."

"The snow made the tracks very unclear," said Alverana, "how did you manage that without any losses?"

"Much of it was down to that bow of Namdarin's, he was killing them before they were anywhere near us. Then, while the rest of us were circling to defend ourselves and the horses. Namdarin and Jayanne were killing wolves, his sword shattered. So he snatched the longsword from its wooden case, and really started killing wolves. That sword is so fast, and so lethal, sometimes a single touch is enough. It was quite a fight, but it didn't last very long, no injuries, we did very well."

"Those were some really big wolves." Said Petrovana.

"We did fine, it was scary for a while, but Jayanne and Namdarin were very impressive."

"She's definitely nice to look at." Smiled Petrovana glancing over to where Jayanne was erecting a tent with Namdarin.

"She is indeed, but she does have a tendency to wander around naked." Said Mander.

"That's got to be great sight to see." Laughed Petrovana.

"She may not have clothes on, but she's always got that axe, normally hanging from its strap. When you hear that haft slap into her palm, then you know fear, you've seen what she can do with that thing?" Said Mander. "And you have seen what it does to men."

"We've seen." Said Alverana quietly. "Have no fear there will be no inappropriate advances made, if she turns up naked somewhere. You should have seen us a few days ago, we were woken by screaming. So what do you do? You grab your sword and head for the fight. Sadly it was only our clerics messing with Crathen's dreams, it was a short time before we realised that myself and Kevana were still naked. So nudity not much of an issue for us, except perhaps Kirukana. He's a bit obsessed by the rules, but he has mellowed a lot recently."

"What about Crathen?"

Alverana looked over to where the younger man was trying to erect a tent, this task made difficult by his inability to take his eyes off Jayanne.

"He may be a problem. She may just have to slap him for him to get the message."

"When she slaps people, it tends to be with the axe. They generally don't survive." Said Stergin.

"We'll try and discourage him from anything stupid." Alverana looked hard at Petrovana, until he got a nod of recognition. Mander stirred the pot slowly, added a few herbs from a pouch at his belt.

"Food is nearly ready, go get your bowls, it's short on meat, and salt, but there's enough fat in it to keep us going for most of tomorrow. Go easy, breakfast is going to be leftovers, so make sure there are some."

"I'll round up the troops, and advise them of the menu for breakfast." Laughed Alverana walking slowly away.

The men all gathered for the evening meal, darkness as all around them. The only light came from the campfire, the flickering shadows made everything around jump and twitch. Though this was nothing that they weren't all used to. Conversation was soft and light, no one wanted to talk about anything important in all this night. The meal was over in short order, for there wasn't much of it. Jangor declared bedtime, and set Kern for the first watch as normal. Kevana set Alverana as first for his group and retired quickly to his tent. In only a few minutes the camp was empty, Kern and Alverana retreated from the fire light. With Wolf at their heels, together they sat with their backs to a large tree. Where they could see the whole camp, the dark gully that contained the stream on the far side of the fire the horses picketed to the left, to the right the slope that lead down to the road. Wolf lay down beside Kern his head on Kern's hip, facing away from the camp, as if watching for anyone approaching through the trees.

"How did your meeting go with Gyara?" Whispered Alverana.

"You mean the first one, the other side of the mountains?"

"You've met her more than once?"

"Yes."

"The first then, that is a location we have in common."

"I saw the temple tree and recognised it immediately, I performed the summoning. She came, in the shape of the black crow, she told us to take the sword to the elves and get their mindstone."

"And this meeting cost you no men?"

"None, she left, as is her wont, and we collected some fallen branches for torches and went into the caves. What about you?"

"I saw the tree, but it took me a long time to remember. Worandana had already started a summoning, he sensed something about the place. We formed a defensive circle and started charging it, while he summoned and talked to Gyara. Gyara told Worandana that she wasn't going to help either side in this conflict. Because both still had the power to release her from her servitude here, by destroying all life. Before she left, she tore apart our circle, and killed one of our men."

"You remembered the tree?"

"Yes, from way back in my childhood, my family were followers of Gyara."

"So you were a member of the church of Gyara?"

"I suppose, but I was only young when I left to join the army of Zandaar."

"You remember the tree, and how to summon Gyara?"

"Yes, it came back to me while I was part of the circle, but I could do nothing about it."

"Do you know how to summon Gyara without a tree?"

"No, I've never heard of such a thing."

"Well it is possible, all we need is three followers, one to be the tree and two to perform the summoning."

"So we need one other?"

"We've Brank, he's a follower as well."

"Why would you want to summon Gyara? She's also called The Trickster, with good reason."

"It's good to have the option, or at least to know that we have it."

"I'm sorry but I can see no situation that Gyara is ever going to make better."

"She is tricky, of that there can be no doubt, but she has had many followers over thousands of years. She has been useful in the past, she may be useful to us in the future."

"That's a desperate place I don't want to be, if Gyara is going to help us then we must be in some deep shit."

"Where are we going? I don't actually envisage shit that could be any deeper."

"You my friend are not wrong. Which one is Brank, I haven't got the names sorted out in my head yet?"

"The big one, you know, size of a tree." Laughed Kern.

"Got him, tree, how appropriate." Alverana laughed quietly. Wolf's ears twitched; a horse stamped in the picket line. The two men fell silent and reached for their swords. A small shape moved slowly into the light around the fire, as it approached the fire its brown and red colouration became clearer. Its bushy tail sweeping low along the ground as it stepped through the trampled grass of the camp. Wolf stood and turned towards the animal, he let loose a deep and resonant growl. The fox turned towards the men, and then away from the fire. In a single bound it was in total darkness, its rapid passage through the trees could be heard for a few minutes as it sped away into the night.

"Thanks Wolf." Said Kern reaching out to stroke the wolfs mane. "He'll not be back for a while."

"From the sounds of things, that fox won't stop running until next week." Laughed Alverana. Kern reached out and ruffled Wolfs mane, until the canine relaxed enough to lie down again.

"Did we get a warning from the horses as well?" Asked Alverana.

"Most likely that was Arndrol, Namdarin's grey."

"That horse is a bit of a character."

"Oh, he's that and more. A true warhorse."

"How long have you been together?"

"We met Namdarin the day after your god burned his house. We passed as strangers on the road. Next day we encountered him dead on the road, while we were investigating the site, he came back to life. We were together for a couple of days, then we split up. A few weeks later we chanced on Namdarin and Jayanne just as they had finished off a camp full of bandits. They were outnumbered fifty or so to two, perhaps three if you count Arndrol, I think he should be counted. That was an interesting meeting, he had a simple sword at that time. She had the axe; she was naked and covered from head to toe in other people's blood. It seems that some of the bandits quite enjoyed raping her, once Namdarin gave her the axe back. She took her vengeance on them, there were more than a few corpses with cocks stuffed in their mouths. I have no way to tell if they were dead when their manhood's were pushed between their teeth, but knowing her, they were still screaming. We've been together ever since."

"You're mercenaries, he's got no money, why are you still with him?"

"Difficult question to answer, his cause is just, that is important. Working with him is very profitable as well, at every turn there are dead soldiers, thieves, rapists, and assorted murderers. All of these have good metal to trade, or gold in their pockets. We're actually making a fortune on this mission, we know it's going to get very dangerous. And very soon. But in all honesty, we cannot turn away now, we have to see this through. We know that we won't all survive, could be that we will all die, but the cause is just."

"We were on a holy mission given to us by our god, then our own people turned against us, until finally our god tried to burn us all, along with a whole city. Actually, two cities. Now we are without a cause, so tagging along with you seems to be a good idea."

"Good enough to die for?"

"Perhaps, we've been close to death a few times on this mission already, the damned cold took some. Gyara took another, the snow demons, that you set on us, they had a good try, and then we got imprisoned in a cave with a snake, that was you as well."

"That was, is that going to cause any problems?"

"Not likely, we'd have done the same, or worse. And now we are one big happy team." Alverana laughed a little too loud for Wolf in the depths of night, a hard stare from the big yellow eyes choked the laugh in Alverana's throat. Alverana cocked his head to one side and whispered, "Wolf, sometimes you're a humourless bastard." A big smile on his face, Wolf's head dropped back down to its place on Kerns thigh. Kern looked around suddenly, and placed a finger over his lips, Alverana stopped and looked at Kern, his raised brows asking a question. Slowly Kern raised an arm and pointed at the stream just down from the camp. The dark band of water was scattering light from the stars, much more than it had been. Then out of the darkness came a small group of white-tailed deer, four fully grown and three smaller. Wolf tensed, as the scent came to him. Kern put a hand on the canine's head to calm him. The three watched as the group passed the camp. Slowly cropping the occasional mouthful of grass, until something changed, and they all took fright. Vanishing in a heartbeat into the dark woods, with a flash of white from the tails of the adults.

"I thought we were short of meat?" Asked Alverana.

"If you want to go chasing deer in the dark, go to it, I'm not going to get brained on some tree in the dark. If we find some in daylight then maybe, but at night. Sorry you're on your own." Laughed Kern.

"Are you aware the Namdarin almost killed me?"

"I didn't know that you had even met."

"We didn't, he invaded Crathen's dream just after Gorgana left us. I was in the periphery of that dream as he tore it to shreds, my consciousness was shredded at the same time. Only Kevana brought me back."

"And still you want to ride at his side to almost certain death?"

"I'm not sure that want is the right word, we really don't have much of a choice. Zandaar has tried to kill us all once, I don't see him stopping. As soon as he gets back up to full strength, he's bound to try again. We cannot survive too many more of those attacks, nor can the people who are around us."

"So, by standing next to Namdarin you might get Zandaar to kill him?" Smiled Kern.

"Perhaps, but that's not likely is it, Zandaar had sent the hounds against us, not him."

"I don't understand that at all."

"Neither do I, perhaps we are more of a threat than Namdarin and that sword."

"How can that be?"

"I have no idea."

"Well, if that is the case, we need to work out what this threat is before we walk into that damned temple."

"Agreed." They both fell silent for a while, just drinking in the peace of the night.

"Who should we get for the next watch?" Asked Kern.

"How about some magicians?" Laughed Alverana.

"We can't expect the old men to stand watch can we?"

"Not really, I'll go and get Kirukana."

"I'll get Gregor." Kern laughed a little too loud and got a stare from Wolf. "There could be some interesting conversation under this tree."

"Get some sleep, don't bother trying to listen in. I'm sure they'll get loud enough if there is anything worth listening to." Together they walked into the camp and woke each of their replacements. Wolf followed Kern and sniffed at Gregor and followed him as he walked over to Kirukana.

"Alverana says there is a comfortable tree just out of camp, over there." He pointed up the slope, and the two turned to walk that way.

"Why do you think they picked us to be next?" Asked Gregor.

"They expect some sort of arguments."

"Are we going to argue?"

"Perhaps."

"Are you going to accuse me of heresy?"

"How can I? I've been using the dark power that Worandana showed me, I can't think of anything more heretical than that."

"How about planning to kill our god?"

"Well there's that I suppose, and that is what we intend."

"So heresy cannot be an issue between us."

"I can agree with that, I just don't understand why you switched places with Crathen."

"That's actually quite simple, I was afraid that you would eventually convince Worandana that I was enough of a heretic to be killed, and I was so sure it would happen."

"But why Crathen?"

"I talked it over at some length with Anya, she asked me not to bring Namdarin and the sword, because the lightning stone would be open and he might take control of it, or more likely he'd start killing everyone around."

"She is a wise woman." Said Kirukana, his voice slow and level. Gregor's eyebrows rose in surprise.

"I never thought I'd hear you say that about any woman, but to continue. I suggested bringing Jayanne."

"That would not have been good."

"No surprise Anya said no, most emphatically no. If Jayanne is in the village, then Namdarin is coming, with only one intent."

"So you picked Crathen as the least of all evils. Surely switching places was more complex than just bringing him here?"

"Actually no, there is a sort of balance in one going each way, it's far simple to balance the forces involved, the only problem I had was that I was going to lose control of the stone. Anya had assured me that she would be there, I knew she would take control of it and protect everyone."

"That almost fell apart."

"What do you mean?"

"I tried to stop her, the others were all stunned by your departure, and she came running up, she screamed at me to get out of her way, I nearly didn't."

"She took control of the stone?"

"Yes, at some extreme cost, she was burned, but she shut the thing down in a short time, but all her clothes and every hair on her body was burned off."

"She was an impressive sight when naked."

"That she was. Kevana made me give her my robe, I struggled with that for a moment, but he was firm."

"I can imagine. Was Anya injured?"

"Yes, but she healed herself. Her body was without a scar, and full of power."

"How do you know that?"

"She showed us the next day, she turned up as we were preparing to leave, she came with her husband, he was walking and talking, which was something of a surprise to Worandana. She also made it very clear, and I do mean very. That we leave immediately and never come back."

"Did she actually threaten Worandana?" Laughed Gregor.

"She advised that accidents can happen." Kirukana laughed at the memory.

"Somehow I'm sad I missed that."

"How did you survive your meeting with Namdarin?"

"I had to swear an oath on that damned sword. Then Namdarin tried to kill me with it, but it wouldn't let him do it. You should have seen the anger in his eyes. He looked at the sword as if it had betrayed him."

"We both had an interesting time that day."

"What of this dark power that you and Worandana are now using? I've never seen it's like."

"Worandana showed it to me quite recently, he was having a very bad day. He found out that all his friends that he had already showed it to had been killed by Axorana. His plan to take over the council was in ruins. So he showed it to me and took me fully into his confidence. That was a huge shock to me, this power is definitely not from Zandaar."

"Where is it from?"

"Something huge and outside the world, but it feels like it is getting closer."

"Something moves in the darkness, this way it comes." Whispered Gregor.

"I suppose it's something like that, why?"

"Because those were the last words of Grinderosch, the undead elven king."

"So he knew that this power whatever it is, is getting nearer."

"The question is, what is it going to do when it arrives?"

"I feel it as a huge hunger."

"But it gives you power?"

"Yes, but I think it's going to want a lot more back when it gets here. We'll have to find something to feed it then, if it actually gets here. I'm hoping it's going somewhere else." Kirukana grinned.

"What are the chances of that?"

"I'd say almost none, sadly."

"At least it will be of some use when we have to face Zandaar."

"Let's hope so." There was a lull in the conversation before Kirukana spoke again.

"How can you store power in that staff? How does that work?" He asked.

"Granger showed me how to do it, and you'd be surprised just how much power my staff can hold, and even more so at the rate it can deliver it."

"I thought he was simply a charlatan."

"That is what the council want us to believe, but they are so wrong, he's a very knowledgeable and powerful old man."

"But old none the less."

"Oh, he's old. Don't challenge him."

"Not a chance, I'm just getting used to all this, so I'm taking no risks."

"Good idea. What do you think we will be facing when we get to Zandarkoon?"

"There are going to be a few of the brotherhood, but not too many, small groups and most likely scattered around the city, they'll certainly be defending the gate."

"There are more ways into the city then just the gates."

"I'd rather not enter my home town through the sewers." Laughed Kirukana.

"I actually know of another small door, it's south of the eastern gate, I'm not sure of its purpose, it's a heavy door, and small, might be difficult to get the horses in that way."

"We'll just have to try. The city is small enough that we could leave the horses outside."

"Sorry." Laughed Gregor. "That's not going to happen, Namdarin will never leave Arndrol behind, and Jangor will not surrender the mobility of being mounted."

"That's true, Kevana will be the same."

"We'll just have to try, let's just hope it's not too well defended."

"What are the chances of the new troops knowing about this tiny gate?"

"That is one of the things in our favour, the path to this gate looks like a little alleyway going nowhere, it's not something that an outsider would recognise."

"We'll just have to see when we get there." Kirukana paused for a short time before continuing. "So, what have you learned to do with your new staff?"

"I've tried all sorts of new things. The first time I used it for something new and important, we were attacked by a group of Elves. Well, one of them released an arrow from his bow, I threw up a barrier spell, that covered the whole group for a few heartbeats. That was so hard I passed out for a few seconds. By the time I had my senses back Jangor and the Elven chief, Gervane, were walking side by side, sharing a flask of some spirit or other, I was lifted into a saddle and we followed."

"How did the barrier spell work?"

"Exceptionally well, though Jangor has forbidden its use. It takes so much energy that I was completely empty for a few hours. That couldn't happen now, I always keep this thing as fully charged as I can." He patted the heavy staff.

"I'll have to find myself a staff, or something similar." Said Kirukana.

"Isn't that contrary to the teachings?" Laughed Gregor.

"Storing energy isn't specifically forbidden, it's just not something that anyone is supposed to know anything about. Anyway, that is completely by the by. The council is dead, everyone is dead. When I think of how much of my life I have given to Zandaar, I get angry. I wasn't expecting fame, or fortune, or power. I was just happy to serve something bigger than just me. I watched the council and their toadies, always manoeuvring, forever scheming, after a little advantage here, a pot of gold there, a morsel of power. And in the end it did them exactly no good at all. I just had a wicked thought."

"Go on, explain your idea."

"Zandaarkoon is dead, unlike Angorak it didn't burn, it is just sitting there empty, other than a rather angry god."

"And?"

"Think of all the work the council have been doing to accumulate power for themselves."

"I don't understand."

"The most obvious indicator of power is wealth, some of them are wealth beyond their own dreams. They use gold to control others, and amass more of it. Their storehouses are full and undamaged."

"That sounds like a plan, the survivors can raid a few on their way out of town."

"I am certain that both Jangor and Kevana have thought of this already, they're a little more in touch with the realities of this world." Laughed Kirukana.

"That's for certain. Do you think we've watched long enough?"

"I think so, even Kevana and Alverana have gone to sleep."

"How long have they been lovers? There was certainly no hint of that before I left."

"I think it started just after you left, remember when Namdarin visited Crathen in the night and tore apart a dream?"

"He said something about it, we had to mount up and ride out before he stopped laughing."

"Well Alverana was watcher, and he was in the periphery of Crathens dream when it shattered, he consciousness got scattered, we had to bring him back. Actually we were feeding power to Kevana. From the look in his eyes he would have died before he would have given up. He got close. Since then they've been getting closer, Worandana gave them a little push in a dream a few nights ago, damn it. That was last night. So much has been going on."

"I would just like one day with nothing happening." Laughed Gregor.

"Who shall we get to watch next? Namdarin?"

"No. He'll have the predawn with Kevana. Though Jangor will join them."

"And Alverana."

"Mander and Petrovana." Giggled Gregor.

"Why?"

"I'd have put Mander with the old you, you have changed. Mander has more wives than there are days to the week. Scattered over a hundred miles."

"The old me would have debated endlessly with him, you are a bad man." Laughed Kirukana. "Petrovana will be a good match. I'll see you on the morrow." Kirukana climbed to his feet and went to find Petrovana. Smiling to himself Gregor went to get Mander.

Petrovana came out of the camp, looking into the dark for the man of the others that he was to stand watch with, Mander waved an arm from his place by the tree. Petrovana settled beside Mander, Wolf wandered out of the dark to join them.

"Drink?" Asked Petrovana, showing a large water skin.

"What you got?" Asked Mander.

"Water."

"Wine." Said Mander lifting a slightly small skin, a grin on his face.

"Should we be drinking on watch?" Asked Petrovana in a whisper.

"I'll not tell, nor will Wolf. Right boy?" Wolf barely raised his head before he returned to sleep. Petrovana reached for the skin, pulled the plug, and squirted a fair portion into his mouth. He looked at Mander and nodded his appreciation.

"That's good." He said.

"Go easy, it's the last one." Petrovana hefted the skin then passed it back to Mander.

"Have you been with Namdarin long?" Asked Petrovana quietly.

"Not long at all, though it does seem like forever, things happen fast around him."

"Things had been quiet for us for a while, then we got the call to go to collect the sword, then the whole world went crazy."

"I know what you mean, you should have seen the mess Namdarin made of Jayanne getting to that damned tree."

"I don't understand."

"You know what guarded that crypt with the sword?"

"Yes, a tree."

"Not just a tree. It was a sleeping willow, everyone who came within its influence fell asleep and never woke up."

"Did they wake up when you killed the tree?"

"No, they slept until they died, then their corpses fed the tree. It was a big tree."

"What do you mean mess?"

"Namdarin realised just before he went to sleep that pain woke him up, so took his belt knife and slashed his left arm, and then Jayanne's thigh, shallow cuts, enough that it hurt like hell and bleed like a bitch, but not enough to kill. After they killed the tree, he woke Jangor. Jangor got the rest of us moving, Kern spent the best part of an hour sewing them up. Namdarin insisted that Jayanne was treated first, only when she was finished did he let Kern tend to his wounds, he made even more mess of himself."

"He sounds like an honourable man."

"Why else would he be here?"

"We are both soldiers, we both have the same sort of experiences. The real question is how are we different?" Asked Petrovana.

"The thing that comes straight to my mind is that you are a member of a religious order, is celibacy really a thing?" Petrovana laughed quietly before he replied.

"It's supposed to be, though the military arm has a little more freedom than the clerics. Marriage is very rare, relationships not so much, and there are often women available at any barracks. These things never change."

"I can't imagine even giving lip service to such a restriction."

"I've heard that you have a woman in every village, now a sad thought just hit me. Did you lose a friend in Angorak?"

"No." Mander shook his head slowly. "I'm currently so far outside my normal stamping grounds that no one even knows of me. Could be that I won't have any time to make new friends. Perhaps on the way home."

"You are actually thinking about a future?"

"Of course, if you think you are going to die, then you will find some way to make it true."

"You believe that?"

"Definitely. When I started out as a young foot soldier our sergeant used to put on clean socks every morning and hang his dirty socks on the end of his bed. I asked him why he did it. 'I always have something to do when I get back to the barracks, the gods love order, and they won't let me die while I still have something to do.' I laughed at his reasoning, but never challenged him."

"How did the sergeant end?"

"He died in a small skirmish, damn him, he took an arrow meant for a youngster that had left himself open." Mander chuckled softly. "His dying words were, 'Wash my socks for me.' We let the youngster have that honour. Then the whole platoon started leaving our dirty socks for the evenings."

"So his strategy didn't work to well."

"Oh, it did. He was well into his fifty's before he died, that's old for an active soldier. Anyway we came back from a patrol some months later and the captain had been into the barracks, he commented on the dirty socks all around. Our new sergeant explained the reasons behind the socks. The captain said carry on and left."

"Strange way to do things." Said Petrovana.

"Not finished yet." Laughed Mander. "Next morning, two men came into the barracks as we were getting dressed for training. They hung a short rail on the wall just inside the door. The sergeant asked them what they were doing, they replied that they couldn't tell. The men left and the sergeant told us to get on with things. After a few moments he shouted 'Attention.' The captain had come into the room. 'At ease gentlemen, at ease.' He said. Then turned to the rail, he hung a pair of socks on the rail. Stepped back and saluted them. He turned back to the room and spoke slowly. 'I remember that sergeant and his damned socks, when I was a youngster, like you are now.' He glanced over his shoulder at his socks, before carrying on. 'Now I have something to do at the end of the day, the gods love order.' He nodded to the serge, we were called to attention again, salutes were exchanged, and he left. After that, he turned up every evening and took his dirty socks to our washroom and spent a few minutes with us. Every morning he hung dirty socks on the rail, in honour of the man who had trained so many."

"Sounds like you had fun with your training?"

"It wasn't too dreadful, but there were bad times as well, battles that went badly. I survived."

"Lucky or good?"

"My training was good and I became good, very good."

"So how do you find enough time to get a girl in every village?"

"Overnight patrols are a good place to start. Staying in various villages to give the local people some confidence in the military might of the local lord. Sometimes the ladies are grateful, very grateful."

"They'd actually marry you after only one night?"

"Not to start with, I started on the young girls that worked the inns. They were fun, but almost never available for a second visit. So I started talking to the slightly older single ladies, they were more difficult to get started, but once they were, they were a whole new education for me. It was a time I thoroughly enjoyed. In some of the regular villages word about me got around, and occasionally a more matronly woman would approach me as soon as camp was set up, those women were wild, surprisingly usually married as well. Again more of an education for me, I think that by the time I was twenty I had more experience of lovemaking than any five men in my unit, perhaps anywhere."

"If you were a woman, you'd be called a whore."

"Not a word I approve of, though there are some that charge for their services, I am not one. You've made use of the camp followers?"

"Occasionally, and yes they always charge." Laughed Petrovana.

"It's sort of essential with soldiers I'm afraid."

"What do you mean?"

"You have no idea how many gifts I have turned down over the years, I don't take gold or favours, for me that would cheapen the love I share with these ladies. Sadly for most soldiers if something has no price, then it has no value."

"I think I understand, is that what the camp women really think about us?

"Many of them, there are some that would do it for free, just for the fun, just to eat at the soldier's kitchens, and drink at their bars, but if they don't charge, then service becomes expected."

"We have an additional disadvantage." Smiled Petrovana.

"Explain?"

"We are a monastic order, celibacy is expected, women are frowned on at best, not actually heretical, but that might not have been far off. The council is dead, so things can change."

"Your god is going to die too, and you're going to be involved in that."

"I suppose. That means that everything changes."

"For all of us that survive."

"Have you a plan for after?"

"We've come across some really bad people on our journey here, Jangor has declared that if we survive, then we shall hunt them down and kill them."

"I'd have to talk to Kevana, but I think I'd like to be part of that."

"I'm sure that you'd be welcome." Wolf appeared out of the darkness and trotted up to Mander, he stopped in front of the man, and let loose a happy puppy sort of yap. He turned away and walk into the trees behind the men, looked back and yapped again.

"I think he's found something," said Mander, "we ought to investigate." He climbed to his feet and reach down a hand to help Petrovana up. Mander jogged down to the fire and recovered a burning branch to use as a torch. Together they followed to wolf into the darkness of the trees, torch held high and swords drawn. They didn't have far to go before they came upon a deer, it had obviously been caught by Wolf, its throat was ripped out, from the marks on the grass Wolf had dragged it a fair way before he came to get them.

"Well done Wolf." Said Mander, ruffling the mane of the huge canine. "Looks like breakfast is going to be something better than leftovers." He took the antlers in his right hand, after sheathing his sword, he nodded to Petrovana, who took the other side of the antler in her left hand. Together they started to drag the deer back towards the camp, with Wolf jumping around them like an excited puppy. They dragged it all the way to the stream, and started preparing it, even though it was still dark. Once the intestine had been removed it was much easier to deal with, and considerably lighter, Mander cut the liver from the abdomen, and presented it to Wolf, well half of it, the people would want their share.

"How long to dawn, do you think?" Asked Petrovana.

"The sky isn't lightening yet, so we have a while."

"Do you think it's time we handed over the watch?"

"You really see Jangor finishing off the butchering?" Smiled Mander.

"Nor Kevana." Petrovana nodded. "We'll finish this then wake them, it should be almost sunrise by then, though they may consider that doing this is not standing watch."

"What can they do? They can't make us stand watch tomorrow night, we'll be damned lucky if there is a tomorrow night."

"That's true. We'll wake them up as the sky starts to lighten, then carry on. We may as well start cooking the thing, we're not going to get any useful sleep now anyway."

"Agreed." Said Mander, as they continued the butchering of the deer. Wolf came back from wherever he'd run off to, to eat his share of the liver. He sniffed around the remnants of the deer, but he knew he would get some more once it was cooked. The eastern sky was just starting to lighten but they still hadn't finished the butchering.

"I'll get Jangor," said Mander, "he'll need to watch this, or the damned wolf will eat it all." He ruffled the wolf's mane as he walked over to Jangor's tent. He scratched gently on the flap of the tent and heard a groan from inside.

"I'm up." Muttered Jangor, only just covering the sounds of him getting out of his bed. Mander walked back to the carcass of the deer, and waved Petrovana off to get Kevana while he continued with the butchering. Very soon Petrovana returned.

"Kevana is coming." He muttered, as he helped Mander with the skinning of a good-sized haunch.

CHAPTER SIXTY-EIGHT

Jangor walked over to where the men were working on the carcass, Wolf was lying off to one side chewing on a thigh bone.

Getting scraps from it, and working on getting the marrow from inside, this was proving to be both loud and difficult.

"Where did that come from?" He demanded, curtly.

"Wolf brought it, he even left most of it for us."

"That's very good of him." Kevana walked up, dressed in his light underclothes, even though his breath made clouds in the air.

"Looks like plans have changed for breakfast." He said.

"Yes." Replied Petrovana. "We're going to need more wood to cook all this, can you two gentlemen watch the meat? I'm sure that Wolf would want more than his fair share."

"Report first." Said Kevana. "What have you discovered about our new friends?"

"They're soldiers as we are, though they serve a master usually, not a god, and they are currently without such a lord, as are we. They seem to be good men, not quite as we were led to believe."

"Mander, report." Said Jangor.

"Pretty much as he says, they're soldiers, and not exactly the monsters Namdarin believes them to be."

"Can we work with them?"

"I'd say yes, but if they pick up with their god again, then we'll have to kill them all quick."

"You could do that?" Asked Kevana, looking Jangor in the eyes.

"We'd have to, because you'd be doing the same. Let's just hope that it doesn't happen."

"We have two dead cities, I don't see how I could ever forget about that, thousands of people killed simply to burn us. I still don't understand why." He paused for a moment before going on. "I'd like to know how the other pairs got along, so you two go get some wood. Jangor and I will keep the hound off the food."

The two walked off towards the trees, leaving the leaders to mind the carcass and to talk about the day to come.

"I wish we had Jayanne with us." Said Mander,

"Why?"

"You should see the way she deals with trees, it's truly amazing."

"What do you mean?"

"We needed some wood for a funeral pyre, she turned up to help cut trees down. There wasn't enough dead fall for her liking, six strokes of her axe and a fully matured tree was down. Side branches as thick as a big man's thigh lopped off with a single stroke."

"Sounds impressive, who died?"

"A merchant, a woman, and her children, raped, tortured and murdered. They got a funeral fit for a king. All those that attacked them were killed, mainly by Jayanne, though she fed the last one to Wolf."

"Sounds like a nice little battle."

"Oh, it had its moments. She was real angry, Namdarin was dead. Again." Mander laughed and bent down to collect a large branch.

"Does he do that often?"

"Not so much, he doesn't really trust that he will return, if he did, then he'd be unstoppable."

"I can see that. Would be a useful skill for a warrior." Said Petrovana collecting another large branch.

"That's the truth."

"We should have enough wood now, let's get back to camp and start cooking." He turned and Mander followed, before they cleared the trees, they could hear steel on steel.

"Is that real, or someone playing?" Asked Mander.

"I heard no call to arms, and I'm sure we would have, so it's not real."

Mander nodded and they walked on, pausing at the edge of the trees just to be certain. Sure enough, it wasn't a real battle, just Jayanne and Brank sparring. Sparks flew from every touch of steel on steel, Jayanne's voice almost as deep as Branks as she spun and turned. Her axe flashing from side to side, intercepting every strike, and every feint, it became a silver blur as they all watched. Brank started to tire, long before Jayanne was even showing any signs of strain. Namdarin stepped in and the blue blade took the edge of the axe, the howl of tortured steel filled the air. The axe of Algoron and the sword of Xeron screamed together, as edge slid along edge. The sword spun into the attack, a blue stripe across everyone's eyes as it turned against the silver of the axe. Back and forth the pair danced, sparks flying at every touch, showering at every glancing blow. Alverana stood alongside Kevana and whispered slowly.

"Remember when I stopped a fencing match, because someone was using magic?" Kevana looked at him and nodded.

"These two are sucking energy in ten times as quickly as you were, at least ten times."

"Are you sure?"

"No. It could be a lot more, ask Worandana, he has to be feeling this." Kevana waved the cleric over.

"Are these two pulling energy into themselves?" He asked.

"Oh yes. Can't you feel it? Every hair on my body is standing up."

"Should we stop them?" Asked Kevana.

"This might be normal for them. We have no idea; we don't know them well enough yet." They both turned to watch the battle. Then Jangor shouted.

"Enough, we have battle to do today. Breakfast then on the road." The two combatants showed no intention of stopping.

"I said enough." Jangor's voice cut through their battle concentration and they stepped apart. Even before the echo of his words had finished the long journey to the nearby hills and back. The lightening of the eastern horizon was the precursor of dawn, that told them all that they may be entering their last day. Two heavy skillets were already on the fire cooking thick venison steaks, ready for the hungry people. Yesterday's heavy broth turned into gravy to go along with them. Wolf got many strokes from the people by way of gratitude for the breakfast he had brought. Mander declared the first batch of venison ready.

"It's not the best you're ever going to have had, but it's the best we can do. This meat is far too fresh, it won't sit still in the pan, it needs a few days to hang really." He apologised.

"It will be fine." Said Jangor. "Eat up, gentlemen and lady, we are carrying none of this with us. There is no saying when or if we will be eating again, so fill up." The pans were refilled, and more thick venison steaks were set to cooking. Mander's cursing of the meat became more vociferous, but he was eating with one hand and cooking with the other. Petrovana's smile grew as Mander's temper worsened.

"What are you laughing at fool?" Snapped Mander.

"You, of course." His smile didn't lessen. "Relax, there's nothing you can do about the meat, just burn it enough for people to eat. They may not be hungry by the time they are finished, but they know that Jangor is right, so they'll eat it all. There's going to be belly ache later, but we'll all have to deal with that."

"It still rankles, my cooking is usually much better than this."

"Perhaps in the near future, you'll be able to far surpass this somewhat substandard offering."

"Thank you so much for those kind words." Mander smiled and turned the heavy steaks over again.

Conversation died as the people ate. Not so much heartily, as determinedly. Even Wolf was eating ravenously, tearing chunks from the cooked meat, far and away his preference. The sun was just starting to clear the mountains when Jangor spoke.

"I think that's enough, anymore and I'll be sick." He looked around to confirm that the others were feeling pretty much the same.

"I agree," Said Kevana, "let's just hope we don't meet any foes for a couple of hours. We're all going to be too sluggish for a good fight."

"We'll manage." Muttered Namdarin letting loose a huge belch. Jayanne giggled and followed suit.

"Right." Called Jangor. "Let's get this camp stripped and get on the road, we have a few miles left to go." Alverana turned to Kevana, the pair were sitting next to Jangor.

"He's quite bossy, isn't he?"

"Yes, but we'll go along with him until the time is right."

"And then what?"

"We'll do exactly as he says, he's usually not too far off right." They both laughed and climbed to their feet. Walking to their tent side by side, to follow the instructions of the commander. Kern stood slowly and went over to the picket line to check on the horses, much would depend on their condition today. The grass around the pickets had been cropped close to the ground, the horses were still eating the last of it. The ones that were used to the presence of Kern calmed the ones that weren't. A quick inspection showed that none were lame, and all the shoes were in good condition. Arndrol and Kevana's stallion weren't happy to let Kern check them, but they did as was expected after some convincing. Once he had finished his inspections he walked over to the edge of the stream and collected two handfuls of thistles. These he gave to the big horses, he fed both at the same time, to help them become friends. It always amazed him, how the much horses loved the succulent, if prickly weeds.

"How are the horses?" Asked Kevana as Kern walked back to the camp.

"Good, they'll serve us well today." Kevana continued to the pickets and collected a packhorse. He took it back into the camp to be loaded with the tent and luggage that Alverana was just finishing rolling up. He turned to the camp in general.

"We may be going into battle today, there could be some serious resistance, so I want packhorses as heavy as possible. Riders must carry weapons only, no luggage at all. Is that clear?" Most of the riders were nodding as they understood that manoeuvrability could be important.

"Bossy, isn't he?" Asked Jangor of the camp in general. There was some laughter, especially from the ex-Zandaars. It didn't take long for the camp to be packed away and everyone nearly ready to ride. Kern took a water skin to the river to fill it, as he walked back to the fire to put it out Gregor called out.

"Stop, I'll put the fire out." He turned his staff towards the fire and focused his mind, in less than a heartbeat he had established the link between the heavy staff and the fire. He decided to try something a little different, feeling the heat and the energy of the fire. He reached into its very heart and pushed it. The fire blazed hotter than ever, he pulled the heat into the staff. He pushed the fire a little harder, it burned hotter and faster, a roaring column of flames reaching up to be quenched by the staff. In only a few moments the fire was completely out of fuel, and all its power had been extracted, stored in Gregor's staff. Gregor shivered and nodded to Jangor, that he could now proceed.

"What in all the hells did you just do?" Demanded Worandana as the column of riders started to form up.

"Well." Replied Gregor. "We've been using fire to store energy in the staff for a while, it is actually a good way to put out a fire. I thought that it was a bit of a waste to leave all that power behind unused."

"So how did you make it burn up so quickly?"

"I felt the resonance of the fire, the way it burns, it's difficult to put into words. I sort of enhanced the resonance, then pulled the power as it was released."

"I still don't understand exactly what you mean, but I hope that you will be able to teach me."

"I'll try, we need to find you some artefact to store your energy in."

"Well I do have this, er, wand. There is no word that fits it so well." Worandana pulled the wand from his belt and flourished it with a flick of the wrist.

"It's not very large." Interrupted Granger. "But it is solid steel, it was a sword, that has been bathed in blood and lives, it was formed into its current shape by the magic of Worandana. I can think of nothing that could be more powerful for you to use."

"You think this will serve?" Said Worandana

"We can only believe." Laughed Granger.

"Belief is everything." Said Gregor.

"That is what we've always been told." Said Worandana, the three formed up into the middle of the column. They followed the path the others took, so that they could continue their conversation. Up at the front of the column Jangor and Kevana rode side by side.

"You know a quiet way into the city?" Asked Jangor.

"Well there is a little used eastern gate, which has a small side door. The forest comes almost up to the wall on that side. It is said to be Zandaars forest, his sole hunting preserve. Not that he actually hunts, in fact I don't believe he has stepped outside the city walls for many generations."

"Is this gate likely to be guarded?"

"I have no idea; in recent times it hasn't been. There is no need it gets so little traffic, but the current occupants of the city are going to be newcomers, as a minor gate it should get at least some guards. If they don't know where to look, they may not see the side door. It's small, and never been used. At least not that anyone remembers. The city hasn't been attacked in hundreds of years. The last large force that attempted such a thing, they all died, they didn't even make it as far as the walls. Even under the cover of night they were visible to the clerics, they were trying to creep up to the walls, and perhaps scale them, or the gates. The attack is well documented, as far as Zandaar was concerned it was a complete victory. The enemy were routed, survivors were enslaved. None returned to their homes, so as far as their people were concerned, they simply vanished."

"So how did you beat them in the darkness?"

"The clerics could see their presence on the other plane. The commanders are different, brighter. I don't really understand this magic, but the leaders were all killed. Before they were within bowshot of the walls the captains were all dead. The next leaders died in the same way, and the next. Who's left?"

"Generals, then captains, then lieutenants. You're down to the backbone of any army, the non-commissioned. They stopped the advance, dug in, and waited for dawn."

"Exactly right, our archers took massive tolls on them as the daylight came up. Then our cavalry rode out and mopped up the remainder, there weren't that many. A few pockets of resistance had to be burned out by the clerics, but only a few."

"It would have been good to let some of the survivors go home, the word would have been spread, further attacks would have been discouraged."

"As it was no one has attacked since, at least not in any overt way. There are always spies trying to get inside and find some way to take the place from the inside. At the first hint of anything untoward the clerics check them out, and without fail they identify the spies. Their brains work differently and show up on the etheric plane. All it takes is a sensitive on the gate and they don't even get into the city."

"So." Jangor spoke slowly. "All it takes is one sensitive watching for us and they'll know we are coming. They know you, and I don't believe that Namdarin or Jayanne with their weapons will be able to hide."

"You are correct. There may be some who know Worandana or myself personally. The sword and the axe, they can't hide. Even more prominent Granger and Gorgana, sorry Gregor. That takes some getting used to, their staves, with all that energy stored, they are really bright. Like a beacon."

"So even if we approach from a never used gate, they'll see us coming?"

"Almost certainly. There is one fact in our favour."

"We could do with just one advantage." Jangor smiled.

"The clerics with the searching powers were mainly based in Zandaarkoon and Angorak, they're all dead. The ones left are second rate at best."

"Weren't the best sent out to teach, bring on new talent from outside?"

"No." Laughed Kevana. "The power is all in the city, and anyone powerful wanted to be there. The dangers were high, but the power that came with a seat on the council was worth the risk."

"What about the ones that only wanted to teach, there must have been some of them?"

"Perhaps, but they were looked on with such suspicion by the council that they tended to die young."

"What about him?" Asked Jangor nodding in the direction of Worandana.

"Special case, and I do mean special. His power is such that the councillors wanted him on their side, more than they wanted him dead. Now they are all dead, and he's walking around with that black power in his hands. These are exciting times to live in."

"Indeed." Jangor laughed. He felt the weight of breakfast lessening, so kicked the ribs of his horse, walking was too slow, he wanted this done.

"How long to the gate?" He asked Kevana once he had caught up.

"Maybe half a day, if we kick a little harder, we could be there before midday."

"I don't want to kill the horses; we may need some speed from them at some time."

"We can still push them a little, your man Kern said that they were in good condition."

"If we pick the pace up now, then we can rest them before midday." Said Jangor, then he turned in his saddle.

"Namdarin, any horses in range?" Namdarin place a hand on the wide neck of Arndrol, then paused for a moment.

"Nothing in range, and with the number of horses we have, range is quite long."

"Fine. Pick it up, I'd like to be at the city before midday." Jangor kicked his horses' ribs and pulled the pace up to a rolling canter. In quite a short time they came to a fork in the road, Kevana guided them to the eastern branch. The much lesser used of the two, it showed little use by the heavy carts that churned up the western road.

"That one goes to the north gate." Said Kevana, by way of explanation. "This one goes to the forest, and on to the eastern gate." Jangor nodded and kept the pace as fast as he could with some margin of safety. After an hour the forest came into view, the road vanished into the darkness beneath the trees. When the trees were still more than a mile away Jangor hauled on the reins, slowing down to a walk, the horses breathing soon settled down. In only moments he noticed a sudden cold and the breath of the horses blowing huge plumes of steam. He turned in his saddle.

"Namdarin, horses? Granger stop pulling so much heat out of the air, we need the horses to dry out before they get chilled."

"The cold isn't good for the people either, it slows them down." Added Kevana.

"Sorry," Said Granger, "we just wanted to be as charged up as we can be."

"No horses." Said Namdarin. "I can't reach far into that forest though; it seems to be cutting down the horses herd mind. I've never noticed it before."

"How far in can you reach?"

"Maybe a few hundred paces, or so. It's difficult to get distances from the horses." He laughed.

"Keep alert, I'd like some warning, even if it's only short." Namdarin nodded by way of an answer, the air around them became warmer, the dark opening into the forest came towards them. The road was clear of any signs of recent travel, no hoof prints or cart tracks obvious. This made Jangor feel a little better. He paused at the entrance and looked round at Namdarin.

"Still nothing."

"Keep watching, we have to go in whatever you can feel." He walked his horse forwards, the gloom under the trees became more oppressive as they neared it. Crossing out of the weak sunlight into the shadows of the trees they all felt the sudden chill. More than one of the horses shied from the path, only to be hauled back into line. Arndrol was not one of those, he snorted at the darkness, Kevana's horse kicked at the ground, hoping to find a stone to flash some sparks off. Slowly they trooped into the relative darkness. It didn't take long for their eyes to become accustomed. The darkness became less oppressive, but the silence was disconcerting.

"Shouldn't there be more noise?" Asked Stergin.

"I'd have thought so." Replied Petrovana.

"It just feels like everything has died."

"Or more likely, been killed. Worandana." He called. "Did Zandaar kill everything here as well?"

Worandana looked over his shoulder and spoke softly.

"I believe so, I can't feel anything alive here, only the plants are left."

"He did this to burn a city?" Asked Stergin.

"It appears so." Replied Worandana, shaking his head slowly from side to side.

"To burn a city?" Whispered Kirukana. Worandana looked at him for a moment before answering.

"I don't think so, looking at the area he has wiped out, he didn't want to just set a city afire, he wanted to burn it to the ground."

"You don't think the city was the target?"

"No, the more I think about it, the more certain I become. He was trying to kill us."

"Why?"

"I have no idea. Perhaps he will explain before he dies."

"You think we can actually kill him?"

"There has to be some reason he wants us dead."

"I'm not sure if that makes me happy or sad."

"I little of each, I think."

"Riders." Shouted Namdarin.

"How many?" Snapped Jangor and Kevana together.

"Five or six."

"How close?"

"You'll be able to hear them in a moment, they're riding hard."

"Take cover." Called Jangor. "We'll attack them as they ride past." Granger passed his reins to Gregor and slid from his saddle, then stood in the middle of the road as the others faded into the trees.

Kevana pulled his horse alongside Jangor.

"What is the old fool doing?"

"The riders will stop to question him, he's a doddering old man, no threat to anyone, they'll stop and talk. Then we kill them."

"We could disarm them and chase them off."

"They are enemies and they'll be behind us."

"You're right, they die." The thunder of approaching hooves stopped all conversation. Granger stooped over, holding his staff firmly in one hand, leaning heavily on it. The riders came around the bend in the road, and there was some shouting as they all reined in to a halt. The leaders horse only a hands breath from Grangers staff.

"Who are you? Old man." Shouted the leader.

"I'm going to the city." Grangers voice cracked and quavered, as if he had suddenly acquired twenty more years.

"There's nothing there anymore."

"I am going to the city." The grey eyes peered out from under shaggy brows.

"We're hunting demons, they could take any shape they want." Called a voice from the middle of the riders. The leader looked down on Granger.

"Are you a demon? Old man." He asked slowly drawing his sword. Granger stood up to his full height, smiled up at the leader.

"Maybe I am." There was a loud snap, and an arrow transfixed the leaders head, he twitched and slid to his right falling to the ground. The next snap put an arrow through the head of the last man in the line, he fell backward from his saddle. Brank's elven mount stormed in from one side, with Jayanne only half a length behind. Alverana came in from the other side. The black robed monks didn't get their swords cleared before the three were amongst them. Grangers staff pointed at the second in line and a huge concussive force lifted the man from his saddle and into the brush at the side of the road.

"I want one survivor." Yelled Kevana.

"I think you were a little slow there." Laughed Worandana.

"That one is only unconscious." Called Granger pointing his staff at the man he had knocked to the ground.

"Petrovana." Called Kevana. "Search them, I want their silver."

While Namdarin was recovering his arrows, Petrovana cut open the robes and emptied all their pockets. Silver and gold he collected, the silver he handed on to Kevana. He saved the survivor until last, by the time Petrovana had finished the rough search the man was starting to wake up. As he became conscious of his surroundings his eyes opened wide in terror. He cringed away as Petrovana yanked his belt pouch, another hefty quantity of gold there.

"Looks like we have been promoted to demons." Worandana said to Kevana. The man on the ground looked from one to the other.

"I wonder why?" Asked Kevana.

"Perhaps someone can tell us."

"Do you think he will?"

"I'm not sure about that, but I do know that if he tries to launch that message back to the city, he'll be dead before it leaves his head." Worandana turned to the supine form and raised his hands, darkness engulfed the elderly fingers and the air crackled with power.

"Whatever happens I am dead." Muttered the fallen monk.

"True." Said Kevana. "There are many ways to die." He looked pointedly at Granger, who was replenishing the power he had used. Dead men turned frosty as his staff sucked the heat from them. "That is a very peaceful way to die, where as Jayanne's axe will take your soul."

"Speak." Said Worandana, tersely. The hands lowered but the darkness remained.

The shaky voice of the monk firmed up as he spoke.

"The people of the city gave their lives so that Zandaar could burn the demons, their bodies are piled ten high all around the citadel. The demons are coming to kill our god, so they must be stopped."

"Zandaar didn't stop with the volunteers, though did he?"

"No, he emptied the city of life, and sent a fire the likes of which has never been seen before."

"He didn't burn us though, he burned Angorak."

"No, the demons were burning Angorak. He tried to save the city, but the demons had taken it over."

"We were simply riding through it at the time."

"You are demons, you will say anything to achieve your nefarious ends. Which of the old gods do you serve?"

Worandana looked away from the monk, the darkness fell from his hands. He looked around the people he had known for such a short time. He caught Namdarin's eyes for a moment then moved on. Jayanne, then Granger. Finally he looked into the eyes of his old friend Kevana. Gregor's heavy staff touched the back of the fallen man's head. "You're thinking a little loud." Whispered Gregor. Slowly Worandana looked down again.

"I begin to think that we serve the oldest of the gods."

"Gyara?" Asked Kern. Worandana's head snapped around to look into the big man's eyes.

"I'd forgotten about her, no. Second oldest."

"I carry the sword of Xeron." Said Namdarin.

"Not him." Said Worandana.

"I have the axe of Algoron." Said Jayanne.

"Not him." Laughed Worandana.

"Who then?" Said Granger, impatiently.

"Why, man of course." He smiled down at the monk. "We are demons in the service of man. Tell us of the city." He leaned forwards and placed a blackened hand against the monk's chest.

"Riders are coming in almost continuously, there were hundreds when we left to patrol the city walls. We found the east gate and decided to investigate this forest."

"You left a guard at the gate?"

"We left five men there."

"Fool. You should know better than to lie to me. You left two."

"There are more men coming in all the time, you cannot get inside, the gates are all guarded."

"Much as I hate to suggest we take up the black again, we could ride up to the main gate and be let in." Laughed Kevana.

"With a woman?" Sneered the monk. In a heartbeat he was surrounded by swords, and one axe.

"You be very careful how you treat the lady." Snapped Granger, the iron heel of his staff touched the man's chest and the monk screamed. The smell of burning flesh filled the air, smoke rising slowly from the man's chest as his shirt started to catch fire.

"Enough." Whispered Worandana. The staff retreated. "Tell us." The monk panted for a while to control the effect of the pain. Slowly he spoke, this time only the truth.

"There are hundreds gathered at the northern gate, and many at the west gate. The dockyards are guarded too. The east gate will have guard presence very soon, it was thought to be of no importance, after all you are coming from Angorak. There are many powerful clerics, and respected soldiers amongst those on the walls. You cannot get through all that, you will die before you reach the citadel."

"We survived the burning of Angorak. We will succeed." Said Worandana. The monk looked up into Worandana's eyes and smiled. In that very instant Worandana pushed his black hand into the man's chest and crushed his heart. Dark blood spurted briefly from the massive wound, pooling in the cloth of the shirt and running sluggishly down the sides of the chest.

"What?" Demanded Kevana.

"He was trying to send a message."

"Did he get through?" Worandana just looked at his friend and shook the blood from his hand.

"Of course not, he was still trying to push through my barrier when he died."

"How much of what he said was the truth?"

"Most of it, though he was exaggerating about some things, there aren't that many defenders in the city as yet. More are coming, but many are still a day or two out."

"Could we storm the main gate, and kill most of them?"

"Perhaps."

"Our losses would be too high; we need to get as many people to the centre as possible." Said Jangor.

"That is also true." Kevana thought for a long moment before going on. "We need to get all the way in before we are discovered, once in the centre chamber we have only three doors to defend."

"The best place to make a stand." Laughed Worandana. "God in front of us and three doors behind us. This is not going to be fun."

"If we can get inside the perimeter before they know we are there, then they'll all be looking over the wall as we are moving around inside." Said Jangor.

"You've done this sort of thing before?" Asked Kevana.

"We've had the occasional covert mission behind enemy lines."

"Successful?"

"Generally, there are always risks with those sorts of missions and always some losses."

"Fine." Kevana paused and looked at the men before him. "We ride through this forest, anyone in our way dies. We ride to the gate, and get inside without the sentries getting word of us to the main force. We'll hide up until nightfall then make our way to the citadel. Kill a god and run for home."

"I really hate to mention this." Said Petrovana with a smile. "This is our home, and I don't think we'll be exactly welcome here."

"Then we find a new place to call home. We could always go and help with the rebuilding of Angorak."

"You think people there will welcome us?"

"They'll be needing all the help they can get, and it wasn't us that burned their home to the ground."

Petrovana shrugged.

"Now we have a plan." Called Kevana. "Let's ride." He turned and leapt up into his saddle, the others following quickly. Jangor was the first to catch him up, as he pulled in alongside Kevana's cantering horse, he looked across.

"If you're hoping to keep them moving before they have time to think about things, then you are far too slow."

"They'll be concentrating on the ride and not thinking too much about what is to come."

"You already know what is coming?"

"As do you." Alverana pulled in alongside Kevana, and Namdarin beside Jangor. Jangor turned to Namdarin.

"I thought that Brank and that horse of his would catch up first?"

"He saw me take off, and he stayed with Jayanne."

"He's a good man."

"Better than we deserve, he needs to survive this."

"We'll keep as many alive as we can, but it's not going to be all."

"I understand that, but I don't have to like it."

"The curse of leadership."

"That's for sure." Said Kevana, looking over his shoulder as the rest of the riders were catching up, he was wondering how many, if any would live through this. Like Jangor he didn't think for a single moment that turning away and running would mean that they all would survive.

They had been riding for the best part of an hour when the path started to widen out, the daylight became stronger. The spaces between the trees became greater. Kevana slowed the pace to a walk just before the wall came into view between the trees. The grey stone wall was about three men high, with castellations along the top. Obviously, a walkway along the top, the gate house had a short tower each side. On the walkway above the gate they could see two men watching. Kevana stopped, the rest followed suit.

"They can't see us from there, we're in the dark here." He said. "We need to kill them before they can give the alarm."

"I can get one, but I'm not sure I can get the other before he can move." Said Namdarin.

"That's one hell of a shot." Said Kevana.

"Good bow."

"I can barely see them." Said Granger. "Sorry." He turned to Gregor.

"There's a wall, and a gate." Said Gregor squinting.

"We spend too much time in dark libraries, with flickering candles. Our eyes aren't up to this sort of thing. We need to be at least fifty paces closer."

"Namdarin," said Kevana, "can you get both?"

"I can have two arrows in the air, the second will be halfway there when the first hits. So long as target two doesn't move too much, I'll get some of him."

"If we give them something to see, they'll stand still for a while." Said Jangor.

"What do you mean?" Asked Kevana.

"They are not going to report that the demons have arrived unless they're sure. So long as Arndrol stays out of sight, they'll not be sure, they give us some time to walk closer. While they're leaning over the parapet, Namdarin can shoot them both." Namdarin slid from his saddle and strung the bow, he stood with his back against a tree. One arrow at the string, and another in the ground, green feathers by his right hip.

"I'm ready." He said. "Go and give them something to watch, don't rush. As soon as I have two shots, I will take them. When they fall, ride hard. You need to get inside and secure that gate. I will be along presently." He settled back against the tree and waited. The rest formed up into a column and walked their horses slowly into the view of the gate guards. It took a while for the guards to notice them, they were obviously busy chatting about something really important. As is the manner of bored guards everywhere. Suddenly they both stood upright and leaned on the edge of the parapet.

Namdarin raised the bow but didn't pull it. Words and looks were exchanged between the guards, then they settled to watch the slowly approaching riders. Namdarin sighted on the furthest target, only really a head in view. He pulled the bowstring to his lips, sighted along the arrow, made allowance for drop and wind, released. He snatched the feathers from beside his hip, nocked the arrow, pulled, released. Namdarin turned, grabbed the saddle horn and pulled himself up. As his backside hit the saddle the first arrow arrived at its target. It buried itself straight into the guard's skull, the second guard looked for a long moment at his dead friend, then he too fell from sight. Namdarin laid his heels to the big grey and set off after the others who were already at a full gallop. Kevana and Jangor crossed the open space to the gate side by side. Once they were up against the wall, they turned left to look for the side door. Just around the tower abutment they found it, a heavy oaken door in the stone wall. It had no visible means of opening it from this side, but that is how it was intended. Worandana dropped from his horse and ran up to the gate, his hands black with power. He felt the surface of the gate and through the heavy wood to the locking mechanism inside. A simple iron beam lifted and fell to the ground on the inside. Creaking loudly the door opened outwards. Grangers staff flashed forwards ready to burn anyone in sight, no targets presented themselves. Granger and Gregor rushed through the narrow door and took up positions in the chamber just inside. The large double door to this chamber was closed but not locked, they opened both doors and light flooded into the room. The street outside was almost empty, there were more than a few corpses about and one living person. The man was groaning and trying to crawl along the street. The chamber started to fill up with riders, Worandana waving them through as fast as they could go. As Kirukana passed he spoke.

"Go help the magicians." Kirukana fell from his horse and ran to the doorway. He saw the man on the ground and ran to him. He turned the man over onto his back and placed a heavy hand on his chest.

"Be still." He whispered.

"Who are you people?" Stammered the injured man.

"Who do you think we are?"

"Zandaar help me." The man whispered. Kirukana placed darkened hands against the sides of the man's head.

"I don't think he's going to be coming to your aid."

Slowly the riders immerged onto the street, last was Namdarin. Shortly behind him came Worandana, leading his horse and Kirukana's.

"Who is he?" Called Worandana.

"I've no idea," replied Kirukana, "I thought you might want to question him, after all we weren't expecting a survivor." He turned to Namdarin. "How did you miss?"

"I said it would be difficult to get both. He moved in time. Though only just looking at the score along his ribs."

"So you knocked him off the parapet."

"Sorry I couldn't claim that one, he just jumped out of the way, and got too close to the edge, but I did get some of him." Namdarin smiled down on the injured man.

"What do you know that could be of use to us?" Demanded Kirukana shaking the man's head slowly from side to side.

"Why should I tell you, you're going to kill me anyway?"

"True, but there are many ways to die. Perhaps given enough time you could even find a way through the barrier I have placed around your mind. Until you do, you'll not be able to call for help."

"All I know is that there are more of us arriving every hour, and they come to kill the demons that burned Angorak."

"Well, your people aren't terribly well organised as yet," said Namdarin, "and completely inaccurate. We are simply men, and we intend to punish a god who burned his own city, this one here, and Angorak as well. His time is over, we will explain that too him."

"You will all die."

"Maybe, but your god is leaving this plane. Then where will your people be?"

"You cannot kill him, so we will have no problems, things will continue exactly as they are now."

"All your people will be happy with the fact that he killed thousands, just to burn some of his own, and failed."

"Everyone already knows that it was you and the demons that burned Angorak."

"And what about Zandaarkoon? Did we kill all these people here?"

"No, they gave their lives freely. To help Zandaar burn the demons."

Kevana pushed through to face the fallen man.

"There is so much death in this city, did the babes in arms give their lives freely fool?"

"Their love for Zandaar would have been so great that they could do nothing else."

Kevana turned to Namdarin.

"You know that plan to rid the world of bad people, I suggest we start with anyone wearing black."

"Much as I'd like to do that, in fact that is the oath I swore. We can't really go killing someone for being stupid, for most of them they don't understand that there is a different way."

"This sort of stupid just keeps on breeding though."

"We'll just have to see how they turn out once Zandaar is dead."

"You cannot kill our god." Snarled the fallen man.

"You may be right." Namdarin looked down at the man, his face sad. "It could be that the belief of people like you could sustain him, but if we drain him enough to drain all his supporters, much like he has already done here. Once all his supporters are dead, then he'll not be far behind them."

"You can't do that; how many will die?"

"Your people burned my house." Snapped Namdarin. "My wife. My child. My people and all their children as well. Innocents all. You and yours burned them with black fire. You believe there are any limits on the revenge I shall wreak? Fool." The sword leapt into his hand, and with a single blurred slash Kirukana staggered away from the monk, the head still firmly held in his hands. The short fountain of blood splashed across Kirukana's shoes; the man had already lost quite a lot from the shattered remnants of a lower leg.

"You could have given me a little warning." Said Kirukana dancing backwards away from the blood flow.

"I don't know." Said Kevana, looking at the cleric's hands. "You seem to have something of a heads up." He laughed as Kirukana finally dropped the dead monks head.

"Let's get this mess cleaned up." Called Jangor, "I want this place to look like they deserted. Hide the bodies. Clear that blood trail. Take the bars off the gate but leave the gate as shut as someone could manage from the outside. We need somewhere to hide out until it goes dark." He turned to Worandana expectantly.

"I know a nearby tavern that should do nicely. Follow me." The old man mounted his horse and led them slowly down a small alleyway. In the narrow confines of the dark alley they came across the corpse of an old man, he was slumped as if he had died mid-step. Wolf sniffed at the man then jumped back, glaring and growling.

"What's wrong Wolf?" Asked Jayanne, a little concerned that something scared her friend.

"He knows that it is a dead person, but it smells wrong." Said Brank.

"Why is that?"

"Because when a person dies there is much inside that carries on living, it starts the rotting processes, these bodies are completely dead, everything has been killed, so it smells like nothing, as far as Wolf is concerned it smells like the man is still alive, but he's obviously dead. Wolf thinks his nose is lying to him."

"That sort of makes some sense, and I'm glad. There's an awful lot of corpses in this town that are going to cause a serious stink, but not for a while yet. I suppose."

"Worandana," called Jangor softly, "how close to the centre is this tavern?"

"The one I have in mind is quite large, and still a fair way from the citadel. If there are any patrols protecting the central temple, we should be outside their perimeters."

"That very much depends on how many there are, enough men and the patrols could reach all the way to the wall."

"Not likely, they can't even man all the gates properly. There will be groups of riders, and lookouts at fixed locations."

"Can we keep to the back alleys, to get to this tavern?" Asked Jangor.

"Yes, that is why I came this way and chose the place. Given the time of day when Zandaar killed everyone, the place should have been fairly empty as well. That'll make the clean-up easier."

"How much further?"

"A few minutes, and only two major roads to cross."

"Good. Kern, front I want your observation skills there." As Kern set off to the front of the column Kevana twitched his head and Alverana set off to the rear. Jangor looked at Kevana and smiled, before he spoke again. "Namdarin horses?"

"Damn, yes. Off to the right, on the street ahead. Not close, but definitely not far off."

Jangor looked around for a moment or two.

"Everyone fall back round the bend in this alley." As the people started to turn round. "Not you two," he pointed at Kevana and Worandana, "pretty coloured cloaks, go and make them chase you, I want them all on your tail. When you come around that left-hand bend keep as close to the right wall as you can. That way they'll be amongst us before they know it. Namdarin how many?"

"Small herd, maybe twenty."

"Good." Jangor paused as they rode around the corner. "Jayanne, Brank, Kern, if there are foot soldiers with them be ready to ride them down. We are behind enemy lines, no survivors." As the alley straightened out Jangor spotted a couple of hefty posts on opposite walls. They may be hitching posts, but they looked strong enough for his purposes.

"Mander." He called, pointing. "Trip line, knee height for the horses, don't get our men though." Mander nodded and ran a loop round the post on the right-hand wall, dropped the rope over the second post and tied it to his saddle horn. Once the friendly riders were passed, he'd pull the line tight, and hopefully take down any following horses. If a horse is running hard, it doesn't take much to disturb its stride and make it fall. They gathered along the left-hand wall, waiting. Swords drawn, fidgeting like excited children. Namdarin dropped his reins, and reached forwards. Arndrol glanced backwards then spat the bit into Namdarin's waiting hand. Namdarin stuffed the bit inside his jacket and patted the horse on the neck. Namdarin guided the big horse hard in against the wall, the whitewashed bricks almost the same colour as the horse. The sound of approaching hoof beats made the tension in the narrow alley almost palpable. Flashing around the corner came two horses close together, one rider in red, the other in yellow. Twenty feet behind them came a group of riders in black. Mander's horse stepped forwards lifting the trip line, which worked very well. The two riders to reach it first went straight over the front of their falling horses, the riders behind colliding with them and falling the same. Five riders managed to haul their horses to a halt before they crashed into the writhing mass, their relief lasted only a second. Arndrol turned away from the wall and spun into the attack. Using his sheer mass he knocked two riders to the ground and stamped on both. The screaming of injured horses was joined by the howls of the fallen riders.

"Jangor." Yelled Kevana over the racket. "They have foot as escort." Jangor nodded and yelled.

"Jayanne. Foot soldiers coming this way, round them up, take Wolf." Jayanne nodded and turned away from the melee, there wasn't much work left to do there anyway. She called Wolf and he followed her. Brank and Kern turned with Jayanne, as did Namdarin. The four were riding abreast as they turned into the straight section of the alleyway, towards them came a squad of twelve. Armed with swords and short spears, not really long enough to be classed as pikes. Without a hesitation Namdarin and Jayanne plunged into the attack, Brank and Kern were a second behind, but moving none the less. The long blue blade of the sword made short work of spears hastily pointed, but not braced. Wielders fell with heads and arms missing, Namdarin rode through the falling bodies. Jayanne slashed her way through two more, with exactly the same results. The cobbles of the alley were getting slick with spilled blood and guts. From the back of the squad Kern noticed one soldier throw down his weapons and shield and turn to run. He glanced around, found Wolf.

"Wolf." He yelled. "Runner, kill him." Wolf turned and ran through the soldiers, jinking left and right, too fast for them to even think about attacking him. Once in the open he turned on the speed, his spine flexing to the limit as his gallop reached out. He hit the man in the back without slowing and as the pair rolled into the open street, he gripped the man's throat in his powerful jaws. A wrench of the strong neck, and the man was dead. Wolf stood over the body growling softly. In the confines of the alley, the fight was almost over, the last three of the foot soldiers threw down their weapons. Still the axe caved in ribcages and the sword took heads, a few heartbeats later silence fell. The stamping of horses and the panting of people the only noises.

"Brank." Said Kern. "Get that corpse out of the street." Brank nodded and walked his horse slowly into the open, checking carefully for observers.

"Good boy Wolf." He said, dropping from his saddle beside the animal. Wolf stopped growling and sat on the ground, his long tongue lolling out of his mouth. Brank tied a rope to one ankle of the fallen soldier, climbed back up onto his horse and unceremoniously dragged him back into the alley.

The clean up was already in progress, the unlocked door of a house was open, and the bodies were being dragged inside.

"We can't do much about the blood, but at least it won't be visible from the street." Said Kern. They returned to the others to find that a similar clean up was almost finished. The only things left were seven live horses and four dead.

"We don't have anywhere to hide the horses, but they're not visible from the main streets, so we'll just have to hope that no-one patrols this alley." Said Jangor.

"I think many of the troops coming in will be strangers to the city, it'll be a few days before they are aware of all the alleyways." Said Worandana.

"We can only hope." He looked around. "Injuries?" Only shaking heads and shrugs as answers. "Damn this is going too well. Something has to go wrong, and soon." He turned to Worandana. "How far to this hidey hole of yours?"

"We cross that road ahead, then a few hundred yards, cross another larger road, and we arrive at the back gate of the hotel."

"Let's try not to be seen again. You lead on. Kern take the rear; the rest be ready to ride down anyone that sees us. Move out."

Worandana led the way, with Kevana alongside, Wolf sniffing at the walls and gateposts as they passed. Worandana checked the road thoroughly before he finally crossed, pushing to a trot across the open space, and into the dimness of the alley. The one was short and straight, before long they arrived at an even bigger open space, this one a tree lined boulevard. Littered with even more corpses, both human and animal. Every tree trunk was surrounded by small feathered bodies, Wolf had a sniff and stepped back again. Again Worandana rushed across the road and into the alley that led to the hotel. The high wooden gates were open when they arrived, so they walked their horses inside.

"Close and lock the gate." Said Kevana quietly, as he slowly dismounted. There were a few dead horses in the stables, many of the stalls were empty. Mander started to ride his horse into a stall, when Kevana spoke.

"No. The horses go inside, they make enough noise to attract attention, we'll drag the dead out here and put the horses inside. Curtains drawn, doors locked, should keep the casual observers out. Get to it."

"That's a great idea, once it gets properly dark, we can sneak up on the citadel and maybe leave the horses here." Said Jangor.

"Personally, I'd rather have the manoeuvrability, we can abandon the horses at the gates to the citadel. Either way we have a few hours before dark, so let's get some rest, once we've cleared this place out." Kevana turned to the door into the hotel in time to see Brank walking slowly out, a corpse on each shoulder. He carried them to a stall and casually dropped them on top of the horse that died there. Mander was behind him, only one. A slow procession of men carrying the dead out of the building, once the first stall was full, they moved on to the second. Jayanne came out of the door with tears streaming down her face, a basket in her hands. She gently placed the basket on top of the pile in the first stall, she dragged the arm of a dead woman across the basket. She stepped back, and slowly turned to face Worandana. She stared into his eyes, her own brilliant green rimmed with red and tears. There was a slap of wood on calloused skin.

"Babies." She whispered. "Babies. I'm going to gut that bastard." Worandana paused for a moment, not breaking eye contact. His arms blackened to the shoulder.

"I'm going to rip his head off, so you better be quick." His voice grated in the constriction of his throat. She held his eyes for a short time then turned away with a snap of the head that threw her long hair up in a red swirl. She almost collided with Namdarin as he came out of the door, his arms full, two young children. Each little more than five years old, one girl and one boy, judging by their clothing. Jayanne snarled at the sight and stepped away so he could carry them to the pile. Once he had laid the two on the pile, he turned to Jayanne. He opened his arms and she rushed to him, he held her and rocked her slowly. Kern came out with an old woman in his arms. Her skirt had ridden high up her spindly legs, one shoe was missing, showing a calloused foot with a large bunion. Her grey hair almost tied in a flowered scarf that was falling off.

"She was the last." Said Kern. "The place is clear, the doors to the street are bolted. The curtains drawn, the casual observer passing in the street will see nothing."

"Good." Said Kevana. "No fires, smoke would be a giveaway. I'm sure there is beer and cold food to be had."

"We have a few hours to rest." Said Jangor. "I suggest we make our move just before midnight."

"When the guards have gotten bored." Laughed Kevana.

"Guards for ourselves?" Asked Jangor.

"Clerics, we need clerics to be sure that they're still searching outside the city for us. If they start looking for us inside, then we have to attack before they find us."

"I don't think we are actually going to need an organised rota; I'm not going to be sleeping. Resting perhaps, but I don't see sleep coming, unless it rides in on a sea of wine, and that's not happening." Jangor shook his head, before going on. "To be honest I'm scared shitless. Before dawn we are going to be facing down a god, with the intention of killing him. Aren't you frightened?"

"I'm shaking like a leaf in a storm, but we can't let the men see that, now can we."

"Truth." Jangor held out his hand, as Kevana grasped it he whispered. "Do you want to live forever?"

"Hell no." Whispered Kevana by way of reply.

The two men followed the last inside and closed the doors, they had a few hours to wait before they could continue their quest.

CHAPTER SIXTY-NINE

The large common room of the hotel had been turned into an impromptu stable. The horses all gathered at one end, most of the tables were piled up in one corner and the chairs grouped around the few tables left.

"Mander." Said Jangor. "Go find beer, wine and food. We have some waiting to do."

When Mander returned from the kitchen he held a huge tray, on which were bottles of wine and jugs of beer. A large ham, a couple of loaves, a pat of butter. He slid the tray onto one of the tables, causing the taller bottles to totter but not actually fall. He returned to the kitchen and came back with plates and cutlery.

"Glasses will be behind the bar; you can get your own." He said, a little irritated that no one had moved to get them. He grabbed himself a large glass and filled it from one of the jugs, then took a seat near where the fire would have been lit.

"Remember people." Said Jangor. "We are going to war; I want everybody sober enough to fight." He took a bottle of wine and peeled the wax seal from it, before pulling the plug and sucking a large mouthful straight from the bottles now opened neck.

"And yourself?" Laughed Kevana.

"Oh, he'll be fine." Replied Stergin. "Just point him at the enemy and let him go." A huge smile split his face.

"Surprisingly." Said Petrovana laughing. "Kevana is much the same. Is it a skill that comes with command?"

"No." Laughed Kevana. "It's a skill necessary before you get command." He snatched a bottle of wine from the tray. "I'm going to get some rest; someone wake me when it gets dark." He stared at Alverana, then walked slowly from the room. Alverana followed only moments later.

"They'll not get much in the way of rest." Said Petrovana, once he was sure they were out of earshot.

"What is it with those two?" Asked Strenoana.

"They're only just coming to terms with the feelings they have for each other and they actually feel death closing in for the first time in their lives. It can be a difficult path they walk." Said Worandana.

"I've fought beside a few such, er, couples." Said Jangor, with a wry smile. "Their connection goes beyond the brotherhood of soldiers, but as a pair, their power is undeniable. You wait until you see them in battle. Tonight should be interesting."

Namdarin grabbed two mugs from above the bar and filled them both with beer. He held his hand out to Jayanne. Together they walked to the stairway leading to the upper floors.

"Try and get some rest." Laughed Jangor, knowing that it was unlikely.

"Will they be ready for battle later?" Asked Worandana.

"Somehow," said Jangor, "I don't believe they have even been tested by the battles we have been in, again tonight should be interesting. Anyone else fancy a little privacy?" There were some glances, but no takers. Jangor chuckled gently to himself. Worandana sat alongside Jangor and reached out for the bottle of wine. Jangor passed the bottle, Worandana took a hearty swig.

"Not bad, but I've had many better."

"Me too." Replied Jangor, taking the bottle back. He stood to draw his sword, and pulled the stone from his belt, the long strokes of the stone clearing the nicks and sharpening the edge.

"Have you ever been tempted by the charms of young men?" Asked Worandana.

"No, well, not to any serious degree, I make do with the occasional camp follower, female of course." He smiled. "You?"

"In my younger days it was difficult, but now, not so much. Since women have been, not exactly banned, but definitely frowned upon. More of the brotherhood have taken to the arms of male lovers. As always some take these things to extremes."

"Some would call your own abstinence an extreme."

"Agreed, but I don't tend to worry about what people think."

"You've always had your special status and your power to fall back on."

"Yes. Not to start with, but I learned fast. Very fast. When I started in the brotherhood, I saw that it was important to be powerful, so I acquired magical skills as quickly as I could. After that I just had to stay out of trouble as much as I could."

"That can't have been easy."

"Sometimes it was very difficult. There are people that just need a slap as soon as they open their mouths, sadly many of these were people with actual power."

"I know the sort you mean, they are everywhere, or so it seems to me." Jangor was finally satisfied with the edge on his sword, he returned the sword to his scabbard, and started on his belt knife.

Namdarin and Jayanne found an empty room, one that

looked like it hadn't had someone die in it recently. As soon as the door was closed, she rushed into his arms, and pressed herself against him.

"How could anyone kill all those children?" She whispered, her voice shaking, tears sliding slowly down her cheeks.

"I don't believe that Zandaar cares for anything other than his continuing existence, unlike us. We are prepared to die to stop him."

"Is there any chance that we will survive this?"

"There's always a chance."

"There is also a chance that we will end all life here and release Gyara."

"True. I suggest we don't worry about it. We'll survive or we won't. Either way Zandaar has to die." He reached down and lifted her chin, then he kissed her, long and hard. There was an urgency about their actions, a desperate need, that had to be filled. They fell to the bed, he pulled her shirt from her trousers and lifted it over her head, her heavy breasts bounced into view and his mouth moved straight to a nipple, his tongue circled it as his lips sealed around it and he started to suckle. She moaned and pulled his shirt from his pants, and her hands went to his belt, she snatched the buckle open and heaved at his buttons.

There was a desperation in her movements, and a need in his. In very little time they writhed naked on the bed together, wrapped in each other's arms, and entwined by the legs, her thighs gripped his hips, his hands her waist. Their mouths fastened with a lust that surprised them both. Tongues duelling for dominance in their shared orifice. The heat around them rose, higher and higher. He rolled on top of her, her legs spread wide and her heels against his buttocks. With a gasp he broke free and pushed his body upwards away from hers.

"Are you sure about this? I never felt you so lustful"

"Yes. I am certain, you will never hurt me. I want to feel this at least one more time. Now get on with it." Her voice rasped in her throat. Her green eyes flashed with passion. Tenderly he reached down and kissed her gently on the lips, as his head retreated her hand snatched him and pulled him back down to her hungry mouth. Her heels moved further down his thighs and pulled downwards so strongly that her body rose up to meet his. She rubbed her mound against him and slowly lowered herself again. Her heels dropped to just behind his knees, he broke the kiss and smiled down at her, slowly his body dropped as he entered her. Jayanne's smile told him everything he needed to know, gradually he moved within her. She rocked her hips in small circles, enjoying both the friction and pressure of his manhood. Their movements progressively increased in both speed and ferocity, until the bed beneath them was bouncing with the energy of their lovemaking. He was trying hard to focus on anything other than the sensations of his body, then he looked into her eyes. The green flashed and became unfocused, her breathing stopped. Her motion ceased. With a groan her whole body tensed up, fierce waves of force travelled within that tension. She shuddered, then Namdarin followed only a heartbeat behind. Bliss filled their minds as they shared the joy born of love. As their heat dissipated, he turned and lay beside her. She rolled away from him and then pushed back against him. She reached back and pulled his arm across her chest.

"That was nice." She whispered.

"Not something you would have thought of not so long ago?"

"No, certainly no. This is not how I understood love to be. Even more I want to kill that bastard again. But now I have you." She tensed briefly. "I do have you, don't I?"

"As long as you want, or as long as we live, whatever you will." His almost silent reply.

"I want this to go on, and on, I want more."

"There are always children to consider."

"You'd want to start another family?"

"In a world without Zandaar, it is certainly an option. Though I am more than a little old to be starting again."

"You don't feel old to me, you feel warm and hard again."

"That's your ass pressed against me, I'm fairly sure that could raise the dead." He chuckled.

"It's only an ass."

"Oh, it is so much more." He sighed. "We need to rest, snatch a little sleep. We can have no future until we have rid this world of Zandaar."

"Agreed." She whispered and wriggled back against him.

"Quit it woman, or we'll get no rest at all." He laughed softly and squeezed her breast gently.

"Says he." She pushed his hand down to the firmness of her belly. They settled down to sleep, at least for an hour or two.

Alverana opened the door of a room on the upper floor, a quick look inside showed a well-made bed. The sunlight through the windows was bright and showed specks of floating dust. The sun was still well above the houses on the opposite side of the street. One pool of light lit the bed, the other window cast light against a wall and a small cupboard. There was a little awkwardness about the two, neither sure exactly how to proceed.

"Show me the wound that Worandana healed." Said Kevana. Slowly Alverana removed his jacket and shirt, exposing his chest. Kevana looked carefully at the scar left on Alverana's hairy chest, it was very white but equally well healed.

"Damn, that looks like it is years old." He mumbled, reaching out and touching the scar. Alverana's pectoral muscles twitched at the warm touch, Kevana smiled. He held Alverana's chest and ran his fingers slowly around the man's nipple. Alverana's breath caught in his throat as his nipple grew hard under the stroking digits. Alverana stepped closer and looked deeply into Kevana's eyes, Kevana's hand didn't move from his friend's chest. He noticed the increasing heart rate, that tried but failed to match his own. Their lips met in a kiss as soft as a butterfly's wing. They both closed their eyes and focused on the feelings. The soft kiss changed slowly into something more urgent and harder. Tongues reached and touched. Probed and poked. Swirled and twisted. Alverana's hand moved to Kevana's jacket and pushed it back off his shoulders, it fell to the floor with a loud thump that made them both jump.

"I'm not used to this daylight." Said Kevana quietly.

"Nor am I, but we don't have much in the way of time, let's get out of these clothes and get comfortable." Alverana smiled.

"Comfortable? Not exactly the words I would have used."

"Why? It feels wrong, but right at the same time. I know what you mean. We've spent most of our adult lives making fun of men who share their love, calling them names, and laughing at them. But here we are." Alverana took the rest of his clothes off, Kevana was far slower. He watched as Alverana sat down on the bed and removed his boots, socks, and then trousers. He stood in his underwear with his fists on hips and smiled at Kevana. Who was still unlacing his boots, the long laces wrapped round and around. Finally the boots were undone, and almost dropped from Kevana's feet. Trousers and socks followed in short order. Alverana stepped forwards and kissed Kevana, he ran his hands down his friends back all the way to his buttocks. The kiss became more intense, Kevana's strong arms enfolded his friend pulling them harder together. Kevana's large hands slid up Alverana's back, and then down again. Pausing briefly on each prominent muscle, down, into his underwear to grip his hard buttocks. Alverana groaned into his mouth and pushed harder against him. Each could feel the others manhood pressed against them, Kevana's breath came in ragged pants. He gripped the large muscles and used his wrists to push the cloth downwards, but he failed, there was something holding them up.

"You'll have to try harder than that." Laughed Alverana breaking the kiss. "Would you like a hand?"

Kevana nodded but said nothing. Alverana smiled and reached between them and pushed Kevana's underpants down. Even at the limit of his fingertips the pants refused to drop, they were hung up on something on the inside. Alverana gave Kevana a brief peck on the lips then sank gradually to his knees. Pausing only to kiss a nipple on his way past. He stopped once his knees reached the wooden floor, he looked up into Kevana's eyes and smiled with his thumbs hooked in Kevana's waistband. Smoothly he pulled the clothing downwards, leaving Kevana naked before him. Alverana stood slowly and stroked Kevana's manhood briefly.

"Your turn." Whispered Alverana, Kevana paused. "Is there a problem?" Asked Alverana looking a little worried.

"I don't know. This feels a little strange, well, more than a little strange. I'm used to the dark confines of a tent, not the broad light of day. I want to take you in my arms and hold you forever. When I watched that sword shatter into your chest I almost died. It was the worst moment of my life. I really couldn't bear to lose you."

"I thought that I was dead until that damned blue sword appeared as if out of nowhere. He saved my life. Then Worandana did the same with his magic. I can't believe that was only yesterday."

"Damn, things are certainly happening fast."

"Not right now they aren't." Grinned Alverana. He dropped his own pants, to join Kevana in nakedness. Then wrapped both arms around his friend, pulling them together in the most intimate of hugs. Kevana slowly relaxed. Alverana rested his chin on Kevana's shoulder, their stubbly cheeks touching. The rasping as they moved together sounded loud in Alverana's ears. "Don't worry my friend. This will all be over soon." He whispered.

"But will we survive?" Asked Kevana

"Do you want to live forever?"

Kevana's answer was considerably slower than usual.

"Suddenly I'm not so sure. It feels so good to be here in your arms, that I want this to continue."

"As do I. We have a god to kill first."

"Can't we just run away, let Namdarin and Jayanne deal with him?"

"We both know you couldn't do that. I believe that we all need to be there, we all have a part to play, even you, and even me."

"I'm still frightened of facing him."

"We all are. We are warriors and we will face him, and if we can we will destroy him."

"That does not fill me with any confidence." Kevana leaned a little more against his friend, feeling the course hairs on their bellies rub against each other. Alverana turned his head slightly and placed a soft kiss just below Kevana's ear, he felt the shudder run through his friends' whole body. Alverana smiled, he pulled away and spun Kevana around, so that Kevana was looking out of the window. Into the bright if descending sun. Alverana pressed up against his back, his manhood resting between Kevana's cheeks. He rested his chin on Kevana's right shoulder and kissed the neck softly. He stroked his hands slowly down Kevana's hairy chest. Down into the coarse mat of hair around his penis, where one hand encircled the thick column.

"How does this feel?" Whispered Alverana.

"It feels nice." Was the gentle reply. Kevana paused for a moment, then whispered hoarsely. "Freeze."

"What's wrong?" Mumbled Alverana.

"Patrol in the street." Kevana nodded forwards. Alverana looked into the street. The low angled sunlight lit them both quite brightly, the flare off the window, and the fact that the only movement was Alverana's slowly sliding right hand prevented the patrol from seeing them. They stood watching, hoping that any sounds from inside would not reach the patrol. Perhaps the sound of the iron shod horses drowned the voices from the ground floor, or maybe the sound of the hooves stopped the conversations. Either way the patrol continued its slow progress, as they passed by Kevana started to breathe a little easier, all of the patrol were looking forwards. None turned, or really looked to the side. They had all become accustomed to the quietness of the city, not unlike that of a tomb. As the two stood in the sunlight, Kevana reached behind himself with his left hand and started to stroke Alverana in a mimic of that man's right hand. Gradually the movements sped up, increasing the intensity of the grips. Until, inevitably both reach their orgasms, Kevana first by only a breath. They stood leaning on each other as their heartbeats slowed.

"That was good." Muttered Alverana, he turned Kevana toward himself and kissed him firmly on the lips. Kevana nodded and smiled as the kiss broke. He glanced at the bed, Alverana nodded. The two lay side by side, facing each other. Their bodies touching along their entire length.

"I want this to continue." Whispered Kevana.

"So do I."

"We have to survive this folly?"

"Folly? I don't think so, if we don't succeed there can be no future for us, Zandaar has gone too far, he's always been a little crazy, but this latest madness. This has to be the end for him."

"It does have a hint of desperation about it."

"More than a hint I'd say."

"He burned two cities to kill us, if that's not desperate I don't know what is."

"That in itself gives me a certain amount of confidence. He's terrified. A god is terrified of us. You know what comes next?"

"I don't understand?" Frowned Kevana.

"He's tried to kill us and failed. Next he'll tempt us, turn us away with bribes. He'll offer to make our dreams come true, whatever it is we most desire."

"I never thought that I would ever think this, let alone say it out loud. What I want is you."

"I feel the same. But what if he offered us eternal life and eternal youth?"

"That would indeed be a dream come true for most people. We were his followers; we know this promise is just another lie. We are soldiers, we know this promise is just another trap. We are men, we grow old and die, if we can do that together that will be enough." Alverana took a deep breath, smiled a big smile, then reached forwards the inch needed to kiss his lover. The kiss burned on and on, hotter and hotter until Alverana broke away panting. Once his breathing was back under control, he looked into Kevana's eyes and whispered.

"Zandaar, we have survived your threats, and your attacks. We are ready for your temptations and your blandishments. When we stand in your throne room you will know true fear." He kissed Kevana again, then smiled and relaxed. They both smiled into each other's eyes as sleep took them.

Jangor moved slowly around the darkened room, carrying the only candle. Waking the sleeping and checking those more conscious.

"What time is it?" Asked Kern, as Jangor passed him by.

"Getting towards midnight, we need a snack and a drink then

off to war. Are you ready?"

"As ready as I'll ever be. I'll check the horses."

"They only have a short way to go."

"I think they'll be fine, but I'll let you know."

Jangor moved on. He shook Worandana by the shoulder, and then snapped a hand over his mouth as he shouted.

"Ssssshh." Whispered Jangor.

"Sorry," said Worandana, "crazy dreams, I'm fine now." Jangor nodded moving on to the stairs. Up he went to the middle floor. Along the corridor, opening doors as he went. At one door he saw Namdarin and Jayanne, they were already dressing, he nodded but said nothing. He pulled the door to and moved on. The next time he found people they were Kevana and Alverana, both naked, spooned together on the bed.

"Gentlemen." He said softly. No response. "Gentlemen." He repeated, a little louder. Four eyes opened and stared at him. "It is time gentlemen. We will be on the final mile very soon."

"We will be with you." Said Kevana.

"Good." Said Jangor, retreating and closing the door on his way.

"Let's get moving." Said Kevana.

"I'm comfy where I am." Said Alverana, wriggling his backside against Kevana to emphasise the point.

"Move your ass." Laughed Kevana, slapping the mentioned item with an open hand. The two rolled to their feet and started dressing. They followed Jayanne and Namdarin down to the ground floor, to find the rest getting ready to travel. Kevana surveyed the room briefly before speaking.

"We are going to battle today, this is not going to be easy, it is almost certain that we will not all survive. We go to face a god, and any of his followers who have arrived here. I want us to be at our best. Alverana run through a quick warm up cycle." The former monks formed up in the confined space of the common room. The others all formed up with them. Alverana called the commands quietly, not with his usual vigour. The flexing and twisting. Jumping and lifting. Soon they were all well on the way to working up a good sweat. Some of the older members of the group were actually strained by this work out, as they hadn't actually performed any exercise in quite a few years. Worandana and Granger were beginning to struggle when Alverana finally declared exercise class over.

"Light meal, and a little beer, I don't want heavy bellies slowing us down." Said Kevana, Jangor smiled.

"Something to say?" Asked Kevana.

"Only what you have already said, this is going to be an interesting collaboration up until the time we disagree." Laughed Jangor.

"I'm fairly sure we will work something out." Smiled Kevana.

"Lady and gentlemen." Said Jangor. "We go to battle; we go to die. Let us not do this with any reservations in our hearts, if there are unresolved problems amongst us let's get them out in the open here and now. Please speak now." Silence fell. It lasted for a long minute, and then another. Kevana looked pointedly around the room. Finally Kirukana coughed and spoke.

"Gentlemen, I have no words to say how sorry I am for my behaviour, I accused so many of heinous crimes, with little reason. I blindly followed the dictates of the council, as if they were god and not men. And now I find myself to be one of you, heretic and proud of the people I stand with. Gorgana, sorry Gregor." Kirukana bowed, Gregor smiled. "I am sorry that my actions made you the first to leave us. Would you do me the honour of accepting me as brother?"

"Kirukana there is nothing to forgive, and you will always be my brother." Said Gregor. "If it were not for you, and that fight in the village. We would not be here now; I would not have had a wonderful night with Carin." Mander laughed. Gregor looked hard at him and cocked his head to one side in question.

"You had Carin too." Laughed Mander. "She was a special one." His smile spread across his face as the memories rushed through his mind.

"She was special." Said Gregor. "Without her I would not have found the secret of the stone, nor made the switch with Crathen. All these events would not have occurred. The old

Kirukana started these, and the new Kirukana could never have done that. You are a different person now; you have changed more than any of us on this road. I will always call you brother. When this is finished, I will find a lover to share the rest of my life, I might even run back to see if Carin has found a husband yet."

"What skill can you bring to a backwoods village like that?" Laughed Kirukana.

"If nothing else I can watch over the lightning stone, with the best will in the world Anya can't have that many years left."

"I think that would be a good place for you to settle." Said Kirukana stepping forwards to hug his friend.

"I might even tag along with that one." Said Granger. "It would be a nice place to live out one's life."

"Kevana." Said Namdarin. "I thought your people to be all bad, murderers and worse. You have proved to me that though there are some bad people everywhere, not all those wearing black are the same. You have shown yourself to be an honourable man, and your friends here are the same. Not as black as I had painted you."

"Namdarin." Replied Kevana. "I saw you simply as a thief, but you are much more, and with some good cause. Though you have killed my brothers, I cannot think badly of you; for I am no longer a brother to most of them. My god has tried to kill me, and I want to know why. Together we will demand answers from him. If we survive this, I will take you to the man that called down the black fire on your house, and together we will gut the bastard." Kevana reached forward his right hand. Namdarin took it and shook. Silence fell again, but not for long. Crathen coughed then spoke.

"Lady Jayanne, you must know that I love you beyond all things. Even life itself. I would free you from your bondage to Namdarin and take you to a new life with me. Tell me you will come with me?" Jayanne looked at him for a long moment, a cold glare in her green eyes.

"I will never love you." She said carefully. "Namdarin is my lord, he is the one I will live my life with if we survive this adventure. You are of no importance to me at all, you may have a part to play in what is to come, I know not what it is. I hope that you live through this and find love elsewhere."

"Lady, I can love no other. You are my moon and my stars."

"Sadly you are not mine. I am certain that there is someone out there in this world for you. But she is not me."

"Lady I love you."

"I cannot love you. Namdarin is my lord, and he will always be so. Live through this and life will find a way for you to love another."

"Lady I love you." Crathen whispered as he fell to his knees. For a short time nothing happened, then there was the characteristic slap of wood on skin. The men around Crathen started to move away from him. He found himself in an empty space facing Jayanne, the axe firmly gripped in her right hand.

"Crathen, you step awful close to the precipice, your very soul is in peril here."

"Lady. I have no wish to anger you, but my soul already belongs to you. How can you take what is already yours?"

"I won't take it. I have no interest in your soul. But the axe will eat it, then pass some of it on to me. You will feed me for the battle that is to come. I would much rather that you fight alongside us, to free the world from the tyranny of Zandaar. What say you Crathen?"

"Why should I not fight alongside you and hope that Namdarin dies?"

"You should not wish for that. If he dies, then everyone dies."

"If she dies, then everyone dies." Interrupted Namdarin, the sword jumped into his hand. The mind stone flashed hot and green. Everyone in the room froze under the baleful green light. The mindstone filled everyone with that intense moment of stillness. Then Namdarin lowered the sword, covering the hot jewel with one hand. Once release from the geas of the stone, all eyes turned to Crathen.

"Lady. I will fight with you and hope to die at your side."

"When a man wishes to die, then he usually finds a way to make it happen."

"If it happens then it happens."

"I'd rather it didn't."

"I will love you until my last breath, if that is taking a sword at your back then my life has not been wasted."

"You live for now." She turned away and silence fell again.

Kevana let the silence run on for a while before finally speaking.

"Anyone with anything else to mention?"

"I have a question more than anything." Said Worandana.

"Ask."

"Granger, I don't know how much power we will still have when our god is dead. Will you help us to learn your ways?"

"I thought that I was a charlatan?" Laughed Granger.

"That title was only given to you to stop the young and foolish of our order from dying. You have to admit it worked quite well."

"It did, I haven't been attacked in my home for a few years now. Well, not until recently." He smiled, looking pointedly at Kevana. Kevana bowed by way of apology.

"Will you help us? We have been magicians all our lives, we are not ready to become pig herders."

"I will help you in any way that I can, if we survive." Granger reached a hand to Worandana. The two shook hands.

"Thank you." Whispered Worandana.

"Anyone else?" Asked Kevana.

"Only me." Said Petrovana.

"Go on."

"How do I get out of this chicken shit outfit?" Laughed Petrovana.

"At this time there is only one way out." Said Kevana, he paused. "Do you want to live forever?"

"Hell no." Was the answer from all around, though Kevana didn't actually answer his own question.

"Kern." Called Jangor. "Check the street. Everyone else be ready to ride. We'll take the horses as far as the citadel, then leave them to Arndrol's tender care."

"Pack animals stay here. Riders carry weapons only." Said Kevana.

"And canteens." Added Jangor, making a show of filling his with wine. Kevana chuckled as Kern returned from the door.

"The street is clear and well lit, we have the major moon from one side, and the small red one from the other."

"Those are signs of ill omen." Muttered Petrovana. "When the main and the blood face each other, nothing good can happen."

"What more bad omens do you need?" Asked Fabrana. "Our god set fire to a city to kill us, and you are worried about lights in the sky." They moved out into the street, Namdarin took Arndrol's bridle and bit. Placing them in a saddle bag, Arndrol shook his mane and curved his neck proudly. He knew he was going to war. Kevana's black stallion was kicking sparks from the flagstones of the street, until Kevana cuffed him gently on the head. As Kern mounted his horse, he looked back at the hotel they had stayed in. Hanging high on the front wall was a large sign board, swinging slowly in the light breeze. The image picked out by the silvery light of the major moon was a huge white bird. A crow by its shape, but white as snow. Kern captured Brank's eyes, then Alverana's, then turned back to the sign. The two took in the sign for a moment then looked back at Kern.

"Petrovana is worried about moons in the sky." Said Brank. "And we slept in the house of the white crow."

"When she comes as the white crow, then death rides with her." Said Alverana.

"Could she bring death for Zandaar?" Muttered Kern.

"Only a madman would bring the white crow." Said Alverana.

"Could we bring the black crow, would she help?" Asked Kern.

"She's not called the trickster for nothing." Said Alverana.

"We'll keep this one quiet for a while yet," said Brank, "I'd rather not be in her presence any time soon."

"Agreed." Said Kern. "We'll see how things go. It's going to get crazy enough very soon."

Alverana nodded his agreement as the horses started to move off along the street. There was nothing they could do about the sound of the hooves, but there were patrols moving. So they could be mistaken for one of those, at least until they came into view.

"Kevana." Said Jangor. "Can we approach the citadel from a back alley?"

"No alleys in this part of the city, large houses with large walled gardens, we have only roads to walk on."

"How many more turns before the citadel is visible?"

"After the next turn we should be able to see one of the side gates." As Kevana spoke a bank of cloud covered the silvery moon, now the only light was the dim red of the blood moon. The two looked at each other and smiled. At least something is going right.

"How far into the building to the throne room?" Asked Jangor

"Outer gate, inner gate, outer door, inner door, short corridor, door to the centre chamber."

"We're likely to be fighting the whole way, how far in can the horses get?"

"They'll not fit through the outer door. We can take the gates and then go afoot."

"That's good, the four heavy horses can take those. Then the rest of us can rush the doors. What are the chances of the gates being locked?"

"Who can tell? If I was in charge the gates would be locked. I've no idea who is in charge. Either way he's going to pay with his life."

"Sounds like a plan to me." Smiled Jangor.

"Four heavy horses?"

"Yes, Arndrol, Brank, Jayanne, and you."

"I've not been in the forefront for a fair while, you know."

"I'm sure you'll remember what to do, once you hit that gate."

"I'll try."

"The trick is not to get between Arndrol and the gate, he's just going to hit it and run through. He's not known for his subtlety."

"I'll follow him in and take out anything that is left."

Jangor looked back and waved Namdarin, Jayanne and Brank to the front.

"You four are going to be hitting the gate, hit it hard, there's another one just inside, hit that hard as well. We'll be behind to mop up. Then it is foot slogging. Everything clear?"

"Sort of." Said Namdarin., he turned to Kevana. "What sort of hinges on these gates?"

"Two on each, heavy pins and collars on the gates themselves."

"Visible from the outside?"

"Yes, why?"

Namdarin smiled and turn in his saddle. He waved Granger and Gregor to the front. The two magicians pulled alongside.

"We are going to be hitting a couple of gates, I need you to weaken them just before we hit. Burn the top hinges on each, that way they'll fold better when we charge them." The two nodded and moved to the outside of the front line.

"Well that takes care of the locked gates." Laughed Kevana.

"And there should be plenty of corpses for you to recharge from." Said Jangor.

"At what point do we start our attack?" Asked Kevana.

"Let's not actually charge until they are sure we mean them harm. We may even get close enough, that the gates aren't even closed." Muttered Jangor.

"So basically we wander up to the gates like we own the place and take them as much by surprise as we can." Laughed Kevana. "Sounds like just my sort of thing."

They turned the corner and ahead could see the gate, it wasn't quite shut, but it was close. They were only a hundred yards from the gate, with the dim red moon behind them, the light hid the colours of their capes, though Arndrol was quite clear as a light-coloured horse, his flanks glistening red under the moons baleful light.

"Is there a guard house at this gate?" Asked Namdarin, barely above the jingling of their equipment.

"I don't remember," replied Kevana, "but I'm not seeing too many men at the gate, they've seen us, but aren't paying too much attention. They think we are just another patrol passing by."

"If there are regular patrols in the depths of the night, then someone is nervous." Namdarin smiled.

"The guards are starting to pay attention. Be ready." Whispered Kevana. He watched the guards closely, one tried to casually shut the gate. Kevana heeled his horse and accelerated hard for the gate.

"Magicians." Called Namdarin as Arndrol took off after Kevana's black stallion. Two staffs levelled and blue bolts jumped to the gates, bathing the upper hinges in hot fire. The upper hinges both failed, and the gates started to topple inwards, the guard at the gate tried to hold the gate up, but its weight was far too great for him. One gate collapsed slowly on top of the guard, the other fell to the cobbles with an enormous clattering sound. Namdarin rode over the gate further crushing the man caught under it, Kevana turned to the left and attacked the guards coming towards him. They were slow and sleepy, but not for long, very soon they were dead. Namdarin turned right and hit the larger group of guards, with Jayanne and Brank at his side, the blue sword appeared in his hand and the green gem flashed into brilliance. The guards stopped and stumbled, as the sword and the axe cut them down, leaving the stragglers to Brank Namdarin turned to the inner gate, this one was locked. The gates though made of heavy iron were more decorative than anything, pretty scrolls of fancy ironwork with many holes. Namdarin used these holes to attack the guards, and once they had fallen back from the gate, he used Arndrol's weight to push the gate open. Even the heavy bar on the inside couldn't restrain the strength of the large horse. Maybe they should have used an iron beam, the wooden one shattered under the force exerted by the heavy horse. The gate crashed open inwards. Guards came rushing out of the room to the right, partially armoured and all armed. The ceiling was high enough that Namdarin could still swing massive overhand strokes, even though mounted. Jayanne killed the guards almost as fast as Namdarin and every kill fed her energy. The corridor was too narrow for more than two horses. Side by side they forced their way towards the inside of the building. Once they were passed the entrance to the inner guard house, there were no more guards, at least none that made it through the doorway. While Mander watched the inner gate, Andel went into the guardroom, with Wolf at his heels. Just to ensure that there were no survivors to cause any further problems. It was Wolf that found the man hiding in an equipment cupboard. Wolf scratched at the door, growling. Andel opened the door and plunged his sword through the man, then Wolf ripped his throat out as he fell from the cupboard. Once the pair had cleared the room, they joined the rest in the corridor. Their attack had been so fast that there had been no alarms yet. Arndrol trampled the last of the guards as they arrived at the door.

"There may be guards on the other side." Said Kevana.

"How many?" Asked Namdarin.

"Does it really matter?"

"I suppose not."

"It's too tight in there for horses." Said Worandana, as he slid from his saddle. Slowly the others did the same, Namdarin thanked Arndrol for his help and told him to take the rest of the horses outside and watch over them. Slowly the horses passed the riders and went out into the streets. Namdarin turned to the door, and pushed hard against it, it rocked inwards a little, but stopped solidly with a very small gap between the two doors.

"Heavy bar on the inside." He said, then turned to Jayanne. "Yours." He smiled. Jayanne stood not quite facing the door and raised the heavy axe. It flashed downwards and carved a huge chunk from the edge of one door, more of the central bar became visible, before she could make a second strike a sword came probing through the small opening, searching for a target. Namdarin stepped forwards and the huge sword came slashing down, the smaller sword stuck in the door shattered as the blue blade passed through it. Namdarin stepped back and the axe slashed down again, this time it bit into the bar on the other side of the door.

"You're wasting time." Called Worandana pushing through the crowd from the back. As he got to the door an arrow appeared in the opening. Worandana's blackened hand, covered the arrow and it vanished with a sudden scream from the other side. Worandana braced his hands against the door and black power filled his arms and covered the face of the door. He turned to the other magicians and whispered. "Be ready." Granger and Gregor came to the front, and Kirukana stood behind Worandana and braced his darkened hands against the old man's back. The two pushing together against the door. Power started to crackle in the staves of the others. The door started to groan alarmingly, and soon the whole inner surface was covered in the dark power. With a sudden crack the bar against the other side failed, the doors flew open and slammed against the walls, only one of them caught a black robed monk, he died in a heartbeat, crushed beyond recognition. The guard force protecting the door fell back from the opening, knowing they had failed. Two staves flash blue power, the archers in the guard fell burned black to match their clothes. Small fires grew on their bodies as they fell. Namdarin and Jayanne pushed through into the corridor and attacked the guards. The battle was short and brutal. The shiny wooden floor of the corridor soon became slippery with blood and cluttered with broken body parts. Wolf surged through the crowd, taking the last man in the thigh as he tried to run away. Jayanne stepped up and finished him. The axe feeding strongly as he died.

The wide corridor was curved, but the ceiling was too low for mounted men, Namdarin looked both ways, then turned to Kevana.

"Which way to the centre?"

"This corridor runs around the central chamber, there are three doors. Once we are inside, we will be facing whatever troops are in there and the god. I hear men coming." He pointed, the group reformed, Namdarin and Jayanne to the fore as normal, the approaching troops stopped as soon as they were within sight. There were swords in evidence, but it was clear these were not to be the primary weapons of this meeting. Three balls of fire leapt across the intervening space, Jayanne took one on the face of the axe, Namdarin slashed another with the sword, and Worandana reached between them to catch the third on his empty hand. He eased between Namdarin and Jayanne, Kirukana came with him. Granger and Gregor push through along the walls. The four stood shoulder to shoulder waiting for further attacks to come.

"Kill the demons" Came a yell from the back.

"We are men." Yelled Worandana. "You have one chance to survive this, and that is to run now. We mean you no harm but Zandaar burned two cities, and for that if no other reason he deserves to die. You stand in our way and you join him. Choose now, choose well." He spread his arms, and called the darkness to them, black to the shoulder he stood. There was a moment of hesitation amongst the monks, but it didn't last long. A surge of both lightning and fire came roaring down the corridor. Gregor and Granger simply absorbed the energy, as they had at Angorak, Worandana and Kirukana darkened and pulled the power into themselves. The barrage of silver weapons died out. Worandana smiled, then his face vanished into the darkness. Then a torrent of dark power rushed along the corridor, driving the monks to the ground and smashing them against the walls. Jayanne and Namdarin push through and set about finishing them off. A couple of shaky monks put up some resistance to the heavy weapons, but they didn't last long. Their swords shattered and they died. Namdarin turned to Kevana.

"Which way?" He asked.

"This way." He turned and led the way back towards the door they had used to enter the circular corridor. "They know we are here; they'll be coming quick." He hurried past the entrance that they had used and followed the corridor round. They came to another large double door, wooden and heavy. Iron studs and plates reinforced the face of it. "There will be guards inside, we have to get in quickly and secure all three doors." He waved Worandana to the fore. "Can you open this quickly?" Worandana stepped up and leaned against the door, his arms spread wide, he paused for a heartbeat.

"Not alone." He nodded to Kirukana, the second cleric stepped up, each took a firm hold of one door. Slowly they both moved their hands around the door, each settled on a heavy iron stud, and on the opening edge.

"Can you feel the beam." Whispered Worandana. Kirukana nodded.

"It's old and weak, the stud is where the hook is on the inside, break the beam and push the door." Worandana looked into his friend's eyes, and together they counted. Down from five. As they reached zero Worandana whispered. "Push." A surge of dark power was held back by the heavy oaken door, but only for the briefest of moments. The beam on the inside shattered and both doors flew open. Smashing against the stops, crushing men along the way. They fell from their hinges and clattered to the ground amongst the wreckage of seats and men. Kevana Jangor and Brank rushed through into the throne room. Three guards had been crushed by the door, five more were peppered with splinters from the shattered beam, two of those were already dying, the others slashed by Jangor and Kevana as they passed.

"I want those doors secured." Yelled Jangor, as he sprinted across the open centre of the room, towards the opposite door. Granger and Gregor swept the soldiers from the inside of the centre door with raging blue fire. Before Jangor could cross the room, the bar was lifted from the hooks and the doors opened. A flash of silver fire and the hinges would never work again. The commander of the guard force knew the importance of open doors, even if it cost him his life to achieve it. He was successful on both counts, Jangor's sword took him in the back as he destroyed the second hinge. The doors staggered like drunken men and leaned at an extreme angle; they would never move again. Kevana and Jangor made short work of the last of the guards. Kevana sent Apostana, Briana and Crathen to the large centre door, it didn't require much in the way of guarding, but they all needed to know if there was any danger of it being breached. Kevana Alverana Petrovana Fabrana and Strenoana took up positions at the second door. Jangor returned to the first door, taking Brank, Kern, Andel Mander and Stergin with him. Across from the main door was a dais, raised upon five shallow steps, it ran the length of that side of the room, the seats in the place all faced the dais. On the wall above the dais was the round emblem of Zandaar, circles of flames and lightning bolts, on a blue background. No sign of the god to be seen.

"Where is he?" Yelled Namdarin, his sword sweeping huge circles as he scans the room for Zandaar. The only answer was a booming on the central door, it shuddered and shook, but it was not going to open.

"Have no fear, he can't reject a summons from this place, much as he wants to. He will have to come." Worandana and Kirukana stood facing the dais, speaking softly. The emblem appeared to turn, slowly at first then faster. They heard the thump of Fabrana's bow, speaking of the arrival of brothers at the open doors. The crash of steel on steel was only a moment or two later. Granger reached out with the blue fire to quench a lightning bolt in the air. He turned to Gregor and yelled.

"Their silver has power. Go steal it." Gregor nodded and ran to the second door, as a black robe came into view he reached out with the power of his staff and drained the energy of the silver the man was carrying, a silver flame came flashing forwards from the monks flying fist. A harmless, if pretty, piece of metal fell to the floor, causing only a tinkling sound. The look on the monk's face was a picture as Fabrana's arrow took him in the heart. Gregor watched as the next monk came into view. He had a different thought this time, rather than stealing the energy that the man was carrying, he just reached into the man's pockets and released it all at once. The monk was consumed in a ball of flame and electricity, he had no time to even scream before he was dead. Gregor heard a similar sound from the other doorway as Granger came up with the same idea. By the time that two had exploded within sight of the doors, the attacking monks were dropping silver to the floor before they came into view. It became a sword battle, something the black robes were not really equipped for. They were the young and the untried, coming up against battle hardened veterans. They died, bloody and quickly. Wolf kept running from one doorway to the other, whenever he lunged through the defensive line more of the attackers died. They were distracted by the huge canine, then the swords or the teeth caught them. Namdarin stood in the centre of the room, watching the emblem on the wall as it spun faster and faster; his sword hanging loosely from this hand. The electric colours on the wall spun into grey then suddenly the deepest black, a tunnel of darkest night opened in the wall and a tall figure approached shining and silver.

"How dare you summon me?" The deep voice echoed in everyone's minds, like rocks grinding against each other.

"Zandaar, we summoned you because your time is over." Yelled Worandana, against the silent roaring that filled all their minds.

"I decide when my time is over, and it is not yet." Laughed the silver figure, brilliant light leaked and scattered from the joints of his armour. If armour it was. Namdarin climbed the steps of the dais, slowly as if moving against a great river. Jayanne climbed from the other side, each approached Zandaar.

"Why did you burn my house?" Screamed Namdarin.

"Your house was nothing." Snorted Zandaar turning back to face the two monks. Namdarin's blue sword flashed in an arc to intercept Zandaar's head, the sword in his left hand swept Namdarin's blade away. Jayanne's axe slashed at his legs. Only to be blocked in a similar fashion. Sparks flew from the clashing edges, and power flowed into Namdarin and Jayanne, but nothing like as much as passed into their weapons.

"Why did you burn Angorak?" Demanded Worandana. His darkened hands raised, tendrils of night fell from his fingers and crept across the floor towards Zandaars silvered feet. Worandana twitched as the power started to flow from Zandaar into him and the darkness. Kirukana did the same, Namdarin and Jayanne continued the attacks, with exactly the same effect. The silver swords blocked everything but still passed on lots of energy, making the people and their weapons even stronger.

"I had to kill a man, but you all survived. Where is he, the traitor?"

"You don't even know which one he is?" Laughed Worandana, his darkness thickening and pushing slowly up Zandaars legs. Soon the god's legs were dark to the knees, not that he was moving. Despite the attacks of Namdarin and Jayanne, his feet never moved, the swords taking the attacks. "Gregor, we need your help." Shouted Worandana. Gregor turned from his position by the second door and levelled his staff at the silver figure. A bar of light so hot that the blue became white splashed across the silver armour and vanished.

"No." Yelled Worandana. "Drain him." The bar of light changed, not so hot now, but still great quantities of energy flowing out of the god figure. Another bar of light leapt from the chest of the god to the wooden staff of Granger. This time Zandaars left foot stepped backwards, his balance disturbed by the energy losses. Namdarin's sword slashed into the shoulder joint of the gods armour. For a moment brilliant white light flooded the chamber, casting the darkest of shadows on the walls. The god's sword swept the blue one away from the joint, and the light went out, the shadows remained. They slowly slid down the walls and crossed the floor in small black rivers, they passed around the people and collected at the feet of the god, to be consumed by the blackness around his feet. Kirukana looked at Worandana, his brows raised in question. Worandana shrugged and went back to the task of draining the gods power. The god took another step backwards, and Jayanne's axe flashed through his armour at the belly, not deep but enough to let more of the light out. The shadows formed on the walls, until the armour healed itself, the shadows flowed into the blackness again. Granger's staff started to crackle with energy.

Namdarin slashed at Zandaar, only to have his attack blocked by the sword, which spun around the blue blade and brushed it aside before plunging straight into Namdarin's heart. The sword of Xeron fell to the ground, followed in a moment by Namdarin himself. Jayanne saw him fall. Her scream of despair filled the room, drowning all sound of battle and making the god turn to face her, he turned both swords against her. Jayanne's howl brought Wolf to her side, he had no idea what to do to help her, so he snapped at the swords as they passed him by. Jayanne spun the axe into the attack, faster and faster it flew until it was a silver shield between her and the gods twin swords. Zandaar lunged at Jayanne, his right sword arm came through the shield on the lunge, but failed to return, the arm was completely severed above the elbow. The god howled and hot light spewed from the stump for a long moment, as it was healing Jayanne danced around to the other side of the god and placed the axe on Namdarin's chest. While the axe was feeding him, she kicked his sword to within reach of his hand. Every instant she dreaded the touch of the gods remaining sword, but he was a little busy healing the stump, if not replacing the arm and hand. Namdarin screamed and sat upright, the sword returned to his hand and he flicked it as quick as a striking snake, to block the attacked aimed at Jayanne exposed back. She rolled to the side and got to her feet, instantly followed by Namdarin, now they had both weapons against the god single sword.

"I'm full." Yelled Granger, he shut down the drain on Zandaar, who stepped forwards as the pressure was released. Again the sword and the axe slashed him, bright light and creeping shadows. Granger turned his mind to the monks attacking the doorways, with a rush of blue fire he swept them from the circular corridor. Leaving blackened corpses behind. His staff drained to almost empty, he turned to Zandaar and started to pull power from him again. Another disturbance and two more openings in the gods armour. More light, more shadows, but still the god was no more damaged. Namdarin was weaving complicated attack patterns against the god's sword, but not actually making contact unless the god was distracted. Jayanne was being less subtle, her attacks were designed to take down trees in a single strike. Every contact fed her energy, stealing it from the sword that was blocking her at almost every point, the silver sword seemed to be everywhere all at once. Every stroke she sent was more powerful than the last, loaded with stolen energy. The god's sword was still blocking but it was shuddering with every touch. Namdarin's blue sword was a curved pattern in the air, spinning to stab and slash, to chop and lunge. Moving so fast now that people couldn't even see it, the flash of contact sent showers of sparks into the air around them. Gregor took his attack away from Zandaar and following Grangers example he cleared out the corridor and the pathways to the outside, a rolling wave of blue fire sweeping everyone away. To be instantly replaced by more monks running in behind the fire, there were hundreds running in to protect their god. While Gregor was clearing the passageways Zandaar staggered forwards, Namdarin slashed deep into the god's chest, then pulled away as the hot light came flooding out. Jayanne changed her tactics, she hacked at the god's wrist, and hit. The wrist was almost severed, again the flood of light drove her back while the injury healed itself. Gregor's staff started to take power from Zandaar and he staggered again, Jayanne failed to score on this occasion but Namdarin punched a hole in the armour right through the chest. Light and creeping shadows as usual. Zandaar looked around his inner sanctum and picked Gregor out of his attackers, his eyes opened wide. A blast of heavy red light reached out to Gregor, as it passed by Worandana the old cleric freed one hand from the black web attacking Zandaar. He reached up and enveloped the red fire in darkness, the black absorbed the red. Dark shadows rippled through the confluence of the forces, until the red was quenched.

"Gregor." Yelled Worandana over the noise of the battle. "Direct the energy you steal into the darkness. It can take anything you can send it." Gregor nodded, his mind focused on the staff and he formed a second channel for the power, this time down into the darkness around Zandaars feet. Moments later Granger followed suit. Again red light came from Zandaars eyes, this time targeted at Kirukana. The young cleric followed Worandana's example and engulfed the red in darkness until it died. Granger shifted his target and focused on Zandaars head, sucking energy out of it as fast as his staff could transfer it. Red light came from the centre of Zandaars belly, heading for Namdarin this time, stopped by Worandana this time. It the battle at the dais was deadlocked, the battles by the doors were anything but, the dead Zandaars were creating problems for the attackers, they were trip hazards that had to be avoided if their swordplay was going to be successful.

Kevana and Alverana were standing shoulder to shoulder in the doorway, Fabrana and Strenoana long out of arrows were lunging through the line occasionally as targets presented. A tap on the knee from the two bowmen was usually enough of a distraction for the monk to lose his life to the foe standing in front of him. Petrovana was hauling seats into the doorway to make it narrower and therefore easier to defend. Alverana had a small injury on his upper right arm, but this wasn't causing him any real problems. Alverana's current opponent reached his sword to his right to slash at Alverana's head, in the moment before he struck Kevana took his sword arm with a lunge to the elbow, while the monk screamed Alverana took him in the throat, blood fountained from the man's mouth as he deliberately threw himself forwards. Petrovana pushed the dying man backwards into his friends, his slowly vanished from view behind the next in line. Each man that came to the front was fresh, vital, and ready. The men guarding the door had no respite, no time to recover, they moved from one opponent to the next. Kevana caught Petrovana's eye, and as his next opponent died, Kevana stepped back and Petrovana took his place. Kevana was panting heavily, sucking air into his labouring lungs and filling his blood with oxygen. He looked at the battle on the dais, he could see it was going nowhere.

"They need some help with our damned god." He called over the noise of battle.

"I have an idea, but I need to be off this line." Shouted Alverana plunging his sword into a man's heart and recovering in an instant. The dead man was yanked backwards and a new one replaced him, before the man had prepared himself for the battle Alverana had taken his throat and he was dying. Alverana stepped backwards and Kevana filled the space.

"What is your plan?" He called without looking back.

"You really don't want to know. Do you trust me?"

"You know I do. Get on with it, and hurry. We're all going to die here."

"Remember." Said Alverana. "We are the fire and the fist."

"Fire and fist." Whispered Kevana. Alverana smiled as he dropped back.

"Fire and fist." Called Kevana. Alverana grabbed Fabrana and Strenoana. "Keep the bastards off his back," he snarled. "if he dies, I'll kill you all." As he turned away, he heard Kevana scream.

"Fire and fist." A horizontal slash took two heads. Followed by a lunge that pierced two chests. A cross body cut took an arm and a leg. Kevana took a step forward.

"Fire and fist." Another step into the corridor, standing on the dead at his feet, he added to that pile with every stroke. Alverana ran around the outside of the room, at the centre door, he grabbed Apostana.

"You go to that door and support Kevana, he may need it. You two come with me."

"What about this door?" Asked Briana.

"Don't worry, Kevana's going to be on the other side of that door very soon. With me." He turned and carried on to the other door. Alverana came up behind Jangor.

"I need Brank and Kern, now." He called.

"No."

"Without them we all die."

First Kern stepped off the line and Andel took his place. Despite the fact that he had taken a cut to his left thigh. With the next death Kern stepped back, and Stergin took his place. Stergin switched with Andel, then Jangor switched with him again. This gave Jangor the centre position, Stergin to his left, and Andel to his right. With Mander as back up, though he was now fighting left-handed, his right wrist having been cut badly.

"How long?" Shouted Jangor, slashing a throat with no subtlety at all, taking the next in line with a lunge through the heart as he stepped up.

"We'll be as quick as we can. Hold."

"We hold." Yelled Stergin, his sword flashing left and right, killing two, much to Jangor's relief as the man in front of him folded in death, a blood fountain reaching the roof as his knees failed. Crathen stepped in behind them.

"What in all the hells are we doing?" Demanded Brank.

"You are the tree." Laughed Alverana looking up at the taller man.

"I can do that."

"What are we doing?" Shouted Kern.

"You know, you take the back. I'll take the front. We are making a summoning."

"Are you sure?" Asked Kern.

"No, but we need to try something." He turned to Brank. "Be a tree." Brank smiled and raised his arms to mimic the branches of a tree, almost exactly the shape of the tree the others had seen up in the mountains. Brank knew what shape the tree should be. Kern stood at Brank's back and formed his arms to match the branches of Brank's tree. Alverana Smiled at Brank then turned his back, he pushed back against Brank and assumed the position of the summoner. Before his right hand formed up against the tree, he pulled something small from his pocket. A shiny black feather, so black that it glowed blue, and green and red. The three shaped as a tree spoke the summoning prayer, softly and slowly. It wasn't necessary for the world to hear it over the sound of the battles raging around them, only one entity needed to hear it and hear it she did. In only seconds the silent sound of feathered wings filled their ears. Gradually the shape came into view, the black crow appeared on Branks outstretched arms.

"Crawk" She spoke loud and hard. Alverana stepped away from the tree that was Brank.

"I have summoned you. You must end Zandaar, send him on his way."

"Why should I do what you command?" Demanded Gyara hopping to the ground in front of Alverana.

"Because you know what is right, and because I carry your feather."

"Right is the most flexible of things." Laughed the crow.

"We know what is right for you, but that will not happen here today. See the dark?"

"Who has summoned Glard?" Called the crow, ruffling her feathers, another dark feather fluttered to the ground, this time not un-noticed by Gyara. She snapped it up and swallowed it. One dark eye glaring at Alverana. He smiled in recognition, Gyara would only be worried about that fallen feather if there was a future for both her and the people here.

"How do we send him back?" Asked Alverana.

"He must be filled, sated. This is not going to be easy."

"How can we do it?"

"You are on the right path, but you need much more power than a single god can provide."

"Now we have two."

"Even I will not be enough."

Zandaars red fire reached out to the black crow. Again Worandana blocked it and poured it into the darkness. The distraction was enough for Namdarin to plunge the sword into the chest of Zandaar, he held the sword inside the gods armour. The light escaping from the wound was so close that the cuff of his shirt started to smoulder.

"Xeron." He yelled. "Xeron." Again. "Xeron, come to me." The power pouring from the wound in the gods chest gave Namdarin's call the energy it needed, behind him a ghostly head appeared. Along with the one Namdarin knew came others that he had never seen before. "Xeron help us in our hour of need."

"We will help you." The voice echoed like it came from the depths of a grave, without sound it resounded directly into their brains. Namdarin withdrew his sword from the god's chest, and the light pouring from the healing wound, cast harsh shadows on the wall, the transparent faces of the gods gathered in the chamber solidified under the influence of this light. Again when the wound was closed the shadows slithered across the floor to the darkness at Zandaar's feet. Namdarin and Jayanne attacked again, the sword of Zandaar blocking them. The god's wrist appeared to be a fraction slower than before, the parries became a little desperate. The faces of the other gods rushed forwards and wrapped themselves around the head of Zandaar, the silver god was held fixed by them. His red light washed all around his head but was contained by the images of the other gods. Xeron's head hung in front of Zandaar's face, the lips moving in some prayer, or spell. No sound was obvious but Zandaar was held almost motionless by the forces holding both his head and his feet. Namdarin took advantage of this stillness and plunged his sword into the gods heart. Jayanne smashed the axe into his groin and held it there. The drain on the gods and most especially Zandaar was immense. The energy flowed down to the darkness around Zandaars feet.

"Help them." Said Alverana to Gyara.

"I don't want to, but now there is no choice for me." With a sudden sweep of the wide black wings Gyara launched herself directly at Zandaar, her beak plunging into the very core of the god's body. Now Zandaar was held in place at head, chest, solar plexus, groin, and feet. The darkness around them all seemed to thicken and slowly come seeping through the walls. Each felt a coldness seeping into their bones. A dark shape started to form, gradually coalescing into a form that tried to fill the entire chamber. The shape solidified into something man shaped with huge bat like wings. Eyes and mouth triangular pits of red fire. The mouth opened wide, pulling the black tendrils from the two magicians, thickening and pulling more power from the restrained god. The temperature in the room was falling quickly, Xeron's head turned away from Zandaar. Focused on the dark figure.

"Send power to the mouth." The graveyard voice echoed in everyone's mind.

Worandana and Kirukana had already lost control of the source of their power, the darkness was walking amongst them and lending out nothing. They both reached inside their colourful cloaks and started casting silver fragments at the open maw. Jayanne and Namdarin pulled their weapons from the silver god, and turned them toward the darkness, together they released all the energy they were carrying. Power from the silver god was flowing through the phantom faces of the other gods, and from the tail of Gyara. Granger turned to join in the group feeding the figure, he knew that this hunger could eat the whole world. He had read of it in some ancient tome.

"Stop." Yelled Gregor over the howling of the energy transfers in the now crowded chamber. "Help, I need to open a channel."

"Where to?" Granger knew of no power close enough.

"It's a long way, I have the resonance, I need someone to steady me at this end." Granger ran across the room and stood behind Gregor, he passed his staff across the younger man's chest and gripped it in both hands.

"You'll not lose yourself now." Gregor leaned his head back and caught the old man's gaze.

"Pray for us all." He whispered, then closed his eyes. Shutting out the noise and horror in the chamber he launched his mind, into the etheric plane he went, pouring energy into his own travelling form. He raced north and east, in only heartbeats he was standing at the lightening stone. He looked down at his hands. Each one holding the staff, more accurately, the projection of the staff, held in ghostly hands.

"No blood." He screamed, howling into the night both in the chamber and on the green. He looked around and behind him he saw an old woman running, running straight towards him, as if the devil himself were chasing her. She ran through him to the stone, crudely slashed both hands, and rubbed the blood into the top of the stone. A wide column of white fire came from the crest of the stone.

"Thank you, Anya." Yelled Gregor, as he took the power from the stone and channelled it into and through the staff. It came through the puddle of blood, and into the staff at the stone, then out of the staff and into the red mouth of Glard. A bolt of light so white that it turned everything else in the chamber into simple shades of black. Granger struggled to hold Gregor still, his mind and body scattered so far across the country. Even the silver god turned grey in the light from the stone. Slowly his formed changed into a shadow like the other gods as his power drained, changed as did Gyara. Her form shrunk and lost its characteristic blackness, the colour drained from her feathers as her power vanished leaving a pure white crow. The two Zandaar clerics moved to support Gregor, each taking a shoulder they braced his pitching form. Gregor looked at Anya, his silver eyes flashing in the night.

"More." He said. She raised her eyebrows but opened the flower of the power even more. The dark figure flinched as the power hit him.

"All the way." Whispered Gregor so many days away. This time she shrugged, opened the bloom to the widest it could go. This time the figure did more than twitch, this time it tried to get away from the light, but Gregor held it, pinned it to the wall like, a butterfly nailed to a board. Glard wriggled and writhed in the heat of a fire it couldn't understand. Then in an instant so short that none could see it, the darkness vanished. The white-hot light did not, it tore a hole through the building and leapt out into the night.

"Thank you Anya, you can shut it down now, you have saved the world today. I will explain if I ever see you again." He snapped his ethereal body back to his physical and slumped in the arms of his friends as the light stuttered and failed. The torchlight in the chamber looked dim and depressing after the brilliance.

Silence descended. There was a scream from a doorway as Kevana came running into view, he saw Alverana leaning against Brank. He threw down his sword and ran to his friend, together they hugged and kissed as if they had been apart for years.

"I thought I had lost you when they all died." Muttered Kevana breaking the kiss. And looking round at the others. Jayanne and Namdarin were hugging and kissing. The clerics and magicians where hugging, but no kissing. Brank and Kern had arms around each other's shoulders.

"They're not dead." Said Jangor. "They're only stunned. They'll be coming round in a while."

"Anyone injured?" Asked Namdarin.

"Fabrana is dead, Strenoana injured, Petrovana will be bringing him." Said Kevana.

"Mander dead, Andel and Stergin injured." Said Jangor.

"Anyone got any power left at all?" asked Worandana taking his wand from his belt. The magicians all shook their heads, even Gregor was completely out.

"I'll steal some from the dead," said Granger, "sort of appropriate." He followed Worandana to the first door.

"Xeron." Snapped Namdarin. The gods translucent head drifted to face the lord of Namdaron. "You will now leave and take Zandaar with you."

"We will, but there is something you must know before we go and a choice you must make."

"I've had enough of your riddles. Explain clearly."

"The energy you have been exposed to here is inimical to your human forms, you will die in the next few days."

"Now we know. What is the choice?"

"We can heal you before we go, or you can die and move on

to the next adventure. Choose there is little time."

Namdarin turned to Jayanne.

"Live or die?"

"Live." She smiled; gripping is hand firmly. Namdarin looked around at the others still in the chamber, then he shouted.

"Do you want to live forever?" The answer was the usual with one or two exceptions.

"Do you want to die today?" He shouted.

"Hell, no." was the answer and universally so.

"Heal us." Said Namdarin.

"Don't forget Wolf." Snarled Jayanne, brandishing the axe.

"It shall be as you ask." Intoned Xeron, a dim blue light pervaded the room and wrapped itself briefly around each of the party, even the heavy canine. "It is done, you shall live out your lives as you normally would."

"Thank you." Said Namdarin. "Now get the hell out of our world."

ABOUT THE AUTHOR

My name is Michael Porter, some call me Roaddog.

Formal training for writing, I have exactly none, I did start reading early, generally before breakfast. I actually learned to read before I started school, many thanks to mother for all the hours she put in. Of course this wasn't popular with the school at that time, some fool had just introduced a new learning system, some sort of phonetic garbage. When asked "Why should children have to learn English twice?" They had no answer. I didn't bother with that phonetic junk, they had to get some old books out of storage for me to read. Yes, a troublemaker from the start. I was only at that particular school for one year, but before I left, I had read every book they had, well, all the ones that were spelled properly. This pattern continued through every school I attended, grammar school was no different, they had a huge library, which I read in less than three years. Much to the despair of my teachers reading didn't help me in my English lessons, spelling, punctuation, these things aren't important it's the story that counts. I'm sorry Miss Boll, Cider with Rosie is boring, I'm not reading it. David Eddings, now he's good. I'm making no friends amongst the English department here.

English exams were obviously interesting, mock 'O' level I scored a massive -30%. This was in the days before students got credit for just being there. The scoring system was simple, you start with 100 points, for every spelling, punctuation or grammatical error a point is deducted, it seems that in only four pages of writing I managed an impressive 130 errors. The real 'O' level was unclassified. No real surprise there. I managed to pass on the second attempt, but only by twisting the proposed essay title, and plagiarising large chunks of the sci-fi novel I was currently reading. Enough ancient history.

For those that don't know me I'm getting along in years, I'd be approaching retirement if the government didn't keep moving the goalposts. I've been writing this story for many years, but only got around to publishing it recently due to pressure from she who must be obeyed. I started this mammoth project after reading a particularly dreadful fantasy novel. I decided that even I could write something better than that. I noticed that most books of the genre were lacking in real violence and proper sex, so this series is definitely for a more adult audience. I have a day job that takes up a lot of my time, I also have an evening job as sound and lighting engineer for a local rock band, which eats a big chunk of my weekends, so time for writing is somewhat restricted. I finally got Doom finished a little after my schedule, but finally it is done.

Keep your eyes open there are a couple more projects in the pipe.

For me reading and writing is all about the story.
Enjoy.

Printed in Great Britain
by Amazon